A Threefold Cord

Bill Crews

All incidents and dialogue, and all characters with the exception of some well-known historical figures, are products of the author's imagination and are not to be construed as real. Where real-life historical figures appear, the situations, incidents, and dialogues concerning those persons are entirely fictional and are not intended to depict actual events or to change the entirely fictional nature of the work. In all other respects, any resemblance to actual persons, living or dead, events, or locales is entirely coincidental.

Cover design by Kerrie Robertson.

Copyright © 2020 Colonial Frontier Press

All rights reserved.

ISBN 978-0-692-14661-3

DEDICATION

To my beloved wife, partner, and best friend, Deborah.
"Therefore, shall a man leave his father and his mother, and shall cleave
unto his wife: and they shall be one flesh."

CONTENTS

ACKNOWLEDGMENTS

I want to start by thanking my wonderful wife and partner, Deborah, for pushing me to begin and, more importantly, to finish this manuscript. She prodded and encouraged me, she read drafts, she helped shape the characters, and she found the money in the family budget to make it happen; she allowed me to have the free time to work at this endeavor by wrangling our three kids. Sweetheart, there is no way I could have done this without you.

No one really writes a novel alone and I am no exception. Critical partners were my great beta readers: Giselle Simlett, Karlie DeMarse; and Gabby Crowley. They gently pointed out plot holes and inconsistencies and inexplicable acts by characters and remained encouraging the whole time. Without their help, the project would not have been possible. Likewise, to my editor Christy Distler of Avodah Editing Services. Her light but firm touch gave me focus on rough places and kept the history from getting in the way of the story.

Thanks are also due to the fine folks who run and give seminars at the War College of the Seven Years War at Ticonderoga, NY; the Ohio Country Conference at Westmoreland, PA; and the Frontier Culture Museum in Staunton, VA. The understanding you provided of frontier culture and politics and economics was invaluable.

Special thanks to my long-time friend and fellow company commander from our youthful days in 2d Battalion, 32d Infantry, Pat Walsh, who is a font of knowledge on frontier life and to Robert Shade, author of the Forbes Road series of historical novels, who inspired and mentored me in this project.

The wild Irish, who had gotten possession of the valley between the Blue Ridge and North Mountain, forming a barrier over which none ventured to leap, and would still less venture to settle among.

--Thomas Jefferson

Chapter One

OUTSIDE OF DANGLING from a gallows, there might be worse fates than being exiled to America.

But Christopher Hawkwood, soon-to-be ex-lieutenant of foot, was hard pressed to think of one offhand. For one who had imbibed the precepts of the English gentry, like fair play and justice, with his mother's milk, the unfairness of his situation warranted unadulterated outrage. He was, however, philosophical to the point of resignation.

No sense in ruminating over what might have been. He couldn't leave a comrade in distress, and it wasn't like he'd intended to break the man's pate with that cobblestone. Bugger all, the man was trying to break his. Just damned bad luck all around. Even worse luck that his daddy was as rich as Croesus and a cousin of the Lord Mayor. What good was it to have the truth on your side when the other fellow had the power?

Hawkwood shivered under his cape as the November wind, carrying the smell of brine, dead fish, and rotting kelp, and briefly dispersed the miasma of peat smoke that shrouded Cork during wintertime.

He paced and fretted in the narrow, filth-strewn alley only fifty yards from the quay—and safety. His batman, a stolid thirtyish Londoner named Billingsley, was in some waterfront tavern trying to find a wherryman to row him and his belongings out to the Virginia-bound merchantmen, *Lady Charlotte,* anchored somewhere in the gloom.

Hawkwood tensed at a sudden burst of noise, then relaxed and chuckled at himself. Only raucous merriment from an ale house, not the sound of a *posse comitatus* on his heels.

He was as helpless as a babe. Soon they would put a name to the man and some magistrate would issue a warrant for his arrest. The bailiffs could be raising a hue and cry for him even now.

He leaned against the dogcart carrying his belongings and looked up at the sky, again diving into the deep pool of misery. Within moments, the sounds of low voices and approaching footsteps startled him again. He whirled, drawing a pair of heavy dragoon pistols from his waistband, thumbed them to full cock, and leveled them at the half-dozen men looming out of the murky mist.

"Easy, Kit. Stand easy." The group's stout middle-aged leader, Terry Molloy, the adjutant of Hawkwood's regiment, looked out of place in civilian attire.

Hawkwood eased the cocks forward and stuffed the pistols back into his waistband. "Terry. What are you doing here?"

"We're seeing you off." Jamie Halkett, the colonel's favorite son, shoved a bottle of brandy into Hawkwood's hand.

"We couldn't let you leave in the dead of the night with no send-off," Molloy said. "That's not how the Forty-Fourth Foot conducts its affairs. Besides, a group of fellows with a bottle draws less attention from the night watch than a single man idling by a dogcart."

Hawkwood both appreciated and resented their presence. They had come at some risk to see him off—and if constables did arrive, they could create enough confusion to allow his escape. On the other hand, he wanted to wallow in his misery alone. "There will be hell to pay if they find me with you."

"Maybe. Maybe not. Colonel Halkett sends his regards and regrets." Molloy reached into his coat pocket, drew out a letter sealed with wax and ribbon, and handed it to him.

Hawkwood stared at it. A letter?

"The colonel has an acquaintance in Virginia, a very prominent man—one of the *ton*, so to speak—in that godforsaken pesthole. This is a letter of introduction. He has also instructed the regiment's agent to sell your commission and property. He will send you a bill of exchange in care of the gentleman."

Hawkwood feared he would be overwhelmed by emotion and

shame himself in front of his comrades by failing to appear game to the end. He'd idolized the colonel since joining the regiment five years ago as a frightened sixteen-year-old ensign and the disappointment he knew he'd caused the old man was in many ways more painful that exile itself.

"Tell Colonel Halkett I can never repay him for his kindness and that I hope to return to the regiment one day." As he swallowed, his lip trembled. "Damned hard this is. Sodding Virginia. Is the colonel certain it must be so? I have relations in Hanover. I could probably cozen my way back into the Austrian Army if need be."

"Sorry, my lad. Once the hue and cry is made, you can be certain they'll twig on to your family on the Continent and your time in Austria. Nay, you must go somewhere they'll never look." Molloy snorted. "Who knows, Kit? This might all be for the best." He took a deep draught from the bottle. "Unless you have family money, you're heading for debt and a life of dodging creditors."

How right he was. None of them could live on their army pay or hope to scrape together the thousand pounds it took to purchase a captaincy. Their colonel had done well by them, but in the other regiments on the Irish Establishment, English officers were being forced out and replaced with the slack-jawed imbecile sons of the lackwit boobies Lord Dorset relied upon to rule the pestilent land. The colonel wouldn't be able to hold out forever.

"Now you have ready chink and an introduction that will help you make a fresh start," Molloy continued. "Take joy of it."

Hawkwood shook his head. "I'm an Englishman, and the army is all I know. The British Army—this regiment—is where I belong. I'll be back."

"You can't come back to us. You'll never be safe in Ireland." Molloy draped his arm over his shoulders and leaned close, his breath tinged with brandy. "You're a damned good officer, Kit. You've fought Jacobites and Turks. Maybe one of the colonies will make you captain-general or whatever the rank is there. In a few years, it'll be safe for you to return to England and buy into a regiment there."

Hawkwood took a swig from the bottle and passed it to another of the group. Molloy was right. He'd never be safe anywhere in Ireland. But there were many good regiments in England. Even Scotland looked appealing when compared to

Virginia.

The group talked in low whispers. Waiting. The octogenarian carter snored heavily.

Damn Billingsley. What could be taking him so long? Not for the first time, the thought of betrayal crossed his mind. Though Hawkwood was well liked by the men in the regiment, there were always a handful of troublemakers, men he'd sent to be flogged at the halberds, who would cheerily see him taken up and hauled off to swing on the gallows. Billingsley had never seemed to harbor ill will, but enough guineas offered as a reward could make even the firmest attachment between master and man a tenuous one.

No, Billingsley was loyal and resourceful. If there was a betrayal, it wouldn't be from him.

A figure loomed out of the blackness, and Hawkwood relaxed at recognizing his batman. All that remained now was to get aboard a merchantman.

"I have a boat a-waiting for you," Billingsley said. "The man wasn't happy about the idea of rowing out in the middle of the night, but I threw some of your coin his way and he shut his gob." He paused, eying him. "Do you wish for me to come with you, sir? I rather like being your batman."

Molloy grunted. "Billingsley. You shouldn't discuss desertion in front of the regimental adjutant."

"Well, Mr. Molloy, sir, it wouldn't be actual desertion. It would be more like me taking my discharge."

Hawkwood clapped Billingsley on the shoulder. "Twouldn't be right to ask you to hazard yourself. I'm sure another of the gentlemen has need for an honest and attentive batman."

The group laughed.

"Right, then. Let's be going. You, man,"—Hawkwood prodded the carter awake— "let's be about our business."

The carter snapped the reins, and the pony eased the dogcart into motion. The solid wheels creaked and bumped over the cobblestone road, and Billingsley led the way with a lanthorn and a shillelagh to discourage footpads.

Hawkwood followed just behind the cart's wheel, glancing around. His heart pounded like a cavalry kettle drum, and his breathing would have sounded like a bellows had he not fought to control it. The group of men stayed a few steps behind him, obviously not nearly as distressed. One of them started singing the regiment's marching song, "Lilliburlero," and soon all were singing. His spirits lifted, Hawkwood grabbed the bottle of brandy from Jamie, took another long drink, and began singing with the group.

As they neared the quay, a burly man stood in the sternsheets of a small boat, leaning on a sweep. The cart stopped on the quay, and the wherryman and Billingsley loaded Hawkwood's trunks onto the boat. Before they had moved the first trunk, the elderly carter was snoring.

"Well, boyo," Molloy said, "this is it. Take care and Godspeed."

Hawkwood shook hands with the other officers. "I'll miss all of you. Now run along before I get maudlin and weepy."

The men vanished into the night.

"Begging your pardon, sir," Billingsley said. "Your baggage is loaded. A mate from your ship asked me to fetch him from the tavern when you were ready to leave. I'll be back in a twink."

Hawkwood sighed. Wouldn't this night ever end? He leaned against the dogcart, took a final drink from the bottle, and tossed it into the harbor.

A hand grabbed him by the shoulder and spun him around, then a meaty palm pressed him against the cart. Before him stood a roughly dressed man carrying a shillelagh.

"Sir, I'm Burchill, called a thief-taker by some." He was shorter than Hawkwood by half a head and though his paunch put great stress on his waistcoat buttons, Hawkwood could tell his stoutness was hard and muscular. "I've been hired by Mr. Charles Jermyn to apprehend the killer of his son Henry. I believe you are Mr. Christopher Hawkwood and you are than man. You need to come with me, sir."

Hawkwood's bowels churned. *Sod me. They've got me.*

The man's politeness was accented by the appearance of two companions. Both were shorter than Hawkwood and older, but they had the broad, sturdy build of men used to heavy labor and an air that said they were no stranger to tavern brawls.

Considering the pistols in his waistband, Hawkwood fingered the hilt of his hanger with his left hand and measured his chances of escape.

The ancient carter snored so loudly that he started from his nap, then sat up and stretched. He blinked at the three men accosting Hawkwood.

Burchill eyed him. "Be a good gentleman, sir. No need to start a row like a common street tough." The thief-taker slapped his shillelagh in his palm. "The magistrate has signed a warrant in the case of the murder of Henry Jermyn. There is a witness, and this witness had an attack of conscience." He smirked at Hawkwood. "He says he tried to dissuade you from fighting, but you were determined."

The old man on the cart glared at Burchill and his lip curled.

"Show me the warrant," Hawkwood said. "If you don't have the warrant, you have no right to detain me. I'm a King's officer."

"That is your view, sir, but you must come with me. I'd prefer you come along peaceably, but if need be, my boys will drag you." His voiced had hardened with the threat, and when he nodded in Hawkwood's direction, his companions circled to Hawkwood's flanks.

Hawkwood pulled the dragoon pistols from his waistband and trained them on the constable's followers. He cocked them, the sound deafening on the quiet street. The men froze, and the carter's head swiveled from Hawkwood to the constable and back.

"Gentlemen, I don't wish to shoot, but rest assured I will."

The thief-taker advanced, brandishing the shillelagh. "In the king's name, I'm commanding you to drop your pistols!"

"Murder! Murder!" the carter howled.

Burchill shook the shillelagh at him. "Shut up, you bleeding fool!"

Down the street, a tavern was emptying. A wanted man had many more friends on the waterfront than did the minions of the law, which gave Hawkwood an idea. Turning toward them, he shouted, "Murder!"

The mob thundered up the street with Billingsley in the lead. He surveyed the scene and placed his hands on his hips. "Boys, the constable here is trying to take an honest man. I say we show him—"

Burchill stepped forward, swinging his shillelagh. The blow caught Billingsley on the shoulder and drove him to his knees. A visceral roar surged through the mob as they moved to surround him.

Hawkwood knelt over Billingsley. The man was breathing, though only someone as close as he would see that. Billingsley opened his eyes slightly and gave him a wink. Hawkwood looked around at the tense faces of the crowd. "He's killed him!"

"No!" Burchill backed up. "No! He isn't dead. Look at him!"

Billingsley emitted a bloodcurdling imitation of a death rattle and shook his arms and legs as if having a final nervous spasm.

"Get them! Murderers!" Hawkwood shouted.

As inexorable as a storm tide, the mob rolled over the constable in a flood of flashing truncheons and a froth of flailing fists. The bellows and wails were punctuated by the meaty thwack of clubs landing on flesh.

Hawkwood pulled Billingsley to his feet. "Can you stand?"

He nodded. "Let's get you out of here, sir. Godspeed. And, sir?"

"Aye?" Hawkwood said clambering into the wherry.

"Virginia can't be all that bad. Can it?"

Chapter Two

HAWKWOOD LAID HIS KNIFE and fork on the delftware plate and gently pushed it away. He was well and truly rogered. There was no sense pretending otherwise.

He'd had enough of the tough and stringy simulacrum of roast beef that comprised the main course. In the dim glow of the myrtle wax candles that flickered in drafts, he surreptitiously checked the progress of the other guests. Outside, the February wind and sleet played a howling tattoo on the shuttered windows of the dining room to Ardleigh Plantation, on the bluffs of the Rappahannock River.

Hawkwood didn't fancy himself an epicure, but so far he'd found the beef to be leathery. The fish course, advertised as trout, was bland and spongy and resembled no trout he'd ever tasted. Roasted wild fowl only slightly larger than sparrows were passed off as partridges, and the cabbage and turnips had been stewed to paste.

He sipped from his claret and suppressed a grimace. It was thin and vinegary, but at any time of the day he preferred it to the rum punch swilled by the plantation gentry. Oddly, the other dozen guests weren't deterred by the quality of the roast, but rather the opposite. It must have been a Virginia trait, consuming enormous quantities of poor quality food and drinking oneself insensible on rum punch.

He sighed and closed his eyes. This had to be what Dante had in mind. If this wasn't hell, it was certainly within a stone's throw. If a week had been this torturous, what would the rest of his life be like?

"Mr. Hawkwood." Richard Crosslin, the host, addressed him from the head of the table. "May I offer you more of this joint?"

"No, thank you, sir. My digestion is still recovering from the passage."

"Send some this way," a short, florid man seated across from Hawkwood said, "and my compliments to your cook. He has outdone himself."

Hawkwood almost laughed. The cook would have been flogged within an inch of his life if there was justice in the world.

A dark-skinned hand removed his plate. One of the most difficult things to adjust to in Virginia had been the presence of slaves. Black slaves had worked as teamsters on the sweeps of the lighters that unloaded and then loaded *Lady Charlotte*, the merchantman aboard which he'd crossed the Atlantic. On Crosslin's plantation, called Ardleigh after the seat of the family where Crosslin's brother was ensconced as baronet, Hawkwood had yet to see a single white retainer other than the overseer and his family. Unlike the cheerful household one would expect in an English country manor, the servants at Ardleigh, who were shabbily dressed in red coats cast off from the British Army and ragged slop trousers instead of a proper livery, were sullen and cutty-eyed.

Hawkwood hoped to God Richard has a food taster. Otherwise, they were liable to be poisoned at any meal. And his fears were not unfounded. The hanging of the slave Caesar and the burning of the slave Eve the previous summer for a conspiracy to poison their masters was still a topic of conversation. He shuddered at the thought of living in fear of servants.

"What are your plans, Mr. Hawkwood?" The question came from a saturnine fellow near the end of the table. Hawkwood had gathered he owned two tobacco warehouses on the Tappahannock waterfront.

Plans, indeed. His first plan was to keep his neck out of a noose. The next was to find some way to escape from this wilderness and take up a normal life again. "I'm examining all possibilities, sir. Our host is still educating me on the ways of Virginia, though I'm not sure I am an apt pupil."

The man guffawed. "Our friend Richard has 'educated' many a cully in the 'ways of Virginia.'"

The guests laughed, and Crosslin toasted the man with his tankard of rum punch as he chuckled along with them.

Hawkwood would never understand Crosslin. He had been called a Captain Sharp to his face and gloried in it. In polite society, such a slur would have resulted in a meeting with pistols early in the morning, but Crosslin treated it as a jape.

"Richard," the man continued, "is acquainted with all the *ton* in Williamsburg and the Colony. He will find something interesting and remunerative for an active gentleman such as yourself."

Hawkwood watched as his host picked at his teeth with a pen knife. This was like watching bedlamites play at having a dinner party, although the house was very nice—well, except for the damned pack of foxhounds that roamed it at will and weren't completely housebroken.

Across from Hawkwood and beside Crosslin, the plantation owner's wife, Jenny, looked to be about twenty years his junior. She was beautiful and high spirited with a slim waist and generous bosom. Since this was the first opportunity Hawkwood had spent time around her, he gathered that she and Crosslin didn't take meals together. The man's social life was demanding, leaving her as something of a grass widow at Ardleigh, and while she held back in conversation, Hawkwood sensed a quick wit about her.

He couldn't help but notice that she was badged, with the base of her left thumb branded with a "T," indicating she had been convicted of theft and escaped hanging by reading the neck verse. At least she was literate and had made quite a step up in the world—from Newgate to mistress of Ardleigh.

She caught his gaze and fluttered impossibly long lashes over her large green eyes. "Mr. Hawkwood, how long will you be with us?" Her harsh accent was more at suited to the St. Giles rookery than a fashionable plantation dining room.

"I think not much longer. Life at Ardleigh is like living in the land of the lotus eaters, but I came to Virginia to make my own way and the sooner I start, the better." Hopefully that wasn't laying it on too thick.

A mottled brown muzzle topped by a pair of luminous brown eyes suddenly appeared from beneath the tablecloth, nuzzled his crotch, and lapped at his hand. He pushed the dog away.

"Do we grow lotuses here?" she asked.

The silly mort was serious. But of course, she didn't know what he meant. They didn't read *The Odyssey* in London stews or Newgate. He forced a chuckle. "Oh, that is very witty. I must remember that."

She looked uncertain for a moment and then laughed with him, her high-pitched cackle silencing the conversation for a moment. "I am so enjoying your presence at Ardleigh, Mr. Hawkwood, though we've had so little opportunity to talk. Our social circle is other planters and tradesmen, so we rarely travel to Williamsburg. It is such a pleasure to have a visitor from England."

How uncomfortable it must have been for Crosslin to introduce his wife, a transported felon, to the governor. Out of the corner of his eye,

Hawkwood caught a glimpse of Crosslin blowing his nose on the skirt of the tablecloth. Well, there could be other reasons too.

"I would love it if you stayed with us longer. It would give us a chance to become better acquainted." The eyelashes batted again.

Something rubbed against the top of his foot, and he moved it. Damned hound. Why did Crosslin let the beasts roam the dining room? Within moments, the rubbing repeated, and this time he stiffened. That couldn't be what he thought it was. When he pressed gently against the pressure, she smiled at him with eyes narrowed and returned the foot gesture.

By God, it was her. The brainless piece was giving him a come-on at her husband's dining table. She would be a good tumble though. Nice dugs. It would be tempting given the lack of other talent in this godforsaken wilderness.

"I think that would be a splendid idea. Alas, I fear I will only be here a short while." He then damned himself. This was quite a situation he'd gotten himself into, in a miserable backwoods populated by the crudest and dullest people imaginable. His host was a notorious sharper, and his wife a felon and a trollop.

Fortunately, Crosslin called for the tablecloth to be cleared and dessert served. As custom dictated, Jenny invited the ladies to join her in the parlor, leaving the men alone at the table.

One of the men produced a set of dice. "Hazard?"

A rumbling of agreement followed.

"A crown a throw?"

More agreement.

"A crown?" another man scoffed. "A crown is a bet for a scrub, for a Scotsman."

"Will a guinea a toss suffice?" Crosslin asked.

Hawkwood swallowed hard. A guinea a toss? He could be skinned before the evening was out. "I'm sorry, gentlemen. Those stakes are too high for me."

The man with the dice gave him a hard stare. "By God, sir, you're not one of those Welsh leaping Methodists, are you?"

Everyone laughed.

"It's hard to trust a man who won't wager."

Hawkwood's ears burned. "I've no objection to wagering, sir. It's only my present situation obliges me to prudence."

Crosslin waved his hand. "Pay him no mind. When our fortunes dangle in the balance with each harvest, it breeds a certain boldness in our wagers."

A slave brought in a tray of long-stemmed clay pipes and a canister of tobacco. Hawkwood accepted one—he'd never developed a taste for tobacco, but it didn't seem politic to refuse in the heart of tobacco country—then took a puff, suppressed a cough, and exhaled.

An older man wearing a very expensive dark brown tie wig that contrasted with his white eyebrows eyed him. "I don't suppose you'd be interested in tobacco planting."

"No, sir, I think not. I'm not familiar with the crop or the country. No offense intended, gentlemen, but I don't intend to remain in Virginia. As soon as is practicable, I shall return to England."

"Return to England? Really?" The white eyebrows raised. "Well, it's true that many of our indentures return at the end of their service. By that time, they've discovered the streets aren't paved with gold."

"Or paved at all." The man with the dice guffawed.

"But it is rare for a gentleman to return to England once he's removed to Virginia. It's even more rare for a gentleman to risk a midwinter voyage."

Hawkwood didn't like where this is going. "The voyage was quite an adventure. Most days none of the passengers— 'live lumber,' I think the sailors called us—were allowed on deck. Then one night, just off the Virginia capes, we were all turned up, even the convicts in the hold, to shovel snow and break sleet from the rigging lest the ship fairly capsize."

"Convicts, you say," a man at the end at the table said. "We don't see a lot of them these days. It would be more merciful to hang the poor wretches and be done with it."

Hawkwood held his gaze. "I would have thought that life in Virginia would offer opportunity once they obtained their freedom. They can own their own farm and be freemen. No one here will care about their past."

The man with white eyebrows shook his head. "Their indenture will be purchased by soul merchants who'll march them in shackles through the backcountry south of the James River, selling them as they go. They will suffer privations and hardships that make the worst corner of Newgate look like a veritable paradise. Most of them that survive will try to return home even though getting caught means the gallows."

"Aye," another man agreed. "They won't work if you don't drive them, and most are so weak when they come off the ship that they die soon after. Thank God we have Cuffees. Give me a good, strong black over some starved gallows bird looking to run any day."

White eyebrows spoke again. "Are you on the run? Got some

gentleman's daughter ankled?"

Hawkwood smiled, but inside he was fuming. These people posed as gentlemen, but their manners were scarcely better than a hod carrier's. "Nothing quite so exciting, I'm afraid." Giving the lie he had rehearsed during his passage from Ireland, he continued, "My father died, and instead of an inheritance I found the estate consumed by debt." Well, there was some truth there. The old man was dead, and he had no inheritance—never mind that he was disinherited. "As you know, a subaltern's army pay is not sufficient to live on without incurring debt you can never repay. So here I am. With some prudence, I shall be able to purchase a captaincy in a year or two and return to the army." Also, true. Within a year or two he should be free to travel to England, and as a captain he could live without indebtedness.

An older and well-dressed man who had also abstained from gaming intervened. "Gentleman, please. You ill-use our guest." He glowered at his companions before turning his attention back to Hawkwood. "Wise move, young man. Many a gentleman has lost everything in tobacco. The competition from the Spanish colonies and Turkey is fierce. And"—he gestured above himself— "the vagaries of the weather can destroy you when your competitors don't."

Hawkwood nodded. "What do you recommend, sir?"

"Anything but tobacco." He laughed and was joined by the other tobacco planters.

Well, they were still in the business and laughing, so it couldn't be that bad. Or could it?

Talk turned to hunting and the latest rumors from Europe, punctuated by the rattle of dice, the clash of the cup on the table, and the shouts of the players.

Hawkwood detached from the hubbub and occupied himself with his own thoughts, musing about Jenny's game under the table and his chances of bedding her without being found out. He wrestled with his conscience over the propriety of rogering the wife of his host and finally decided he shouldn't do it, even though she was clearly neglected and he would not be insinuating himself into a happy marriage.

Then his thoughts drifted to the night in Cork that had precipitated his flight to Virginia. A knot formed in his throat, pressing like a hangman's hemp, and a dull ache throbbed behind his eyes. *Dear God, you know I'm not one of your most successful projects. If you're trying to give me a foretaste of hell, well, you've made your point. But please help me out of this shitten mess I've got myself into.*

From the depths of his despair, he suddenly became aware of someone addressing him.

"Ha! There he is. I knew he was in there somewhere," Crosslin said over the top of a tankard of rum punch.

Hawkwood flushed with embarrassment.

"I've been thinking, Kit." Now with the setting more informal, he used Hawkwood's nickname. "The ideal position for an adventurous young man, a military man like yourself, is land speculation. Last year, the Crown granted the Transmontane Company a patent for eight-hundred thousand acres of land in Virginia west of the Blue Ridge. Think of it, Kit! A parcel of land the size of Kent, uninhabited, a wilderness. Not even red Indians. It's there for the taking. All the company has to do is survey land and find families willing to settle. You as a military man, especially with your experience in the wilds of the Carpathians, would be a logical choice to plan the location of forts to protect the settlements from French and Indian incursions."

"Where does the company plan to find settlers?"

He thought that flying pigs would be just as easy to find as inveigling entire families into abandoning their lives and decamping to the Virginia wilderness.

"Released bondsmen." Crosslin stabbed at the air for emphasis. "The Irish trash that is pouring into Pennsylvania." Another stab. "The restless and landless in England. Trust me, Kit, there is no shortage of families. You could buy land on your own account and resell it. By working with the survey parties, you would have first pick of all the parcels. The most desirable acreage."

It could be just so much moonshine but Hawkwood found himself intrigued. The idea of exploring and hunting while earning enough chink to buy a captaincy had a strong appeal.

"That sounds very intriguing. Wild country, you say?"

"There are only a few hundred families west of the Blue Ridge from Lord Fairfax's lands into the Carolinas. A lot of those are Germans in what's called the Lower Valley. But you wouldn't have to find tenants. All you'd have to do is hunt and keep the surveyors safe."

He nodded. "I must say, Richard, that sounds most agreeable." He glanced over Crosslin's shoulder to the parlor and saw Jenny staring at him, all slitted eyes and pouty lips.

When she was sure she had caught his attention, she puckered her lips in a kiss and cupped her breasts with her hands.

* * * * *

HAWKWOOD RAN HIS FINGERTIPS over the buttery honey-colored leather as if he were caressing a lover's cheek. "This is beautiful work, my man. How did you say you came by it?"

"A recently deceased gentleman, sir." The saddler, an old man with a stained leather apron stretched over his paunch, tsked. "His widow is selling his effects to finance her return home. Most folks prefer the heavier-type saddle. Planning on racing, are you?"

He chuckled. "At thirteen stone I don't get called upon to race very often, but I find the lighter saddle sits better for long rides."

"It comes with a brace of pistol buckets should you want them."

"Aye. That will serve nicely. Would you have a carbine bucket as well?"

"I do indeed. I shall have it all delivered to Ardleigh by nightfall." The saddler leaned forward and lowered his voice. "Begging your pardon, sir, and I don't mean to pry into your affairs, but seeing you're a friend of Mr. Crosslin, I have to ask. Is there any reason the constable would be asking after you?"

Hawkwood's heart skipped. "A constable? Asking about me?"

"Indeed, sir. He was asking about the tavern. Wanted to know where you sailed from and what your business was here."

Hells bells. Hawkwood felt his heart skip beats, That could only mean they were onto him. His mind raced, and in blurred mental images he relived the drunken clash between himself and a clutch of Irish bucks in a Cork side street. It had left him battered and one of his opponents dead by a cracked skull. "I've nothing to hide, sir." The hell he didn't, but now wasn't a good time to cast a false scent. "I've some business to attend to in Baltimore, and from there I shall travel to New York. I hope your saddle will serve me well."

The old man cackled. "Constable Boulware is probably just satisfying his curiosity. He thinks he's more important than he is."

Hawkwood paid his bill and he'd just stepped into the street when he was accosted by an unlikely pair of men. One was tall, perhaps two inches taller than Hawkwood's six feet, and looked starved and a tad dimwitted. The other was a short, stout man with a prominent belly who looked oddly familiar.

"Do you be Christopher Hawkwood?" the John Bull-looking one demanded in an accent that could only have come from Cork.

His mind returned to the night on a Cork quay. *Sod me. It's the thief-*

taker, Burchill, and he's brought a charley with him.

"What business is it of yours who I am?" He was determined to brazen his way out of the situation by counting on the natural reluctance of men from the lower classes to clash with gentlemen. "Now stand aside or you will damned sure find out what I am if not who." Rather than walking around them, he tried to push his way between them.

The Scarecrow stuck out his arm, blocking his passage. Hawkwood shoved his arm aside and received a glower for his efforts. The man may have wanted to take a poke at him, but he hesitated, probably afraid of the consequences if he made the wrong decision.

Burchill brandished a cudgel at Hawkwood. "Stand fast, boyo. You may not remember me, but I remember you. You set a mob on me in Cork. Well, now I have you and you must come with me."

"Not bloody likely. Who are you any-bloody-way? And who the hell is this gawk?" He jabbed his thumb at Scarecrow.

"Oh, you know me. And to make it all legal, this is Thomas Boulware, a constable for Essex County."

Burchill was trying to bluff him. If he had a warrant, he would have clapped hands on him rather than ask questions. "Well, Burchill, old sod, do you have a warrant?"

"One is coming by the next packet, the same packet that will take the two of us back to Ireland."

"If you don't have a warrant for me"—Hawkwood looked Scarecrow up and down— "and a lot better help than this fellow, you'd better stand aside." He rested his hand on the hilt of his hanger and stared at the pair of them. "A word of advice, my fubsy friend: a tripes-and-trillibubs fellow such as yourself would be well advised to be careful where you point that stick, else your friend may have to extract it from your fundament. Now stand aside, the both of you, and let me pass." After pushing his way between them, he turned. "Oh, and Burchill, why don't you find yourself a nice bog to trot upon until your packet arrives."

He sauntered down the street toward the stable. Though he could feel their eyes burning into his back, he gave no indication that he was aware of their presence. They were going to be back—and when they did come for him, they weren't going to forget the rowing he just gave them.

* * * * *

After a light supper of yesterday's cornbread crumbled in a bowl of buttermilk, Hawkwood rested his gaze on Crosslin. "Richard, as I intimated to you, I left Britain due to some personal difficulties. I fear those particular harpies have pursued me to your home. A constable and some fellow from Cork called Burchill stopped me in the street today and tried to take me. I sent them packing, but I have no doubt that next time they will have a warrant."

Crosslin scowled. "Damned bad luck. What did you do that someone would pursue you to Virginia?"

He closed his eyes and exhaled. "I killed a man. It was an accident. I mean I didn't intend to kill him, but it was during a street brawl. As it turned out, he was an only son and his old man has more money than Croesus himself. He's hired a thief-taker to serve me up."

Crosslin nodded slowly, and Hawkwood thought he saw a trace of a smirk.

"You mentioned the possibility of an agency with this land company of yours," he went on. "I don't wish to impose, but that position would kill two birds with one stone. It would give me self-sufficiency and get me out of sight for a time. That is, if that position is available. Regardless, I need to leave within the next two or three days."

"Hmmm." Crosslin propped his elbows on the table and steepled his fingers as though in deep thought. "The company partners will not meet again until midsummer. I hadn't anticipated you would have to leave before then. It will be a damned difficult journey across the Blue Ridge mountains in winter."

Hawkwood filled with growing dread. Crosslin seemed to hem and haw about the support he would give, and without his aid, Hawkwood knew he would be forced to flee Ardleigh. If Burchill succeeded in raising a hue and cry against him, he'd be taken up in short order as he had neither friends nor family in America. "It will be an even more difficult journey across the Atlantic in irons."

He paused and pulled his face as if in deep thought, then clapped his hands. "I have it, Kit! You and I will be partners."

Hawkwood blinked. "Partners? How?"

"I'm a partner in the Transmontane Company. That is, I own some number of shares. I understand you have a bill of exchange in your favor due in the next packet, correct?"

"Yes, the proceeds from the sale of my commission and my personal effects."

"Endorse the bill of exchange to me. In return, I'll transfer to you half of my shares in the Transmontane Company and I'll invest the remainder for you."

An answer to prayer, indeed. "That would be perfect. In a year or two when this Irish problem blows over, I shall go home with enough rhino to purchase a captaincy in a decent regiment."

Crosslin smiled and extended his hand across the table. "What do you say, Kit? Partners?"

Hawkwood shook it. "Partners. Richard, I'm forever in your debt."

He'd have to take him at his word—and hope Crosslin wasn't giving another cully an education.

* * * * *

HAWKWOOD SHIFTED IN BED, trying to fall asleep but without much luck. At first light he would leave for the Shenandoah Valley. His personal effects had been crammed into a pair of leather trunks that, along with his camp chest, were in the stables and strapped to packhorse pannier.

The Blue Ridge would be a hard four-day ride, and once he crossed that obstacle, there would be another two or three days' journey to his final destination, the home of a Randolph Welbourne, the gentleman who saw to the Transmontane Company's interest in the Shenandoah Valley. Though the weather had been mild, crossing the Blue Ridge in midwinter was a risky undertaking, though one that would probably deter a constable and a paid thief-taker.

He sighed and tossed in bed. At least now he had a chance. One good year speculating in land along with the return on his ready money that Crosslin would invest should give him sufficient funds to purchase a captaincy. A solid county regiment posted in England would be best, but he couldn't risk returning to his old regiment or any other regiment on the Irish Establishment. He'd also have a small nest egg to cover expenses. A year or two in Virginia shouldn't be too big a price to pay for his future security. He just needed to focus on his objective—and stay alive.

A cold draft infiltrated the sash of the shuttered bedroom window, and he pulled the quilt over his ears. Instead of relaxing, he found himself trying to anticipate the difficulties of the trip ahead. Hopefully he could find a place to stay for the first four or five nights, but he expected to be sleeping rough once he crossed the Blue Ridge at Woods Gap.

The door latch to his bedchamber clicked.

Damned hounds. The one thing he wouldn't miss about this place was the hounds. Well, and the food … and the slaves … and Crosslin's low friends… and Crosslin. But he especially wouldn't miss the hounds.

He raised himself on one elbow to shoo the beast out, but there was no beast. Instead, a lithe silhouette slipped into the room. His pulse raced, and he rubbed his eyes, shook his head, and strained to focus in the dark. "Who is that?"

"Shhh," a husky feminine voice said.

Surely it wasn't … "Jenny?"

Though almost invisible, he could sense her presence beside the bed. "What are you doing here?" A stupid question. She wasn't bringing him breakfast, that was for sure.

"You're leaving tomorrow." Her shift whisper against her skin as it drifted off her shoulders to the floor, then she lifted the covers and eased into the bed. Nuzzling her back against his chest, she dragged his free arm over her. "It would be bad manners to let you leave without giving you a present."

Hawkwood pulled his arm away and sat up. "Look, I'm not denying you are stunning or that were things different I'd be in hot pursuit of you." Well, that might be laying it on a bit thick. It would be a cold day in hell before he'd ever chase after a badged bit of laced mutton—but she didn't know that. "But Richard is not only my host, but he has also aided me greatly. I could hardly cuckold him, and not under his own roof."

She turned to face him and draped one arm around his neck. Her hardened nipple brushed against his chest as her other hand found its way under his nightshirt. With only a brief touch, she had him fully erect.

Dammit. There was only room for one head doing the thinking.

Her tongue darted about his ear, and he felt gooseflesh raise on his spine.

"Stop it, Jenny. The servants will hear."

She laughed softly. "They know everything, dear Kit. They own us, we don't own them." She stopped stroking him for a moment. "They know that I'm in your room, just as I know that Richard is with one of his mulatto wenches down in Fredericksburg. You aren't cuckolding Richard. He doesn't care about me or my favors. He needs a white wife for entry into the right social circles." She sighed. "I envy you, Kit, being a man and able to fly to the backcountry and make your fortune."

She leaned against his chest, pushing him off balance. As he fell, she slid one long, slim thigh over him, grasped both of his hands, and mounted him.

"Wait," he gasped as he slid into her. "You can't do this."

She giggled. "But I am." Pulling his hands up to cup her breasts, she started grinding her hips down on his.

He closed his eyes and felt his eyeballs roll up in their sockets. "Ah, sod me," he muttered. "Might as well be hanged for a sheep as hanged for a lamb."

Chapter Three

Hawkwood started from a sound sleep at the cacophony of a barking foxhound pack. Amidst the furious barking, fists pounded on the front door of Ardleigh manor. Jenny lay sleeping beside him.

"Quick, Jenny. Get up and out of here." He rolled from the bed and opened the window sash, then peeked through the gap in the shutters. In the dim pre-dawn light, he could see horses and men clustered by the portico. After clearing his eyes, he opened the shutter a little wider. John Bull and Scarecrow.

He moved away from the window and grabbed his breeches from a chair. "The constable is here for me." He pulled them on and tucked in his shirt. "Delay them. Keep them at the front of the house. Have one of your servants get my horses ready."

She was already pulling on her shift beside him. "Don't worry, Kit." After brushing her hair back behind her shoulders, she gave him a gentle kiss on the lips. "They're no match for me."

As he struggled with his top boots, Jenny's voice at its harshest began to remonstrate with someone. The rough Cork voice that responded could only be John Bull's. Crosslin's voice didn't join in, so he hadn't made it home from his night of carousing yet.

At least Hawkwood was already packed. He tossed a few personal items into a small canvas bag as Jenny answered the door and continued rebuking the men in language more appropriate for a Billingsgate fishwife than the mistress of Ardleigh. A rap sounded on his chamber door, and he drew his hanger and opened the door a crack. A black woman holding a candle peered back at him, her eyes wide with fright. She mumbled something in a dense plantation creole.

"What? I don't understand."

"Mr. Hawkwood." She closed her eyes and concentrated on her enunciation. "You come with me."

Hawkwood grabbed his bag, keeping his hanger drawn, and followed her. She led him down the rear stairs, into the central hallway and out the back door. Gravel crunched under his feet as he jogged behind the slave woman. At the stable door, he was met by a liveried groom holding his mount, a handsome chestnut gelding, and a dubious bay mare packhorse. He fished about in the pocket of his coat and found two coins, both crowns, and pressed one into the hand of the maid and then the groom. That should keep them silent for a while.

"Thank you, very much. And give Mistress Jenny my thanks too. Tell her I will write as soon as I can." He swung into the saddle, hauled his mount's head to the west, and touched the horse's flanks with his boot heels, leaving behind the barking dogs, shouting men, warm bed, and Jenny.

* * * * *

HAWKWOOD'S SADDLE CREAKED as he shifted on the big chestnut gelding and checked over his shoulder. A hunted man could not afford complacence. Behind him his packhorse ambled on a plaited leather lead, carrying all his worldly possessions under an oilcloth cover. He carried a brace of dragoon pistols in holsters on either side of the saddle pommel, an infantry officer's hanger on chains at his left side, and a wicked little *sgian dhu*, a Scottish dirk he'd been given by his Jacobite captors, tucked in his boot top. The butt of his Austrian *doppelstutzen*, the heavy over-under rifle and smoothbore musket combination favored by Empress Maria Theresa's Grenzers and an affectation from his three years with them, rested in a carbine bucket behind his right heel.

This was the fifth day of his trek. The first day he had pushed his horses hard, fearing a pursuit that never materialized. For four days, farmsteads had appeared at regular intervals, and the householders had been all too willing to extend hospitality to him. A stranger, especially an English gentleman, seemed to be a long-awaited interruption in their mundane lives.

Today, however, he followed the narrow road as it climbed the gentle grade through Wood's Gap, the gateway between the sparsely settled Piedmont and the virtually empty Shenandoah Valley. As he ascended into the heights of the Blue Ridge, the relatively moderate temperature transitioned to bitter cold and the north-facing draws and hollows scored into the foothills and mountains were choked with snow. He leaned into the cutting west wind, pulled his cloak tighter about him, and damned February for its lack of warmth.

Late in the afternoon, he reached the crest of the Blue Ridge and began to descend into the Shenandoah. Sleet pelted him, and he pulled his muffler up to cover his eyes and rode blind. He had resigned himself to a night roughing it, shivering near a campfire with no sleep, when he caught the fragrant scent of wood smoke on the wind. The sleet abated, and just as darkness descended, the road entered a roughly cleared field.

Rather than properly clearing the field, the occupant had girdled trees, waited for them to die, and then planted around the dead stand. The field was a stubble of chopped stalks of Indian corn accented by large tree limbs that had fallen from the dead and were now matted with dead weeds. The field showed no evidence of having been plowed, so the owner had likely used a pointed stick or similar device to plant seeds in hills.

"Shabby work, this," he muttered.

Hawkwood pushed on until he reached a ramshackle cabin. The walls, a precarious trapezoid with no windows, were undressed logs chinked with mud and stones. Rough cut shingles held in place by a combination of wooden poles and stones formed the roof. A steady stream of wood smoke rose from a wattle and daub chimney. He dismounted, stretched his legs, and massaged his buttocks back into sensibility. After tethering his mount and packhorse to a meandering split-rail fence, he approached the cabin.

A half dozen ragged hounds charged him, barking, and he skipped back beyond the rail fence. The dogs pulled up, satisfied that the ·interloper had been thwarted.

"Halloo! The house!" he called.

The front door, set on crude and sagging leather hinges, opened, and a man emerged dressed in rough osnaburg trousers and a leather smock. He called the dogs off and then addressed Hawkwood. "Welcome, friend. Come share our hearth."

Inside, he took a seat on a crude puncheon bench in front of the smallish fire. His host was from some obscure Ulster burg that Hawkwood had never heard of, but he nodded as though he knew just where it was. The man pressed a crock jug of harsh liquor onto him, and though tempted to refuse it, he didn't. As far as he could tell, the entire house didn't possess a single drinking implement other than the ladle for the water bucket.

The man's wife squatted by the hearth, stirring something in a three-legged cast iron cauldron. She might have been attractive at one time, but the harsh life in the backcountry had aged her beyond her years. Both the man and his wife were in their thirties, though on first glance they could have been twenty years older. Three children huddled in one corner of the cabin, uncertain at what to make of the visitor.

"Do you care for some supper?" she asked in a near impenetrable Ulster Scots accent.

Hawkwood looked at the unidentifiable substance simmering in the cauldron. It uttered nasty popping sounds as bubbles burst in the surface scum. Did he dare risk it? He didn't look forward to a day of squatting trailside, shitting his insides out.

"Madam, you are most kind, but the long day in the saddle has killed my appetite. Do you perhaps have an egg or two that you could roast for me?"

"Aye, I do. I can also toast you some Indian bread." She fetched a pair of duck eggs from a basket on the table, produced a long needle, and deftly punctured the shells, then rolled them into the hot ashes at the edge of the hearth. As the eggs roasted, she hewed a slice from a pone of cornbread and arranged it on a cast iron harnen near the flames.

Hawkwood and the man chatted about innocuous topics as he waited for his food. They swapped the jug, the man drinking in throat-pulsing drafts while Hawkwood pretended to drink. The woman picked her teeth with the same needle she'd used on the eggs, then rolled the eggs from the ashes and tested their doneness by spearing them with the needle.

Hawkwood felt his gorge rising. Then she retrieved the bread from the harnen, gathered on her thumb and forefinger a dollop of what looked like slushy butter from a crockery jar on the table, and wiped it on the bread. He suppressed a gag. *These are the people I'll be living with? By God, they're worse than the planters.*

He nodded at the woman and began peeling an egg. "Thank you for your hospitality, madam. This is a meal I shall always remember."

* * * * *

HAWKWOOD RELAXED IN THE SADDLE as the cabin disappeared in the distance. He had survived the hospitality of his hosts with nothing more serious than a few lice and a persistent rumbling in his bowels.

Having skirted the county seat, a rustic hamlet called Staunton, he continued south, deep into what was called the Upper Valley. Based on his conversations with locals, he would arrive at his destination in two more days.

At a small leaf-gorged stream that cut across the trail, he stopped to give the horses a rest. As they slurped noisily, he drew a tin flask from the capacious pocket of his coat and pulled the stopper. He didn't usually drink spirits this early in the day, but the wet, gray morning, the boredom of the ride, and his general melancholy over the ruins of his life made the brandy a welcome diversion.

He looked up, squinting, and jammed his heavy beaver tricorne low on his brow and surveyed his surroundings. The mountains were nearly bare and a somber patchwork of muted colors. The grays and browns of the tall hardwoods dominated, but the gullies and ravines that scored the mountains were picked out in dark green by thick growths of greenbrier. Here and there, a hollow sheltered in the perpetual lee of one of the multiple ridges and spurs running off the spine of the Blue Ridge still bore the bright reds and yellows of autumn. On the upslope, brighter green marked heavy thickets of mountain laurel, called slicks by the locals. Off to the west lay the vast openness of the Shenandoah, a veritable ocean of grassland, which he had glimpsed from the crest of Woods Gap.

When he judged the horses had drunk their fill, he nudged his mount with his knees and resumed his journey. Soon he came to a hairpin turn in the trail, where it narrowed and dropped off steeply to the right. A sluggish creek had undercut the bank. As he pressed tight against an exposed jumble of boulders on his left, he saw another rider some thirty yards distant, dismounted and examining a fore hoof of his horse.

"Halloo!" he called to announce his approach.

The man looked up and waved at Hawkwood, then deposited his pen knife in his pocket and approached him. He was a big man, perhaps in his late thirties, though it was hard to tell beneath the heavy copper-colored beard. His kinky hair was clubbed into an untidy queue under a shabby tricorne, and he wore a homespun linsey-woolsey hunting shirt, osnaburg trousers, and moccasins. A broad smile spread below hard eyes that reminded Hawkwood of a snake's.

"Good morning, young sir," he said as Hawkwood brought his horse to a halt. "Where are you bound?"

"The Welbourne place. Is there a problem with your mount?"

"She pulled up lame, and I fear there is no way of setting this right.

Could I trouble you to ride me double?"

Hawkwood pursed his lips. *Not bloody likely.* The man was big enough to lame his horse as well, and he stunk like a badger. "I think not. My horse has to carry me far today and bearing both of us would tax him greatly. I doubt we are ten miles from a farm or ordinary. I'll stop at the first one I come to and have someone send a horse."

The man screwed his face into a frown. Without warning, he lunged forward, seized the reins, and jerked them from Hawkwood's grip. The gelding whinnied in surprise and sidled dangerously toward the sheer edge where the trail dropped ten feet into the shallow stream.

Hawkwood dropped the packhorse's lead rope, grasped the gelding's mane with both hands, and brought him under control. "Shite!" He'd have to fight his way out of here. The man would kill him if he didn't.

"Boys!" the man bellowed. "Come on! I have him!"

Up the hillside behind the boulders, shouts and heavy thrashing sounded as the man's accomplices vaulted from their hiding place.

He booted the highwayman's face, connecting solidly with his chin and sending him staggering. The man growled a curse and reached underneath his shirt. He glimpsed the gleam of a pistol's brass lock, but when the man tried to draw it from his waistband, its lock snagged on his shirt. He fought to free it while trying to keep his balance and retain his grasp on the reins.

Hawkwood kicked again, his boot heel thudding on the man's shoulder.

The man grunted, reeled sideways, and regained his footing. Somehow, he still managed to draw his pistol and aim it at Hawkwood. "Down off the horse, boy!"

He twisted the gelding sharply to the left and kicked at the man's pistol as he cocked it. The pistol discharged over the horse's neck, engulfing Hawkwood in a cloud of acrid smoke and sending the ball warbling into the trees. Hawkwood jerked the reins from the highwayman's hands, shouted, and raked his mount with his spurs. The gelding leapt forward, glanced off the highwayman and sent him sprawling in the trailside brush.

The man unleashed a volley of curses, dropped the empty pistol, and drew the tomahawk from his belt. "Goddammit, boys! Get down here a give me a hand!"

Hawkwood pulled on the reins, reared his horse up on its hind legs, and drove the highwayman off balance again. Now holding the advantage, he whipped his dragoon pistol from its saddle holster and thumbed the hammer back to the full cock position. The motion caught the man's attention, and his eyes bulged when he found himself looking down the .62-caliber muzzle.

The gelding was on the verge of panic. His eyes rolled and he bucked and caracoled. Hawkwood fought to bring the horse under control with his left hand and tracked the highwayman's movements with the pistol in his right. The man dodged under the horse's neck and out of view, then hands grabbed Hawkwood's foot. He caught a glimpse of the man near the horse's breast, and without a moment of hesitation he tugged on the stiff trigger. A flash and spurt of smoke came from the frizzen, followed instantly by a loud report as the main charge exploded into the man's face. The pistol recoiled, blasting a thick cloud of gray-white smoke as it spat three buckshot followed by a lead ball weighing a little more than three-quarters of an ounce. The shot shredded the crown of the man's hat, and he squalled and ran for the brush.

Damn it all. He'd missed. The shots still ringing in his ears, Hawkwood spun his horse about and bolted to his packhorse, which stood by like a disinterested observer. Without a wasted motion, he palmed the dropped lead rope and pulled the gelding into another tight turn just as four rough-looking men bounded out of the laurel onto the trail. He ducked low over his horse's neck, whooped at the top of his lungs, dug the short shanks of his spurs into the beast's flank, and drew his second pistol.

Hawkwood thundered through them, his knee colliding with one and bowling him aside. He cocked the pistol, pivoted in the saddle, and aimed at the group. Though he had only the barest chance of hitting one, he squeezed the trigger. The pistol bucked in his hand, and the ball and buckshot went wide, ripping a shingle-sized slab of wood from the trunk of a young sycamore and sending them scurrying for cover.

He yelled in exultation, but when he looked back, the barrels of three muskets foreshortened into black dots were aimed at him. "Sod me!"

The three men fired in a slow ripple.

The first shot splattered in the tree branches overhead, while the second went wild. The third ball whipped by his head, nicking his ear just as he felt a sharp smack to his shoulder blade followed by a hot poker probing his flesh.

He hugged the gelding's neck and dug his spurs in again and again.

Chapter Four

H AWKWOOD HISSED THROUGH CLENCHED TEETH as he explored the wound on his back as best he could.

Not all that bad. The ball had missed, thank God, but he caught two buckshot. He rolled his shoulder. Nothing broken. Probing the oozing wounds, he grit his teeth and inhaled in a long hissing whistle. The lump of one shot was palpable, so it was close to the surface. The other was deeper, with not much bleeding. After examining the blood coagulating on his fingers in the cold air, he flicked it away and wiped his hands on his waistcoat. The damned thing was ruined anyway.

He cut a section of mostly clean linen from his shirttail, folded it into a pad, and stuffed it under his shirt to staunch the steady seepage of blood. That should hold for a while. He should be fine—well, unless the blood poisoned. Damme, but that was a close-run thing.

He fished into his coat pocket for his flask and took a long pull of brandy to deaden the throbbing in his back. Before him, a wide expanse of meadow stretched without end to the west, its grass as high as the withers of the pack horse. While he found something comforting about the closeness of the forest, the utter emptiness of the meadowland filled him with foreboding.

As he scanned the horizon for any sign that he was being pursued, music carried on the breeze. Not a tune that could be identified, only stray notes. What the hell? Was he losing his mind? He concentrated a cocked an ear to determine the direction, and the music grew louder—the tune of *"Mattie Groves."* He drew one of his pistols and rested it on the saddle's pommel concealed by his cloak, pointed his horse toward the sound, and rode to meet the musician.

An old man sat on a log, his back resting against a massive maple, tootling on a flageolet. He didn't notice Hawkwood's approach, or if he did, he paid it no mind. Scattered about him were a double-bitted axe, a maul, and a half dozen or so iron wedges. A small fire heated a cast iron pot, probably for brewing tea, and by the old man's leg was a one-gallon crock jug stopped with a corn cob.

"Hello there," Hawkwood called.

The man stopped playing, scratched his week-old growth of silvery whiskers, frankly appraised Hawkwood, and seemed to find him wanting.

"Pardon me, my man." Hawkwood felt vaguely uncomfortable under the man's silent gaze. "Where is your master?"

The old man jetted a long black stream of tobacco juice from the corner of his mouth, wiped his lips, uncorked the jug, and took a long draw from it. "My master, d'ye say? Well, sir, I reckon that son of a bitch ain't been born."

* * * * *

"HOLD STILL, BOY! YOU'RE MAKING THIS a damn sight harder than need be," the old man growled.

Hawkwood arched his back, clenched the roll of leather hard in his teeth, and gave a loud grunt to keep from crying out as the old man pushed the probe into the wound. When he felt the probe pulled free, he spat the roll of leather to the floor. "Dammit, you cunny-thumbed old butcher. I'm not dead yet, though I shall be if you keep going the way you are." He groaned and collapsed on the floor.

The old man—he had introduced himself as Bram Rankin while bringing Hawkwood to the farmhouse—muttered a sound that seemed to signify satisfaction, then he held the blood-smeared wand of white pine in front of Hawkwood's eyes. "See that black mark on the end? That's from the buckshot. See how deep it is?" He marked a place about four inches from the end of the stick with his thick forefinger. "It went in at an angle. If I take it out, I'm going to have to filet your back to get to it. Based on my experience, and I've been shot more'n once or twice, it'll serve you better to leave that shot in. I'll make sure the wound is clean and patch it. The other one is close to the top. I'll just pop it out."

"Wait, wait, dammit." Hawkwood rolled onto his back. "Why don't you just leave that one in, too?"

"Better to get it out. You double the chance of mortification by leaving it in. The other one may yet have to be drawn, but it will be very painful, not that a big man such as yourself would mind." He chuckled and took a swig from his crock jug. "Now be a good lad and roll over and let's be at it."

"Wait! No! And get them out of here." Hawkwood pointed at the semi-circle of spectators, six children all sitting with wide eyes and mouths agape in wonder as Rankin worked on Hawkwood's wounds.

The door banged shut. "Do you need help here, Mr. Rankin?" a boy who Hawkwood judged to be in his late teens asked as he shucked his buckskin blouse and then hung it and a black felt slouch hat on a wooden peg by the door.

"Aye, Master Hugh, I do. Could you flip this fellow onto his belly so we can be done with this?"

Hawkwood appraised him. He wasn't much more than sixteen but already had the heavy shoulders and arms of a yeoman farmer and was nearly as tall as Hawkwood.

"Stand fast, you." Hawkwood pointed at the boy, then looked at Rankin. "Go ahead, take it out." He chomped down on the mouthpiece and rolled onto his stomach.

"Just a second, Mr. Rankin." A softer voice came from the stairway.

Hawkwood dropped the mouthpiece and sat up. A young woman stood at the base of the stairs, clad in a tight green bodice over a homespun linen shift with that was low-cut to the point of scandalous. Her skirt was taken in snug about her hips and hemmed short, about three inches above nicely turned ankles. Above a smile that might be sly or shy—he could not decide which—her green eyes were lambent in the firelight.

She was a little too tall for his taste and a tad gawky, but she might fill out in a year or two. Truth be told, she tended toward homely. Of course, there wasn't much for a man to choose from out here. Even so, there was still that red-copper hair and the deluge of freckles cascading from her high forehead down her pert nose and washing over her cheeks. He wasn't sure how a man could ever get used to red hair and freckles, and these Irish women dressed near indecent. Self-consciously, he crossed his arms over his chest and looked around for his cloak.

"Don't be so bashful, sir. I helped birth half of my brothers and sisters and dressed Father's broken ribs. I've seen men more naked than you."

He flushed and started to speak but realized there was little he could say.

She touched his shoulder, causing Hawkwood to start. "Here. Turn around and let me look at it." She was now so close that he could feel her breath on his back. "I'm afraid Bram has terrorized you beyond reason with his roughness. Lay back down. I can see the ball just beneath the skin. I'll have it out in a trice."

Hawkwood opened his mouth to protest.

"Shush," she said. "By the way, I'm Emma. You've met Hugh,"—she nodded toward the young man standing near Rankin—"and these are Susan,"—a nod from a girl who looked to be twelve—"Thomas, Tabitha, Charlotte,"—the latter were obviously twins and waved and smiled in mirror images of each other—"George, and the youngest is James." Each had nodded or waved when named.

"We're the Pettigrews." She did a quick curtsey that was either flippant or polite, he wasn't sure. "Mr. Rankin is living with us for the nonce. Mam is an invalid, and Da has just taken ill. They're in their bedchamber. I was tending to them when you came in." She shrugged. "So, I'm the head of the household until Da recovers." Her fingertips caressed the lump covering the buckshot. "It might be better if you kneel and arch your back."

Hawkwood did as instructed, then picked up the leather roll but decided to not use it. He glanced over his shoulder at her. "You don't seem quite as barbarous as Mr. Rankin, so I shouldn't need this."

Rankin handed her a short, wide-bladed knife.

She placed the point against her index finger, twirled the blade, and smiled—a smile so filled with gentleness and good humor that he was stunned into submission. "Let's see if you hold that opinion once I am finished."

* * * * *

THE PETTIGREW HOUSE WAS LARGER and better appointed than the other homes Hawkwood had lodged in on the way from Ardleigh. He appraised it as similar in comforts to what one might expect to find in the home of prosperous yeoman farmer back home in Devon.

The house was built in two sections or pens of chestnut logs adzed square, both measuring about twenty feet by twelve. Each pen was two stories, and they were connected by a one-story dogtrot. The main door of the house entered the dogtrot from a covered south-facing porch.

The main section of the house had a tall and deep-mortared stone hearth, and a trestle table and four chairs were centered in the room. A fine spinning wheel occupied one corner, well-thumbed copies of the

Holy Bible, Foxe's *Book of Marytrs* and Bunyan's *Pilgrim's Progress* lay on the mantle, and a ten-string cittern stood in the corner.

Delft pattern plates were in a rack on the dressed and whitewashed log wall, though wooden trenchers were used for meals. The windows were glazed with greased newspapers, older numbers of the *Virginia Gazette,* set in wood frames with whitewashed shutters. On the puncheon log floor, planed smooth and glowing with linseed oil and beeswax, a pelt from a bear and another from a mountain lion served as rugs. Upstairs was the bedchamber of Bart and Peggy Pettigrew and a sleeping loft shared by their brood.

The other pen was the kitchen. One rough plank table that held wooden bowls stood on a straw-covered packed-clay floor, and the hearth had a small cauldron suspended from a cast iron crane. The walls were festooned with neatly tied bunches dried herbs, sliced and dried squash, dried beans strung together, and hard-smoked cuts of meat. Above, a second story was a partial loft that served as a larder. Hawkwood slept in a folding settle bed by the cooking hearth, while Rankin occupied a small lean-to cum tool shed attached to the rear wall of the kitchen.

Even though Emma's parents were confined to bed, the farm work was continued by Hugh with the assistance of Rankin. Emma, who Hawkwood learned was nineteen, managed the household with the able assistance of Susan, nicknamed Sukey, who acted a sergeant-major for the platoon of children.

On the evening of his second day at the farm, he and Rankin stood together on the kitchen porch. Hawkwood sipped a large mug of scalding tea while the old man worked on whatever he carried in his crock jug. They looked out on the huge flakes of snow falling, cutting visibility to about thirty yards and accumulating with alarming rapidity.

"I must say," Hawkwood said, "the Pettigrews are a cut above the people I've encountered so far. Their fields are well kept. The house is sturdy and clean and orderly. The food is quite good. They have a barn too, the first one of those I've seen in the Valley."

Rankin nodded. "They're good people. Mr. Bart, as I understand it, was apprenticed a blacksmith. He ran off with the daughter of a gentleman farmer, and Mistress Peggy's parents never forgave them and made life hard for them in Ireland. They came to the Valley about six years ago, I reckon." He scratched his chin. "That would be just a little after I came here. You can see Mistress Peggy's hand in everything on this place. She is quite a lady. Miss Emma is just the spit and image of her in every respect. If you're still here when Mr. Bart gets up and about, you'll like him. He's one of those fellows that other men follow. You don't really know why, you just do."

"How did you come to be here, Mr. Rankin?"

Rankin looked out as the snow gathered velocity and density. "We don't get no proper spring like you're used to in England. It will be as cold as a witch's tit. You'll get a few pleasant days, and then it will be as hot as the hinges of hell. Same with autumn. A few days of autumn such as you're used to, then it'll turn off cold and you're full on into winter."

Hawkwood laughed to himself at the way the old man had ignored his question. *Guess there are more men than me who don't want to talk about their reasons for being here.*

"You said you had business with Mr. Welbourne? Would that business be keeping you in the Valley?"

Hawkwood inhaled through clenched teeth. He liked the man, but he sure was nosey. "I'm partner in the Transmontane Company, and I've come here to assist Mr. Welbourne in forwarding the aims of the company."

Rankin gave him a shrewd appraisal. "Don't get me wrong, Kit. Mr. Welbourne is a fine gentleman, but what these land companies are doing just don't seem right. And it ain't just Welbourne's. Take the county lieutenant, Colonel Patton. Now he has a company that he calls the New River Company. His cousin, John Lewis, owns the Greenbrier Company. All the nabobs in Williamsburg are part of what they're calling the Ohio Company."

He took another pull from the jug. "Then there's the Loyal Land Company. But they're all about the same thing, snapping up all the good land. There ain't an inch of river bottom nor a spring in the Valley what ain't been surveyed and claimed by one of them. A free man has to buy the land from them and"—he shook his finger for emphasis— "pay a quit rent or he has to settle on wasteland. This may be a 'new world,' but the rich and those with interest still rule."

"The Crown owns the land, and the Crown wants settlers on it to hold the French at bay," Hawkwood said, recalling a conversation with someone at Ardleigh. "The companies are claiming most of the best land, that is true, but they must also settle the land or they forfeit their claims. They have invested substantial sums, and they have much to lose. Mr. Rankin—Bram—I sympathize with your views, but it is the way of the world."

Rankin shrugged. "I suppose so. But it don't make it right. You were a lobster? An officer, I suppose."

"Yes, I was a lieutenant of foot. Lee's Regiment. How did you know?"

"It sure weren't second sight." Rankin held up his hand with the fingers splayed. "You were carrying a hanger when we met." He pulled down one finger. "And you have a camp chest." Another finger came down. "Your hat has a Hanover cockade. You carry yourself like a soldier, and you appear to be a gentleman." He closed his hand into a fist and dropped it to his side. "A word of caution, Kit. The backcountry is full of men on the run."

Hawkwood suppressed a grin. The old man didn't know the half of it.

"No small number of them have deserted. They'll bear no love toward an officer, past or present. We've also got our share of Jacobites what were turfed out after the Forty-Five. Walk small around them. If you tangle with one of them, you'll have to fight the whole pack. And, of course, we have our criminal element. Like the ones who peppered your back. I'll bet my last farthing that was Ute Perkins's bunch."

Hawkwood met his gaze. "You know these men?"

"Know them? Of course, I know them. Everybody knows them. Perkins and his boys ply their trade on the Seneca Trail, the wagon road from Pennsylvania to Carolina. They don't hurt anybody." Rankin wheezed a laugh. "You must've rowed them something fierce to get them to put buckshot in you."

"The authorities allow these men to operate?"

"*Mo buachaill*, there ain't no bleeding authority out here but what you got in your own strong right hand."

Hawkwood exhaled. What a fucking mess he'd gotten himself into. He was working for a cause no one respected, and his neighbors were highwaymen, blackguards, and traitors. "Thank you kindly for the counsel. I'll keep it in mind."

The door to the main house opened, and Sukey, breathless and flushed with worry, stepped onto the porch. "Mr. Rankin, can you come quick and look at Da?"

Rankin and Hawkwood hurried into the house and up the stairs. Emma was seated at the bedside of her father, sponging his forehead with water from a basin.

"I'm sorry to call you, Bram, but Da won't eat and he don't recognize me." Concern reflected on her face and in her voice.

Hawkwood stepped closer. "May I?" When she nodded, he took a seat on the edge of the bed and rolled Bart's eyelid open using one thumb. The whites of his eyes were bright red.

Emma gasped and covered her mouth.

Hawkwood folded down the quilt covering him and opened his nightshirt. His skin was hot, dry, and splotched in a color so dark it could be mistaken for charring. He turned to Rankin and Emma. "I've seen this before, when I was in the army. It's called black pox."

Chapter Five

E MMA GRIPPED THE BEDCLOTHES with both hands, slowly twisted them she was like wringing wet laundry, as her lower lip trembled.

"I'm sorry, Miss," Hawkwood said, "but I've never heard of anyone recovering. Has he been in bed with your mother the whole time?"

She nodded as tears streamed down her cheeks.

"Miss, I need for you to check your mother."

She checked her mother's eyes and sobbed in relief when they were normal.

He stood. "Now open her nightgown." He and Rankin turned their backs.

"Dear God!" she exclaimed.

Hawkwood moved around the bed to Peggy. The visible skin, that of one shoulder and her upper chest, was covered in red dots. He touched her and could feel tiny lumps as though she had bird shot just underneath the skin. "Smallpox." He looked at Rankin. "Have you ever had smallpox or cowpox?"

The old man shook his head. "Not so far as I know."

"I have." Hawkwood raked his hair back from his forehead, revealing the faint line of pitted scars going from his right cheek to his hairline. "I can't catch it again. Mr. Rankin, you need to stay out of the main house. Be sure to send visitors on their way. Tell them we have the smallpox, and don't let them inside the rail fence."

"Aye, right you are," he said. "The smallpox spreads like wildfire."

"While you're at it, tell Hugh he's to move into your lean-to until this all passes." He touched Emma's cheek and turned her face to his.

"Emma, I fear you may be infected. You need to stay away from your siblings until we see. Understand? I'm not a doctor, but I am protected, so I will see to your parents' needs."

She wiped her tears with the sleeve of her shift and nodded.

* * * * *

BART PETTIGREW DIED THE DAY AFTER EMMA had asked for help, and Peggy followed two days later. Hawkwood dragged their bedclothes and mattress some distance from the house and burned them, knowing it was more of a gesture than a prophylaxis, but the thought of doing nothing at all was unbearable. Rankin then dug the graves and Hawkwood removed the bodies, and together they prepared them for burial. Hawkwood presided over the funeral, reading the Service for the Dead from his *Book of Common Prayer*.

The graves of Bart and Peggy were barely filled when Emma developed an ominous series of symptoms—fever, pain in the lower back and neck, and then the pustules. Two days later, Sukey and all the remaining children, save Hugh, were stricken on the same day. Hawkwood was up at all hours, providing such succor as he could.

The youngest children were the first to join their parents in death, passing one after the other. The twins, Charlotte and Tabitha, exited the world as they had entered it, together. Emma's case was mild, and it was clear she would recover with minimal scarring. Sukey looked to recover, but after a brief rally her fever returned, and she slipped into a coma and then passed through that thin twilight to death. Hugh, alone, avoided infection. While Hawkwood tended the sick, he and Rankin worked the farm and cooked and dug the graves.

Rankin tried to make coffins, but the number of the dead, actual and anticipated, overwhelmed the supply of lumber, his skills, and his spirit. In the end, Hawkwood wrapped Sukey in a blanket, and he and Rankin lowered her into her grave.

When Hawkwood spaded the last of the earth onto the grave mound, he leaned heavily on the shovel handle and wobbled with exhaustion. "I think we're through it, Bram." He mopped his brow with his forearm.

Rankin snorted. "Are we? We've got a field full of new graves, and we got a boy and girl on their own. I think it's just starting."

* * * * *

HAWKWOOD GLANCED AT RANKIN AND EMMA as they all sat at the table. Her eyes were red and swollen, and a line of ugly scabbed pustules bulled a highway from under her shift, up the left side of her neck, and onto her forehead. She appeared weak and tired and was beyond tears, a look he had seen before. That time it had been Serb villagers standing dumbly in a row, bereft of hope and waiting their turn as his Grenzers herded them to the gallows.

Instinctively, he reached out to comfort her but then caught himself. *Damme, what am I to do? Nothing I can say or do is going to help her through this.*

Hugh entered through the door opening on the dogtrot, carrying an iron skillet filled with fried squirrel and some of the dwindling stock of potatoes. He sat the pan on a charred place in the center of the table, and the burned wood brought to Hawkwood's mind color of Bart's skin at the end.

"Miss Emma," Rankin said, "I know you're brokenhearted, but we have to decide what you're going to do. I can work for you, but you and Master Hugh aren't going to be able to stay here alone. There are shiftless folks about who'd take what you have and think nothing of it. Your da was a strong man, but the two of you will be eaten up."

She nodded. Whether in agreement or mute acknowledgment of words being spoken, Hawkwood couldn't tell.

Hugh filled the wooden trenchers with food and placed them in front of everyone. He served Hawkwood first, then Emma and Rankin, before taking a seat across from Hawkwood.

Emma kept her face lowered, likely to hide the smallpox scabs, as her neck and the sides of her face were obscured by the long copper hair she'd parted in the middle and draped over her breast. She looked at Hawkwood from under her brow much as a beaten dog would look at its master.

Hugh took a squirrel haunch in his fingers and began gnawing at it while observing, with a Spartan stoicism, the proceedings that would shape his life. Amazingly, his appetite seemed unaffected by the deaths of his parents and most of his siblings.

Emma suppressed a sob and stiffened as she brought herself under control. "Hugh and I have an uncle in Philadelphia."

Hugh's eyebrows arched and he paused from worrying the squirrel bone, then they returned to normal and resumed eating.

Hawkwood looked from him to her. Perhaps Hugh disliked his uncle that much? Or maybe his father and uncle had had a falling out?

"I shall write of our plight," Emma went on. "Mr. Hawkwood, if you could stay until I receive a response, I shall owe you a debt of gratitude. As Mr. Rankin says, there are men here who coveted our farm when Da was alive. Hugh and I will be no match for them."

Hawkwood considered the request. A month or more would probably pass before they could contact their uncle and receive instructions. It was early March, and, truth be told, he had no desire to spend time out of doors until the weather broke. According to Rankin, by April he could rely on mild weather. As well, Emma was an amusing lass, even a bit attractive in an Irish sort of way. She'd never turn heads, not even in Cork, and of course now she was scarred by the smallpox, but he could do much worse for company.

After the kindness they showed him, it would be cruel and un-Christian to leave now. Besides, he felt sorry for Emma and Hugh and didn't think Rankin would be all that well suited to defending their interests.

"I would be honored to be of assistance to you, Miss Pettigrew," he said.

* * * * *

COLONEL JAMES PATTON GUFFAWED, rocked his chair back on its rear legs, and slung a booted foot up on his writing desk. He rested his elbows on the chair arms, holding a pewter tankard of grog. Beyond the window, the sun was setting in its blood-red splendor, and he was exhausted from a long Sabbath of preaching. Though he wanted nothing more than to enjoy his grog and then an early bedtime, there was business to be tended to.

He regarded his nephew, William Preston, fondly. The boy was only twenty-two but was already indispensable to managing Patton's business interests and the affairs of Augusta County, to the extent that those affairs were not, in fact, the same thing. "Old Man Huntzinger's tenants are really his livestock?" he asked in mock disbelief.

Preston, tall and athletic, held a dog-eared folio in his hands and had a pencil tucked behind his right ear. "So, it would appear, Uncle. Clendenin spent a few days crisscrossing Huntzinger's grant and didn't find a single cabin. So, he dropped by and told him he was looking for Jakob Hahnchen, Heinrich Rind, Peter Ferkel, and the other two families he'd sworn were settled there. Clendenin said Huntzinger was nearly in tears as he confessed he hadn't recruited a single settler. He just made up the names from his animals. Hen, cow, piglet, and so on."

Patton threw back his head and roared again.

"Uncle, Huntzinger's time to find families has expired. His grant is no longer valid. Shall I order him off the land?"

Patton took a sip of the grog and stared at the whitewashed ceiling planks. "Evict Old Caspar? I think not. He's loved by all the Dutchers in the county, and he's related to those who don't love him. Evicting him would cause me a lot of problems. It does pose a problem for me though, because I've reported those same families as part of the settlers I have to bring to the Valley."

He paused in thought. "No. I have a better idea. Have Clendenin tell Caspar that I expect each of those families to produce one tithable … Hell, neither Clendenin nor Old Man Huntzinger will know what that means. Tell them I want him to produce one male over the age of sixteen for each family and I want to see them recorded at the courthouse."

Patton took another sip of the grog and peered out the window at the rickety courthouse, dilapidated jail, dozen nondescript cabins, and muddy, rutted street that comprised Staunton. "Tell the old coot that even if Colonel Patton, the commander of the militia, doesn't require their presence at musters, then Mr. Patton, the president of the county court, demands they pay their taxes."

Preston broke into laughter. "Will do, Uncle."

In addition to those positions, Patton was also president of the county court, president of the vestry of Augusta Anglican parish, and president of the commissioners controlling the largest Presbyterian congregation in the county. He was county coroner, county customs collector, county sheriff, and the escheator—the official charged with disposing of property belonging to the intestate. He was also the largest single landowner, save George II. In a county that was larger than most European countries, Patton was undisputed master.

He rose from his chair with much more grace than one would have supposed from a man of his size and bulk and strode to the fireplace. A roaring fire held the March chill at bay. Picking an oak billet from the stack of firewood, he tossed it on the fire.

"One more thing, Uncle. The Transmontane Company has sent out a man to work with Ran Welbourne. Word is that he's supposed to place caveats against all our claims along the New River and the Holston."

"Do tell. What do we know about this man? Is he another cully they've skinned and are letting him think he's making his fortune?"

"He's a young'un. He was a lieutenant of foot in Cork. In fact, he came out in your *Lady Charlotte*. He's of some acquaintance to another of the company's partners and bought shares. He may be in some trouble in Ireland. I'm trying to find out more."

Patton faced him. "Well, find out what you can. If he came out in *Lady Charlotte*, the master may know something of him. Let me know what we can expect from this boy."

* * * * *

TWO DAYS AFTER THE LAST BURIAL, a visitor appeared at the Pettigrew place, his approach announced by the baying of the Pettigrews' hounds.

Rankin got up from the table and opened the door to investigate, then turned to those sitting at the table. "It's Reverend Huntsman come calling."

Huntsman turned out to be an unattractive specimen. He was around thirty and short, and a prominent nose and equally prominent underbite and narrow lips gave him an air of perpetual pugnaciousness. Dressed in a black ditto suit topped with a white neck stock and Geneva tabs, he gawped in surprise when Hawkwood walked out onto the porch, much to Hawkwood's delight.

After allowing a moment of silence, Hawkwood introduced himself and invited the man inside. The three men took seats around the table, with Huntsman beside Emma. They chatted for a few minutes, and Huntsman made unctuous noises of comfort and quoted the Bible at length. He then appraised both Emma and the room and furnishings as though he were a Scots horse trader, and the conversation became his soliloquy to Emma.

Hawkwood watched in disbelief. *Stap me! The dog is courting her.*

Huntsman took Emma's inert hand in both of his. "You poor child. Whatever shall you do?"

Not marry you, you hound. Hawkwood sat up straighter. "Perhaps, sir, I can set your mind at ease. For the time being, I've agreed to protect the interests of Miss Emma and"—he nodded toward Hugh— "Master Hugh, who is also affected by this tragedy."

"I see."

"Emma," he continued, taking pleasure in seeing Huntsman flinch at his familiar use of her Christian name, "you're looking very tired. I'm sure Reverend Huntsman would understand if you retired for the evening."

"Of course, Miss Pettigrew. You've been through quite an ordeal, and rest would do you well."

As the reverend was speaking to Emma, Hawkwood caught Hugh's eye and nodded at the dogtrot door. Hugh stood and excused himself, leaving Hawkwood and Rankin alone with Huntsman.

Hawkwood eyed him. "It seems to me, and please correct me if I am wrong, that your interests have evolved, so to speak, from providing succor to the bereaved survivors of this calamity to paying court to Miss Pettigrew."

Huntsman swallowed. "Well … ah … um …"

Rankin fidgeted in his chair, though Hawkwood couldn't imagine why.

"Exactly. That is unseemly, sir, trading upon your calling to gain entry to her home and taking advantage of her grief. Emma"—the man flinched again at her name— "has asked me to protect the interests of Hugh and herself until such time as she's been able to contact relatives. When that has happened and she has a guardian, then you may press your suit. For the nonce, sir, I can offer you a bed in the kitchen, near mine, and in the morning you can perform your clerical duties at the graves of Miss Pettigrew's family. I don't expect to see you again until Miss Pettigrew has a guardian."

Minutes later, Hawkwood and Rankin stood on the porch and watched Reverend Huntsman, astride his shabby pony, recede down the road in front of the house.

"Looky here," Rankin said, drawing the word *here* out into two syllables. "I know you had Miss Emma's best interests at heart, but you did her no favors."

He faced him. "How so? The man had all the tact of a vulture. These dissenting hedge priests or ministers or however they style themselves are a rapacious lot. Sukey is only barely in the ground and Emma still covered in sores, and he's seeing what pickings there are to be had."

"You only get one chance to be nice." Ge raised his index finger in front of Hawkwood's nose. "You can be mean and hard as often as you want, but you get one chance to be nice. You just pissed that chance away. And while we're talking,"—he shot a stream of tobacco juice over the porch railing—"you may not like Reverend Huntsman, but a minister is a man of substance, and Miss Emma is going to need to take a man if she's going to hold what's hers. She could do worse than the reverend … and because of you, she may. I got work to do. See you at dinner." Rankin turned and walked away.

Hawkwood stood on the porch, mouth agape and flushed with embarrassment. What had he done?

* * * * *

RANDOLPH WELBOURNE LOOKED OUT THE expensive leadlight window—one made in England and set with his coat-of-arms—at the two men dismounting just beyond the white-columned veranda.

"I suppose that is the new man sent out to us, Sarah," he said to the young woman beside him.

One of the men was young, about the age of his wife, and dressed in stylish clothes that one did not see in the Valley. His fine horse was equipped with excellent tack. The older man he recognized as the Pettigrew's hired man, Bram Rankin. As they approached, a black groom dressed in a red-checked shirt, buckskin breeches, and Hessian boots with silver tassels took their horses.

Welbourne appraised his wife. Wearing a dazzling dark green gown with white lace fichu over her shoulders, and with her ebony hair combed back from her forehead and temples into a flow of ringlets cascading down her back, Sarah would turn heads anywhere in the Western world. He was well aware that he still had a colt's tooth in his head and he should have wed an older woman—a woman with a dot—rather than a mort thirty years his junior. But when he'd espied Sarah on the docks at Tappahannock, dressed in rags and with the still red and raw brand on the brawn of her thumb, he fell head over heels in cream-pot love. At least here, west of the mountains, there were no young bucks slobbering after her and providing her with temptations he wasn't sure she could resist.

"Cicero," Welbourne said, "please see that our guest is offered refreshments."

A young black man, clad in a red and black livery of fine broadcloth, nodded and retreated from the room in silence.

Welbourne turned to Sarah. "Well, dearest, what do you make of our guest?"

She canted her head back slightly and looked down her nose. "Handsome lad, he is." Her heavy Bow Bells Cockney accent still made him wince. "A gentleman. Don't know how he will make out here among this Cohee trash."

Welbourne had dressed to impress his visitor, and an immaculate wig perched on his head. He entered the parlor on shoes with high, red-lacquered heels, which, while uncomfortable, added a precious three inches to his otherwise lacking height. Even so, his guest was nearly a head taller.

Christopher Hawkwood grimaced when he sipped the port he had been served. The man clearly knew his wines, but he needed to try harder to conceal his opinions.

Welbourne greeted him, then took the proffered letter of introduction, opened it, and studied it. He already knew the contents, as Crosslin had sent him a fair copy by fast messenger, but he gave the impression of seeing it for the first time.

He folded the letter and handed it back to Hawkwood. "So, you're acquainted with Richard?" He extended his hand toward a pair of wing-back chairs arranged near the fire that roared in the large stone fireplace. "I've met him several times. Once I was a guest at Ardleigh. It was most generous of him, sharing his interest in the Transmontane Company with you. This is an exciting time for an enterprising man, a man of ambition."

They sat down in the chairs.

"Let me set the scene for you, if you will. Our company has a charter to survey and claim lands north of the border with Carolina, wherever the hell that may be"—he chuckled— "and in the watershed of the Ohio River. This, my young man, is the chance of a lifetime." He paused and drank of his glass of terrible port. "No, this is the chance of a century."

Leaning close to Hawkwood, he placed his forefinger along the side of his nose. "There is some subterfuge involved in your work, you see. Colonel Patton's company, the New River Company, is laying off land in areas where our company and the Ohio Company have charters. On the other hand, our charter and that of the Ohio Company are in different areas. So, if you find good land that the colonel has claimed, record the location and I will enter a caveat to his claim. At some later point, the Privy Council will sort the matter out."

Hawkwood remained silent for a few moments. "I see. We are to lay out our own claims and deter Colonel Patton from making claims within our charter. Does he know what we're doing? I should think he'd be unhappy about it."

"This is the way the game is played. We all know the rules, and it isn't personal." Welbourne poured him more port just to see if he could elicit a reaction from him and was pleased when he saw none. "Other than the surveys, the biggest problem we have is the people. Richard said you were posted to Cork, so you know the scum you will be dealing with. We call them Cohees. Most of these people are Irish Dissenters. We have some lowland Scots, a handful of Geordie trash, and a smattering of Jacobites who were exiled after the Forty-Five. None of them are loyal to the Crown. Their only saving grace is that they hate papists more than they hate Tuckahoes."

Hawkwood raised his eyebrows. "Tuckahoes, sir?"

"That's the name given to English from the flatlands east of the mountains. By their lights, we are weak and effete and too lazy to labor on our own behalf. The anger that bringing a mere handful of Cuffees to serve me has created is simply amazing. They seem to think my slaves are taking food from a free man's table." Welbourne eyed him. "Beware, sir. They hate you and me. They are insolent. They are arrogant. They are violent. They will slit your throat just for the sport of it. I wish to God the Crown had decided to populate the Valley with good Englishmen or even Germans. We will reap a whirlwind one day because of this."

"I see, sir."

"Wish to jump right in, eh? Well, you're in luck. I have a survey party departing from here two days hence. You'll be back for Easter."

Hawkwood leaned forward in his chair. "Not to be a croaker, sir, but there is an issue that prevents me from leaving then. You see, sir, I was wounded by highwaymen along the way." He waved his hand dismissively. "Just two small shot in my back. I'm fairly recovered thanks to the kindness of the Pettigrews."

"Yes, the Pettigrews are good people. From County Antrim, I believe. We need more such as them. Even though they are Irish, they are well behaved."

"Sad to say, sir, smallpox struck the family while I was there and carried off all save Miss Emma and Master Hugh."

So, Bart Pettigrew was gone. That changed everything. The other Ulstermen looked to him for leadership, and he could keep the wilder ones in check. And he was damned near English, for a Cohee.

"I hardly think it would be proper to leave the people who cared for me when they need help," Hawkwood continued. "So, I promised Miss Emma that I would stay with them, and that their man, Rankin, and I would keep their property secure. She has written an uncle in Philadelphia to tell him the news. When she has heard from him, then I will be free to begin my duties."

"Uncle, you say? I didn't know Bart or Peggy had kin in America." Welbourne shrugged. "Then again, I didn't know them all that well. But you make a good point. The Pettigrew land is prime farmland and has a stream or two that could power a mill. There are many rascals in this country that would take the Pettigrew children's patrimony without a thought. Pettigrew was a stalwart, always ready to aid anyone in need. The least we can do is to see his children safe."

He paused to consider his next move. The boy before him would make a fair match with the Pettigrew girl, and she would never consent to leave the Valley. Hawkwood was English and someone Welbourne might be able trust. "So that there will be no doubt, I will write Colonel Patton directly and have the appropriate action taken by the county court to have you made the legal guardian of the Pettigrew orphans. In the meantime, it will make a superb place from which you can become familiar with the Valley."

Hawkwood grinned. "Thank you, Mr. Welbourne. I won't disappoint you or them."

He smiled to himself, having converted an inconvenient situation to his advantage, then stood. As Hawkwood followed suit, feminine voices carried into the room. Sarah and her black maid. The boy stopped, transfixed and jaw agape.

Welbourne bristled. "Ah, Sarah, my dear. May I present Mr. Christopher Hawkwood. He's one of my business partners, just out from England, and will be living in the Valley for the next few months. Mr. Hawkwood, my wife, Sarah."

Hawkwood made a deep bow, right leg forward, and received a small curtsey in return.

"Pleasure to meet you, sir," she said, turning her head ever so slightly to one side. "You must visit us often. I'm dying to hear the latest from London. There is ever so little entertainment here in the wilderness. I keep asking Ran to take me into Williamsburg. I would gladly spend nights in the rough for the chance to visit a milliner or for real conversation at dinner. Ran is a sweet old thing"—she flashed a smile at him but returned her focus to Hawkwood— "but the lack of guests who can talk about anything other than their latest land claim is tiresome. Ran, have you prevailed upon Mr. Hawkwood to sup with us and spend the night?"

Welbourne gave Hawkwood a leery glance. "No, my dear, I'm afraid that isn't possible. The Pettigrews have all been taken away by the smallpox, save Emma and Hugh. Mr. Hawkwood will be their guardian until the estate is sorted out." From the corner of his eye, he saw his wife smile and bat her eyelashes at the newcomer. "And he is headed there even now to see to their well-being."

* * * * *

As HAWKWOOD LEFT THE HOUSE, he approached another man waiting to enter. He was young, about Hawkwood's age, and wore a matchcoat over a homespun hunting shirt, woolen leggings, and moccasins. Lithe and though he seemed at ease, he slouched with his forearms crossed on the muzzle of an iron-mounted long rifle—alert and his body tense, like the mainspring of a cocked musket. His long red-blond hair flowed over his shoulders from underneath a dark blue Monmouth cap festooned with a pair of eagle feathers, and heavy silver pendants were inserted in his earlobes, which distended them until they almost brushed his shoulders.

"You Welbourne's new gundog?" the man asked, his question carrying a challenge with it.

Hawkwood stopped, noticing the crude tattoos—arrows, tomahawks, and animals—about his neck. "Pardon me?"

"You Welbourne's new gundog? That's what I hear. I hear you're staying at the Pettigrew place." He smirked. "That's got to be entertaining, spending all that time with Miss Emma."

"Who are you, sir?"

"Jemmy Clendenin." He fixed his glacial blue eyes on Hawkwood and extended his hand in as much a sod-you dare as a greeting. "Since we're going to work together, I thought it might be best if we got introduced."

The man was spoiling for a fight, but damned if Hawkwood would accommodate him. He took his hand without hesitation. "Kit Hawkwood, at your service. What is it you do for Mr. Welbourne?"

"I guide and hunt for his survey parties."

"What you've heard is correct. I am staying at the Pettigrew place but under rather unfortunate circumstances. Most of the family passed of the smallpox, and Mr. Welbourne has made me temporary guardian for the children."

He looked pensive for a moment. "Sorry to hear that. Mr. Pettigrew treated me fair, and the mistress was always very kind to me before she took sick. Did Miss Emma survive the smallpox?"

"Yes, she and Hugh were the only survivors."

He nodded and pursed his lips. "They're both strong'uns. It'll be hard, but they will prosper. How's your back, by the way?"

Hawkwood stiffened. "What do you know of my back?"

"Ain't no secrets out here, Boo." He grinned and winked. "People ain't got nothing to do but talk."

* * * * *

EMMA, CLATTERING ABOUT THE KITCHEN, woke Hawkwood from a deep sleep. Sensing that it was well before dawn, he propped himself on his elbow in the settle bed, yawned, and watched her go about her tasks.

Her hair hung midway down her back in a loose braid, and she was barefoot and wore only her shift and an apron. She had rolled the sleeves of her shift above her elbows, which garnered his attention. The flexing of forearm as the hearth's light made a coppery nimbus of the down on her arms fascinated him.

As she worked, she crooned *"A Blacksmith Courted Me."* It comforted him to hear a woman singing and watch her sure and economical movements as she prepared the hearth for the day's cooking.

"Good morning to you, Mr. Hawkwood. Tea will be ready directly," she said without turning from the fire.

His cheeks warmed at having been caught so brazenly observing her.

She turned from the fireplace, where she stirred the cauldron suspended from the cast iron crane and took a seat on a low stool near him. "You came in very late last night. We had expected you to spend the night at Chestnut Grove. Was something amiss?"

"On the contrary, Mr. Welbourne is writing to the county lieutenant to have me made the guardian of you and Hugh until your uncle decides what is best for you."

She smiled, clasped her hands, sighed, and looked at the ceiling. "That is very good news. My father once said Colonel Patton and Mr. Welbourne are very close." She rose, glided across the rush floor to the hearth, and retrieved a brass tea kettle from the ashes. Then, with an air so casual that Hawkwood felt it had to have been practiced, she unlocked the tea caddy and filled a delft pattern china teapot with fragrant tea and hot water.

"Since I am going to be here for a while, I would prefer that you stop calling me Mr. Hawkwood. I'm not much older than you. My friends call me Kit, and I would be honored to count you among them."

She blushed and raked a stray strand of hair behind her right ear. "And you shall call me Emma."

Chapter Six

H AWKWOOD LEANED AGAINST a tree and watched Hugh hard at work splitting cord wood. The boy wielded the nine-pound maul with the same sure ease and economy Emma had shown in the kitchen while making tea.

"You know, Hugh," he said, "you'd make quite a grenadier. A well-knit young fellow like yourself, you'd be a sergeant in just a few years."

Hugh leaned on the end of the maul handle. "My mam used to say that she'd rather dress herself in mourning than see me in a red coat. Even though she's passed on, I see no reason to ignore her advice. Here." He held the maul out to him. "You want to give it a go?"

Hawkwood laughed. "Not me. That's too much like work for me to be interested." He removed his tricorne and used his fingers as a Welsh comb to smooth his hair. "What will you do here? In Virginia? Do you intend to spend your days beyond the edge of civilization, trying to make a prosperous farm from this"—he gestured broadly— "wasteland?"

"I don't see it that way, Mr. Hawkwood."

"Kit. Please, call me Kit."

"Very well, Kit. Here I'm my own master. There is no landlord to run me off my land like happened to my da. There are no tax collectors, no recruiters. Now the life may be boring for you, you being a lobster and all." Hugh paused, his eyes twinkling. "But this suits me fine. Da left us a good bit of land, a solid house, and a dry barn. He showed me where he wanted to build a sawmill once we were able. There's a nice girl that I have my eye on. I'll get married and live out my days right here." He turned to go back to splitting but faced him again. "Kit, if I may ask, if you dislike it here so much, then why are you here?"

Hawkwood grimaced. With manners like that, he'd better stay in Virginia. For a moment he considered fobbing the question off, then decided to answer. "Are you usually so blunt with your seniors?"

Hugh grinned. "You'll either tell me or you won't. Why not ask?"

He laughed. "Sad to say, Hugh, but money determines our future. If you have it, you have comfort. If you lack it, well, then you live in perpetual want. A lieutenant has to spend more than his pay to survive. If you don't have a remittance or income, you're perpetually skint. Inevitably you slide into debt and are reduced to dodging creditors." Hawkwood shrugged. "But if I'm a captain, I can afford to live. Not high on the hog, as our Mr. Rankin would say, but I can be comfortable. I can even afford to wed. To become a captain I need money, and there is money to be made here."

Hugh paused. "How long do you plan to be here?"

"I don't know. Originally, I'd intended to stay here a year. Now I have this guardianship thrust upon me—not that I mind, I owe you and your sister a huge debt for your aid and kindness—so the one year may extend to two. But as soon as I can, I shall leave Virginia and return home. By then my purse will be fat and I shall purchase a captaincy and return to the army. Finding a new regiment is the least of my problems. I have buckets of experience, and my old colonel will speak well of me."

He nodded. "I need to get back to work." With a series of small taps, he began seating a wedge into a log.

Hawkwood sensed displeasure in his action and, for a reason he couldn't explain, felt a need to keep their conversation going. "Do you hunt?"

"You mean with horses and dogs?" The maul crashed down on a wedge.

"Any kind?"

"No. Da had an old Dutch fowling piece, but he never used it much. I'm not even sure it works. He always said he found cows, pigs, and chickens put more meat on the table than game."

"Can you shoot?"

"Never tried."

"Finish that log later. I'll let you try my rifle." Hawkwood looked about for a mark and picked a squirrel's nest in the crotch of a chestnut tree about a hundred yards away. A challenging shot, but not an impossible one. He pointed out the target to Hugh and handed him the rifle. "It has two triggers. The rear one fires the rifle barrel on top. The other fires the musket. Go ahead and shoot both of them."

Hugh took the rifle in his largish hands, bit his cheek in concentration, and shouldered the firearm. At the first shot, dry twigs erupted from the nest.

"Aim a bit high this time," Hawkwood said. "The musket ball drops much more than does the rifle."

The second shot hit low on the nest and sent it spinning from the tree.

Hugh grinned and waved the gun smoke away with one hand as the report of the rifle died in the damp air. He handed the *doppelstutzen* to Hawkwood, massaged his right shoulder, and made an exaggerated sour face.

He laughed. "You did well, Hugh. You've a talent for shooting. I well remember my first experience. I was an embarrassment to myself and everyone watching. This evening after supper, let's get your father's fowler out and see about its condition. If it is in working order, we should go hunting. As you said, there are no landlords or gentry here with rights over the game."

Hugh snorted. "Hell, Kit, you've made my shoulder so sore I can't work anymore today. Let's head back to the house."

* * * * *

WAT TURNBULL TOOK IN THE SURROUNDINGS with satisfaction as he and his sons neared the Pettigrews' cabin. He'd had his eye on their farm for some time. Wat had tried to intimidate Bart Pettigrew but discovered he was a tough man. But now Bart was dead. Nothing stood between Turnbull and owning the land. In fact, he'd decided, a strategic marriage between one of his offspring and Emma would be just the thing.

Turnbull nodded to his son Tim as they neared the front door. "Go ahead. Open it."

Tim hit the door with his shoulder, splintering the wood around the hinges.

He cuffed Tim on the ear. "Goddammit, boy. We're here to court the girl, not scare the bejeezus out of her." His sons and hired men might be younger, stronger, and more vigorous, but no one would ever say Wat Turnbull didn't rule his clan with an iron fist.

Emma was sitting at the spinning wheel in the parlor when he, his four sons, and two hangers-on pushed their way into the room. She jumped to her feet. "Mr. Turnbull, what do you think you're doing? This is my house! Get out!"

"We need to talk, girl," he said as they all closed in on her. "You can't run this place on your own. You're in need of a husband, and my boys need a wife. Pick one."

Her eyes narrowed. "Pick one of your gits? I'd sooner lead apes in hell than be mounted by one of these noddies."

Tim—tall, wiry, and with unkempt greasy locks spilling out from under his hat—slapped her. "Watch your mouth, you bitch."

She staggered back a step under the blow.

Bandy-legged Ned, with only one eye and a scarred face, grabbed him by the shoulder. "No need for that, Tim."

Tim shook free of his grip. "Look to yourself, Ned. You don't have any say here. Right, Pa?"

Turnbull scratched his chin. "Well, Ned is the oldest. If he wants her, I reckon he can have her."

Emma lunged to the fireplace, grabbed the poker, and lashed out. She caught Tim across the back and drove him to his knees. Before she could slash it again, Robbie grabbed her arm and tossed her to the floor. She struggled to regain her feet, but he held her down.

"Pa, this one needs some taming," Robbie said.

"Please, Pa, just give me some time with her," Ned pleaded. "She's scared, that's all."

Robbie shifted his weight, grabbed the hem of her skirts, and pulled them up around her waist. "Not much meat on her, Pa, but she's right nice looking." He groped up between her thighs.

She braced against the floor, bucked him free, and lashed out with a foot that caught Tim in the kneecap. Tim let out a sharp yelp, and right away the other men were on her. Hands gripped her ankles and wrists, and Robbie crouched by her and tore her shift and skirts away, leaving her naked.

"Your brother is right, Ned. She needs to be broken in," Turnbull said over the scuffling. "She won't have one of you, so she can have all of you."

Ned faced his father and placed one hand on his shoulder.

"Pa, this ain't right."

Turnbull addressed Robbie. "Let all the boys get a taste, but don't hurt her much. Maybe that will help her pick a man." Then he turned to Ned. "You can take wait till they're done. She'll be more in the mood to talk to you then."

A Threefold Cord

* * * * *

HAWKWOOD AND HUGH WALKED SIDE BY SIDE, Hawkwood leading his horse as Hugh didn't have one to ride. The wind, a perpetual feature of the Valley as far as Hawkwood could tell, was brisk from the Upper Valley, its gusts bending the small hickories along the streambed that paralleled their trail and creating undulating waves of the endless acres of chest-high grass.

As they walked, Hugh pointed out where new fields of wheat, buckwheat, and Indian corn would be laid out, and explained how his father had planned to expand the plot of flax once the pond for retting the flax stalks had been enlarged.

"By the bye," Hawkwood said as the Pettigrew house came into view. "It looks like we have company." Though they were nearly two furlongs away, he could count eight horses grazing near the house and see two men moving about outside.

Hugh stopped short, shaded his eyes with a hand, and stared at the scene. "Fuck. It's the Turnbulls come calling." He dropped the maul and raced toward the house.

Chapter Seven

WAIT!" HAWKWOOD CALLED. "Who are the Turnbulls?"
Hugh didn't answer other than to wave Hawkwood
onward.

He swung onto his saddle, raked the horse with his spurs, and in a
flash had caught up with Hugh and cantered alongside him. "Here. Grab
my stirrup strap and hang on."

They thundered downhill, cutting a swath through the waist-high
grass as the horse's hooves cut dish-sized divots from the thick sod.
Hugh kept pace with impossibly long strides, grasping the stirrup strap
with one hand while the other was flung wide to keep his balance. A wild
raspberry thicket stood in their path, and Hawkwood thought about
steering around but was afraid Hugh, who was only barely holding onto
the stirrup strap, would be lost.

"Sorry, Hugh!" he shouted. "We've got to go through the thicket."

Hugh spat and nodded in assent.

As they barreled toward the thicket, Hugh reached up and gripped
the saddle's pommel with both hands, hauled his legs off the ground, and
glided over the briars. He then resumed his frantic, oversized strides
alongside Hawkwood's boot. Together they splashed through the broad
run at the base of the hill and leaned into the shallow slope leading to the
house. Hugh was now holding the stirrup strap with both hands, gasping
for breath, red-faced with exertion, and struggling to remain upright.

Hawkwood slowed the pace, but Hugh looked up at him and
grunted, "Faster!"

The boy couldn't hold on if he went any faster, but he was man
enough to ask for it. Hawkwood scraped his spurs along his mount's

flanks, and the horse gradually accelerated. Then he sawed back on the reins, bringing the horse to a turning halt near the rear wall of the house. Hugh let go of the stirrup and raced around the corner as Hawkwood slung his right leg over the pommel of the saddle, released the reins, and slid to the ground.

"Emma!" Hugh screamed. "Emma, where are you?"

"Damme!" Hawkwood cursed aloud. The rifle wasn't loaded, and his pistols were with his other gear. Hearing shouts from the front of the house, he pushed his way around his horse and raced in pursuit of Hugh. As he turned the corner of the house, he found Hugh in the grips of a scrawny, lank-haired man. Hugh struggled to free himself, but the man kept his arms pinioned behind his back.

"Hey! You!" Hawkwood thundered in his best parade-ground voice. "Let the boy go."

The door of the house slammed open, and several roughly garbed men boiled out. "Who might you be?" an older man demanded, and he planted his fists on his hips. "What's your business here?"

Hawkwood sized him up. He carried himself with an air of authority and barely restrained violence. Hawkwood swallowed a sharp retort and decided to try to extricate himself, Hugh, and Emma with their skins intact. "Hawkwood, sir." He lifted his hat slightly. "Kit Hawkwood. I've been appointed guardian for Master Hugh and Mistress Emma until such time as a permanent guardian is found. Be so kind as to have your man"—he jerked his head toward the man restraining Hugh—"release the boy. There's no reason to hold him."

"When the young'un cools down, we'll let him go. Right now, he's better off with Tim." The man worked a cud of tobacco while appraising Hawkwood. "Guardian, eh? Says who?"

"Mr. Welbourne made the appointment."

"Did he? Well, he made a mistake. Considering the circumstances, you don't seem to be doing much of a job." He shot a stream of brown juice from the corner of his mouth to splash near Hawkwood's boots. "This is how it's going to work, Mr. Hawkwood. You gather your things and leave. Me and my boys are going to stay here to make sure these young'uns and their property is protected."

"That may not be possible, Mr. ...?"

"Turnbull. Wat Turnbull. Of course, folks in these parts call me Hairless Wat." He doffed his hat and sketched a bow.

Hawkwood gasped. At the crown of his head, a hand's breadth of hair and scalp were missing, leaving exposed an expanse of yellowed skull roughly transected by a darker seam.

He straightened and replaced his hat while fixing his eyes on Hawkwood. "I was scalped and left for dead by Indians up on the Youghiogheny. They're still regretting not doing the job right. But the experience has made me a patient man."

Guffaws came from his men.

"You were about to tell me why something may not be possible?"

"Indeed, sir," Hawkwood said. "I'm bound by my honor to act as guardian for the Pettigrew children. And I have pledged a two-hundred-pounds sterling surety bond against my performance of that duty." A lie, but he feared he had no choice. "So, you can see, even if I desire to agree to your demand, I am in no position to do so."

The door to the house opened again, and Emma shuffled onto the porch. Her hair was loose as she clutched a blanket tightly about her shoulders. Red-rimmed, slitted eyes exuded rage as surely as molten iron radiated heat. As she moved, the blanket swung open, exposing her leg to the hip.

"Emma!" Hawkwood took a step toward her, but a large hand pushed against his chest, restraining him. Its owner was a squat man whose muscles stretched his homespun hunting shirt taut across his shoulders. He wore a yeoman's broad-brimmed hat pulled down to the single eyebrow that crawled like a hairy caterpillar across his forehead, shadowing one translucent blue eye and an empty socket where his left eye should have been. Both cheeks were furrowed with a latticework of scars.

Hawkwood was a head taller but half as wide through the shoulders, and the man outweighed him by at least thirty pounds. Showing fear was not going to be helpful with these men, so his only hope was to brazen his way out. He knocked his hand away.

Turnbull took a step forward. "Stop. Don't take another step. I don't care about your honor nor about your money. Ned here"—he nodded at the man confronting Hawkwood— "is also a patient man and slow to anger. I'd suggest you keep that in mind." He turned to the other men. "One of you boys get the girl inside. She don't look decent standing outside like that."

There were snickers from the men.

Two men on the porch took her by the arms, and with a rough shove propelled her back into the house.

Hugh took advantage of the distraction. He slammed his heel down on his captor's instep; the man howled in pain. Hugh twisted himself free and ran to Emma. The lank-haired man, Hawkwood now knew he was called Tim, recovered from Hugh's attack, landed a thunderous punch between Hugh's shoulder blades and drove him to his knees. Hugh struggled to stand but caught a kick to the side of his head and went down.

Well, thought Hawkwood, *we're in for it now.* He took a step and landed a hard right jab to the back of Tim's neck. His head snapped over and he fell to his knees. A blow from behind caught Hawkwood on the ear, and he staggered and tried to turn, only to have another fist rebound off his right cheek. He lashed out with a flurry of punches and was rewarded by a grunt of pain.

Someone grabbed Hawkwood's queue, jerked him backward, and slammed him to the ground. The impact sent shock up his spine and rattled his skull. He willed his body to move, but the shock slowed him considerably. Ned stomped a moccasin-clad foot hard on his chest, and he exhaled with a resounding grunt as the man dropped onto him.

Lightning flashed before his eyes as his head bounced off the ground. The man's hands searched for his arms, and one with a grip like a blacksmith's found his right elbow and pinned it to the ground. Hawkwood suppressed a gag as his nostrils filled with the reek of the long-unwashed body and fetid breath of his foe.

He punched with his left fist and landed a blow, a weak one, on the man's jawline. He punched again. This time an iron hand caught his wrist and forced his arm to the ground. Hawkwood pushed down with his feet, grunted, and arched his back, trying to dislodge his opponent. His heart hammered in his chest as his breath came in short gasps.

Ned's companions cheered him on.

"Gouge him, Ned!"

"Beat him!"

Fear telescoped time for Hawkwood. He watched—it seemed to take forever—as the man drew back one of his huge hands and formed it into a fist. The man gritted his teeth, and Hawkwood was pleased to see a tendril of blood trickling from the corner of his mouth and tracing an erratic course down his chin. Then, with a detachment that bordered on disinterest, he observed the descent of the meaty mallet. Hawkwood tried to move his head from the path, but the fist cracked hard into his face just above his eyebrow. His head ricocheted off the ground and his teeth bounced in their sockets. There was no pain, but he was sure that would come soon.

Another blow landed, this one thumping his cheek and eyebrow. He felt his face swell, and the vision in his left eye reduced to a slit. The man stood, pulling him erect, and a fist thwacked into his abdomen. He doubled over in pain, letting out a coughing groan. Another blow glanced off his short ribs, and he lurched to the side and went down on one knee.

Hawkwood tried to clear his head. If he didn't break his grip, he was dead.

A fist caromed off the crown of his head, and more fireworks exploded before his eyes.

Even if he did get out, he still might be dead. *God, not here. Don't let me die now.* He drove his left fist into Ned's gut with all his remaining strength. Ned stepped back as Hawkwood's fist thudded home but still kept a tight grip on Hawkwood's coat collar. He lashed out with his right hand and caught the man's crotch in a death grip, twisting his privates like he was wringing water from an old rag.

The man roared and rose to tiptoes. Hawkwood grabbed a roll of cloth and flesh on the man's chest with his left hand, lifted the man off the ground—growling and grunting with the exertion—and dumped Ned on his head. The man hit the ground hard.

Hawkwood lost his balance, stumbled, fell onto his arse, and groped his way back to his feet, struggling to see through eyes that were nearly swollen shut.

His opponent rolled to his knees and drew a long-bladed knife from a sheath at the small of his back. "I was just going to whip you," he growled, "but now I'm going to gut you."

Just then a musket shot cracked.

Chapter Eight

IN SPITE OF HOW EVERYONE ELSE LOOKED in the direction of the shot, Hawkwood kept his attention on Ned and his knife. Blood streamed from Hawkwood's nose and the cuts on his forehead, dripped off his chin, and hit the dusty earth in fat plops. When he glanced over, Clendenin held a smoking rifle in his hands. Beside him sat Randolph Welbourne astride a strong bay mare. For a man who moved somewhat clumsily in his own home, he had a fine seat and cut a commanding figure on horseback. Behind them at a distance was Rankin.

"Men," Welbourne announced in a firm tone, "you've had your fun, and it's time to be on your way."

"Wait! Wait!" Hawkwood turned to Emma, who was back on the porch. "Emma! Are you hurt?"

She spat. "These mollies can't hurt me."

Hawkwood faced Welbourne. "What about the girl? Look what these bastards did. I'm her guardian."

Clendenin sidled closer. "Never mind about the girl, Boo," he said under his breath. "Let Welbourne get these boys out of here while they're still of a mind to care what he says."

* * * * *

HAWKWOOD SAT ON A STOOL ON THE PORCH, his head tipped back as far as he could manage. Emma washed the dried blood from his face with a cloth soaked in warm water while Hugh and Rankin gathered chickweed for a poultice that Rankin swore would reduce the swelling of Hawkwood's face.

"This is becoming a habit," he said through swollen and split lips.

Her face tightened and she said nothing.

"Me getting hurt and you dressing my wounds, I mean."

Silence.

He tried again. "Does it look bad? Because it hurts like the very devil."

She still didn't respond.

"I'm glad they didn't beat you."

He straightened and looked at her, but she averted her eyes from his.

Gently, very conscious that this was the first time he'd been so bold, he touched the line of her jaw with his fingertips and coaxed her head around until their gazes met.

"What is it? What's wrong?"

Her lower lip trembled. "Those bastards!" she sobbed. "Those sons of bitches!"

Tears coursed down her cheeks, and her shoulders heaved as she covered her face with her hands.

He reached out to give her a comforting pat but then withdrew it. Crying women always left him unsettled. You never knew the right thing to do until you did the wrong thing.

She snapped her head up, eyes fierce, red, and dry. "It wasn't enough for them to violate my home and my bedchamber." Her voice rose as she spoke. "No. They had their fun tearing my clothes off and mocking me. Nothing like a bare-naked girl to make a little man feel big."

"Let me ride to Welbourne's. He can have the sheriff on them if you complain."

She laughed, low and angry, and shook her head. "You just don't understand, Kit. There is no law here save"—she gripped his right hand with both of hers, raised it in front of his eyes, and curled his fingers into a fist— "your own strong right hand. No man will stand with you if you won't stand for yourself. You are an outsider, a Tuckahoe, and you have no name among the Valley people. And truth be told, even if you did, damned few will stand with you against the Turnbulls. What they did here today was to shame me. They stripped me naked—in my own home."

She combed her hair back behind her ears with her fingers, wiped a single tear from the corner of her eye, and looked into the sky. "Heaven only knows what stories they will spin about me, and no man of quality will touch me because they'll think I was had by one of the Turnbulls." She sighed and wiped her eyes on her shift sleeve. "Here, Kit." Dipping the cloth into the kettle of tepid water, she grasped his face with her other hand. "Let's get this cleaned up. Hugh and Bram should be back soon, and then we'll fix your poultice."

* * * * *

HAWKWOOD PEEKED AROUND THE DOOR from the dogtrot to the kitchen area. Emma and an old woman squatted side by side at the hearth, the woman's arm slung possessively over Emma's shoulders. They rocked and swayed together, chanting in a low sing-song voice as the crone added ingredients to a small cauldron simmering over the fire.

The woman had appeared three days after the Turnbulls left. She was tiny, barely as tall as Hawkwood's shoulder if she would have been able to stand erect rather than being stooped and reliant upon a walking staff. Since her arrival, she had slept in Emma's bedchamber, said scarcely a word to anyone save Emma, and taken meals with Emma alone. They spent much of the night doing what they were now.

"What are they doing?" Hawkwood whispered.

"Granny Nixon's a witch woman," Rankin said. "She makes potions that heal all manner of things that a regular sawbones can't cure. She has second sight. She can just hold your hand and tell you your future. Folks say she can put a hex on you too."

Hawkwood started to guffaw, then realized that Rankin was serious. "You jest, surely. Witchcraft and second sight? Humbug and more humbug."

Rankin shrugged. "Granny Nixon and Peggy Pettigrew were grand friends. Mistress Pettigrew would probably have become a witch woman herself in due course."

"Why's she here?"

Rankin shrugged again.

The women stood.

Hawkwood closed the door, and he and Rankin retreated into the parlor. The two women came through the door, arms about each other. Emma, who was much taller than the old woman, nuzzled her cheek atop her head.

Granny Nixon stopped and faced Hawkwood. "Sir, I'll be on my way at first light," she croaked. "You've been most kind to an old woman. I can tell by your face that you think this is some sort of humbug."

Hawkwood stiffened at the use of the word. She couldn't have overheard him.

"I'll not try to convince you otherwise." She held out her tremulous hand.

Hawkwood hesitated, recalling Rankin's words, and then took it. She clasped his hand with both hers, her walking staff clattering on the floor of the silent parlor, then brought it to her lips and kissed his fingers while her otherworldly coal-black eyes fixed him like a snake would freeze a bird.

"This is my gift to you, sir." She closed her eyes. "You'll never leave this Valley. As the Good Book says, 'Moses fled from the face of Pharaoh, and dwelt in the land of Midian.'" She cackled. "And you are truly seated by the well."

Chapter Nine

HAWKWOOD STUDIED THE LINE where the gray-green peaks of the Blue Ridge disappeared into the low pewter clouds. "Looks like rain, Bram. Maybe we should call it a day?"

Rankin glanced at the sky. "It ain't going to rain if there's enough blue in the sky for a Dutchman to make a pair of breeches. You stick to that harrow, young man."

He exhaled. It was one thing being a gentleman farmer, and quite another to be a farm laborer. Maybe this is what the papists meant when they spoke of purgatory. He needed to be shed of this guardianship responsibility and get on with his life. Otherwise he'd be scratching in the dirt forever. Leaning on the pair of smooth handles used to guide the triangular spike harrow, he watched the yoke of Red Devon oxen amble toward the end of the field. This wasn't so hard, really. He tugged on the handles to straighten the harrow.

A week after the Turnbulls had invaded the Pettigrew house, Hawkwood still smoldered over his manhandling by Ned Turnbull. Often, he awoke in the wee hours of the morning, breathless and with his nightshirt soaked in sweat after reliving the fight, thinking of what he could have done. The mood around the place had become grim as Hawkwood, Hugh, and Emma withdrew into themselves in the aftermath of what had happened. "One day there will be a reckoning, Ned," he muttered. "For my beating and for what you did to the spirit of that girl."

"Hold there, Kit!" Rankin shouted. "You're supposed to be guiding the yoke, not the other way around."

Hawkwood looked over his shoulder at the snake-like path cut by the harrow.

"When you turn around, go back over this again and do it right. We need to get the flax in the ground next week, and at the rate you're moving, we'll be damned lucky if that happens." He spat tobacco juice and took a nip from the demijohn he carried.

"Bram, tell me again what you're doing?"

"I'm making sure you do this job right, young sir." Cackle. Spit. Nip.

Hawkwood engaged in a fierce battle of wills with the yoke of oxen but, in the end, convinced them to turn and then forced the harrow back onto the row he thought he had completed. As he steered the yoke to a halt, Hugh arrived driving a large Conestoga horse hauling a sledge piled with split rails. Dismay spread through Hawkwood's belly. "Are you and Bram building that fence?"

Hugh laughed. "No. You and me are."

They unhitched the animals, hobbled the horse, and left them to graze. Rankin leaned against a tree, fished a plug of chewing tobacco and a clasp knife from his pocket, and offered it to Hawkwood. "Want a chaw?"

"Thank you, no." What a foul habit. The chewing and spitting. The brownish teeth bedewed with blackish particles of the cud. Never. He stripped off his waistcoat and tested the weight of the flat river rocks that weighted down the harrow spikes. After choosing one that weighed about five stone, he lifted it and pressed it above his head.

"What are you doing, boy?" Rankin asked. "Ain't you had enough work for a morning?"

Hawkwood lowered the stone. "My business with this one-eyed Turnbull is not settled." He flexed and pressed the stone overhead. "I can best him bare knuckles, but he's too strong to wrestle." He lifted the stone above his head again.

"What are you doing with the rock?"

He grunted and pressed the slab of granite overhead. "If you recall, the Greek Milo of Croton—"

Rankin and Hugh laughed at the reference.

Hawkwood glared at them, grunted, and pressed the stone again. "As I was saying, there was a Greek cove, hundreds of years ago, who lifted the same calf every day ..."

"Why would he do that?" Hugh asked. "That doesn't make sense."

Rankin snickered.

Hawkwood realized he was being tweaked and ignored it. "And by the time the calf had grown into a bull, our Greek could lift the bull." Hawkwood grunted and pressed the stone overhead.

Rankin gave his croaking laugh. "You best steer clear of Ned. He don't care about you, and you'd be wise not to give him cause to care. If you fight him, lifting all the rocks in the world ain't going to save you. There is fighting, and there is fighting. When you were nose to nose with Ned, what did you notice about his face?"

"It was too ugly and too close."

Hugh guffawed.

Rankin set down his demijohn and faced Hawkwood with his arms crossed.

"Fine," Hawkwood said. "He was missing his left eye, and his cheeks were covered with scars. Thin ones. Perhaps from a knife?"

"Ned had his eye gouged out by Tom Cribbs down on the Yadkin. And while Cribbs was taking out Ned's eye …" Rankin extended both arms, inserted his fore and middle fingers into Hawkwood's hair just in front of his ear, and with a flick of his wrist wound Hawkwood's hair around his fingers. As Rankin's hooked thumbs grazed a furrow up his cheeks, Hawkwood gripped his wrists and tried to move his head away before the thumbs reached the inner corner of his eyes. "Ned popped out both of Cribbs' top lights."

He rotated both thumbs upward, and Hawkwood inhaled in surprise as Rankin extracted his fingers from Hawkwood's hair. "Ned is a rough-and-tumble fighter. Those scars on his cheeks are from the thumbnails of men who were trying to take his eyes out. They didn't."

"What's this rough-and-tumble fighting? Is the only purpose to take out the other fellow's eyes?"

"The main point when you fight rough-and-tumble is there ain't no rules other than doing what it takes to win. You bite. You kick. You gouge. If you knock the other man down, you stomp his head. I saw a fellow have his nose and lips bit clean off by a man who'd just lost both his eyes. Lifting all the rocks in the world ain't going to help you in a rough-and-tumble with Ned. It takes a special kind of man to fight like that, more of an animal than man, really. If you want to tangle with Ned, do it with your firelock or a knife. Don't fight him hand to hand."

* * * * *

HAWKWOOD, RANKIN, EMMA, AND HUGH SAT CLUSTERED together on the porch in the gathering gloom of dusk. For once it seemed that they were making progress on the farm, and they'd decided to take time to congratulate themselves. Rankin played his flageolet, Hawkwood strummed the ten-string cittern, and Emma leaned her head on Hugh's shoulder as she sang an Irish Gaelic song in a soft soprano voice.

When she finished, Hawkwood asked, "What song was that?"

"It's an Irish song I learned back home, called *'I Am Stretched on Your Grave.'*" She smiled. "It's a sad song, as you might imagine. A sad song from a sad country."

"Do you speak that language?"

"Not more than a word or two. Few Ulster Scots deign to learn Irish. What's the need? The Taigs speak English. An old woman taught the song to me. I could be saying most anything, but it sounds beautiful."

"How about you, Kit?" Hugh said. "You sing us a tune."

Hawkwood tried to beg off but finally relented. "On one condition. That Emma sings with me. Her voice is so angelic, it will divert attention from me."

Emma grinned again. "Oooh. A girl can't resist blandishment like that, sir. What do you have in mind?"

He strummed the opening chord of *"Over the Hills and Far Away"* from *The Beggar's Opera.*

"Were I laid on Greenland's Coast,
And in my Arms embrac'd my Lass;"

—he winked at her and set her blushing—

"Warm amidst eternal Frost,
Too soon the Half Year's Night would pass."

She looked skyward and sang,

"Were I sold on Indian Soil,
Soon as the burning Day was clos'd,
I could mock the sultry Toil
When on my Charmer's Breast repos'd."

Hawkwood leaned toward her, waggled his eyebrows, and gave her a comic leer.

"And I would love you all the Day."

She blushed again.

"Every Night would kiss and play."

They leaned their heads close together and sang the final words together:

"If with me you'd fondly stray;
Over the Hills and far away."

As the note from the cittern died, Rankin and Hugh applauded. Emma gave him a quick, not-quite-sisterly peck on the cheek.

Hawkwood smiled. *I'll be damned. I'm not sure what just happened, but I think I like it a lot.*

Emma stood, all bright eyes and happy. "Wait here and don't turn around," she said to him. "Promise?"

"Very well." He chuckled. "I promise."

Her footsteps hurried into the house and then returned to the porch. "Now turn around."

He did.

In her hands she held a Virginia hunting shirt of deep brown linsey-woolsey. It was triple caped, with each cape heavily fringed, as were the cuffs, hem, and waistband. He assumed its rich color had come from dye made from black walnut husks.

My God, the chit thinks I've become a Cohee. Why would I want this?

"You have to leave us soon to go exploring with Mr. Welbourne's men, and I wanted you to look the part. Like a true timberbeast. We can't have them thinking you're some soft-handed Tuckahoe."

"This is beautiful, Emma," he lied. "Let me try it on." He removed his coat and waistcoat, then pulled the hunting shirt over his head. It came down to his knees and, to his surprise, fit perfectly.

Her eyes twinkled. "Wait, there's more." She handed him a pair of forest green wool leggings, a breechclout, and a pair of moccasins worked with dyed porcupine quills.

Blushing despite his best efforts, he tried to laugh his way through his embarrassment. "See here, you don't expect me to try this on." He held up the breechclout. *She can't seriously think I would wear this garb ... can she?*

She covered her mouth and laughed. "Oh, heavens, no." She reached out and took his hands. "Though you would cut a fine figure in them."

"Is it true what they say, Kit?" Hugh asked. "That you are on the run?"

Hawkwood forced a chuckle to draw attention away from his embarrassment. "There really are no secrets out here, are there?"

Hugh looked anxious for his response. "All folks have to do is talk."

He pulled his chin. "I've done a lot of thinking about that. Yes, I am on the run. I was in a stupid drunken street brawl in Cork, and I had the misfortune of killing the wrong man—the son and heir of a very rich man. His family has hired a thief-taker who has pursued me to Virginia. I was nearly taken up in Fredericksburg but escaped."

Emma gave him a comforting touch on the forearm. "There is no shame in that, Kit. Many men in the Valley are wanted for something. That is why men come here, to start a new life."

"Right. Of late it occurred to me that I have spent the last five years running from one thing or another. I served in the Austrian army for couple of years. I told myself it was for the adventure and to get the hell out of Flanders, but I was running from my colonel's displeasure, which"—he held up both hands— "is another story. Service there was not all beer and skittles. We—I—did some very cruel things in the Balkans. It was so bad that for some months I could hardly sleep. So, I ran back to my regiment. Maybe here I will have time to discover what I should be running toward instead of running from."

Rankin took a draw from his jug. "Maybe if you stand still for a minute instead of running after one thing or another, you might find that what you want has come to you."

Chapter Ten

EASTER SUNDAY DAWNED CLEAR AND UNSEASONABLY warm for early April. Dew drops sat in their battalions on the grass stalks, and the wind carried the heavy scent of honeysuckle and the hint of a scorching summer to come.

Hawkwood surveyed the gathering crowd. He estimated there were at least two hundred people of all ages anticipating the field day with more arriving. Merchants of all types gathered to hawk their wares, and smoke from dozens of small cooking fires sooted the crystalline morning sky.

Most people had arrived the day before so they wouldn't miss Reverend Huntsman's sunrise service. Some had come in two-wheeled farm carts and slept under osnaburg shelters, while most had traveled on foot or astride rough-coated cobs and slept beneath the sky wrapped in a blanket or matchcoat. Hawkwood had tried to beg off, but Emma insisted they all attend. She stood entranced as the minister filibustered from the gospel of Saint John for nigh on two hours.

With the Easter service and breakfast finished, Hawkwood arrived at the drill field an hour before his militia company was due to muster. He had an idea of what to expect. In Britain and Ireland, he had witnessed the pitiful efforts of the militia, more county fair than martial assembly, and doubted that the Virginia backcountry was going to produce a more warlike gathering.

He'd dressed in a bottle green broadcloth coat, buckskin breeches, and brown top boots, not so much for military necessity but to make an impression on the ladies who would show up to watch. For several minutes, he'd considered breaking out his regimentals for the day but decided that wearing them would more likely make him a laughingstock than overawe the locals.

As he waited, he sulked. *Private man, mine arse. By what possible method of reasoning would Welbourne enroll me in a company of foot as a private man? I'll be the only man at muster who has ever stood watch in His Majesty's coat.*

The muster had been ordered for ten in the morning, but the time came and went with no sign of anyone having either the authority or interest to assemble the waiting men. Hawkwood, with Emma holding his arm and Hugh following close behind, mingled with the crowd, taking in the sights and sounds of the backcountry.

"This is quite a gathering," he said. "I had no idea that there were this many people hereabouts."

"They come from all over to a militia muster." Emma nodded at a passing couple. "Some of these people have traveled up from the Watauga Country. It's difficult for folks to get together. Working a farm takes a lot of time."

"Indeed. I'm sorry to have to leave you and Hugh with so much work to be done, but I must look to my obligations to my partners. At any rate, Mr. Welbourne assures me that the Turnbulls will not bother you while I'm gone."

Emma's eyes tightened and her mouth hardened. "Easy for him to say. We'll manage, Kit. Mr. Rankin will be around, and if necessary we can hire another man for a time. The plowing and planting is done"—she smiled up at him— "thanks to you."

His face flushed at the praise.

"Are you still angry?" she asked.

"I was, but I've accepted Mr. Welbourne's explanation. This Captain Hogg is a cater-cousin of the famous Colonel Patton, so he has the necessary interest to be appointed captain of foot." He abruptly wheeled on her. "Despite him being a rebel against his king."

Emma giggled, and they resumed walking.

"I accept that this Hogg's kinsmen will be lieutenant and ensign. I accept that I am fated to be a private man in his company. Mr. Welbourne tells me that this is not a grave imposition as the militia only drill briefly for two days per year. I suppose he is correct, but it is deuced difficult to be a gentleman and, having held a commission, to be reduced to the status of the meanest laborer."

Emma clutched his upper arm and leaned her head briefly on his shoulder. "Listen to Mr. Welbourne, Kit. Don't despair. Everything in the Valley is controlled by Colonel Patton. He may favor his kinsmen, but he shows preference to those who know what they are about. I'm sure that in a short time you'll be recognized. It's a misfortune to be in Hogg's company. He's a crude man, given to violent fits against those who can't respond in kind, and avaricious in the extreme. Never trust him with money or property."

"You've had dealings with him?"

"I've said too much," Emma said. "The Bible tells us 'whoso keepeth his mouth and his tongue keepeth his soul from troubles.' Spreading tales is not Christian behavior, but take care around him, Kit."

"What was it like in battle, Kit?" Hugh asked from behind them.

"I've been in several skirmishes, but I've only been in what you would call a battle once, and then for only about half an hour," he said with a wry smile. "And that was quite enough. You're familiar with the Forty-Five? The Young Pretender or Bonnie Prince Charlie,"—he sneered the name in his best imitation of a Highland accent— "as our Mr. Hogg would call him. When the rebellion broke out, I pestered my father until he purchased me colors as an ensign in Long's Regiment of Foot. I'd barely turned sixteen and, fool that I was, I was keen for battle. We marched and countermarched in the Highlands. Trying to intimidate the clans, our general explained."

He stopped talking as they neared a cluster of men, thinking better of slurring the Jacobite Rebellion about those who might well have been rebels themselves. Once out of earshot, he resumed his narrative. "September twentieth. Monday. We camped on a hill near an insignificant collection of hovels called Prestonpans. We knew the Pretender was nearby. Our general, Sir John Cope, had good information that we were evenly matched in numbers and many of their men were without real weapons. Just billhooks and pitchforks and shovels and the like.

"Were you scared?" Hugh's wide eyes made him look much more like a youngster hearing his father's tale than the confident young man Kit had come to know.

Hawkwood chuckled. "Aye. I was scared. The bagpipes and war cries in the fog. The guns firing. Not seeing a bleeding thing but knowing they were coming for me. But it got worse. Their charge hit the dragoons holding both our flanks first, the ground opposite them being firmer. The horse fairly flew to safety. Then the rest of the army followed them. Our lieutenant colonel, Sir Peter Halkett, tried to rally us, but the men ran like hares. I was with about a half hundred officers and old soldiers who took shelter in a sunken road.

"The rebels ignored us until the field was theirs. By this time, I was on the extreme left flank of our line with a musket blazing away into the fog. I suppose that it was good experience for what I will be doing in our militia. Suddenly a huge *ghillie* was in among us lying about with that bloody great claymore they are so fond of. He must've decided I wasn't worth the trouble of killing because he slapped me with the flat of the blade. Knocked me bloody senseless."

"Were you made prisoner?" Emma asked.

"Nay. Sir Peter held out for a while longer after I'd been nearly brained. The rebel general, Drummond, gave him terms that allowed us to march away, in return for our word that we wouldn't bear arms against the Pretender. That caused many of us great difficulties with our colonel, and indeed with our monarch, but without honor, what is a man?"

"What of your general and the men that ran?" Hugh asked.

"They say Sir John was the first general to ever announce his own defeat, so fast did he ride from the battle. But a court-martial cleared him. Too many men ran to punish them all. If I'd been older and had more experience, I would probably have run too. I often wonder whether holding true to my parole was driven by my love of honor or my fear of facing another Highland charge."

Emma met his gaze. "I don't believe that, Kit. You could have run from the Turnbulls and no one would have known. But you didn't. I don't think running is in your nature."

Hawkwood made a deep bow to her so she couldn't see him blush.

* * * * *

PEOPLE CONTINUED TO ARRIVE THROUGHOUT the morning, pitching camp on any open piece of ground and milling about with no apparent purpose. He watched them intently. The men were rawboned, tanned to match the maple and walnut of their gunstocks. They dressed in cheap trade cloth shirts and baggy trousers, and a few wore caped and elaborately fringed hunting shirts over leggings of buckskin or wool.

Off to the edge of the gathering, associating with no one, lurked the hard-bitten men the settlers called timberbeasts. They rarely came into the white settlements and lived mostly solitary lives or who had taken up with Indian women and lived among the Ohio Valley tribes.

With the men came their women. The young women were lithe and moved with an animal grace. Most were not what Hawkwood would have called attractive, with their faces tanned and their hands roughened by ceaseless labor. They were as rawboned as their men, but the confidence and sensuality in their walk and bearing drew his attention. Their dresses were hemmed just high enough to show the beginning of the curve of the calf and taken in tight about the hips and waist, and the necklines of their shifts and dresses were scooped low. The older women were as worn and rugged as the men, bearing the indelible brand of life in the backcountry. Their faces were deeply lined, and their hair prematurely streaked with gray, so much so that the women seemed to be transformed from young women to bent crones with hardly a pause.

Everywhere there were children. Running children. Screaming children. Fighting children. Cursing children.

And everywhere there was red hair. Red hair and freckles. Red hair in all its variations. Deep mahogany red, brown shot with red, carrot red, spun-copper red, flaxen with a reddish sheen. His own dark brown hair was in a distinct minority. He had not seen anything like it since his stay in Scotland.

Never one to neglect a near-captive audience, Reverend Huntsman unleashed another hour-long sermon extolling the virtues of militia service, using chapter thirty-three of the book of Ezekiel as his text.

Shortly before noon, the company commander, Captain Peter Hogg, arrived with his retinue on scrawny, ill-groomed horses. Hogg was in the lead, dressed in a short snuff-colored Highland jacket, tartan sash over one shoulder, nankeen breeches, and riding boots. His outfit was topped off by a faded blue Scotch bonnet with a white Stuart cockade, and he carried a basket-hilted Highland broadsword at his left hip. Two men who, by their features, appeared to be his kinsmen followed. Another half dozen men trailed behind, all carrying long arms and wearing the omnipresent bleached linen hunting shirt over buckskin leggings. One of them carried a military drum under his arm.

Hawkwood frowned. He, himself, wore the black Hanoverian cockade on his beaver tricorne, and the idea that Hogg would be so bold as to wear a Jacobite cockade—a sore reminder of the Forty-Five—on his bonnet rankled him.

Hogg dismounted, hitched the waistband of his breeches higher on a waist that was destined to become magnificent in the coming years, braced his feet apart, and surveyed the crowd. He nodded in the direction of the drummer, but the man, entwined by the instrument's shoulder strap, missed the signal. Hogg stiffened, pivoted on his heel, took two quick steps, and cuffed the would-be drummer on the ear. The man staggered and fell to one knee. Hogg cuffed him again, and the crowd grew silent.

Hawkwood pursed his lips. *Wonderful. A petty tyrant. If he lays a hand on me, I'll see his heart's blood.*

The drummer struggled to his feet, came to a rough semblance of attention, and began a ragged tattoo on the drum. Men, about half of them with muskets, ambled casually from the crowd and coalesced in a mob about Hogg and his companions. A few had crude pikes, one a scythe, and several carried wooden staffs, but the majority were unarmed.

The drummer continued to flam the drumhead as Hogg and his brothers shouted, pushed, and otherwise chivvied the men into two roughly equal ranks of about a dozen each. Hawkwood moved into the front rank by instinct. In a British regiment the tallest men were in the first rank, and Hawkwood stood half a head above most of the men. The rolling of the drum rose to a ragged crescendo and ended with a flam.

Hawkwood snapped to attention. Around him the other men laughed, joked, and generally ignored Hogg and his drummer.

"Silence!" Hogg shouted above the din, his voice cracking.

The noise lessened but still didn't abate. Hawkwood remained at a rigid attention while watching the happenings with a growing sense of amusement.

Somewhere in the rear rank, a man muttered in a stage whisper, "Eh, fuck off, you Sawney bastard."

The company erupted in laughter.

"Silence!" Hogg's shout broke into a screech midway. An uneasy silence reigned over not only the company but also the crowd. "Men! When the drum stops you will be silent."

Hawkwood laughed to himself. If he kept shouting like that, he wouldn't have a voice in another half hour. He closed his eyes and exhaled slowly. What kind of a mess had he gotten himself into?

"Look at this new man. He knows what he's about," Hogg went on.

Hawkwood snapped out of his reverie. *Damme. I didn't want this.*

He stopped a pace in front of Hawkwood and looked him up and down. Hawkwood focused on a distant point and brought his firelock up smartly in front of his body. Hogg was about four inches shorter, fiftyish, and his sandy hair was streaked rat-gray. His eyes were a transparent blue and set too close to his prominent Roman nose.

"A lobster, were you?" His Lowland Scots accent made Hawkwood want to grind his teeth.

"Sir!" he replied. No private could ever do very wrong by replying, "Sir!" to any question from an officer.

"Which regiment?"

"Halkett's Regiment of Foot. Sir!" Hawkwood's voice, trained on the parade ground since he was sixteen years old, carried across the field.

Hogg grimaced, turned about, and marched to the front of the company. Gazing balefully at Hawkwood, he ordered, "Shoulder your firelocks."

Hawkwood shouldered the musket in three crisp movements, but he was alone in this accomplishment. The formation resembled a field of grass in a heavy wind as the company struggled to move their various weapons onto their right shoulder.

The company drilled haphazardly for the next hour, blundering through one basic maneuver after the other. Hawkwood bristled as he attempted to fathom and respond to commands that were made up as needed. Neither Hogg nor his officers and noncommissioned officers seemed to have the vaguest idea, or interest for that matter, in military drill. The only benefit he garnered from the morning was surreptitiously flirting with the girls watching.

He caught the eye of one girl with shocking red hair, freckles, and luminescent green eyes, then winked at her. Though she covered her mouth and giggled, she met his eye steadily and then turned and whispered to her friends. One of them, tall, lean, and with coppery hair spilling from beneath a mobcap, blew him a kiss as he was moving his musket from right shoulder arms to present arms. He puckered his lips in an exaggerated kiss in response and was rewarded by laughter.

Another girl, middling height and freckled, held his gaze and moved her hands up her sides, as if they were those of a lover, then cupped her smallish breasts and winked. His jaw dropped and he missed a movement in the drill, which seemingly went unnoticed to everyone but himself and the girls.

The flirtation continued sporadically until the company was dismissed to find dinner. Hawkwood looked around for his admirers, but they were nowhere to be seen. Also absent were Emma and Hugh. Disappointed, he considered where to eat.

Many of the men were accompanied by their families and ate with them. The single men, however, had formed an informal mess in the shade of a towering maple. They were frying bacon and potatoes in a cast iron skillet.

"Hey, lobster," a raw Ulster voice called.

At first, he was inclined to ignore what he took as an insult, but then he decided to confront it. One of the men, a paunchy middle-aged man sharing the copper hair of his neighbors, waved him over. He immediately saw that the call of *lobster* was not a jibe; they simply didn't know his name.

"Hawkwood," he said on approaching them, raising his fingertips to his hat brim in an informal salute. "Kit Hawkwood."

"Pull up a chair, Hawkwood," a gap-toothed adolescent said, making a sweeping gesture with his arm.

Everyone laughed.

"Why, thankee, sir." He sat and then, observing the others, reclined on one elbow.

"Care to join us? We have a mess of bacon and potatoes nearly done." The offer came from the man who had waved him over.

"I would be obliged to you, sir."

They were hard-looking men who carried themselves without a hint of deference to anyone or anything. Their easy camaraderie indicated they were all familiar with one another.

"You were a lobster?" another man asked, also in an Ulster accent.

"Late of the Forty-Fourth Foot at Royal Barracks in Cork."

"What brings you out here, Hawkwood? We don't see many Tuckahoes out here."

"Same as you."

"You mean running from Jack Ketch?" another japed to everyone's amusement.

Hawkwood waited for the laughter to die. "I'm trying to better my standing in the world."

Some of the men groaned, while a few nodded in agreement.

"Be careful, young sir, of flying too high." A rugged-featured man next to him spooned potatoes and diced bacon onto a slab of bark that served him as a trencher. "Those what have power are very reluctant to share it. The best land is reserved to those who fancy themselves as lords. They might have their rivalries, but they're blood kin. At the first danger, they cleave together. Stay in your place, and you'll get along fine." He passed the skillet to Hawkwood and occupied himself with his food.

A neighbor offered him a square of bark, and Hawkwood heaped it with food, then passed the skillet.

"Aye," another said, "so long as you stay in your place, you'll have no problems from Patton or Lewis or Beverley. But step outside the bounds and try to claim your own land, and you'll find your house pulled down about your ears."

Hawkwood raised his eyebrows. "Really? They'd do that?"

"Look about you." A short man with the shoulders of a blacksmith gestured. "What do you see? A lot of open land and very few people. Yet we all pay quit rents to one of the big men in the Valley. If you travel down Valley to Frederick Town, you're beholden to either Heydt or Fairfax for your land. They claim all the best land for themselves and leave the barrens and wasteland to people like us. If you give them trouble, suddenly they find problems with your deed and you're tossed off. All your work forfeited. You, your woman, and bairns left to starve." He spat to one side. "They think they're great lairds and we're but tenant farmers. Damme, they'll not do that in this country. I'll move beyond the mountains first."

"Don't pay any mind to Joe here," said a tall, lean man who looked as though he was spawned from braided rawhide. "He's just sorry."

The other men hooted, and the blacksmith stirred uneasily.

"If you try to grab a flat meadow or an old Indian field by a stream or river, you can expect that one of our worthies has already laid claim to it. Joe's right. Beverley and the like have taken all the best land. But all you need to do to get four hundred acres in your own name is make a tomahawk claim. Mark your land, build a house, and plant a crop. So, find yourself a nice piece of land that has a spring, throw up a lean-to, and scatter about some Indian corn and potato eyes. Of course, eventually you have to work to clear the land, and that's what Joe objects to." The rawhide man extended his hand. "Sam Farris. This here is my brother Joe. We're from down toward New River." He waved vaguely to the southwest.

A crock demijohn passed amongst the men. It came to Hawkwood, and he took a long drink of fiery Jamaica rum and passed it on. Some of the men stretched out in the spring sun for a nap. One produced a Jew's harp, leaned heavily against the maple trunk, and began playing "The Escape of Old John Webb." The gap-toothed boy sang accompaniment, and conversation ceased as the boy's clear tenor held them rapt.

The food and companionship made Hawkwood feel at peace with the world. He fished into his coat pocket and pulled a flask of brandy, then took a sip and handed it to Sam Farris. He took a draw from the flask, paused as he considered taking another, and then passed it to his brother. Most were considerate of their fellows, taking only a sip, and the one man who took too large a drink drew jeers and catcalls.

As the boy sang "Twa Corbies," Hawkwood's flask was returned empty. Knowing he had no chance of finding more brandy out here, he slid the flask back into his pocket.

Hawkwood was sleepy but resisted the idea of stretching out on the grass and dozing. He stood, strolled to the top of a hillock beyond the spread of the maple's limbs, and gazed in contemplation at the Alleghenies towering in the west. Soon he was joined by Sam Farris. His approach was so quiet that Hawkwood sensed his presence rather than hearing his footsteps.

Farris stood beside him, also looking off into the distance. "What do you intend to do here, Mr. Hawkwood? Not many Tuckahoe gentlemen are interested in clearing trees, grubbing brush, and planting crops."

"Quite honestly, sir, I don't have a clear plan. I have some small amount of money, and I'm examining opportunities for myself."

"You know there ain't much difference between a lie and half a lie."

Hawkwood bristled and opened his mouth to protest.

Farris motioned him into silence. "I understand you're working for the Ohio Company to protect their claims by helping the Transmontane Company enter caveats on Colonel Patton's deeds."

Hawkwood stared at him as his mind raced. The only person who knew that was Welbourne. "I take umbrage, sir, at your accusation."

"Umbrage, eh?" Farris drawled. "Well, I don't know what that is, but I'd be excited too if these boys found out I was trying to make the deeds to their homesteads invalid so a bunch of Tuckahoe planters could turn a fast guinea." He faced Hawkwood. "Look here. You seem like an honorable man. But you haven't invested five, ten years of your life carving fields from the barrens. These boys have. You get involved in this; you're going to get hurt."

Hawkwood opened his mouth two or three times as he alternated between protesting Farris's statement and being silenced by the magnitude of his revelation. If it became common knowledge, he'd find himself dead by a roadside. And he wouldn't blame them in the least.

"I heard you got connections across the Blue Ridge," Farris continued, "But look around. Did you stop to consider why every man-jack in the county with two shillings to rub together is rated an officer in the militia though they have no idea what they are about? And you, the only experienced soldier in the Valley, excepting, of course, our captain,"—he grinned and winked— "they make a private man? You ain't kin and you ain't a part of their club. Welbourne and Patton and Lewis, they're thicker'n thieves and they squabble over land patents for entertainment. They'll throw you to the wolves if it serves their purpose."

Farris turned to walk away but then stopped. "As long as I'm handing out advice on how you should run your life, son, let me put this on the table. Sarah Welbourne is a fetching woman, no doubt about that.

But don't think that Welbourne don't keep a close eye on her as any colt's tooth with a brain in his head would do.

"And she's not to be trusted. Keep that in mind when you're making calf eyes at her. And while we're on the subject, you ain't the only fellow with his eye out for one of those chits you were flirting with. The wrong man might think that girl is his and take—what did you call it? — 'umbrage.' One man can only handle so many women, and it looks like your hands are full already."

Chapter Eleven

B RIGHT SUN SPILLED UNDER THE PORCH ROOF AS EMMA spun wool into yarn on a spindle.

Hawkwood, standing beside her, helped in a modest way by holding the distaff. "What did you think of the militia muster?"

She shrugged. "It was good to be away from the house for a day." A crease formed between her eyes and her lower lip jutted, the way it did when she was perturbed about something. Without looking at him, she said, "You had a grand time."

"Hardly. Our captain is not only a rebel but an ass and a fool. Lucky for us we'll never see active service or he'd get the lot of us killed."

"I'm talking about the girls you were making calf eyes at."

Hawkwood fumbled with the distaff. He recovered and tried to ignore her comment.

"Emma, I wasn't making eyes, calf or otherwise, at any of them. It was just a flirtation."

She shook her head slightly. "The one running her hands all over herself, Sally Crofter, is nothing but a bunter. She's lain with most every man in the county. I heard someone ran onto her riding Saint George."

"Emma, that language is very unbecoming."

"Don't you mind my language, Mr. Hawkwood. She was found with one of the Crockett brothers in the weeds. If you're interested, she'll fall over for six pence; a thruppence if she takes a fancy to you." She gave him a cold stare. "And she did take a fancy to you, that she did. I'm doing you a favor by telling you her price. I wouldn't want her to look at your fancy clothes and think she could gull you."

"Emma, please. I have no romantic interest in anyone."

She straightened her back and raked stray wisps of gossamer hair back behind her ears. "Well, I must be getting supper on. Come in when you are ready." She stood and went inside.

Hawkwood stared at the spindle dangling idly from the distaff. *What the hell was that about?*

* * * * *

JEMMY CLENDENIN CROSSED HIS ARMS on his saddle pommel and rested astride his shaggy cob as Hawkwood dismounted and walked to the edge of the precipice. The New River was hard below the cliff but obscured from view by the dense growth of trees along its banks. The surveying party was likely hard at work laying off a parcel that included an Indian field and a couple of streams fed by springs gushing from fissures in the limestone bedrock.

Fishing into his coat pocket, Hawkwood produced a green shagreen-covered spyglass, extended it, and surveyed the land lying to the south. The sun was fading, and the April wind was brisk and cold in the mountains, though the vague warmness that augured spring, already in full bloom in the Valley floor, was fast approaching the mountain tops.

They had been on horseback for three weeks, exploring the New River and the streams that fed it, marking the best lands for the Transmontane Company. He intended to take off on his own to explore for land, confident in his ability to reunite with the surveyor and his chain crew, but Clendenin had insisted that he come along. Hawkwood had seen little of him on the trail, as Clendenin had been occupied by supplying meat for the work party while the surveyor showed Hawkwood the finer points of picking the best parcels.

"Looking for anything in particular? Or just looking?" Clendenin asked in his nasal Ulster accent.

Hawkwood passed his flask, filled with cheap rum, to him. "Everyone seems mad for land, so I thought I'd join the bedlam."

"What's a squireen like yourself want with land out here? Didn't you say you were here to make your fortune and run back to England? Pardon me for saying so, Boo, but you don't strike me as a farmer."

"I'm not, Jemmy. I'd like to raise horses. I've seen a few of those Conestoga horses. In fact, the Pettigrews own one. They're beautiful animals. With the right pasturage, I think I could start a good herd."

"The first thing that would happen would be the Shawnee would run off your stock and lift your hair. If they didn't, then Ute Perkins and his boys would take them. He might take that buckshot back from you too."

Hawkwood gave him a sour grin. "The land is near free for the taking. If I can't raise horses, maybe I can find someone to buy the land from me. What about up here on this mountain? It's about a thousand acres. Most of it is already meadow, and there's a spring that feeds a creek. Plenty of trees for a cabin and firewood. What do you think?"

"I think what the Shawnee don't steal, Perkins will."

Hawkwood snapped the telescope shut as Clendenin handed him the flask. He took a deep drink. "If I may ask, Jemmy, where did you get those tattoos on your neck, and why do you wear those weights in your ears?"

"No secret, Boo. My family was killed by the Shawnee, and I was taken prisoner. They adopted me and made me a warrior. These tomahawks here"—Clendenin indicated his neck—"are men that I killed in raids."

Hawkwood could count eight above his collarbones.

Clendenin lifted the hem of his hunting shirt, exposing his bare leg above his blue wool legging. "The arrows mark the raids I went on when we took prisoners or scalps. Some of these here"—he pointed to some geometric shapes and crude animals—"are just decoration. Shawnee men—hell, most Indian men—wear their ears like mine." He touched the heavy silver pendants within distended earlobes. "Once you get them stretched out, there's not much of a way of getting rid of them."

"What was life with the Indians like?"

Clendenin shrugged. "Not bad once you're adopted. It took a long time before I could forget my mam's scalp being scraped and mounted on a willow hoop … and Pa being burned alive." His jaw clenched. "When they trusted me enough to stop watching me all the time, I ran away, down the Ohio to the Kanawha and here." He faced Hawkwood. "I hate them for what they did, and they'll be given no quarter by me." He held out his open hand, then took a few shallow sips when he handed him he flask. "How'd you get crosswise with the Turnbulls?"

"They were abusing Emma and Hugh, forced their way into their house, so I stepped in. Needless to say, I was grateful when you showed up with Welbourne. What's their story?"

He snorted. "North Country Geordie trash by way of Newgate. One step ahead of the sheriff's men and a short cart ride to the gallows. Wat is clever, and a more evil man you'll never meet. I think he's a bit tetched, but you have to credit a man who has been scalped and lived to tell about it."

Clendenin took another sip. "The big'un, Ned, can be a decent sort, but mostly he's mean and strong. Ned will kill you, or gouge out both your eyes, if he gets a chance. Wat's boy Tim, the one whose cock you knocked in the dirt, caught the short end of the stick. He's dumber than Ned but on the scrawny side. That's a bad combination out here. Then there's Robbie. Now he has all the brains in the family, not that it amounts to much. And Willie, who's smart and sneaky. He was in the bunch you tangled with but didn't get involved in the scrap. Willie never gets involved in a fight. You'd do well to steer clear of them."

"I was afraid to leave Emma and Hugh to come on this trip, but Mr. Welbourne assured me that Wat wouldn't bother them again."

"Did he now? The Turnbulls are villains, but Patton and his circle find them useful. If it comes down to a fight, you can't count on anything but—"

"I know, I know. My own strong right hand. That's what Emma told me after the Turnbulls left."

"Told you that, did she? That's damned good advice." He grinned. "How do things stand between you and Emma? I hear she's sweet on you."

Hawkwood bit his lower lip as he considered his answer. "My intentions toward Emma are that I safeguard her and Hugh until a permanent guardian appears. She's written an uncle in Philadelphia, and we hope that this matter will be settled shortly."

Clendenin stared at Hawkwood for a long moment, then nodded. "I heard you run the preacher off when he came a-courting. He would have been a good match for an orphan girl. Why'd you do that?"

"He annoyed me, the greasy, unctuous little twit."

"Maybe so, Boo, but he was a good match, and unless you intend paying court to her yourself, it was a selfish act. What was the fable about that? The Dog in the Manger? Emma's a handsome woman. Better by half than most of the trulls you find here. If I come paying court, Boo, and you try that on me, we'll have more than words."

"Jemmy, Emma has a mind of her own. If you wish to pay her court, you'll find that I won't stand in your way. I came to Virginia to repair my fortunes. When I have done that, I shall return to England. Me paying court to Emma would be dishonest and wrong. She would never be any more at home in England than I will in Virginia."

Hawkwood slid the empty flask back into his pocket. "Now can you blaze some of these trees for a tomahawk claim? I'm going to build a lean-to over by the spring." Grinning, he delved into his saddlebag and pulled out a handful of small, shriveled potatoes that were sprouting eyes. "And plant my first crop."

* * * * *

"Mr. Buchanan, am I correct that a chain is sixty-six feet?" Hawkwood asked.

Buchanan, the surveyor as well as Colonel Patton's son-in-law, was short and about fifty, with his red-blond hair thinning on the sides and having completely abandoned his crown. He looked up from his journal. "That's right, sir, sixty-six feet or a hundred links."

"Well, I'm not a surveyor, but I am a horseman. A hand"—he held up his open palm and indicated the distance between the lowest thumb joint and the outside edge of his palm— "is four inches. My hand is not exactly four inches, but it is very close. A link should be just shy of eight inches, but when I examined one of our chains the links are nearly three hands long. How can that be?"

Buchanan looked at him hard and went back to scribbling. "As you know, there are all manner of measurements with the same name. A mile in England is not the same as a mile on the Continent. A French *avoirdupois* pound is an eighth-part heavier than an English pound. I assure you, sir, this instrument is proper. The chain is a different length than Gunter's."

Hawkwood bit the inside of his cheek. He knew the man was lying. Moreover, Buchanan's face said he didn't credit his own lies. But he could see no advantage to calling the man on the lie.

"Ah, of course, sir. My mistake." What had he tumbled onto here? Damme, but Buchanan was looking too cutty-eyed and got busy writing too damned quick for there not to be something amiss.

Hawkwood stood and strolled down to the bank of the New River, stooped, and selected a sandstone pebble worn into a saucer shape by the current, then skipped it at a brace of blue herons high stepping their way around a half-submerged tree trunk, sending them into panicked flight. After scooping up a handful of pebbles, he tossed one idly toward midstream. Others followed it with increasing velocity as he pondered the chain.

Of course. They made a claim based on this long chain and payed quit rents to the Crown based on that measurement. The chain crew was none the wiser, so they couldn't talk out of turn. Then they sold parcels at the normal chain length and collected payment and quit rents from the buyer. One acre claimed from the Crown was nigh on two acres on the ground. And no one was the wiser.

"Damn my eyes," he muttered. "This is a nest of thieves."

* * * * *

HAWKWOOD GESTURED UP A SMALL HOLLOW near the New River as he and Clendenin were ranging ahead of the survey party, scouting for the best potential farmland. "What's that?"

Disgusted, he'd had enough of watching the survey party at work. He thought about his conversations with Farris, the men at the militia muster, and Clendenin. They were men on the make who had few scruples when it came to acquiring wealth, particularly acquiring wealth at the Crown's expense. If they would disadvantage their sovereign, who had power of life and death over them, then what chance did he have, being only a passing acquaintance of Welbourne and Crosslin?

"Looks like it might've been a cabin once upon a time. Let's take a look." Clendenin checked the priming in his rifle and motioned for Hawkwood to move abreast of him by about ten yards.

Hawkwood drew his rifle from the carbine bucket and checked the priming in both pans, then nodded to Clendenin. They urged their horses forward at a slow walk, making scarcely a sound.

The roof of the cabin had fallen in, and what had been a porch had collapsed, taking the front wall of the structure with it. The wattle-and-daub chimney, choked with honeysuckle, stood sentinel over the ruins. First Clendenin, then Hawkwood, dismounted and surveyed the scene.

"Look here, Boo." Clendenin scuffed aside a clump of calla lilies. "A tombstone."

Hawkwood knelt, gently rubbed his fingers over the face of the stone to remove lichens and peered at the faint engraving. "'Mary Porter. Killed by Indians November 28, 1742. Beloved wife of Joseph.'" He stood and brushed the debris from the knees of his breeches. "Did you ever hear of this Porter?"

Clendenin shook his head. "When he lived here, there were damned few whites west of the Blue Ridge."

"I wonder what makes a man leave civilization behind and move out here with just himself and his wife?"

"Don't know." He shrugged. "Could be he wanted to raise horses."

They mounted up and rode for another half hour.

Hawkwood didn't understand these people. What had compelled this Porter cove to not only remove himself to Virginia, but once he was here to fly west of the Blue Ridge? And what kind of love or loyalty did Mary Porter have that convinced her to go with her man?

But he could ask the same of Bart and Peggy Pettigrew, he supposed. They weren't the rude and dirt poor Cohee trash that abounded in the Upper Valley. They didn't live in squalor, and they had books in the house, for heaven's sake. They could have prospered in Ireland or stayed east of the mountains, but they'd come here and brought their children with them.

Hawkwood spied a bald knob and decided to ride to the top to get a better idea of the countryside. With Clendenin by his side, he plodded up the shallow slope and over the forest floor cobbled by husks from old-growth black walnut trees, to a find the promontory was actually a vast plateau covered with waist-high grass. He opened his spyglass and scanned the horizon. Tendrils of smoke rose above a copse of trees on a bare knoll, and he shut his spyglass and pointed. "What do you make of that?"

Clendenin hawked and spat. "Most likely squatters. No war party would make that kind of sign. Let's go have a look-see."

The men nudged their mounts forward through the endless expanse of wither-high grass, across a broad run, and upslope to the source of the smoke. They reined up a furlong from the crest of the knoll and checked the priming of their muskets. A nod from Clendenin and they spread out and crept their horses forward. That way one musket shot, typically a ball and three buckshot, couldn't hit them both.

The cabin hardly deserved the name. The stacked log walls were not stripped of bark, with their gaps unchinked. A deerskin served as a door, and the chimney was the usual wattle and daub, but the builder's energies had flagged once the job had been completed as high as a man could reach, so smoke leeched out its sides.

Hawkwood shook his head as he surveyed the haphazard garden beginning to sprout from random hills of dirt set between the dead-stand trunks of girdled trees. By the assaulting smell of ordure, these people hadn't even bothered to dig a jakes. He caught Clendenin's eye, frowned, and shrugged.

"Halloo the house!" Clendenin called.

A scrawny dog rushed them, snarling and barking, but stopped well short. A man pushed his way past the deer hide and motioned a woman back inside.

"Beg your pardon," Hawkwood said. "I'm Christopher Hawkwood, and this is my associate, Jemmy Clendenin. Who, may I ask, would you be?"

"Tom Shafto," the man said with a touch of defiance in his voice.

Hawkwood apprised the man. He was middling height with ratty brown hair falling loose over his shoulders. Wearing a ragged, blue-checked shirt over buckskin breeches and moccasins, he had bare and spindly shanks. He was one of the world's put upon and very unlikely to cause Hawkwood and Clendenin any trouble.

"Well, Tom Shafto, how did you come to be here?"

"What business is it of yours?"

"This land"—Hawkwood motioned with his arm from horizon to horizon— "has been granted by Virginia Colony to the Transmontane Company. We are surveying it."

The slow drum of hooves and the jingle of curb chains made him turn in his saddle. The surveyor, Buchanan, and two chainmen approached.

"What is this, Mr. Hawkwood?" Buchanan asked.

"This is Mr. Shafto. He has settled here. I can send out the chains and mark his parcel, and he can settle up with Mr. Welbourne for his quit rent."

Buchanan cast a dubious eye on Shafto and shook his head. "Nay, this Captain Queernabs isn't likely to be able to pay a quit rent." She looked at Shafto. "Do you have two farthings to rub together?"

Shafto seemed to shrink and said nothing.

"Thought as much." Buchanan turned to one of the chainmen. "Pete, tear it down."

"Wait," Hawkwood said. "Why don't we give him the chance to pay quit rent? If he can, then we have a family against our quota."

"We can't do that. If we let him get by, then we'd be beset with dozens like him." Buchanan eyed Shafto. "Anything you wish to keep, best get it out of that hovel before we tear it down."

The woman wailed from inside the cabin. Moments later her keening was taken up by other smaller voices. Shafto looked at the ground, then shuffled inside.

Pete and his mate tied the end of a stout rope around the exposed end of one of the logs near the door. After looping the free end over the pommel of Pete's saddle, Pete gave his horse a sharp smack on the rump. The horse leaned into the rope and pulled. The log tumbled free with remarkably little effort, and with it came the front wall, then the roof fell in, catching fire as it knocked the chimney down. White smoke boiled up, then flames, and suddenly the whole pile was ablaze.

A woman, whom Hawkwood estimated to be in her late twenties, stood to one side. She was thin and clothed in cast-offs that likely would have been rejected by a beggar in Ireland. A boy, equal parts grime and truculence, stood beside her, glaring at the proceedings with balled fists on his hips. The woman was suckling a babe, and two others of indeterminate sex clung to her skirts. She cried as if her heart would break as she and Shafto stood amidst the heap of their possessions, watching their cabin burn.

"I'm done, Jemmy," Hawkwood said.

"What do you mean, done?"

"I evicted tenant farmers in Ireland, and I swore I'd never do it again. It's an ugly business, pulling a man's roof down about his ears. I'm not cut out for this. I'm going home."

"Pah!" Clendenin snorted. "Such is the way it's always been. Them that has, takes more. Them that has little, loses what they do have. Like as not, we did him a favor. Him and his family were going to starve. Though I do feel sorry for the girl and her wee'uns." Clendenin shook his head. "They ain't worth quitting the company over. Hell, I just got used to working with you."

Hawkwood knew he was right. Quitting now wouldn't change Shafto's future but it would change his own. And yet the injustice of a man being thrown out of his house for squatting on empty land by a man who was stealing from the Crown infuriated him.

"What'll they do? There is no parish here to take them in."

"They got out here without your help, Kit. They'll get out of here without it."

"That may be true, Jemmy, but I'll have no part of it."

Chapter Twelve

HAWKWOOD PULLED THE SADDLE'S GIRTH STRAP TIGHT. The gelding was prone to holding his breath to keep the strap loose, so he kneed him in the stomach to make him release his breath, finished tightening the girth strap, and checked it for fit. He had been back from the New River trip for two days and was still angry about the blatant thievery he'd encountered. Gentlemen didn't steal, and they didn't associate with those who do.

Emma met him as he led the horse from the crude stable he and Hugh had built. "Why so downcast, Kit?"

Emma was a sweet girl. She had a good head on her shoulders, and he needed to talk to someone. "I'm dished," he said. "Caught between my honor and my interests. Forgive me for not being more specific, but I've seen things I just cannot abide. I'd be better off back home, even if I have to go into trade."

She laid her hand gently on his forearm, a gesture he found both endearing and intimate. "Oh, Kit, I'm so sorry to hear that. Don't despair. You'll find a way through it. I know you will."

He didn't know why, but his situation no longer felt hopeless. His face began to flush, and he did as he always did when flustered by a woman—doffed his hat and bowed. As he straightened, Bram Rankin trotted up on an undersized pony.

"Did ye hear?" he said without preamble. "The McClintock place burned night before last. Everyone is gathering at their place to raise a new cabin for them."

"Of course," Emma said. "I'll put together a victual basket for them. Hugh and Kit will lend a hand."

Hawkwood held up his hand. "Beg pardon. I'm leaving for Staunton courthouse. Mr. Welbourne has charged me with recording the surveys."

Her eyes narrowed. "But, Kit, the McClintocks are neighbors. If our house burned, they would be here to help us rebuild."

Still, there was nothing he could do. "I'm obliged to look to the interests of my partners. Besides, it isn't like there will be a shortage of willing hands."

Leaning close to him, she whispered, "But your hands won't be there, and it will be noticed. You may need these people to help you one day. You can't just not show up. They'll call you that Tuckahoe squireen who's too good to help. Please, put off your trip and lend a hand."

"I'm sure most will understand that I have obligations that demand my attention. Those that won't understand would find something else to be critical of."

She took a step back from him and crossed her arms. "You really don't understand us, do you? The Bible tells us 'a *threefold cord* is not quickly broken.' None of us stand alone. We need each other. And people have long memories for when help was denied. Go then. Go and be damned." She turned on her heel and stalked away.

"Damn it all," he called after her, which stopped her in her tracks. "I don't want to understand these people. I want to be shot of them. I'll be damned glad when your uncle arrives and I can be on my way."

She flinched as if slapped.

"Wait, Emma, I'm sorry. I didn't mean that." He started to go after her, but she dropped her head, arms tight across her chest, and walked faster.

"You fairly stepped into that, didn't you?" Rankin said. "She's right, you know. No one will ever forget that you didn't help the McClintocks, and your name attaches to the Pettigrews."

"So say you all." Hawkwood went back to his horse and swung up into the saddle. "I'm damned sorry Emma's feelings are hurt, but I'm not going to be here long enough to worry about needing help."

Touching the gelding with his spurs, he headed north to Staunton.

* * * * *

AS BEST AS HE COULD DIVINE FROM his conversations with travelers the day before, he was about thirty miles from Staunton. None of the backcountry yokels seemed to have much of a concept of either distance or time. If he was thirty miles away, he would arrive in Staunton in late afternoon, take care of his business at the courthouse on the morrow, and begin home.

Assuming that Emma hadn't thrown his stuff out of the house or used it to cook dinner. She was so damned headstrong and often very unladylike in her manner. Perhaps life on the edge of civilization and having to run a household put a rough edge on a young woman. One thing was for certain, though, any man who wedded her was going to have his hands full. And that was going to make his job of finding her a suitable husband much more difficult. He wished he could understand her.

After a breakfast of johnnie cakes, he shaved, scrubbed trail grime from himself as best he could, beat the dust from his coat and breeches, and dressed.

He planned on stopping again, just short of Staunton, to sponge his coat and wipe the dust from his boots so as to give the best appearance possible. A courtesy call on Colonel Patton would be necessary, even though his primary business would be to register caveats against any land claims made by Patton's New River Company along the New River or Holston River. That was sure to cast a pall over any meeting.

The road to Staunton was a well-worn track called the Seneca Trail, though he had heard some refer to as the Great Wagon Road. An overstatement in Hawkwood's view, as it was roughly graded, heavily eroded, and scantily marked. The countryside bored him; a vast expanse of rolling meadows interspersed with groves of mixed hardwood trees. The day was unseasonably warm, and the rocking motion of his mount caused him to doze as they ambled along.

Suddenly, the horse stopped. Hawkwood straightened himself from drowsing and looked about, jerking fully awake upon finding himself looking down the cavernous muzzle of a cavalry musketoon.

Behind it stood a large man, with red hair and beard, whom he recognized. "Stand and deliver, boy!"

Hawkwood dropped his right hand to the pistol bucket at his pommel.

"Stand fast or I'll cut you in half!"

Chapter Thirteen

HAWKWOOD FROZE. "I YIELD."

"Now if you would, sir, slide down off that horse. I won't make the same mistake I made last time. Come on out, boys. We have him."

Two men joined him from the forest, both grinning at his predicament.

He did as instructed. Everyone said the man was a highwayman, not a killer, so he might as well put the best face on it. "Ute Perkins, am I correct?"

The man gave Hawkwood a courtly bow. "Indeed, I am, sir. And you would be Mr. Christopher Hawkwood. Pleased to make your acquaintance at long last. Our first meeting was a bit hurried. I heard tell you caught a buckshot. I'm sorry for that, but I was agitated after you parted my hair with a pistol ball. That was my best hat you put a hole in. They tell me that you've been made guardian of the Pettigrew kids. When you next see them, please tell them that Ute sends his condolences, and he hopes they will understand why he didn't drop by for a visit. Their pa was a good man. One of the best."

"Hey, Ute, look at this." One of the men held up Hawkwood's firelock.

Ute inspected it. "Never seen anything like that." He returned his attention to Hawkwood. "What is it?"

Hawkwood glanced surreptitiously at Perkins's men for any sign of inattentiveness. No such luck. His only option, he realized, was to be polite and cooperate.

"It's called *a doppelstutzen*. The top barrel is rifled. For a time, I was in the service of Empress Maria Theresa of Austria. Her borderers carried such as these."

"Ah, I'd heard you were a lobster. Nobody said nothing about an empress."

"I was that too. It's a long, boring story. Trust me."

"Fair enough." Perkins glanced over Hawkwood's horse. "On your honor, sir, are you carrying gold or silver? I don't mind a man trying to blow my head off. That's just the game. But I can't abide a liar."

"I have a few shillings in my purse." He slid his hand into his coat pocket, extracted an embroidered leather bag, and held it out to him. Perkins took it, hefted it to judge its weight, and dropped it inside the collar of his hunting shirt.

"You were a bold gentleman on our last encounter and one of the few who have bested me at my game. Were it not for my reputation being at stake, I'd let you continue unmolested." He smiled and shrugged. "Tell you what. You can keep what you're wearing."

"Now hold on, Ute," one of the men protested. "Those boots look damned fine, and all I got are these broke-down shoes."

"Simmer down, Jack. I'll make sure you get new boots," he said without taking his gaze off Hawkwood. "And you're only ten miles from the courthouse. You'll be there by nightfall. And the road's clear, so you won't have any need of your weapons." He touched his hat brim with his fingers in a rough salute, took the reins of gelding, and mounted it. He began to wheel the horse away to the south, then stopped. "On second thought, you did ruin my hat, so it's only fair that you replace it." He leaned over and grabbed Hawkwood's tricorne.

The three headed off, and as they reached a bend in the trail, Perkins turned in the saddle and gave a jaunty wave. "Take care, boy. We'll be seeing you again."

Hawkwood couldn't help but smile. If one had to be robbed one could much worse than meeting with Ute Perkins.

* * * * *

WILLIAM PRESTON CLOSED THE ACCOUNT LEDGER. "Well, Uncle, I've found out a lot more about Ran Welbourne's new man."

Patton sipped from a tankard of grog, glad to be finished with the official county business. "Does he look like a problem?"

"Depends on what you mean. He had a run-in with Ute Perkins crossing the mountains and damned near blew Ute's head off."

Patton threw his head back and laughed. "I would have paid good money to have seen that."

"He's been out on one expedition with Welbourne's boys. Their guide was Jemmy Clendenin."

"Wait." Patton set his tankard on the desk in front of him. "Is he the sly-boots that figured out the long chain?"

"The same. But there's more. If you recall, a few weeks ago Welbourne sent word that Bart Pettigrew and his family had passed from the smallpox. The fellow he put forward as guardian for the kids is the selfsame—Christopher Hawkwood. Clendenin said he's a bold fellow. He's also run afoul of the Turnbull clan. Ned nearly gutted him."

"How'd that happen?"

"They invaded the Pettigrew house and roughed up the boy and girl. Our boy got stuck into it defending them."

"So, he takes his job as a surveyor and guardian deadly serious. That's good."

"He made his first militia muster. Welbourne, that hen-head, put him in Hogg's company. They didn't hit it off. According to Welbourne, they were on different sides of the line at Prestonpans."

Patton sighed, closed his eyes, and pinched the bridge of his nose. "That could be a problem. Cousin Peter never submitted himself for a pardon. I told him he needed to do that for safety's sake, but he'd have none of it, sang me a bit from 'Wee, Wee, German Lairdie' to make his point. We'll just need to keep an eye on this. I'm guessing that our Mr. Hawkwood was put out by being made a ranker in Hogg's company?"

Preston nodded. "But to his credit, he did his duty and didn't give Hogg any problems. Now this is interesting—"

The cabin's heavy door slammed open, and a short, wizened old man burst into the office. "Shit, shit, g-g-goddammit, Colonel," he stuttered.

"Belay that, Jack, or I'll have you flogged for your blasphemy," Patton snarled. Whenever surprised or upset, he tended to lapse into the nautical jargon he'd learned while working as a midshipman in the Royal Navy many years before.

"B-b-but, C-c-colonel, g-g-goddammit, shit, shit, shit, look out the window. It's a gentleman coming, Colonel, and he's alone and on foot." His stutter rose to a screech.

Patton and Preston exchanged glances, Patton arching his right eyebrow, and they walked to the narrow window at the cabin's front. "Well, well," he said. "Will you look at that."

A Threefold Cord

* * * * *

DUSK NEARED AS HAWKWOOD FINALLY TRUDGED DOWN the rutted-out dirt road that served as Staunton's main street. The temperature wasn't quite as hot as the hinges of hell, but it was damned close—and this was April. What would late August bring?

He had removed his neck stock and carried his coat draped over his back. His shirt stuck to him, soaked with sweat, and the interiors his boots had surely been transformed into fetid pools. At one point he had considered stopping to refresh himself before entering town, but there was no way of putting a good face on what had happened.

Those bastards. They could smile and offer their sympathies, but inside they were laughing at the Tuckahoe, the squireen, who had been humbled by one of theirs. The only saving grace had been that the evening was so damnably hot that no one was stirring.

Ahead, two men stepped out of one of the rude cabins dotting the sides of the furrowed thoroughfare. The older one was tall, powerfully build, and dark, while the other was slightly shorter and fair. The taller man shoved a black tricorne down on his head and strode purposefully toward Hawkwood with an air of authority.

Hawkwood stopped as the man approached and greeted him with a bow.

To his surprise, the man extended an oversized hand. "Colonel James Patton, sir. May I present you my nephew, Billy Preston." Patton made a broad gesture at his companion. "We've heard of you from Ran Welbourne. Tell me, do you always walk when you travel?" His eyes twinkled, then he laughed and draped his arm over Hawkwood's shoulders as if they were close relations. "Come to my offices, sir, and join Billy and me for a drink. You look in need of refreshment. I take it that you didn't set out on foot. What happened?"

Hawkwood shrugged. "I ran afoul of Mr. Ute Perkins about ten miles south of your town. He relieved me of my horse and tack, weapons, purse, and even my bloody hat."

Patton nodded. "Perkins does that with some frequency. But he left you your fine coat and boots. In most cases he'd take those as well." He looked at Preston "Find Mr. Hawkwood a replacement horse and make him a loan of that musket in the courthouse. Can't have him walking back home."

"Much obliged, sir. This Perkins seems to have some grudging respect for me after our last encounter."

"Ah, yes." He laughed. "I'd heard you gave him quite a scare with a dragoon pistol."

"It was more than an even exchange, sir. He peppered me with buckshot."

"As I hear it, you've been quite busy."

Hawkwood eyed him. *And you, sir, have been quite busy yourself. I never imagined my doings would be of interest to the county lieutenant.*

He followed the two men into the single-roomed locust-log cabin that Patton used as an office. Surprisingly, the walls were whitewashed and the plank floor had been sanded smooth and glowed from linseed oil. A sturdy fireplace of mortared fieldstone was set into one wall, and two unglazed windows admitted light and the occasional breeze into the sweltering room. A simple secretary desk, a pew-like bench, four plain ladder-back chairs, a sideboard, and two bearskin rugs filled the room.

Once pleasantries had been exchanged, Hawkwood was comfortably seated with a tankard of rum punch in his hand. Patton was clearly a bluff man, used to asking direct questions and getting direct answers. He asked Hawkwood about his arrival in Virginia, his family in England, his army career, and his service in Ireland and Scotland.

Hawkwood steeled himself for the next inevitable question. This was damned uncomfortable. The man was a generous host and had loaned him a horse and a firelock, and he was supposed to fuck him over.

Patton stared at him for a moment and nodded slightly. "And you've come to Virginia to make your fortune. Good for you, sir. Good for you. There is a fortune to be made here for a man of enterprise and energy who is not afraid to risk all. And the Pettigrew children continue to prosper?"

"Yes, sir. Hugh is a fine young man, and Miss Emma is every inch a lady. By chance, do you hear when their uncle will be arriving? Miss Emma wrote him when her mother and father passed."

Patton shook his head. "I have heard nothing. I had only a passing acquaintance with Bart Pettigrew. He was Irish like the rest of us, but he came to the Valley from somewhere near Richmond. He had a small holding there and came here for more land. I think I recall that he had tried his hand at tobacco but without much success. I take it you're anxious to end your guardianship?"

"Not anxious, sir. But it is what I imagine being a parent to be like, and I'm not ready for it."

He sat back in his chair behind the desk. "Ran tells me that you're doing fine, and you stood up to the Turnbulls manfully."

Preston leaned forward; his natural intensity barely contained. "You must understand that your skirmish with the Turnbulls has made you a number of enemies. You will find them to be ruthless and crafty. They have long memories and are unencumbered by honor or scruple."

Hawkwood involuntarily stiffened.

"Let me explain," Preston continued. "There is a lawless element in our county that steals and extorts with impunity. This impunity exists for two salient reasons." He extended his left thumb from a clenched fist. "Firstly, no one will come forward to make a complaint for fear of retaliation. Barns are burned, livestock driven off, witnesses disappear." The index finger jutted upward. "Secondly, and most importantly, there is no government in this county capable of suppressing them or bringing them to account."

"Colonel Patton, you are the law, sir," Hawkwood said. "Do you send your constables out and arrest them where they may be found?"

Patton snorted. "If only it were it that easy, young Hawkwood. My constables are volunteers who receive a small per diem paid in tobacco warrants. They are loathe to undertake a mission that may end in their death or injury. Billy?"

Preston produced a half-inch-thick stack of writs from his leather folio. "See here. This one not executed because the constable was turned away by force of arms. This one, because the subject had fled the colony. In this one, the constable was chased off by the subject wielding an axe—"

"So there is nothing to be done?" he retorted with disdain. "Against a handful of bully bucks the law is helpless?"

Patton scowled and his voice dropped an octave and sounded like a rasp working an ironwood plank. "Mr. Hawkwood, do keep your judgments to yourself until you understand what we must deal with here. The Turnbulls and their like are nothing to mock or make light of."

Hawkwood was aghast that Patton was so brazen about his impotence. He'd have felt much better if the man had spun him a plausible lie, but to just admit that the county lieutenant, the Crown's representative, was powerless in the face of a handful of scoundrels was something he never could have imagined.

"My apologies for my tone, sir. I do appreciate your warning, and again, I apologize for my lack of understanding for your situation. I have plans of my own, and I will not let a handful of ruffians interfere."

Patton and Preston exchanged glances, then Patton slowly rose from his chair. "Very well. May I suggest that we adjourn for dinner and to arrange quarters for yourself for the night? In the meantime, perhaps you will let your plans be revealed to us."

As the three men walked from the office to the ordinary, Hawkwood watched with curiosity as Patton played the role of local squire. The lack of subservience on the part of the petitioners surprised him. They approached Patton a dozen times, demanding that a license for a mill or ordinary be granted, that a road be built, and on and on. Not once was a cap doffed or a forelock touched, a far cry from anything Hawkwood had experienced in Europe or even in the Virginia Tidewater. It seemed that Patton's influence was based upon his ability to provide favors rather than any inherent social position or official grant of power.

The colonel deftly avoided directly committing himself to any action, always deferring to the county court as the final arbiter. Amusing, since everyone knew that Patton was the county court for all intents and purposes.

"Rude, these people," Hawkwood muttered to Preston.

"Hardly, Hawkwood. I refer you to the eighteenth chapter of the gospel of Saint Luke."

Hawkwood groaned with annoyance.

"Don't pull the long face," Preston said. "If you live in the backcountry, you had better accustom yourself to hearing Scripture quoted. Anyway, Saint Luke relates to us the parable of the widow and the unjust judge who, by virtue of her persistence in demanding justice, the unjust judge eventually relented. This is not to say the colonel is unjust." Preston gave Patton a wink. "Far from it. He often helps people, much to his detriment financially, who are not grateful for the service they have received. But as you will have noted by now, a man here is valued according to his abilities, not his pedigree."

"And this, this republicanism, is tolerated by the Crown?"

"The Crown's writ runs very thin here," Patton said. "West of the Blue Ridge there is no government save we ourselves. Williamsburg is wise enough to understand that the main prize is the possession of these lands by a people who look to England and not to France. Government such as that in the shire counties will come here eventually. In the meantime, having nothing to give us, they are wise in asking for nothing in return."

Hawkwood kept a straight face but was stunned by the statement.

"Nothing to give you? Surely you are being facetious, sir."

"I wish to heaven that were the case. We provide for our own defense from Indian raids. We provide our own currency. We collect and impose our own duties. We elect our county court. We appoint our militia officers. Our trade is down the Valley to Pennsylvania or up the Valley to Carolina. Little that happens in Williamsburg concerns us."

"Extraordinary." Hawkwood nodded. "So, you are the law from here to the sunset?"

"Precisely, sir. But in a way you will not find in England. I am a major landowner in the Valley, but my real power comes from my ability to convince people to do what I wish them to do, and I do that by my ability to do things for the people of the county."

"Then you are riding a tiger, so to speak, are you not? One cannot truly govern when one is beholden to the passions of the mob."

Patton looked at him sharply. "We do quite well, sir, and if you stay with us for a time, I'm sure you'll come to see that the 'mob' has a level of wisdom that their betters often lack."

* * * * *

PATTON STOOD BY PRESTON AS THEY WATCHED HAWKWOOD ride off on his borrowed mount. "Did he fuck us, Billy?"

Preston laughed. "No, Uncle, he didn't place caveats on any of our claims. He did—and you'll find this interesting—file his own claim for a thousand acres on that bluff above the New River trace. Truth be told, I think he decided before arriving that he wasn't going to place the caveats."

"A man of honor, eh? Damned few of those around. Wonder what he's going to do with land up there?" He scratched his chin. "I don't suppose Ran and his partners are going to be pleased. Did he mention to you the long chain Buchanan is using?"

"Not a word."

"Good. He knows how to keep his own counsel. That's a rare talent among we Cohees. We have the need to speak well beyond the point of wisdom. What did you make of him asking after an uncle of the Pettigrew bairns?"

Preston arched his eyebrows. "A puzzle. I knew Bart as well as any man in the Valley. As far as I know, Bart and Peggy were alone in America."

"Indeed. The Hawkwood boy's a bold'un. Few men have tangled with the Turnbulls and walked away from it. If he lives long enough he may be of use to us."

Chapter Fourteen

HAWKWOOD'S HOMECOMING WAS NOT AS MELODRAMATIC as he had expected. Emma was more than cordial, actually apologetic, and he let the matter of their argument drop, having no desire to disturb the harmony of the household or engage in recriminations over an incident so trivial. He had been raised with two sisters, so he was familiar with how a sweet-tempered girl could metamorphose into an unbearable termagant in an instant.

As the supper table was cleared, Hawkwood went out onto the porch and watched the sun set over the Appalachian ridge to the southwest. The barn would need new shingles come next spring, and they'd need to clear another dozen acres for the south pasture. He needed to get Hugh to show him where Bart had wanted to build a sawmill, since having a mill would make life much easier.

A quiet laughed escaped his lips. *I'm beginning to think like a bloody farmer.*

The door opened and Emma joined him. "I haven't said it and so I must," she said. "I'm sorry for being such a scold with you. You gave me no cause for such behavior. You have every right to pay attention to young women, and it was most un-Christian of me to spread calumny."

"There's nothing to forgive, Emma. For my part, it is all forgotten. I was thoughtless in my actions and resolve to behave differently in the future."

She leaned against the railing and crossed her arms. "What are you going to do, Kit? You can't continue to serve Welbourne when you've formed such a low opinion of him."

"I don't know." He sighed. "But you're right, it can't go on for long.

I'm in a quandary. I can't return to England because I have no prospects there. I have enough money to buy another commission but not enough to live if I do. I can't go into trade. And I have no family income."

His gaze met hers. "But I don't feel at home here. The land is simply too wild and too empty. I'm an Englishman, a Tuckahoe as you call it, among Irishmen—or should I call you Cohees? —who have no love for England or Englishmen. There are outlaws who do as they will, and there's no authority to stop them. Our Sovereign is cheated on a grand scale by men he has entrusted with responsibility. I'm at a loss for what to do."

"You said you placed a claim on land. Why don't you go there, build a cabin, get married, and start a family? That's what we all want to do. There is no dishonor in making a life out here."

"I have obligations. My colonel, a man who is very nearly my father, vouched for me to his friend, Richard. And he in turn used his good name to find me this position. I can't dishonor either. Even were I so inclined, I couldn't. All the money I have in the world is tied up in this venture. I can hardly just walk away. Perhaps I will tell him that I don't find my situation to my liking. Then I could leave with my head up."

"You don't need Welbourne's approval to hold your head up," Emma insisted. "No man should hold that power over you."

Hawkwood nodded. "And I have an obligation to you and Hugh. I do wish your uncle would write. It isn't fair, him keeping you and Hugh hanging on like this this."

"You have to look to yourself, Kit. Hugh and I will manage. Mr. Rankin is here to help us with the farm. Things will work out for us." She stared at something on the floorboards, and her voice lowered to a near whisper. "Though we would like for you to stay with us as long as possible."

* * * * *

WELBOURNE SCOWLED AND HIS LOWER LIP curled outward in a pout. He couldn't believe the temerity of this puppy. Hawkwood had waltzed into Chestnut Grove as bold as dog in a doublet and demanded an interview. God's beard. Two months ago, he had been an English gentleman and now he was damned near a Cohee, all but treating him as his equal.

"Really, sir? You are resigning over the eviction of squatters. I had thought more of you. After your scuffle with Ned Turnbull, I imagined you had bottom." Welbourne waved his hand. "Very well. You have made your decision, and I shan't try to dissuade you. But mind this, sir. I take offense at your insinuation that I have acted wrongly in throwing those scrubs off my land."

Hawkwood clenched his jaw. "Damme, sir. There is a continent out there for the taking, and you begrudge a poor man and his family a cabin. You may not have acted illegally, but you most assuredly acted wrongly."

"Hold, sir! Hold! Are you now one of these leveling Cohee bastards? You will not address me in such a manner in mine own home. And don't come looking for my patronage, for it will not be forthcoming."

"Have no fear on that account, sir. I have had enough of the lawlessness and the shameless peculations of men—men like yourself, sir, in whom our king has placed great, and, as it turns out, misguided, trust and confidence. I intend to depart Virginia as soon as I have my affairs in order and wish you the joy of your venture. Now if you'll excuse me, I have many miles to travel before dark."

Caught off guard by Hawkwood's exclamation, Welbourne's mouth pulsed open and closed.

Hawkwood clapped his hat on his head, turned on his heel, and fairly marched from the room, through the double doors onto the veranda, and down the broad steps to where a groom waited with his horse.

This was dangerous. Could the boy be so ignorant of the ways of the world? Of course, Welbourne lined his own pockets. Why did Hawkwood think anyone entered into any undertaking for the Crown other than to enrich oneself while serving? It was expected, and it was why one had to pay bribes for government posts that exceeded the salary paid. But if Hawkwood made noise about it, that would cause problems. There were always enemies just waiting on such revelations to engineer a man's fall and ruin.

Welbourne watched through the window as Sarah approached the agitated Hawkwood and spoke to him. She offered him her hand, and Hawkwood looked Welbourne in the eye and smirked before he bowed and kissed it.

Welbourne fumed. *Damn him. He's as much as announcing his intention to cuckold me.* Once Hawkwood had rode off, he fairly flew down the steps to his wife. "What the hell do you mean, carrying on with that boy in front of me? Dare you think—"

She placed a citrus-scented finger on his lips. "So long as he thinks I'm within reach, he will moderate his anger. After all, any damage he does to you will be done to me."

He sighed, somewhat mollified. While he didn't entirely trust her, what she said made sense. If Hawkwood's lust for his wife kept his anger in check, it would be a small price to pay.

* * * * *

"YOU'RE CUTTING OFF YOUR NOSE TO SPITE YOUR FACE," Rankin growled from across the table.

The evening breeze coming through the open door mitigated the heat but foretold a hot summer was close at hand. A fly buzzed in ever-narrowing circles around the three-candle wrought iron chandelier dangling above them.

Hawkwood leaned back in his chair, wondering if his path resembled that of the fly. "You may be right, Bram, but I've made my decision and there's no going back. I don't fit in here."

"You won't let yourself fit in, Kit Hawkwood," Emma said. "You would fit in nicely if you'd come down off your high horse and try."

He was speechless for a moment. "Emma, that isn't fair."

"The truth isn't fair or foul. The truth is the truth." She shook her head. "Why, you wouldn't dirty your hands helping the McClintock's when their cabin burned."

"Dammit, Emma, I had business."

"Dammit yourself." Color rose to Emma's cheeks. "You could have delayed your trip by a day, and maybe you'd still have your fine horse and guns, and Ute Perkins wouldn't be wearing your hat."

"There's no call …" Hawkwood cast a pleading look at her, only to be rebuffed by a fierce gaze that warned him not to expect mercy. He turned his attention to Hugh and Rankin for support, but they had averted their eyes from the argument.

She took in a deep breath. "And I'd thought us friends, but you wouldn't deign to wear the hunting shirt I made for you." She slammed her palms hard onto the table, stood, gathered her skirts, and glided away as if he didn't exist.

"She's right, you know," Hugh said. "You could fit in here. That showed when you were working with me and Mr. Rankin. But here we are. What's your plan?"

"I'm going to go back to Fredericksburg and make arrangements to collect my money. I'll come back and settle affairs here, then leave and take passage back to England. You and Emma can have title to the patent I recorded. It'll be worth something. Maybe it will suit you, Hugh, when you decide to wed."

"Welbourne ain't going to let you keep that land," Rankin groused.

"He doesn't have a choice. I did this on my own account, and Billy Preston assured me that the patent would stand."

Rankin exhaled. "How soon do you intend to take passage for England?"

"As soon as their uncle arrives." Hawkwood looked to Hugh. "Would you know if Emma has heard from him?"

Hugh shook his head. "I've heard nothing."

"Very well then. I'm leaving at first light. Expect me back in a week to ten days."

He would be damned glad to see the last of this Valley and its troublesome people.

* * * * *

HAWKWOOD LAY AWAKE, STARING INTO THE DARK. His throat was dry, and his heart was drumming. He knew this was the right decision and hated to take rattle and quit, but he could never be one of these people. *My God, plucking one another's eyes out. Even the gentlemen are Captain Sharps, stealing from the Crown and from one another as a bloody sport.* He hated that Emma was angry, but what did she expect him to do? Become a fucking Cohee?

"Are you awake in here?" Emma whispered into the darkness.

He sat up, straightened his night shirt as best he could, and bunched the coverlet about his legs. "Aye. What brings you here at this hour?"

"'Tis nearly time to build a fire in the oven." In the faint moonlight that filtered through the greased paper window glazing, her silhouette crossed the kitchen and sat on the stool next to the cold hearth. "I don't know how you do it, Kit Hawkwood."

"Do what?"

"Get under my skin and have me make an ass of myself."

He snorted. "It's a talent, I suppose."

She giggled. "I seem to be making a habit of having to apologize to you. I'm sorry for treating you in such a … an unladylike fashion and beg your forgiveness."

"It's nothing. You were right. I haven't tried to learn the ways of these people, but now it's too late. I have no means of support now that I'm estranged from Welbourne."

"Ah, Kit, you're a strong man. Have more faith in yourself. You can make your fortune here much more easily than you can in England. You'll find these people are a kind and forgiving people, if you just give them a chance."

Hawkwood thought of England in autumn. It would be a year since his misadventure in Cork. No one would be looking for him. He could find a regiment somewhere. If not in England, then in Hanover or one of the other German states. If they sold this farm, then Emma and Hugh would have enough money to get by. By God, he'd be glad to see the last of this benighted land.

"I don't know that I'm that strong or patient. Do you have relatives in Ireland? If your uncle doesn't write soon, we have to assume he has either passed or removed himself far from his last address. You and Hugh could sell this farm. We could take passage together."

"That's a wonderful offer, Kit," she said, and in his mind's eye he could see her cheeks dimple as she smiled. "See, I told you that you had the kindness you needed to win friends and admirers." Even in the pitch darkness, he knew she was staring through to his soul. "My home, what remains of my family, and my people are here in Virginia. I would rather be a free woman in Virginia than a governess or housekeeper for the richest man in Ireland."

* * * * *

THE RAIN HAD STARTED BEFORE DAWN AND, though never heavy, had turned the rough dirt road to a soupy morass while slyly working its way through Hawkwood's oilskin watchcoat. He steered his horse onto the verge of the road, avoiding the worst of the muck. On both sides, gangs of slaves, working under the Sphinx-like gaze of armed and mounted overseers, transplanted tobacco seedlings into knee-high hills. In England, a gentleman passing someone like an overseer would have been acknowledged by a tip of the hat, but not in Virginia. Even low sorts such as these thought themselves the equals of any man.

He patted his rough-coated cob on her neck. "I'll be damned glad to remove myself from this place. And I need to steer clear of Jenny. She was a damned good piece, for certain, and quite a ride, but I can't take the risk of being caught out by Welbourne while I'm trying to get my money back."

His mount crunched up the pea-gravel drive to the front portico of Ardleigh. As he dismounted, a black groom emerged from an outbuilding to take charge of his horse. The groom showed no hint of recognition, though Hawkwood was sure he was the same man who'd seen him off months ago. He shrugged off his impulse to engage the man in conversation, bounded up the front steps, and rapped on the front door.

A black butler opened the door.

"Christopher Hawkwood to see Mr. Crosslin," he said.

"Mr. Crosslin isn't here, sir."

"You are dismissed, Titus," a husky feminine voice said. "Mr. Hawkwood is always welcome at Ardleigh."

Hawkwood looked at the doorway leading to the parlor to see Jenny standing there, immaculately turned out in a sack gown of pale blue silk brocade. A large silk bow drew attention to the daring *décolletage*, and she had kilted up the front of her gown, *a la polonaise*, to reveal embroidered silk shoes with silver buckles and white stockings. The image of her naked in the moonlight in his bed flashed through his mind.

She crossed the room, extending a hand to him. He took it ever so lightly, bowed, and kissed it.

As the butler vanished, she relaxed from her pose of formality. "Kit, whatever brings you to Ardleigh? Is Richard expecting you?"

"I have pressing business with Richard," he said. "When is he expected home?"

"Later this evening. He's out riding the fields, he said. More likely he's riding some Cuffee wench in the slave cabins. Your arrival is an unexpected pleasure." She took his arm and led him to the imposing staircase leading to the upper floors—and her chambers.

"Jenny, please. I don't think this a good idea. What if Richard arrives?"

"Why, Kit, you weren't this shy on your last visit." She leaned her head against his shoulder and stepped onto the first stair.

"I'm not shy now. It would be inconvenient if Richard arrived and we were playing rantum-scantum upstairs." Despite his words, he took the first stair.

"Mistress," Titus called in a clear baritone voice. "Mr. Carling to see you."

Jenny raised on her toes and kissed Hawkwood gently, the tip of her tongue as light as a summer breeze on his lips. Suddenly, he was possessed of an abundant erection and meager willpower.

"Your choice, fair Kit," she said. "Do you want me? Or should I see to Mr. Carling?"

He closed his eyes and sighed, nuzzled her décolletage, and whispered, "Send him the hell away."

Chapter Fifteen

CROSSLIN DIDN'T MAKE IT HOME UNTIL THE EARLY morning hours, long after Jenny and Hawkwood had untangled themselves, dressed, and enjoyed a quiet supper together. This was followed by another bout of lovemaking.

She's really an amusing mort, he thought while laying alone in a thoroughly ravaged bed, *and plays the lady much more convincingly than most women of her station.* He didn't know what Crosslin could possibly see in slave women and tavern doxies. Jenny was as enthusiastic a lover as one could hope for. From his bedchamber, he heard singing as Crosslin arrived, then a banging of doors and a loud and unintelligible argument between husband and wife.

Hawkwood slept late, waking shortly before noon. After dressing, he went downstairs to find Crosslin seated at a finely inlaid secretary desk in the parlor, still in a silk dressing robe, poring over ledgers.

Crosslin looked up, rose from his chair, and greeted him. The broad smile he offered was a study in dissonance with eyes that were equal parts angry and fearful.

Kit returned the smile. *Shite on a biscuit. He knows I'm rogering his wife.*

"Titus! Bring us a bottle and a couple of glasses." He shook his head and muttered, "You simply can't teach these Cuffees to be good servants. Any English butler—hell, even a brute Irishman—would have anticipated such a basic task."

Minutes later, Crosslin poured brandy, about one finger's breadth in Hawkwood's glass and three in his own.

Hawkwood sat back in his chair and took a sip. It tasted like wine cut with raw spirits, but Crosslin was drinking the swill, so it must have been

114

his normal fare.

"What brings you back to us, Kit? I thought this would be the prime season for surveying."

Hawkwood considered his answer for a moment. He was torn between his instinct, which was to give a diplomatic reason for his decision to sever his business dealings with Crosslin and his companions and perhaps retain a personal relationship with the man, and his desire to damn Crosslin to Hell for putting him in this quandary to begin with. He reflected on his time in Virginia and threw caution and diplomacy to the wind.

"I suppose there's no need to beat around the bush, as the Cohees say. I'm through with land speculation. Your partner, Welbourne, has the ethics of a crimp. The surveys are fraudulent. The tenants they purport to have recruited are nonexistent. And the people are violent, and the rule of law is not to be found. If I continue in my current position, I'll become as degraded as they. I wish to sell out my shares in the company and then go home and see what Dame Fortune has to offer."

"That is a harsh statement, Mr. Hawkwood. I'm a friend of those men, and I must take exception to you painting them as rogues."

"I don't wish to offend." A brief image of Jenny, legs wrapped around his hips and face flushed in passion, flashed through his brain. He felt a fraction of a second of remorse, paused, and then plowed forward. "But the particulars of their conduct are without dispute. I witnessed it. I've come to terminate my arrangement with the Transmontane Company and recover my investment. As I purchased my shares from you, I'm offering them back to you."

Crosslin shook his head. "It isn't as easy as that."

"Why not? Do you wish that I call upon some of the other partners and sell them my shares?"

He took a slug from the glass of liquor. "I'm afraid your money is gone."

Sod me! "Gone?" Hawkwood stood. "Are you barking mad? I invested near six hundred pounds in shares in this venture! All the bleeding money I have in the world! How can my money be gone?" He near panted with the tension squeezing him.

Crosslin languorously crossed his legs and shrugged. "There are no shares. I had to sell them."

"What the fuck do you mean, sir?" Blood hammered in Hawkwood's temples.

He took a glass, stood, and clasped his hands behind his back, ignoring Hawkwood and walking to the French doors opening onto a formal garden. "The tobacco business is very unpredictable. You have the vagaries of the weather …"

Hawkwood took three long strides, grabbed a fistful of Crosslin's dressing gown and bicep, and whirled him around. The glass spun from his hands and shattered on the parquet floor. "I … don't … give … a … fuck … about … tobacco. What did you do with my money?"

"Last year was a bad year, Kit."

"Don't 'Kit' me! You've ruined me!"

"And my Glasgow factor was threatening to foreclose on Ardleigh, and you came along at the perfect time. Ran Welbourne is a friend. His Sarah and my Jenny are cousins."

Damme. They did look alike. The eyes. The impressive breasts. "Damn it to hell!" Hawkwood pivoted and stomped away. *Damn his eyes! He's as good as killed me.* He strode to the desk and snatched out a drawer.

"What are you doing?" Crosslin wailed.

"What do you think?" Hawkwood emptied the contents of the floor and kicked through them with the toe of his boot, then pulled out another drawer and turned on Crosslin. "Shut up! Stop your mewling. You took my money, and it's only fair I take what I find here."

Two more drawers yielded their contents before Hawkwood discovered a smallish linen drawstring bag with an assortment of coins. Some of them were gold. "Damn you to hell, Crosslin."

He spread his arms in supplication. "I meant no harm. You have to believe me. I needed the money. You needed a position and a place of safety. I'm certain this year's crop will make me whole again and I can repay you."

Hawkwood looked at Crosslin's pathetic figure and his anger faded. He was near bankrupt, and he was a cuckold. It was only a matter of time until he lost all of this and ended up in the gutter. "Bah!" He gave Crosslin a dismissive wave of his hand. "The only reason that you don't have your hand badged like your good wife is that you haven't been caught. That money is gone for good. I may be bushed, but you won't be far behind me. Take joy of this fine estate, Mr. Crosslin, for you have damned little time left to enjoy it."

Hawkwood tramped out of the room and was immediately accosted by Jenny. The little mort had likely been listening at the door.

"Oh, Kit, I'm so sorry," she simpered.

"Eh." He shrugged. "What's done is done. Your husband has skinned me as neatly as any cod's head, and there's precious little I can do about it. I can't go to John Law because of mine own difficulties. Besides, he's established and I'm a new-come. I'll make do somehow." How, he wasn't sure. With no money, no family, and no interest, he didn't know what he'd do.

"Are you staying the night?" she asked, placing her hand on his chest.

Hawkwood felt his mouth gape. The brainless chit wanted to tup after he'd rowed her husband. "I don't think so. My continued presence would be as upsetting to your husband as his is to me."

She pouted as her eyes twinkled. "Are you certain?"

"Very certain, love. Could you give me a better horse? The nag I came in on is hardly presentable."

"Let me take you to the stable. Richard has a fine dapple gray mare. I'll have the groom saddle her for you."

He grinned. "You're a darling, Jenny. My tack is poor repair. If you could, replace that as well?"

* * * * *

HAWKWOOD GENTLY APPLIED SPURS TO THE beautiful mare Jenny had gifted him, and the horse accelerated from walk to canter, eating up the miles.

"I knew it was a mistake, following her to the stable," he said to no one. "I should have known what the mort was planning. Can't really blame her, can I? I was more than willing." He raised his right hand to his nose, inhaled deeply, and savored the erotic mixture of *eau de cologne* underlaid with her musk.

Closing his eyes to the glare of the late afternoon sun, he recalled her braced against a post in the stable, petticoats hitched up about her waist, and her lovely lactescent bum arched up high over slim, coltish thighs. So inviting and accessible. "I'd have had to be a thorough-going backgammoner to turn away such an offer."

He planned to take a circuitous route back to the Pettigrew farm, which, for better or worse, he had to consider home for the time being. Crosslin either knew or suspected he was shagging Jenny, though it seemed that he wasn't her only lover. In the closed Tidewater society, that couldn't have escaped Crosslin's notice. Hell, she'd made so much noise in the stable that Crosslin would have to have been stone deaf to not hear.

After their parting, Crosslin had no way of knowing that Hawkwood wouldn't lodge a complaint with someone in authority. He also knew of Hawkwood's own legal problems. Calling the constable would be a quick and effective way of ridding himself of an annoyance and taking revenge. Even the barest modicum of prudence dictated that Hawkwood not make a beeline home.

Now as he traveled northwest, paralleling the Rappahannock River, he intended to push hard and overnight at the Culpeper courthouse. From there he would bypass the South West Mountains to the west, swing southwest through the wilds of Orange County, pick up the Three Notch'd Road, cross the Blue Ridge at Woods Gap, and enter the relative safety of the Irish Tract in the Valley. Hawkwood shifted the musket balanced on the saddle pommel and then adjusted his rump, trying to get comfortable.

The landscape fell into a monotonous pattern. To his right was the Rappahannock, broad, green, and languid. Trees flourished along the numerous streams draining into the it and served as woodlots for homesteads and plantations. Every inch of arable land was covered with the conical dirt mounds festooned with newly transplanted tobacco plants. Every few miles he would pass a large plantation house, few quite as splendid as Ardleigh, surrounded by a cluster of outbuildings and slave cabins.

Hawkwood shook his head. This was a recipe for disaster. Such reliance on a single crop made all the planters vulnerable to blight, weather, and the vagaries of the European tobacco market. "Even a fool can see it's a matter of time until they lose everything they own," he muttered. "And they'll lose it to some other fool who'll make the same mistake."

For the first few hours, he kept an eye over his shoulder. There was always a chance that a hue and cry would be raised against him, and the last thing he wanted was a prolonged chase or a gunfight that might leave several people, himself among them, dead or wounded.

It was one thing to be a wanted man in Ireland; most of Virginia, it seemed, was wanted in Ireland or Great Britain for one crime or another. It was an entirely different matter to be wanted for killing a Virginian. He might find refuge among the Cohees, but they might be as likely to sell out an outsider as protect one. By noon it became apparent that there was no pursuit.

The road shrank from a broad, rutted wagon road to a narrow packhorse trace. Soon, sign of human habitation was limited to the occasional cabin situated with its front porch a scant few feet from the road. These farms had been settled long enough for trees to have been cut, stumps pulled, and brush grubbed. The fields were plowed, and he didn't encounter the fields of dead-stand trees and untidy hills of corn, beans, and squash that were standard in the backcountry.

He pushed the mare hard and arrived in the hamlet growing around the half-finished Culpeper courthouse just as night fell. Whereas his English accent, clothing, and manner marked him as a member on the minor squirearchy and was the source of unending friction in the Valley, Hawkwood found that it offered him advantages in the Virginia Tidewater. When he inquired about lodging at a crossroads ordinary, the innkeeper, without hesitation, guided him to the home of a vestryman who oversaw the chapel of ease for Saint Mark's Parish.

The vestryman was a plump man in his late forties with an equally round wife and two adolescent daughters in the house, and he seemed as grateful for the visitor as Hawkwood was for the meal, the company, and the clean bed.

In the morning, he was treated to a huge breakfast of smoked ham, eggs, trout, partridges fried Devon style rather than stewed to rags in a Valley simmering pot, and hominy, accompanied by fresh baked bread, butter, cheese, and persimmon preserves. By the time he'd finished, he doubted he'd be able to haul himself into the saddle.

The country was deserted after Culpeper. The road south was a poorly maintained narrow dirt track that frequently disappeared altogether. It didn't lend itself to hard riding, which, after the massive breakfast his host had served up, was fine with Hawkwood.

Just before noon, he paused at the village that was emerging around the Orange County courthouse. To give his horse and himself a rest, he stopped at a shabby tavern. Inside, a stout man who wore a laundered and ironed publican's apron greeted him.

Hawkwood looked around, surprised to find he was the tavern keeper's only customer. "I say, how much farther until I find this Three Notch'd Road?"

"Nigh on twenty mile." The man pushed a stone tankard of ale to Hawkwood without asking, then pulled another for himself. "Where you bound?"

"Staunton."

He spat on the rush-covered floor. "Pah. Fuckin' Irish. Thank God for the mountains. That keeps most of them out. A lack of ambition does for the rest."

Hawkwood laughed and took a cautious sip of the ale. It was cool and amazingly good.

"Just be careful of those damned Cohees. If you aren't a kinsman, they'd just as soon cut your throat as look at you. Maybe cut it even if you are a kinsman. You live there?"

Hawkwood nodded.

"You know, don't you, that no matter how long you live with them, you'll always be an outsider and a Tuckahoe?"

* * * * *

AN HOUR LATER HE FOUND HIMSELF STILL MULLING over the innkeeper's counsel as he rode south. "Are the Irish that bad?" he wondered aloud. Since his first trip to the Valley, he'd found that he dealt with solitude best by talking aloud. "They're clannish, for sure, but with good reason. Who can I trust? Rankin?" He paused and scratched his chin. "Within limits, I trust him. I'd never put him in the position of doing something really hard, but I trust him as much as any man. Clendenin? Don't know. He's Welbourne's man, but he knows he's just another Cohee to him. That gunsmith, Farris, was a good man and would have your back in a fight. Emma and Hugh, I trust with my life. Hah! The only one I really don't trust is Welbourne, and he's as English as I am."

Near Three Notch'd Road—the most direct route from Richmond and the settlements and plantations along the James and Rappahannock to the Valley via Woods Gap—he encountered cabins and farms that bore outward signs of prosperity. Most were fieldstone and clapboard rather than log. The road widened, and sections of corduroy road laid in marshy areas eased his passage.

"I'm still in a bind. I was gulled. Most of my money is gone," he mused. "When Emma's uncle arrives, I'll have to find a place to stay. He'll likely sell their farm and take them with him. I do have that claim I filed. I can build a cabin there. Maybe I should interview Colonel Patton on the way home. I am passing through Staunton, and he seemed to favor me. Ho! What's this?"

He tugged the reins of his horse, bringing her to a stop. Ahead, some hundred yards off, he could see a two-story clapboard house set on a fieldstone foundation and surrounded by a broad expanse of meadow and cultivated land neatly divided by low stone walls and the beginnings of English-style hedgerows. A dozen horses, mostly unkempt cobs, were tied out front.

Hawkwood pulled his watch from his waistcoat pocket and opened the case. Four in the afternoon. He'd had a good ride today, and it would be dark in another three hours. This would be a good place to seek lodging for the night, and if he had a bit of luck, he could cadge a meal in the process.

He rode on to the house, dismounted, tied his horse to a rail fence, and went up the steps. The front door was open, allowing the gentle breeze to ventilate the crowded front room. Hawkwood removed his hat and was immediately greeted by an elderly man in shirt, waistcoat, and apron. After asking for cider, he pushed his way through the crowd, none of whom paid attention to him. The old man brought him a leather tankard of cold cider fresh from a spring house.

Hawkwood turned to a middle-aged man, roughly garbed in patched buff coat, nankeen breeches, and shoes that had seen better days. "What's the occasion? When I rode up, I thought it was a foxhunt."

"In a manner of speaking, it is," he said. "We're a *posse comitatus*, a hue and cry, raised to run down a notorious murderer."

Hawkwood's throat tightened. "Is that right? Did he kill someone nearby? I see your glass is empty, friend. Can I fill it for you?"

The man grinned. "Thankee, sir, that's mighty generous of you. Most of these fellows"—he jerked his thumb toward the other men— "are so tight, they squeak when they walk. No way they'll stand a man a round." He leaned closer as if sharing a great secret. "The man we're after killed a man in Ireland. The man's family were so in a tweak over his death that they paid a thief-taker to come to Virginia and hunt him down."

Hawkwood's eyes flitted about the room. "Are you hot on him?"

The man shook his head. "The constable said he's headed for the Irish Tracts. If he gets there, he's safe as houses. The king's writ doesn't extend beyond the mountains. I think we'll spend the night here and head home on the morrow."

He knew he should leave, but he couldn't resist. After waving the innkeeper over, he dropped a single guinea in his hand. "This is for these men. Pour them drink until it is gone."

A cheer went up as the innkeeper brought out a crock jug of rum and set it on the trestle top. Hawkwood said his farewell to the old man and walked to the door—just in time to come face-to-face with Constable Boulware and the Irish thief-taker, Burchill. Scarecrow and John Bull.

Scarecrow leered at him. "My, my. Who do we have here? Bold as a dog in a doublet, you are."

Chapter Sixteen

HAWKWOOD TOOK A STEP BACK. The men of the hue and cry made no indication of noticing the confrontation at the door, but he knew that would only last for a moment. John Bull thrust out a meaty hand and grabbed his upper arm. Hawkwood pivoted and wrenched his arm free, but the man retained a handful of coat. Hawkwood shrugged his shoulders, left John Bull holding his coat, and bolted for the window where his drinking partner was sipping free rum.

Grabbing the tabletop with one hand, he shoved it back into what he hoped were his pursuers. The tavern was quiet for a moment, then filled with angry shouts. Hawkwood shouldered the old man against the wall and launched himself headfirst through the window. The diagonal muntins splintered, the glass exploded into a shower of shards, and Hawkwood, sans coat and hat, cannoned onto the packed earth yard near the steps. He slapped the ground, the breath nearly driven from his body, and scrambled to his feet as the mass of his pursuers forced their way through the door.

"Stop your shoving! Damn your eyes!" someone yelled from the doorway.

Another voice called for him to halt.

He vaulted the split-rail fence, jerked his reins loose, spun the horse about, and leapt into the saddle. Raking the horse's flanks with his spurs got the animal moving, and they accelerated through an open field south of the tavern. A glance over his shoulder revealed a half dozen riders hot on his trail.

His horse thundered through the thigh-high timothy grass, and

Hawkwood forced his uncertain mount over a low wall and hedge and landed on the far side, scattering a covey of farm laborers taking an afternoon break from mowing. He dug in his spurs and slapped the horse's haunches with the free end of the reins as he leaned low over its neck. Over his shoulder only three riders still pursued, with the rest milling in confusion on the far side of the jump.

Putting his faith in the mare's latent strength, he pointed her up a long shallow hill. One of his pursuers, his horse short of leg and blown, was now headed back toward the tavern. None of the men who had stopped at the jump had continued the pursuit. But like avenging harpies, Scarecrow and John Bull hung on his trail.

Hawkwood and his mount shot over the crest of the hill. Stretched out, ambling across his path was a long ribband of wooly, dirty sheep.

"Fuck! Move! Move!"

But the sheep continued to munch and meander as if doom was not bearing down on them. Hawkwood continued to scream. After what seemed like hours, one of the beasts looked up, its legs stiffened, and it bolted away. Other sheep followed suit, and when Hawkwood hit the edge of the herd, it was a swirling mass of confused and frightened sheep.

Ahead were a handful that hadn't perceived the activity. He clutched the mare between his knees, took a handful of mane in his right hand along with the reins, and coaxed his mount into a jump. Her haunches bunched, and she levitated over the suddenly active sheep and landed in full stride on the far side.

He stole another glance behind him. Scarecrow was enmeshed in the herd of frightened sheep and ceased to be a threat. John Bull, however, had pushed through the herd in Hawkwood's wake and had closed the distance a length when Hawkwood had been forced to vault the sheep. He was now no more than thirty yards behind. Hawkwood applied the spurs again, and the mare surged even though she was breathing hard and her coat sweat-mottled. They smashed through a thicket and into thin air.

The thicket had masked a deep-cut creek bed. Neither horse nor rider had time to react. For a moment the mare tried to balk, her legs becoming rigid poles as her back arched. But she was already in full flight. Hawkwood hugged her neck to keep from being thrown.

The cut was about four feet deep, and the mare hit with her forelegs first, staggered forward, regained her footing for a moment, and then lost it again on the cobbles in the creek bottom.

"Oh, shit!"

Her forelegs buckled and she heeled over. Hawkwood extracted his right foot from the stirrup, pushed down hard on the horse's neck, and levered himself out of the saddle and away from the horse. She went down hard on her right shoulder and neck as Hawkwood twisted slightly in the air and slammed into the side of the creek bed flat of his back. The horse's haunches flipped over her head, and she lay stunned in the shallow creek. Hawkwood lay stretched out, benumbed, looking at the sky.

His momentum had scarcely been spent when John Bull, in feverish pursuit, encountered the same obstacle. His bay stallion saw the chaos unfolding in front of him and balked, sending him arse-over-tea-kettle into the creek.

Hawkwood's mare wormed her way to her feet, shook her head, and drifted woozily to the side. Hawkwood rolled to his stomach and forced himself to his hands and knees, taking great wheezing gulps of air. He stood, staggered backward for a couple of steps, righted himself, and lurched to his mount.

She appeared to as healthy as could be expected after the tumble she had taken. A few hours on the road would tell him if she was hurt, and he'd cross than bridge when he came to it. His musket hadn't fared as well. The stock was snapped just behind the lock, which didn't matter since the lock was wrenched from the stock. He put a foot in a stirrup and with effort pulled himself into the saddle.

John Bull lay face down in the creek but was struggling to rise. Hawkwood gritted his teeth so hard his head ached, then sucked in air through his teeth. The gotch-gutted bastard damned near killed him. To stop his business here and now, he'd have to kill him. He dismounted, stomped over to the fat man, and dealt him a solid kick in the kidney. John Bull groaned.

Stepping on the back of his neck, Hawkwood held his face beneath underwater. The man struggled, his wide arse jerking from side to side and his hands clawing at Hawkwood's boot. He pressed down harder, and John Bull's struggles became more frantic.

But he couldn't do it.

He made one final shove with his boot, then released him. Bull jerked his head up, coughing and struggling for breath.

Hawkwood knelt beside him, grabbed one of his ears, and twisted it. "I don't know how much money that man's family is paying you, but you have to consider if it's worth your life. That man was a Captain Hackum who picked a fight with the wrong man and got just desserts. I'm tired of you and your friend and your silly game. Yeah?"

In the distance, Scarecrow hallooed for his mate.

John Bull glared at him.

Hawkwood grabbed his queue, slammed his face into the creek bottom, and then jerked his head up so their gazes met. "What did you say about me? A dog in a doublet? Well, you're a bold fellow yourself to act so uppish to a man who would just as soon crash you as not."

He released his grip on the man's hair, stood, and paused for a second, then crouched and backhanded the man across the nose and lips, splattering his own breeches with droplets of bright blood. "Don't let me see you again. Ever."

He mounted his horse, climbed out of the stream, and cut across a pasture. Soon he came to Three Notch'd Road, and within minutes the track started downhill. He laughed aloud as the tension fled him. Now he was in the Valley, and for once he was glad that the wild Irish who inhabited the area were hostile to outsiders and to any law but that of their own.

* * * * *

HAWKWOOD FELT AS NEAR GIDDY as an English gentleman could be, even in complete privacy. He'd evaded the *posse comitatus*—though at the loss of his coat and musket. And now he was in territory where he knew they feared to tread. Staunton was less than twenty miles distant, but day was fast fading. Making the journey in the dark was possible, but would be a close-run thing and wouldn't be good for a horse that desperately needed forage and rest.

At the foot of the Blue Ridge, the road broadened a bit and ran parallel to the path of the narrow, meandering South River. He stopped, let his horse water and graze on the tall meadow grasses, and stretched. The fall had left him bruised and sore but otherwise none the worse for wear. He pulled off his boots and worsted stockings, seated himself on a sun-warmed boulder, and rested his feet in the chill water. After a few minutes rest, he tugged his boots on, mounted, and continued on his way.

"Damn Richard to hell," he muttered for perhaps the hundredth time since leaving Ardleigh, though now he could do so without feeling the urge to froth in rage. Crosslin had near ruined him. He has too much interest with the powerful for Hawkwood to prevail in a lawsuit, and even if he did prevail, it would be damned difficult to collect. And damn Welbourne too, for being a low, thieving hound.

He chuckled. At least with Richard he got some of his own back in trade. He didn't think Welbourne could manage Sarah all too well either. She seemed as interested in sport as Jenny. Hawkwood couldn't imagine a tripes-and-trillibubs like Welbourne could keep an active young piece like that satisfied. Since he was going to be stuck here for a while, he might just take a run at her and see what happened.

His stomach took a fit of growling. And damn it all, but Emma was right. If he going to have to live among these people, had had to become a part of them. Otherwise every man's hand would be against him.

The sound of horses close behind jerked him from his reverie. He turned just as three men reined their horses to a halt beside him and found himself looking into the solitary and malignant eye of Ned Turnbull.

Hawkwood's stomach soured. *Sod me. I'm dead.*

"See, boyos, I told you it was him. Riding alone on a fine horse," Ned said to his companions.

Hawkwood recognized one of them as the man Tim, whom he'd beaten to the ground at the Pettigrew house.

Ned eyed him again. "You're looking the worse for wear, boy. No hat or coat. Is that how all"—he imitated an Oxonian drawl— "the *ton* are dressed these days?" He guffawed at his own joke and was joined by the others.

Hawkwood had to brazen his way out, but he couldn't fight and couldn't run. He forced a smile and touched his forehead in salute. "Good afternoon, Mr. Turnbull. Yesterday I was set upon by highwaymen and was able to escape at cost of my coat and weapons. Would you know of a place nearby where the people are accommodating to visitors?"

Ned goggled in amazement and then recovered. "I don't think you'll need accommodations tonight, once we're finished with you."

Well, so much for that plan. Let's try something else. Hawkwood flicked his wrist, whipcracking his reins and landing them with a flat smack across the bridge of Ned's nose.

He howled and grabbed his face. "My eye! My eye! He's blinded me!"

Before Turnbull's squall had died, Hawkwood spurred his mount hard, and, tired as she was, she responded with the heart he had come to expect.

"Get him, you useless buggers!" Ned howled.

Hawkwood looked over his shoulder. He'd gained a lot of distance on them, and his mare was a much superior mount to their scrawny ponies. But his mount was badly jaded, and a little bit of bad luck could see him in their grasp. He jerked the reins hard to the right, raced across a narrow meadow, and plunged through riverside growth of greenbriers and cattails. After plowing through an alluvial mud flat, he blasted across the shallow river and up the other bank.

The mare exhaled loudly, shook her head, and shuddered to a walk. Hawkwood applied his spurs beyond the point of usefulness and yelled himself hoarse, but the mare wouldn't move faster than a plodding walk. A furlong away, Ned's companions came into view.

To Hawkwood's right was a steep, wooded hillock that would at least give him a chance. Then the mare stopped, blew a great breath, and sidled like a woozy old woman. He vaulted out of the saddle and sprinted for cover just as the mare collapsed. The men whooped in victory as they raced after him.

By the time they came to his horse, Hawkwood had reached the tree line. With knees lifted high and legs churning, he drove himself up the hillside. It was too steep and too wooded for horses, and they yelled at him when they reached the verge of the forest and stopped.

"Come on down, boy! Nowhere to go!" Tim screamed breathlessly from behind him. "It'll go hard on you if we gotta chase you!"

Fuck that. He broke through the trees on the rim of a sheer drop of twenty feet above the river. The water was scant inches deep and the riverbed a mix of slab boulders and cobbles that guaranteed a broken leg. Hawkwood groaned as the men beat their way up hill behind him, then looked left and right. With no clear advantage in either direction, he shrugged and bolted to the left.

His lungs ached and his legs felt like lead. If he got out of here alive, he'd train himself until he could run like the wind. A cramp seized his left side, doubling him over, and he pressed the heel of his hand hard into what he imagined to be the locus of the pain but continued to run. His abdomen contracted and he stopped, rested his hands on flexed knees, and retched.

Please Lord. I know I'm not the best man, but no one deserves to die at the hands of these animals. If you can see your way clear to help me out of this spot, I promise to mend my ways.

Hawkwood crossed himself, took a deep breath, and started to run again. Soon he stumbled, tripped over a low log, and went sprawling. He clambered to his feet and forced himself to run though he could scarcely lift his feet. As he gasped for breath, he smelled and tasted wood smoke.

He stopped, sniffing the air to be sure. Yes! It was wood smoke.

Even so, he couldn't detect the faint breeze that carried the scent of salvation. He attempted to moisten a finger but found his mouth was desert dry. After working at creating saliva for a few seconds, he wetted his finger, found the direction of the wind, and then turned into it and ran.

Now he was heading downhill at breakneck speed, arms windmilling to balance his overlong strides. He leapt over one low log, then running hard upon a large tree trunk lying across his path, he deftly placed one hand atop the log and vaulted over. The smell of smoke became stronger. A little luck and it would be a cabin with either a horse or a firelock he could use, whether the occupants were willingly or not.

Hawkwood perceived rather than saw a tendril of smoke rising above the trees. Reaching deep into himself, he threw his last reserves of energy into a final race to either blessed salvation or ignominious death. In the clearing sat a crude three-sided lean-to with a smoldering cooking fire in front of it. A five-gallon cast iron cauldron suspended above it from a tripod of iron rods.

"Halloo! The house!" he shouted.

No sound from the lean-to, but it drew a blast of obscenities from the men chasing him.

He yanked aside the deer hide covering the open side of the lean-to and looked in. Saddles, blankets, and other items covered the floor, but no musket. Maybe he could hide under that stuff? A second look convinced him that his fatigue was doing the thinking. They'd winkle him out of there in a minute, and even if they didn't kill him, he'd be laughed out of the Valley. He stepped away from the structure and turned to run, but his confidence was failing fast.

Movement in the forest caught his attention, and he saw his salvation—horses. He sprinted toward them but was stopped short by a haphazard fence of poles tied between trees with rawhide thongs. He grabbed one of the poles, braced his feet, and pulled against it with all the force he could muster. The sinews in his neck and jaws contracted and the muscles in his shoulders rippled as he grunted with the effort. The thong nearest him gave way, and he ran into the pen, picked a piebald mare, and grabbed her by the mane.

"Stop! Stop right there!"

He wheeled to face the voice, composing his excuse for being caught taking a horse. Then his shoulders sagged, and he sighed in resignation.

"Mr. Perkins," he said, touching his forehead. "How do you do?"

Bill Crews

Chapter Seventeen

MR. HAWKWOOD." THE BIG MAN LOWERED HIS MUSKETOON. "You have a way of getting around. Are times so tough that you've become a knight of the road yourself?"

"I've had a run of bad luck and—"

Perkins nodded his head at something behind Hawkwood. "Is that there some of your bad luck?"

He turned just as Tim and his companion broke into the clearing. "That would be a large part of it at the moment."

The two men stopped running, composed themselves, and walked toward Perkins and Hawkwood. "How do, Ute?" Tim said, his hands on his hips.

"How can I help you, Tim? Did Ned let you out without your governess?"

He indicated Hawkwood with a toss of his head. "Ned has some business with this boy."

"That ain't going to happen. He's on my place and tried to take my horse. So I'm the one who decides what to do with him. Go back and tell Ned that I've got him and when I get done with him, I'll let him know."

"Ned ain't going to like that, Ute. You know how he gets. He told us to bring this boy back and we got to."

Ute stared him down. "What kind of business could a one-eyed hector like Ned have with a man like this?"

"I don't ask Ned his business. Nobody does."

"Tell you what, Tim. You and your boy clear out of here. Don't think about coming back. If Ned has business involving me, then he knows where to find me."

"You're making a mistake."

Ute snorted. "It's been known to happen."

* * * * *

AT LEAST IT WAS PLEASANT DAY FOR STROLL. Hawkwood walked down the main road through Staunton, barefoot and in shirtsleeves. Perkins had reminded him, gently, that he was a knight of the road. A highwayman. As such, he had a reputation to keep up, for a highwayman without reputation was forced to use violence more than was Perkins's wont.

It wouldn't do for him to let Hawkwood escape unscathed, and as his man, Jack, had expressed an interest in Hawkwood's boots in their last encounter, it was only fair that he give them up. Jack was also short a good waistcoat, so it was only fitting that Hawkwood contribute that to Jack's wardrobe.

Hawkwood couldn't help but be amused at Perkins's kindness in sheltering him and all the while adhering to his code as a highwayman. In the spirit of the moment, he'd thrown in his worsted stockings and told Perkins where his mare had collapsed so he could retrieve her, should she still be alive, along with the tack.

Perkins and his men had fed him, treated him as a companion around the fire, gave him a clean bed of pine boughs, and sent him on his way at first light—sans boots, sans waistcoat, and upon his word of honor that he wouldn't betray their camp.

Patton and Preston stood on the porch of Patton's office cabin, and he gave them a cheery wave. They exchanged puzzled looks and returned the gesture.

Hawkwood squared his shoulders, Welsh-combed his hair, and walked toward them. "Good morning, gentlemen." He touched his brow with his fore and middle fingers in greeting. "Could I trouble you for the loan of a mount and then I'll be on my way?"

"Christ commands us to feed the hungry and clothe the naked. I'm sure the loan of a horse falls within what is required of us." Patton guffawed. "I swear to heaven, Hawkwood, every time you show up, you have less than what you started out with." His expression became serious. "Come in and take some refreshment and let your journey be revealed to us."

* * * * *

"WHAT DO YOU WISH ME TO DO?" Patton asked as he stared at the ceiling and stroked his neck.

Hawkwood sat forward in his chair. "Why, restrain them, of course. They've already invaded the Pettigrew house once and would have killed me and perhaps Hugh had Mr. Welbourne not acted to stop them. Now they waylay me on the road and attempt to kill me. From their actions, I can only assume that my falling out with Mr. Welbourne has emboldened them. He has designs on Miss Emma, for certain."

"What lies to the west of those mountains?" Patton jerked his thumb in the general direction of the serried skyline of the Appalachians, his voice taking on a higher pitch.

West of the mountains? "I'm sorry, sir, but I don't see how geography bears on this problem."

"Damn it all, Hawkwood. It has everything to do. The French are west of the mountains. It was barely a year ago that a French expedition left markers—lead plaques, for heaven's sake—along the waters that flow into the Ohio. The New River doesn't flow north to the Potomac or south to the Carolinas. It flows west to the Ohio. The French claim the very land we are sitting on at this moment. Why do you think the Crown has encouraged Irish Dissenters to settle the Valley?"

Patton slapped his palm with a forefinger the size of a sausage. "Because Ulstermen dislike papists more than they dislike Crown authority." The finger slapped again. "Because many of them have had experience fighting rapparees." He paused. "And because some of them, like the Turnbulls, were a damned nuisance at home, but in the backcountry they might be of some use."

Patton took a deep breath. "When war comes to this country, and it will come as surely as dark follows day, our colony and the Crown will need rogues and ruffians like the Turnbulls. As it stands now, I have no cause to act against them. Indeed, I must ask myself, what if I did raise the hue and cry against them and no one answered? What would become of this county then? I am ashamed to admit this, young Kit, but many people fear the Turnbulls more than they fear me."

This struck Hawkwood like a thunderbolt. He'd never imagined the county lieutenant could doubt his own ability to enforce the peace without popular consent or that he had no real power beyond what he was perceived to have.

"What do I do?"

"You're charged with protecting the interests of the Pettigrew children's estate until they reach majority. Perhaps you should consider betrothing Emma to Ned, if he's set his good eye on her?"

Hawkwood opened his mouth but couldn't produce a sound for a moment. "Sir, that is grotesque. It is unseemly. Emma is a sweet and gentle young woman. She will wed eventually but not a low-bred ruffian like that."

"In that case, all you can rely upon is your own strong right hand and the support of your followers. If you have no followers, you stand alone. 'And if one prevail against him ...'"

"Aye, I know," Hawkwood said "'Two shall withstand him; and a threefold cord is not quickly broken.'"

"Did she now?" Patton laughed. "She must be wise far beyond her years."

"Very well, sir. I see. In that case, if you could loan me that horse you mentioned earlier, I'll be on my way." He stood.

"Stand fast, Hawkwood," Patton growled. "You are entitled to think less of me because of this. Hell, I think less of me." He grinned. "You have a place in this county. When the French come, we will need men who know what they are about. You can master the Turnbulls if you put your mind to it. Two final thoughts for your consideration. Welbourne is not your friend. He relies on the Turnbulls to do a lot of his dirty work. Second, and forgive me for asking this, what are your intentions with Emma Pettigrew?"

Hawkwood gawped. "I admire Emma, sir, but she has no interest in me and I am in no position to wed. Further, sir, I would never take advantage of someone placed under my protection."

Patton stared at him, his narrowed eyes dark under a furrowed brow and augering into his soul. Hawkwood held his gaze for a few seconds, seconds that seemed like days, as Preston watched in silence. Then Patton nodded and extended his hand. "Billy will get you that horse. I trust we'll be seeing you again soon. And not on foot."

What do you think, Uncle?" Preston asked as he and Patton watched from the window as Hawkwood rode away.

Patton exhaled. "I think that boy is as good as married, though he don't know it yet. We know that Bart Pettigrew don't have no kin in Philadelphia. That girl has spun him a story to keep him around for a reason. The only question is if he lives long enough figure it out."

"What if he's killed?"

"Then he won't be the first Tuckahoe to be killed in the Valley. We'll cross that bridge when we come to it, but our man Hawkwood seems to be a survivor. And the Pettigrew girl sounds like she can keep him from making too many stupid mistakes. I wish him the best. I'm tired of loaning him my horses."

* * * * *

"DAMN THE MAN. DAMN HIM TO HELL," Hawkwood muttered as his questionable nag jolted her way south. How was he supposed to deal with this crew of blackguards?

Hawkwood chewed on the thought as though it were a particularly tough chunk of gristle. And what possible interest would he have in Emma? Sweet though she was, the country mort had no dot other than her share of their farm and not enough breeding to hold her own in society in England. On top of it all, she was really a Cohee in her thinking, and he'd never think like them.

He had been riding bareback for a day and a half—Preston's charity may have extended to a broken-down nag but not to a saddle—and his mood grew darker by the moment. It was late afternoon when he reached the branch in the trail. To the left lay the Pettigrew farm, and to the right a shebeen, an illegal ordinary operated by one of the multitudinous McDowell sept that peopled the western Valley. He knew little about it other than Rankin was a regular visitor.

Though he had been invited to accompany Rankin a couple of times, he had no interest in drinking with Cohees who were violent enough when cold sober. But he didn't feel like going home either. He tugged the reins, and the docile old horse meandered to the right.

The shebeen was similar in layout to Ute Perkins's camp—a three-sided structure with a flat roof sloping down to the rear of the structure. The front was open, with a rough covering of deer hides laced together with rawhide cord. That protected the front in inclement weather, but tonight it was rolled up out of the way and secured with ties. A low fire kept a cast iron cauldron filled with unidentifiable stew simmering. Rankin sat on one of the puncheon benches near the fire, balancing a battered tin mug on one knee while gesturing and yarning with his companions.

Hawkwood tied his mount to a sapling and approached them. "Good evening, Mr. Rankin."

The old man gave him a quick look up and down, then extended his hand in greeting without getting up and introduced him to the other men.

They eyed him curiously, taking in his hatless head, sweat-circled linen shirt, stained buckskin breeches, bare shanks, and old and broken shoes.

Rankin drew his flageolet from a pocket on his smock, one of his companions produced a battered fiddle, and soon they were squealing their way through "Boyne Water."

A burly man in his thirties—the shebeen's proprietor perhaps? — approached them. "Is he drinking with you?"

"Aye," Rankin replied between tootles.

The man handed Hawkwood a cup and left. Leaning over, one of the men in the group poured Hawkwood a healthy measure from a demijohn. Hawkwood sniffed it, recognized the drink as raw corn whiskey, and took a cautious sip. The liquor burned his throat, and the fumes singed his sinuses. He took another sip, this time larger, and it hit his stomach like molten iron flowing from a forge. He nodded his approval at the men who were watching him, clearly testing his reaction.

"So, as I was saying," one of the men said. About thirty, he didn't have a pinch of spare flesh on his walnut-brown body.

All conversation ceased.

"There I was on the Youghiogheny, minding my own business, bringing back a canoe load of prime plews. A whole season's worth of trapping in the Ohio Country—"

"Youghiogheny?" Hawkwood said. "Isn't that where Wat Turnbull became Hairless Wat?"

The group chuckled.

"Indeed, it be." The man's eyes looked agate hard in his smiling face. "Anyway, I round a bend and there they are. No shit, boys. A Shawnee war party."

Hawkwood sipped the whiskey. "Shawnee, you say? Jemmy Clendenin was held captive by them, wasn't he?"

"Right. There had to be thirty, thirty-five of them, war-painted every last one. Out for blood and scalps."

Hawkwood leaned forward, and the other men nodded and murmured assent.

"The river weren't more than shin deep, and they came charging toward me. I hopped out of my canoe and ran for the other shore. Now I'm a fast runner,"—some chuckling came from the audience— "and I started pulling away, you see. I cleared that riverbank, had to be six feet high, as clean as any buck you've ever seen."

Hawkwood took a drink. "Six feet? I say, sir, that is quite a leap. Most amazing."

The man's eyes glinted in the light of the setting sun. "Well, it was a choice of jumping high or losing my hair, so I jumped."

The group guffawed.

"I clawed my way through the greenbrier, and you boys know how thick the stuff is there. Tore off my hunting shirt, tore off my fucking breechclout, scratched me up worse than some two-penny whore. I came out of the brambles in my birthday suit, bleeding like a stuck pig,"—he paused for dramatic effect—"and I found myself smack-dab in the middle of the rest of the war party."

The man took a couple of throat-flexing gulps of whiskey, wiped his lips, and continued to his rapt audience. "I looks to me left and there's war party from the river, hootin' and hollerin' like Billy Hell. So, I took off running again, but I was tired, you see, and all the blood I'd lost made me weak and I could hear them gaining on me. So, I figured if I could climb a tree, I could get out of sight and lose them. Well, sir, I gave it everything I had, near about sprung my guts, I did. I hit this big old chestnut at a dead run and went up it faster than any 'coon you ever seen."

Silence hung over the group, and the man swirled the whiskey in his cup and stared into it.

Hawkwood took a drink. "And then what happened?"

He stared him in the eyes. "Well, hell, boy, they pulled me out of that tree and killed me." With that, he threw back his head and guffawed, and the crowd joined in.

Hawkwood flushed with anger and rose to leave.

The storyteller grabbed his arm. "Just having some fun, son. No harm meant. These other boys have heard all my stories a hundred times. Bram, why don't you fill the gentleman's cup?"

Hawkwood took a few moments to examine the man to see if he was being mocked, decided he wasn't, and took his seat. Stretching his legs, he closed his eyes and realized how much he missed visiting a tavern or coffee house. He found his mug empty and just as quickly refilled, and he kept drinking.

He soon knew he was chirping merry and well on his way to being as drunk as Davy's Sow—and he didn't care. The emotional turmoil of the past few days—leaving the land business, finding Crosslin had betrayed him, the pursuit by the hue and cry, being hunted by the Turnbulls, getting robbed by Perkins, and, finally, being abandoned by Patton—was too much to comprehend at one sitting. Or to comprehend while sober, anyway.

The storyteller produced a twist of chewing tobacco and offered it and a clasp knife to him. "Chaw?"

Hawkwood shook his head. "I know you Cohees are fond of it, but I don't see the attraction."

"Well,"—he shrugged—"it keeps you awake when you need to stay awake, keeps you from being hungry when you can't eat, and it makes the best dressing for any wound. Once my woman told me that she couldn't abide chaw, that it was either her or the chaw. I told her I'd never had bad chaw, packed my bag, and I ain't seen her since."

The men chuckled and nodded.

"Let's have a song, boy," said a short man, not much older than Hawkwood, with the same weather-beaten and sinewy look as the storyteller.

Hawkwood shook his head, but the others took up the call. He held up his hands for silence. "D'ye Cohees know '*Scarborough Fair*'?"

They laughed, and Rankin essayed a couple of notes and the fiddler nodded and drew his bow. Hawkwood let them feel their way through one bar before beginning:

"O, where are you going? To Scarborough Fair.
Savoury sage, rosemary, and thyme;
Remember me to a lass who lives there,
For once she was a true love of mine."

Feeling the liquor taking more effect, he closed his eyes and plugged one ear with his finger so he could hit the notes. His clear tenor cut through the raucous noise of the shebeen and served as a fitting counterpoint to the crimson ball of the sun touching the Appalachian ridge line.

"Tell her to make me a cambric shirt,
Savoury sage, rosemary, and thyme;"
A few voices joined him:
"Without any seam or needlework,
Then she shall be a true love of mine."

"Ha!" Hawkwood turned to the voices and found they belonged to Ned Turnbull and the two men who had chased him at the base of Woods Gap. "They sing nearly as good as they run."

Chapter Eighteen

HAWKWOOD STOOD, HOLDING UP HIS HANDS. His mind and heart raced, and he was in no shape to either fight or run. Blood roared in his ears and pounded at his temples like a farrier sergeant working a bar of iron, as his guts churned. "Turnbull, you and your boys had your fun yesterday. There's no reason to bring trouble into this place."

"I'm not bringing trouble here, Hawkwood. I'm bringing you"—he jabbed a finger at him— "fair warning. Soon. Real soon. I'm coming to pay court to Miss Emma. I intend that we be wed. You'd best not interfere."

Hawkwood nearly sighed in relief. *Is that all he wants? He's welcome to give it a try.* "Do as you will. She's of age to make up her mind. If she wants you, you'll have no difficulty with me."

Ned gave him a piercing stare with his single evil eye, shook his head, spat on the ground, and walked away. The men who had been gathered near Hawkwood drifted away, and Rankin looked up at him, a dark glower bespeaking his disapproval.

"What?" Hawkwood said. "What was I supposed to say?"

"D'you think so little of that girl that you'd see her bred with that ape?"

Hawkwood gave the old man a cold stare. It was damned easy for someone who was not in danger of being gutted by Ned Turnbull to judge the man whose life was on the line.

"Well, she can make up her own mind. It's not my place to decide for her."

"Bah! What kind of a man are you?" Rankin picked up his flageolet, nodded at the fiddler, and struck up "Hey, Johnnie Cope."

Some of the men knew the words and began singing. Hawkwood stood there, his ears burning with humiliation. He felt as though every man there knew he had been with Cope at Prestonpans. And now they had seen him flee Ned Turnbull with the same alacrity that marked Cope's wild ride to Berwick Castle. Men who had been his comrades only moments ago now either averted their gaze from his shame or boldly laughed in his face.

Fighting back tears, he dropped his tin cup and stumbled toward his horse in the gathering darkness.

* * * * *

IN THE FAR HINTERLANDS OF HAWKWOOD'S consciousness, barking dogs raised a racket. He tossed in his bed, and a hand shook him from sleep.

"Get up, Kit," Hugh said. "The Turnbulls are here."

His head rumbled like a kettle drum, and his mouth felt coated with river clay. He blinked and looked about. What time was it? Afternoon? Really, it could have been anytime. "Turnbulls, you say? How many?"

"Ned, Tim, and Robbie."

Oh, sod me. Hawkwood shook the wool from his head and stood. His shirt reeked of sweat with a bouquet of dried vomit hovering over it. "Right." After opening one of his portmanteaus, he extracted a nearly clean shirt and pulled it on. Then he took his infantry officer's hanger from under his mattress.

"Kit, you're not going out with that, are you?" Hugh stared at the hanger. "If they see that long knife, it will set them off sure as shooting."

"I know. Get your fowling piece. Follow my leader and don't say a word."

Hawkwood propped his scabbarded hanger against the wall just inside the door and pointed where he wanted Hugh to lean the fowling piece, then opened the door and stepped onto the porch. When his eyes adjusted to the bright sunlight, the Turnbulls had tied up their horses and were walking toward the house.

"Good afternoon, Ned," he said. "May I help you?"

The Turnbulls stopped. Ned regarded Hawkwood with a scornful squint of his one eye. "No. You can't, but you can tell Miss Emma I've come calling and I would obliged if she would step out and walk with me."

"Very well, Ned." He turned to Hugh, who stood beside him. "Would you bring your sister out?"

Hugh began to protest, but Hawkwood silenced him with a stare. He then went into the house and came back onto the porch with one arm draped protectively over Emma's shoulders. She took small, reluctant steps, her eyes averted to the floor.

"Emma," Hawkwood said, "Ned has asked you to walk out with him. What is your will?"

"Hold on, Hawkwood," Robbie called. "We didn't ride here to see if she wanted to walk out with Ned. We came here to do it."

Emma shuddered, drew herself up straight, and looked at Ned. Her lips trembled. "I'd sooner die and go to hell, Ned Turnbull, than share your bed. But if it will get you to leave us alone, I will take a turn about the yard with you."

The four men watched in sullen silence, giving each other cutty-eyed looks as Emma and Ned Turnbull walked the perimeter of the house once. At the end, Ned made a clumsy bow, motioned for his brothers to join him, and they mounted up and rode away.

Emma covered her face with her apron, her shoulders heaved as she sobbed, and then she ran for the house.

* * * * *

HAWKWOOD EXTENDED HIS ARM ACROSS THE doorway leading from the kitchen to the dogtrot, blocking Emma's path. "I'm not moving until you speak to me."

She glared at him; her lips pursed under eyes that were nothing short of glacial. The tell-tale vertical crease between her eyebrows appeared and deepened. "Fine," she said without emotion. "I spoke. Now stand aside, sir."

This was the first time Emma had spoken to him in three days. She had been cold toward him when he arrived at the house in the early morning hours in the latter stages of a solid drunk. He deserved that, considering he'd been gone from the farm for some days and when he returned his first stop was the shebeen. Not exactly considerate. Then the Turnbulls arrived. After their uneventful departure, instead of the mood lightening, it had turned arctic in the house. She prepared meals but served them in silence. Hugh averred ignorance, but Hawkwood suspected his loyalty to his sister prevented him from sharing any information he did have.

"Emma, please, what have I done? Tell me. Let me make amends."

She inhaled as though she had been stung, then released her breath and closed her eyes. "What have you done; you ask? Really? You can stand there after buttock-brokering me to that one-eyed Turnbull git and ask what you did?" Tears welled in her eyes and she slapped him hard across the cheek.

He stepped back, shocked.

She came at him, flailing at him with her fists. "You bastard! You whore-son!"

He brought his arms up to shield his face as she belabored him. "Please, Emma, stop this. I can explain."

She stopped mid-blow, covered her face with her hands, and sank to the rush-covered floor. Hawkwood sat close by her and reached out to put his arm around her, but then stopped. In the pet she was in, she might gut him or take his nutmegs off. He gulped and did it anyway.

"Kit, how could you? How could you give that awful Turnbull your permission to call on me? You're supposed to protect me and Hugh and our property. I thought you were my friend. How could you?"

"I had no choice. Ned and his men tried to kill me on the trip home. When he showed up at McDowell's place, I was just trying to get out of there in one piece."

"And you gave him the freedom of my thighs so you could be safe?"

"Emma, I did no such thing! I never promised you to him!"

She wiped her cheeks with her fists, reminding Hawkwood of a little girl as she dried her tears, and his heart melted. "I'm so sorry, Emma. I am so sorry."

She took his hands in hers and looked into his eyes. "I have no men to stand for me, save you and Hugh. And now you need me to protect you. If I can't depend on you to keep me and Hugh safe, then I need for you to say so."

"But, of course—"

She shushed him, placing a work-roughened finger to his lips. "And if you can't do that, I need for you to leave—"

"Now, that isn't called for."

"Straight away." Her voice was firm. "You need to leave if you can't protect us because"—tears welled again in her eyes, coursed down the sides of her nose and around the drooping corners of her mouth, and hit the rushes with sad plops—"there is no uncle."

"What?" Hawkwood's mind raced with the implications. He had viewed the guardianship as a temporary measure, a duty that would take up his time for a few weeks or months until he was relieved of his duties by her kinsman. No uncle meant he was on the hook to watch over both of them and safeguard their property for another year or two. "What do you mean, there is no uncle? Are you saying you lied to me?"

She stood, straightened her skirts, and wiped her eyes dry with her sleeve. Turning on her heel, she walked away.

Hawkwood jumped to his feet, took her by the shoulder, and spun her to face him. "You lied to me, and you've nothing to say? You can't just walk away. Don't you see what you've done to me?"

She brushed his hand from her shoulder. "What have I done? Are you saying Welbourne and his lot would be honest men if I hadn't lied to you? That you'd have all your money back if only you'd known? I'm so sorry I lied to you, Kit, but I needed a man of character, a strong man, to help run this place until a more permanent solution appeared. Hugh and I are alone. And you need to decide if you are standing with us or running."

Chapter Nineteen

HAWKWOOD BREATHED LIKE A BELLOWS wiped the sweat from his face with his forearm, clasped his hands over the top of the scythe blade, and leaned on the curved snath.

"Kit, you need to whet that thing," Hugh said over his shoulder, moving ahead without sign of tiring. "You're starting to beat the hay down."

"Right." He extracted a whetstone from a pocket of the wide-legged pantaloons the late Bart Pettigrew had owned, then gave the blade a few brisk scrapes until the edge looked sharp.

Hercules complained about the stables of Augeas, Hawkwood thought, surveying the endless meadow oscillating in rhythm with the whims of the southern breeze. *Fuck all did he know about endless labor. He just had to worry about a few bloody cows. I'd trade places with him in a moment.* He spat on his raw and aching hands, gritted his teeth, clenched the scythe's grips, and resumed mowing the thigh-high grass.

Beyond Hugh were a pair of hired men who were working for room and board. At a distance behind them, Emma and Rankin worked in tandem, raking the mown hay into windrows. Emma had shed her bodice, skirt, and petticoats, now working in a shift she had kilted with a rope belt that left her legs bare well above her knees. All of them wore wooden clogs, though Emma had stained hers a vivid red-purple using pokeweed berries.

Hawkwood stopped and stared at her for a moment. The sunlight silhouetted her body through the sweat-dampened fabric that clung to her, and he gave a low whistle and shook his head. Damme, she was a fetching mort. Damned nice legs. He watched her breasts bob with the movement of the rake. Her bubbies weren't that large, but they were pert.

He felt a stirring in his groin.

She was so capable too. She ran the household alone and still helped with the heavy work. Not at all like any other woman he'd known.

Emma caught him staring and frowned. He shrugged. She looked around to locate Rankin, then seeing his back turned, cocked one hip and lifted the hem of her shift for a second, giving him a brief view of her thigh and one enticing buttock cheek. He made a courtly bow, hefted the scythe, and returned to work, thankful for the capacious trousers that concealed his erection.

What was that all about? All she'd done since he'd been here was give him Billy-O for one thing or another. She could be a fair termagant at times. Was Patton right, that he should wed her? He was fairly stuck here in these back settlements. A sheriff would take him up for sure if he went back across the mountains. And Emma's family was several cuts above most of their neighbors. She did have a certain grace, a trace of proper breeding. Where he'd once though her rather homely he was now quite sure that properly dressed she would turn heads in Cork—even in London. Well, maybe not in London. There was that red hair and all those freckles.

Hoofbeats approached, and he turned to find two riders coming. Even at a distance he recognized them as Billy Preston and Jemmy Clendenin. They both gave Emma an appreciative glance as she plied the hay rake and pointedly ignored them.

"Greetings." Hawkwood tipped his broad-brimmed straw hat. "What brings you this way, Billy?"

"Spreading the word, Kit. There's an Iroquois war party heading south to raid the Catawbas. There will be a feast for them near the Lewis place on the Seneca Trail two days hence. The colonel desires as many of the people as possible attend."

By now, Hugh, Emma, Rankin, and the hired men had stopped working and joined them. Emma had pulled her shift from beneath the rope belt, and it now hung down to the tops of her clogs. His fellow workers' eyes were alight with anticipation, likely because a gathering was welcome in the backcountry, where most homesteads existed in isolation. If the gathering promised exotic entertainment, like wild Indians, so much the better.

"Day after tomorrow, eh? We'll be there." Hawkwood turned to resume mowing hay.

"Farming's woman's work, Boo," Clendenin said. "Nothing good ever came to a man from farming." He touched his heels to his horse and galloped away, shouting a war cry.

* * * * *

THE IROQUOIS WAR PARTY WAS QUITE a sight. Under the terms of the Treaty of Lancaster, the group bore a writ signed by the Crown's Indian commissioner in Albany, William Johnson. They checked in at each county courthouse as they moved south along the Seneca Trail and were given an escort to see them safely through the county.

From what Hawkwood had heard, they had passed through Frederick Town without incident. Lord Fairfax feted them royally, though not so much as to host them at his Greenway Court estate.

A Frederick County constable then preceded them on their march by a day and warned the farmsteads along the Seneca Trail that thirty-odd Logstown Senecas were on the move. Ulstermen scurried to round up their free-ranging cattle and hogs and drive them to the safety of the Blue Ridge foothills while the Germans clucked disapprovingly at the slovenly nature of the Irish, a people who lacked barns and sties. At those farms where the war party stopped overnight, they were fed. The reckoning, of course, was remitted to the county court. As a result, Tanacharison's expedition committed only mild atrocities on unsecured livestock and passed unmolested by irate farmers.

Even under the weather, the war party moved remarkably fast, leaving a wake pungent with the reek of bear grease and rum-sweat. They traveled single file at a dog trot and arrived by themselves, having run the constable and judge out of sight earlier in the day even though those worthies were mounted. Most of the warriors were taller than the typical denizen of the Virginia backcountry, and they appeared markedly healthier. Though lean and superbly muscled, they lacked the bulk developed by life behind the plow.

Showing no interest in the polyglot throng staring at them from trailside, from perches in trees and on horseback, they stayed silent and impassive. Their eyes relentlessly flicked from side to side as if continuing to search for prey, reminding Hawkwood of a pack of wolfhounds in the midst of a kennel of cur dogs.

Amidst the monotony of farm life, the party provided great excitement. Unlike their neighbors to the north and south, Virginians in the Valley had very little contact with Indians. Pennsylvanians and Marylanders lived side by side with Lenape and several minor and near-extinct tribes. Carolinians were in close proximity to Catawbas and Cherokees. The Valley, by contrast, was virtually unoccupied by Indians.

As word of the war party's imminent arrival and the location of the rendezvous spread through the countryside, families began congregating. The Germans, who lived north of the Irish Tracts, mostly arrived in wagons. A few drove the behemoth Conestoga wagons or the slightly smaller Virginia road wagons, each carrying two or three families and drawn by a half dozen large horses of the same name.

Others arrived in the lighter wagons or, like the Pettigrews, in a two-wheeled cart. Welbourne arrived with Sarah in a fashionable two-wheeled calash pulled by a striking chestnut gelding. Most, be they Scots or Ulstermen, arrived either on foot or mounted on scrawny horses that were barely larger than the ponies found in Virginia's Tidewater. England, as far as Hawkwood could determine, was represented by himself and the Welbournes.

Once the Indians arrived, the crowd settled in for the night, making rude camps under the trees. The peoples rarely mixed, with Germans camped with Germans, and Scots and Ulstermen camped with their own.

Hawkwood had considered wearing the hunting shirt Emma gave him, but in the end wore what remained of his best clothing—a snuff brown coat, cream silk waistcoat, and buckskin breeches. He would have preferred his top boots, but they adorned the feet of one of Ute Perkins's henchmen, so he wore his shoes with silver buckles and white silk stockings. His hat, he had to admit, was less than satisfactory. He had pinned up the brim of one of the black farmer's hats that has belonged to Bart Pettigrew to make a tricorn, and Emma had made him a passable black Hanover cockade from spare ribband.

Emma, on the other hand, looked gorgeous in a pale blue bodice that she'd embroidered with wildflowers. Her skirt was goldenrod yellow with a saucy red petticoat peeking from beneath the hemline. She had gathered her dense red-auburn hair under a mob cap topped with a homemade flat straw *bergère* hat, and a fine lace fichu covered her shoulders and what Hawkwood knew was a generous display of *décolletage*. She was a creature set apart from the other women of the back settlements.

Hawkwood had to admit he enjoyed walking through the throng, Emma's hand resting ever so lightly on his forearm, conscious of the jealous glances of men and women alike. Then a braying laugh caught his attention. When he heard it again, he steered Emma and Hugh toward it.

Leaning against the dull red wheel of a German's Conestoga wagon was a large, burly man talking to a traveling gunsmith. His back was turned, but Hawkwood didn't need to see his face to recognize him. "Mr. Perkins," he said in his best parade-ground voice.

Ute Perkins started and whirled about, drawing a pistol from under his hunting shirt. Then he relaxed and broke into a wide grin. "Mr. Hawkwood." He took a step toward him and extended his hand.

Hawkwood shook it. Both Hugh and Emma seemed impressed by meeting the legendary highwayman. "Are my horses, pistols, rifle, and boots serving you well, sir?"

Perkins guffawed and clapped him on the shoulder. "They are indeed. That second horse recovered nicely with a little care. You are a game one, young sir. I'll give you that. Now if you will excuse me, I have business to attend to."

Hawkwood whispered to Emma, "Most extraordinary, a notorious highwayman walking about bold as brass."

"You have much to learn, Kit," she said. "Mr. Perkins is well regarded. He only takes from them what can afford it and often shares his swag with those in need."

"A regular Robin Hood, is he?"

"I don't know of this Robin Hood, but he seems to admire you." She gave his arm a warm squeeze. "And that will be noticed by everyone."

* * * * *

HAWKWOOD, EMMA, AND HUGH ROSE EARLY, while the hollows on western slopes of the Blue Ridge were still shrouded in darkness, and joined Rankin, Sam Farris, and Farris's wife Mary at their fire.

"Should be quite a day today," Farris said as they all partook of boiled hominy grits and tea, both sweetened with dollops of maple syrup. "I hear that Patton is offering a purse to the winner of a horse race, and Welbourne is doing the same for a shooting match."

Hawkwood sighed. "Too bad I don't have a horse or a firelock."

"You think you'd have a chance?" Farris's eyes were hooded in skepticism.

A looked at the others showed that they were doubtful too. "I've seen you Cohees ride, Sam. No offense, but you all have a seat like a bag of meal. And with my rifle, I know I could beat any man here."

"Tell you what. I'll loan you my horse and rifle. If you win, you split the purse with me."

Farris's rifle was a beauty. The stock was dark red-brown curly maple with brass mountings, and the barrel and lock had been rust-blued to a dark gray-black. It weighed about ten pounds but was beautifully balanced and was nearly a foot longer than the Land Pattern musket used by the British Army. Hawkwood's stolen *doppelstutzen* was a fine weapon, but for workmanship and artistry, it wasn't in the same class as Farris's rifle.

"Now the sights are set for a hundred yards," Farris said. "Add a foot drop for a hundred and fifty yards. Another foot at two hundred. The balls are thirty-eight to the pound. Use this measuring pot for the powder."

Hawkwood took the brass measuring pot he offered. "Why aren't you shooting, Sam?"

"Too many people know me, and it'd make for a lot less fun. You know if you win, you're going to make some dangerous men unhappy, don't you?"

He dropped the measuring pot in his coat pocket, looked at Farris and said, "I've come to the conclusion that I'm going to make people unhappy no matter what I do."

The competition was straight forward. A tree fifty yards from the firing line was blazed and a silver crown spiked to the center of the blaze. Nearly three dozen men of all sizes and shapes clustered about Billy Preston as he laid down the rules.

Each man would fire one shot, and the ten contestants with strikes closest would move back twenty-five yards and shoot again. The five best shots would move back another twenty-five yards. From there, the closest shot would win. All shooting had to be done from a standing position with no support.

"And the winner gets a purse of five guineas and the crown piece nailed to the tree," Preston announced, "and the colonel will buss his blind cheeks."

The crowd roared with laughter at the earthy humor.

The men queued up and the competition began. The first shooter was the storyteller from the shebeen. Hawkwood wished his bullet to fly wide, but he was disappointed. A chip of bark flashed away from the edge of the blaze, and the judges marked the spot with a stub of pencil.

Another man, one of the Germans, fired and hit the tree outside the blaze. Then two men in a row missed the tree entirely, with the last shaking his musket and cursing it as though the gun and not the shooter had come up short.

As Hawkwood focused on the shooters, someone shouldered their way into the queue in front of him. "If you shoot as good as you run, you'll win this," Ned Turnbull said.

Hawkwood ignored him.

"I'm not finished with you, boy. Your reckoning is a-coming. You act so all high and mighty. Like you're better than the rest of us. Everybody knows you have the white feather. You had that girl fight your fight for you the other day. For all your airs, you're nothing but a dunghill cock."

He clenched his jaw as his face flushed. Men around him were watching him for his reaction but said nothing.

Ned spat and turned away.

When his turn came to shoot, Ned's shot was a fair strike that looked to be about two inches below the coin. His supporters cheered as though he'd won the competition. Hawkwood had studied him as he shot and wasn't impressed. He was sure, even beyond his dislike for Ned, that the shot was luck. Then it was his turn to shoot.

He checked the flint to make sure it was snug in the cock. Stepping forward with his left foot and shifting his weight to it, he raised the rifle and cocked it with his thumb as he snugged it into the pocket of his shoulder.

The barrel floated for a moment in response to his breathing, and he steadied, exhaled half his breath, and swallowed. The sight stopped dancing on the blaze and settled to a point an inch below the target. He gently squeezed the trigger. Powder flashed in the pan and the rifle fired, sending a cloud of gray smoke into the still and damp morning air.

"He hit the mark!" one on the judges called.

After a pause, the crowd broke into whoops and cheers. Emma bounced on her toes, applauding. While Farris touched the brim of his hat with his fingers, Wat Turnbull pulled his face with one hand and the dozen or so men with him looked glum.

"Luck," Turnbull groused.

After the last man shot, Preston pulled himself up onto the hub of a Conestoga wagon's wheel. "Only one shot hit the mark, so I'm awarding the purse—"

"Now, wait up there, Mr. Preston," Turnbull shouted. "Nobody said nothing about a hit on the mark winning. The rules were that these boys would keep shooting until one man won."

"He's right, Billy," Welbourne called from his seat. "There was no mention in the rules of a strike on the mark winning the contest."

Hawkwood clenched his jaw. The bastard was just trying to get his own back over him quitting. "That's fine by me, Mr. Preston!"

The crowd turned toward him.

"I can hit it again just as easy as I did the first time."

This brought more cheers and, for the first time, some catcalls directed at Ned.

"That's a big boast for a Tuckahoe cock-robin," Turnbull called across the crowd.

More cheers and catcalls followed, some directed at Hawkwood and some at the Turnbulls.

"Well, Mr. Turnbull, the one thing I've learned living here is that it ain't boasting if you can do it."

A low laugh rumbled through the crowd.

"Let's go to the next round, Billy," Hawkwood finished.

The ten remaining men moved back twenty-five paces. They fired one by one, but Hawkwood alone struck the mark. Then five men remained—Hawkwood, Ned, the storyteller, and two other men whose hunting shirts and breechclouts marked them as timberbeasts.

The storyteller walked over to Hawkwood. "I know a better shot when I meet him. The first hit might have been luck, the second one couldn't be." He extended his hand, and Hawkwood shook it. "It has been a pleasure, sir, but I'm going to bow out. I can't see wasting the powder and lead it would take to lose to you next round."

A cheer of acclamation rose from the throng.

One of the two timberbeasts touched his forehead in salute. "I'm out too."

The other nodded. "Yep, that was some fine shooting, but I'm done."

Ned, clearly unsettled by the other men pulling out, protested with them over their decision. In the end, the men turned and walked away to watch the contest while Hawkwood and Ned moved back another twenty-five yards.

They flipped a coin for order of shooting, and Ned went first. His shot went wide of the tree, bringing some groans from the crowd.

"That's not fair," he protested. "My piece went off by accident. I need another shot."

Preston glanced at Hawkwood.

"If he says so, Billy." He gave Ned a smirk. "I don't mind him shooting again."

The contest ended in anti-climax. Turnbull managed to hit the tree but missed the blaze. Hawkwood placed his shot squarely in the blaze and near the coin. As the smoke dissipated and it was clear than Hawkwood had won, the crowd pressed in around him, pumping his hand and slapping him on the back. Emma planted a big kiss on his cheek to chorus of whoops and ribald calls.

After the crowd drifted away, Hawkwood handed the purse he'd won to Farris. "Buy me the best rifle you can find with my share."

* * * * *

BY THE TIME HAWKWOOD THUNDERED ACROSS THE finish line astride the ugly beast he'd borrowed from Sam Farris, he was a minor celebrity. Hawkwood's horse was not the best horse in the race, but he was by far the best horseman. He had cinched his stirrup straps high, like a jockey riding at Ascot, and taken some good-natured ribbing from the crowd over his style—and some not-so-good-natured abuse from the Turnbull clan—but the results spoke for themselves.

Hawkwood had melded into the horse, creating a single unit bent on winning, while the backcountrymen bounced along. One man winning the shooting match and the horse race was big news, and that the man was a Tuckahoe and had bested all the local talent was the stuff of legends.

Rankin pushed through the crowd surrounding Hawkwood, put an arm about his shoulders, and steered him away, shooing small boys who tried to follow them. Their relationship had been icy since the incident at the shebeen, making Hawkwood suspect that Rankin had told Emma about his encounter with Ned Turnbull, and he blamed the old man for causing his difficulties. Since then, Rankin had avoided Hawkwood outside the day-to-day farm work, and the late-evening talks on a darkened porch while passing a demijohn had ended.

"You're courting trouble, Hawkwood," he said. "You've shown up a lot of these boys, and many of them don't take kindly to a Tuckahoe beating them at their own game in front of kin and friends. 'Specially, they don't need someone attracting the eye of the women folks. If I were you, I'd watch myself."

Hawkwood stepped away, glaring. "Tell me, Rankin. Why all this concern for my welfare? Could it be you're jealous that I'm winning the respect of these people? That maybe they'll see that I'm not a helpless boy? I needed your help at the shebeen, and it wasn't forthcoming. Why should you give it to me now?"

"To hell with you," he spat. "You are such a toplofty little shit. You think only of yourself. You don't think or care about people around you who are hurt or put in danger by your actions. Have your fun, Hawkwood, and take joy of the day." The old man wheeled and ambled away into the crowd.

Sod him. All Rankin had done since he'd been here was act superior and try to make him look small by comparison. He was just jealous that he was finally coming into his own.

A man passed him a jug of rum and slapped him on the back, which he downed in one drink.

* * * * *

BY MIDAFTERNOON, HAWKWOOD FOUND HIMSELF halfway cup-shot. Soon he and Hugh wandered over to join a knot of young men gathered to watch a game of Indian ball. The ball was the size of a middling apple and made of tightly wrapped iron-hard rawhide.

The war party and many of the future spectators had built dozens of crude racquets shaped like a shepherd's crook with an irregular mesh of rawhide lacing the open area. Two trees about a half mile apart, one on either side of the meadow, made up the goals. A warrior hoisted on a comrade's shoulders stripped off a man's height of bark about six feet off the ground and smeared the bare trunk with vermilion paint. To score, the ball had to hit the painted area.

"You playing, Hawkwood?" a man who he'd never met asked.

Hawkwood smiled. "Sorry, no. I don't think my clothes would survive."

"I'm sure we can find something for you to wear," another man offered.

A challenge. Didn't these people have anything else to do to amuse themselves? "If I could borrow clothes for myself and my friend Hugh—"

Hugh laughed, his eyes dancing at having a chance to play. Hawkwood hoped to God that they couldn't come up with spare clothes, but that was short lived. In a trice, he and Hugh were dressed in breechclouts and moccasins.

"I feel buck naked, Kit." Hugh laughed nervously.

"We are buck naked," he said sourly. Grasping his racquet in one hand, he cut the air with it as though it were a rapier and then walked onto the field. Off to the side, Emma stared at him with eyes bugged and both hands over her mouth, while Farris and Rankin doubled with laughter. "Fuck it, Hugh. Let's make the best of this."

"Damn right, we will. See those girls?" Hugh waved his racquet at a covey of young women. "That pretty one there on the right, that's the girl I told you about. She's the one I'm going to marry."

She was wearing a daring bodice—cut so low that one imagined a hint of areola peeping out—and her skirt and shift ended six inches above her well-turned ankles. Smiling, she waved back.

For two hours they chased a rawhide ball, slashed at fellow players with their racquets, and received many good blows in return. They wandered from the field, exhausted, then retrieved their clothing, found a deep pool in the meandering creek that ran along the fringe of the meadow, and stripped naked. After washing away the grime of the game, they dried themselves by lazing in the sun-warmed grass.

A giggle startled Hawkwood from his daydreams, and he sat up and instinctively reached for his clothes. The girl with the low-cut bodice walked over and sat down beside Hugh, who made no effort to cover his nakedness.

"Kit, this here is Maggie McDowell. Her da runs the shebeen. Maggie, this is Kit Hawkwood, the Tuckahoe gentleman that is staying with me and Emma."

What the hell. He stood, stark naked, and took her hand and kissed it, "Enchanted, Miss McDowell."

The three of them broke into laughter.

"If you'll excuse me, Hugh, Miss McDowell, I'll be going. I'll see you both at the dance tonight."

"Sure, Kit." Hugh pulled Maggie down to the ground. "See you at the dance."

* * * * *

THE VELVETY WARM JUNE NIGHT SKY, draped with the gauzy trail of the Milky Way, served as the roof while the trampled grass of the meadow, lit by a bonfire, became the dance floor. Three fiddlers standing in the bed of a Conestoga wagon provided the music, first as an ensemble and then in competition.

Hawkwood began with Emma as his partner, but custom demanded that he dance with other women and her with other men. Though a bit bruised and stiff from the Indian ball game, he felt pleased with himself.

No longer was he an anonymous Tuckahoe. People greeted him and knew his name, including the women, both Irish and German.

He avoided the company of Sally Crofter, whose attentions at the militia drill had caused him so much trouble with Emma. Still, he couldn't help but notice that she looked stunning in low-cut bodice that was cinched tight, pushing her breasts up high, and the skirt she'd hemmed a couple of inches higher than the already risqué standard of the unmarried Irish women. However, he couldn't avoid Sarah Welbourne.

As Hawkwood stood at the edge of the firelight, taking a pause for refreshment, he felt her presence at his elbow. "Mistress Welbourne." He made a leg.

She nodded. "Did you know that Ran is most displeased with you? Quitting was not wise, Kit. A man who is not with him is a man who is a threat. You may not respect Ran, but he can be very dangerous."

He looked around to locate Emma, didn't see her and decided it was safe enough to stand near Sarah for a time.

"Indeed, madam. I've already been put on notice that I can no longer rely upon his favor. Ned Turnbull made that quite clear to me."

She laughed harshly, with no trace of mirth. "The Turnbulls are useful to Ran's enterprise. So long as Wat rules there, they will do Ran's bidding. You're right to be wary of them. Ned has his good eye on that Irish piece you're besotted with."

"I admit to having become an admirer of Miss Pettigrew. She is a virtuous young woman"—he paused to give the words more weight—"and I may pay court to her someday if the situation permits."

"Virtue, my dear Kit, is dreadfully boring and overrated." She offered him her hand as the fiddlers began a reel. "Dance with me. I haven't danced with anyone who is acquainted with the art in ages."

He led her into the firelight, her hand lightly on top of his. They danced three dances, with Welbourne's eyes flashing daggers at him and Hawkwood smirking openly in Welbourne's direction, before Hawkwood decided he was heading into dangerous territory. There was a fine line between antagonizing Welbourne and seeming to make him a cuckold.

As Hawkwood escorted her from the dance line, he asked, "Why have you never mentioned that your cousin Jenny is married to that blackguard Crosslin?"

She stopped, mouth agape. "When—"

"Never mind when or how, but let your cousin know that I have no intention of seeking the ruin of her husband. It would serve no purpose." Over his shoulder, he saw Maggie McDowell emerge from the darkness.

Hugh approached the firelight from a different direction. "Suffice it to say, I'm becoming reconciled to the idea that my stay in Virginia may be longer than I would wish, and I have enough problems as it stands without creating yet more enemies." But did he mean that?

She chuckled and in an intimate gesture touched the point of his chin. "And I, for one, will be most happy for you to remain. If you wish"—she leaned her head toward him as though speaking to a fellow conspirator— "we can meet away from here. Ran is a dear, but he's hardly suited to keeping a young woman happy. I haven't tarried with a man the likes of you since I came to Virginia."

He hesitated and glanced around. Welbourne stood with Billy Preston and Colonel Patton but was giving Hawkwood and Sarah furtive disapproving looks. Emma talked with Mary and Sam Farris, and when he caught her staring at him, she turned away quick as a flash. A couple of the Turnbull gang were across the dance area in the shadows of the bonfire, watching him grim and hard-eyed.

Damme, was there anyone not watching him? He doffed his hat and made a leg to Sarah. "Madam, I'm forever in your debt for your kind offer, but I think it would be better for both of us if we say goodnight."

She gave a brief curtsey. "Maybe some other time, Kit."

Hawkwood approached Farris just as Emma was led to dance by a roughly dressed young man not quite her height and about Hawkwood's age. She turned her head from him and lifted her chin.

"Looks like you're in hot water, Kit," Farris said and nodded at her.

He shrugged. "I can't win with her, Sam. No matter what I do, I end up in trouble. I'm guessing she's mad about me dancing with Mistress Welbourne."

Rankin joined them and gave a coughing laugh. "Not half so mad as Old Man Welbourne. He was fit to be tied."

"He had reason to be angry, Bram. Emma doesn't. I behaved myself for once. I didn't have to. Emma is one of the sweetest and most amusing women I've ever spent time with, but I'll be heartily glad to find a suitable match for her and let someone else deal with her."

"Women are a mystery," Farris said.

"Pah!" Mary shook her head. "The problem is as obvious as the nose on your face. She's smitten with you, Kit. She saw that minx making cow eyes at you, and you"—she wagged a finger at him— "making them right back, and she's hurt."

"I assure you, Mary. Emma has no interest in me." Then images of her grinning as she bared her thigh to him while raking hay and her anger over Sally Crofter flashed in his mind's eye. "Oh, damn my eyes." He held his forehead. "You're right."

"So what are you going to do about it, *mo buachaill?*" She sat her hands on her hips. "You'd be a damned fool to let one such as her slip away. She's a treasure, and you—"

A scream rent the festive atmosphere, rendering everyone still. Hawkwood cocked his head, trying to determine the direction of the disturbance. "Emma?" he called.

Another shriek followed—one he recognized all too well.

"Emma!" He rushed in the direction it had come from.

Chapter Twenty

A CROWD HAD FORMED, MOSTLY MEN jostling each other to get a view what was going on. Hawkwood elbowed his way through the shouting, jeering mob. In the center, Emma struggled as Robbie Turnbull held her by the wrists. Her bodice had been torn away and her shift ripped to expose her breasts.

Hawkwood grabbed Robbie, spinning him around. Emma slipped free, crossed her arms over her chest, and ran.

Robbie smirked and faced the Turnbull men in the crowd. "Damned nice bouncers on her."

They all laughed.

Blood roared in Hawkwood's temples, and the words he'd heard several times since coming to the Valley resounded in his mind: *All you can rely upon is your own strong right hand.* A glance at Emma showed that her face was crimson, even in the firelight. "The girl didn't deserve that, you son of a bitch." He shoved Robbie hard and sent him staggering into the crowd.

Robbie charged toward him.

Farris appeared at his side and held up his hand. Robbie stopped, glaring.

"The girl's fine, Kit," Farris said. "Let's go."

Hawkwood pushed Farris to one side and faced Robbie. "Damn you, sir, for a low-bred hound."

More derisive laughter from the Turnbulls. Some of the people in the crowd also tittered as Robbie turned his back and ignored Hawkwood's ire while mugging for his cronies.

"Don't you dare let him go, Kit Hawkwood!" Emma screamed, on the verge of tears. "You slap his jaws or don't you dare come home."

Some in the crowd hooted.

Hawkwood looked at Emma, then to Farris.

Farris shook his head. "Don't do it, Kit."

"You're right, Sam. It would be foolish." Hawkwood took a step toward Emma and then whirled and drilled Robbie in the temple with his fist, felling him like a pole-axed ox. The crowd laughed as Hawkwood wrapped Emma in his arms. She gave him a kiss on the cheek, to even more acclamation from the crowd.

From behind, a hand grabbed Hawkwood's coat and whirled him around. He instinctively raised his arms to cover his face, and a thunderous blow hammered his shoulder. He staggered backward, shrugging his coat off as he did, and wheeled about in fighting stance to face his assailant.

Ned Turnbull stalked forward on bandy legs. "You're dead, Hawkwood!"

Fuck this. It would be a fight to the death, with no way out. He might be dead, but by God he'd show these Cohee bastards that he would go game. "Piss off, you one-eyed jackanapes. You're big on talk, but when it comes to fighting, you're not much. Want to tell these good folks how I left you holding your eye and bawling like babe? You and your noddy brothers are big men when it comes to pushing a girl around, but damned scarce when you have to face a man."

The crowd howled with laughter while Ned's face turned strangled-man purple.

He took a half step forward and jabbed at Ned's nose in a feint, then caught him with a hook to the temple that landed with such force that Hawkwood was sure he'd broken fingers. Someone in the crowd started shouting, "Rough-and-tumble!" Several others took up the cry. Hawkwood felt his bowels roiling. The idea of fighting to the death was abstract. Being left blinded and disfigured was a lot easier to imagine than mere death.

Ned crouched and advanced on him, fingers spread claw-like. Hawkwood feinted to the left, stepped right, and hammered him twice in the face. Blood oozed from Ned's lips and nose and dripped from his chin, but he continued to advance. Hawkwood tried to step back in retreat, but someone grabbed him by the waistcoat and propelled him into Ned. Some of the crowd roared in laughter.

Ned's hands flicked toward his head. He knew Ned would try to twist his sidelocks about his forefingers and use that as leverage to gouge his eyes out with his thumbs. He ducked his face and raised his elbows to block Ned's hands, but the man was too quick. In a flash, Ned's fingers were entangled in his hair. Thumbnails dug into his cheekbones at the bridge of his nose.

He grunted in pain as the nails tore furrows in his face, grated on his cheekbones, and worked their way up to the corners of his eyes—and blindness. He shook his head back and forth, up and down, trying to stop the inexorable movement of Ned's claw-like thumbnails toward his eyes.

* * * * *

PATTON, PRESTON, AND CLENDENIN STOOD at the edge of the firelight and watched the contest. Ned Turnbull had Hawkwood's hair knotted about his fingers and his blackened thumbnails—everyone said he hardened them over a candle flame just for the purpose of rough-and-tumble eye-gouging fighting—inching their way toward Hawkwood's eye sockets. Hawkwood leaned his head back as far back as he could, his hands locked in a white-knuckle grip about Ned's wrists. Their feet moved as though in some grim dance, matching each other step for step.

"What do you want to do, Colonel?" Preston asked.

"If it was up to me," Clendenin said, "I'd let them go at it for a while."

Patton nodded. "I agree. The boy don't look to be in danger of losing an eye right now. He needs to show some grit, and right now he is."

* * * * *

HAWKWOOD CAUGHT A GLIMPSE OF WELBOURNE and Sarah at the front edge of the mob, close to the action. Welbourne's face was the picture of smug satisfaction. Sarah was animated, her eyes glowing with excitement as the two men locked in a panting, sweaty death struggle. Welbourne wasn't going to stop the fight this time.

His eyes filled with tears as Ned's thumbs pressed on his eyes, blocking his vision. He hoped the tears were due to the pain, but he couldn't swear to it. Both men growled and grunted as they pushed and tugged on one another, trying to achieve some small advantage. Unlike their last fight, Hawkwood didn't feel overmatched by Ned this time. A bit of confidence pushed forward in his brain and staunched, but it didn't vanquish the rising, bowel-quaking panic struggling to free itself and do whatever it took to preserve his sight.

Hawkwood hooked Ned's ankle with his foot and tried to upset him. Ned stumbled but regained his balance, then lunged forward. His teeth snapped a hairsbreadth from the end of Hawkwood's nose, leaving Hawkwood's sinuses filled with the stomach-churning smell of Ned's breath.

Hawkwood head-butted him square in the nose, causing him to roar in anger, then he chopped down hard on Ned's wrists. He knocked Ned's left hand away, but at the cost of a hank of hair that remained twirled about Ned's fore and middle fingers.

He punched Ned in the mouth and felt something break. Pain howled through his fist and screamed up his arm. He wasn't sure if it was his hand or Ned's teeth that had broken—or both. Slamming the heel of his hand into Ned's face, he clawed for his one good eye. Ned whipped his head out of reach, but the fingers of his right hand were still entwined in Hawkwood's hair.

As he fought for his life, Hawkwood glimpsed Emma standing by Farris's side, wearing a borrowed hunting shirt over her torn garments. Her eyes blazed as she screamed, cheering for Hawkwood along with Rankin and Hugh. Farris stood by, impassive, his arm around Mary who had her eyes covered.

* * * * *

"Hoo-ee!" Clendenin said in a low voice. "I believe the boy may best Ned. Now that would be a story."

Preston crossed his arms. "If he wins, he's not making it out of here alive. Wat ain't going to stand by and have two of his men beat."

"You're right, Billy," Patton agreed. "But let's let him get a few more shots in. Ned needs to learn some manners."

* * * * *

Breaking Ned's grip on his hair and removing the jeopardy to his eye was his foremost thought. He had freed himself from one hand at the cost of the shilling-sized piece of scalp and hair still dangling from Ned's thick fingers. While holding that hand away from his face, he had halted the progress of Ned's other hand. Hawkwood twisted, brought his head down, and clamped his teeth hard on Ned's forearm near the elbow.

Ned hammered him on the back of the head. Sparks flashed and floated before his eyes, but he tasted warm, salty blood—blood that wasn't his. He bore down harder and harder, growling deep in his chest like a mastiff at a bull-baiting.

Ned roared in pain and rage, then he felt Ned's hand release his hair. He pushed off Ned, spat a mouthful of blood at him to the huzzahs of the crowd, retreated a half dozen steps, and went back into fighting stance. Out of nowhere, hands grabbed his shoulders and pulled him back. More men grabbed Ned's arms and restrained him.

"That's enough!" Colonel Patton ordered, stalking into the trampled area of the combat. "Both of you! There'll be no more of this nonsense. Hawkwood, you leave now—"

"Sir, he should be the one leaving," Hawkwood gasped. Now that danger was past, his chest heaved, and he found it difficult to keep his gorge down. He leaned forward with hands on his knees, watching the night-blackened droplets of blood from his face splatter in the fire-lit dust. "He—"

"Shut up! You still got your top lights, boyo. Take joy of it." Patton turned to Wat Turnbull as he and his men protested. "Wat, you and your boys are staying here until morning. If any of you so much as look like you want to follow Hawkwood and take this up again, I swear by the Great Jehovah, I'll raise the county and burn the lot of you out."

"Damn. Robbie's dead," someone said.

Hawkwood faced the voice. A man knelt beside the man he'd knocked down. *Ah, damn it all to hell. This just gets worse.* He stood and wiped the blood from his face mentally prepared himself for more fighting.

"He had it coming," Farris said. "He took liberties with Hawkwood's woman. Can't fault a man of defending what's his."

Hawkwood gaped. *Christ shat on a biscuit! My woman? Defending what's mine? Where in the name of God is this coming from?*

"That's right," another man said.

The crowd murmured a consensus that Robbie's death wasn't a bad thing.

Preston knelt beside the prostrate man and put his ear near the man's nose. "He ain't dead, Uncle. Hawkwood just laced his jacket for him."

The crowd laughed as the Turnbull clan eyed Hawkwood with ill-concealed rage. Wat Turnbull looked like he would eat his hat or start chewing on a wagon wheel. Ned glowered, still restrained by two men. His nose and mouth oozed blood, and it seeped from the wound in his arm, soaking his shirt sleeve.

"This ain't over by a damned long shot, Hawkwood," Ned said. "I warned you before there would be a reckoning."

Hawkwood stooped, picked up his coat, and put it on. *You've made a mistake, Ned, old boy.* People had seen Hawkwood beat him, and Ned had hurt one of his. There would be a reckoning. He could count on it. "So you say, Ned. So you always say."

"And you, Sam Farris." Ned pointed his finger at him. "None of this was your business. I won't forget this day."

Farris squinted at him hard. "You'd be smart to try to forget it. I ain't no Tuckahoe gentleman."

The crowd laughed, causing Ned to growl and pull against the two men holding him.

Farris held his gaze, his eyes narrowed. "You might get hurt."

Chapter Twenty-One

CLENDENIN RODE UP TO THE SPLIT-RAIL FENCE, slid from his horse, and dropped the reins, leaving the horse to wander. "Hey, Boo. How're you feeling?"

Hawkwood stood from his chair on the porch and walked out to greet him. On his face he held a cloth wet with an herbal brew that Rankin vowed would heal the deep cuts over his nose and cheeks. "Damned glad to be alive, Jemmy. My face is gouged all the hell, but I know I can beat that one-eyed son of a bitch. And he knows it too."

"That was a rare show you put on; I'll give you that. It'll buy you some time while they scratch their arses and try to think about what to do. You challenged them in a way they ain't used to. They'll be back, though. You can count on it."

Hawkwood reached behind the post supporting the porch roof and pulled out the Pettigrew's solitary fowling piece. "I know. That means we all have to be armed now. What brings you out our way?"

"I wanted to see Miss Emma." Clendenin's eyes challenging him. "I told you I might call on her one day. Well, this is it."

Did he really think Emma would agree to wed him? As the Cohees said, he didn't have a pot to piss in nor a window to throw it out of. "Sure, Jemmy. Let me call her."

Clendenin patted him on the shoulder. "Never you mind, Boo. Take your ease and tend to those cuts. I'll tell Emma I'm here."

Minutes later, Hawkwood and Hugh sat on the porch watching Clendenin and Emma walk to and fro under the wide-spaced chestnut trees just beyond the fence. She matched his lose-limbed gait with her own long, prancing stride, swinging her hips and rising high on her toes with each step.

They walked side by side, just inches apart, with Clendenin clasping his hands behind his back while Emma kept hers together in front. When he said something, she stopped and laughed. He joined in, and they walked along the line of the fence toward Clendenin's horse. Emma cast a sly glance at Hawkwood and winked.

Hawkwood bristled at the looks they were giving each other. He liked it when she looked at him like that and when she laughed at his japes.

She and Clendenin paused to talk, and he stooped and plucked a handful of wildflowers growing alongside the fence. When he bowed and presented her with the bouquet, she laughed and gave him a chaste peck on the cheek. Then they strolled back to the shade of the chestnuts. She cast a glance at Hawkwood, and when she saw she had his eye, she lifted her skirt to mid-calf for a second, dropped it, tossed her head, and went back to chatting with Clendenin.

What was that minx up to? Why, she was spooning Jemmy and flirting with him. Wait. What was he worried about? He had to get her married to someone before he left. But Jemmy? Hawkwood laughed aloud at the thought, and Hugh gave him a questioning glance. He shrugged.

It would be amusing to see Clendenin yoked with Emma though. He'd run back to the Indians after dealing with her temper. But did Hawkwood want her? She was a pretty girl. Witty, though not so much as to unsex herself, and she was gentle natured even if she wasn't genteel.

Fiery, yes, but she wasn't likely to age into a Billingsgate fish wife. She didn't have money, but neither did he. For sure, she was a strong one. She'd never give her man cause to doubt her. And he was fairly marooned out here. Eventually he would have to take a wife, and it would be from among these people. But Emma? What would people think? He was her guardian. They'd certainly think they'd been madly rutting the whole time he'd been here. But did he care?

After what seemed like hours, the visit ended. Clendenin made a clumsy bow to Emma and held out his hand to Hawkwood. "That was mighty sporting of you, Boo. I'll be seeing you again."

As he rode off, Emma waved until he was out of sight. "Ah," she sighed. "That Jemmy is such a rogue, but he could win a girl's heart no matter how big a mistake she knew she was making."

* * * * *

AFTER SUPPER, HAWKWOOD LAY ON THE PORCH, his head on
Emma's lap as she rubbed a salve of bear grease and what he'd been
assured were healing herbs into the deep, ragged cuts on his face. With
Rankin at the shebeen and Hugh probably off with Maggie McDowell,
they were alone.

"You seemed to have a good time with Jemmy," he said. "What did
you talk about?"

She cocked her head, and her unbound hair fell like a cinnamon
waterfall over her shoulders. "That would be none of your business, Mr.
Hawkwood."

"I'm your guardian, so it is my affair if he intends to ask for your
hand."

"If Jemmy wants to ask for my hand, I expect he'll talk to you about
it. Why are you so concerned about my doings with Jemmy?" She
stopped rubbing the salve on his face, and he opened his eyes. She smiled
and wrinkled her nose. "You wouldn't be jealous, would you?"

Hawkwood's cheeks warmed. "Don't be ridiculous." He closed his
eyes and waited for a minute or two, then said, "You know you damn
near got me killed, yeah?"

"Ah, not really. It wasn't your time." She kneaded the salve into a
deep gouge at the corner of his left eye.

"What?"

"The Bible says, 'The number of his months are with thee.' I knew it
wasn't your time. Granny Nixon told me you'd have a long life. You want
me to say I'm sorry, Kit? I'm not sorry." She laid her hand on his cheek.
"I'm very happy you're alive and in one piece, but a woman can't hold
her head up if her clothes are torn off and her tits waved about in front
of a crowd and there's no price paid. And what's more, her man can't
hold his head up either."

"Hold on a bloody second." He sat up. "Since when have I become
your man?"

She shrugged, smiling. "Everyone thinks you are, so you might as
well be."

"Does Jemmy know this?"

"I said everyone, didn't I? Though I shan't be bound by what people
think, should the right man pay me court."

He laid his head back on her lap and closed his eyes. "If I am your
man,"—he smirked— "when do I get the benefits?" He slid his fingertips

under the hem of her shift and ran his hand up her thigh.

She was still for a moment, then slapped his hand and pulled it from beneath her skirts. "Stop that, boyo. Everything has a season, don't you know." She giggled, dabbed more ointment on his face, and cooed, "You're going to have some manly fighting scars on your phyz. That'll make men walk small around you."

Hoofbeats approached, disturbing any further plans Hawkwood was entertaining. Sam Farris soon rode up, and as he dismounted and tied his mount to one of the cedar porch posts, Hawkwood stood to greet him.

"You're looking the worse for wear." Farris cocked his head and examined the gouges down his face. "You taking care of him, Miss Emma?" He gave Hawkwood a knowing look.

A faint blush colored her cheeks. "Of course, I am. Kit stood up for me. I'm obliged to him for that."

Hawkwood snorted. Had everyone decided that they were yoked? He then cleared his throat and changed the subject. "What brings you this way, Sam?"

"Look here." He walked back to his horse, extracted a long bundle wrapped in oiled osnaburg, and handed it to Hawkwood. "Go ahead. Untie it."

As Hawkwood loosed the twine bindings, he could tell by its shape and heft that it was a rifle. But he hadn't expected it to be such a gorgeous, glorious marriage of artistry and gunsmithing.

It was five and a half feet long from octagonal muzzle to the dark brass butt plate, crafted of red-blond curly maple that had been oiled and waxed to a mirror gloss. A set trigger allowed the main trigger to be pulled with the lightest of pressure. Its accoutrements—shot bag, powder flask, measuring pot, and shot mold—were of equally fine quality.

Hawkwood breath caught. "This is a fine rifle, Sam. Where did you get it?"

"A man named Stephen Emery makes rifles down in Frederick Town. Damned fine gunsmith he is. I knew where one was, and I bought it with your purse. Got a good price because you had guineas. The bore is fifty-eight balls to the pound. Smaller ball reduces the kick, and you use less powder and lead. You'll want to get yourself a powder horn. Backcountry men"—he winked and clapped Hawkwood on the shoulder— "don't use a flask. Hey, take a walk with me."

Emma turned to go back in the house.

Hawkwood hesitated, noting her pursed lips and the deep furrow between her eyes. She didn't like being shut out of the conversation, though she was obedient to the custom that didn't admit women into all discussions among men, and vice versa.

"What now?" Farris asked as they strode away from the cabin. "The Turnbull problem ain't going to fix itself, Kit. They're either going to kill you or burn you out. Or both. How do you plan on dealing with them?"

"Colonel Patton put them under a peace bond. Surely they'll honor that."

Farris gave a bitter bark of a laugh. "That don't mean shite, boy. They're going to come after you ... and Emma ... and Hugh. They're going to come after me and Mary too. We got to hit them first."

He shook his head. "That's not right, Sam. We're civilized people. They would attack me, but they won't bother Patton. Colonel Patton represents the Crown."

Farris stared at him with eyes as bleak as a January midnight. "You're wrong. Blood feud is the law here. Patton got you home safe and maybe bought you a few weeks, but they're coming back. You need to decide what you want to do, and soon. My brother is gunsmithing in the Ohio Country for some Pennsylvania traders. He wants me to join him. If you don't settle these boys, I'm going to take him up on it. Want to come along?"

Hawkwood stopped, facing him. "You'd run out? Leave your farm?" He'd thought Farris was made of sterner stuff.

"Better a live dog than a dead lion. Think about it."

* * * * *

A GRIM MOOD PERVADED THE ROOM at dinner that evening.

"So that's where it stands," Hawkwood said to Emma, Hugh, and Rankin as they sat at the table. "Sam is of the view that the Turnbulls will take retribution on us. Jemmy shares that opinion. I trust that Colonel Patton can restrain them. They were put on notice that he'd raise a hue and cry against them."

"So he said, Kit." Rankin leaned back and crossed his arms. "Whether he can make that stick is an entirely different question. People are scared of the Turnbulls. There are a dozen or more men in that clan, and they can call on kin up in the Watauga Country. Sam may have a point about leaving. There's plenty of land to be had in Pennsylvania or down in the Carolinas. No reason to die here."

Emma scowled at him. "I won't run, Bram Rankin. My family is buried here. If you want to turn tail, go ahead, but I shall not move."

"I don't like the thought of running either," Hugh said. "Maybe this will all just blow over. Kit is right. The colonel told them to leave us alone. They'd never dare gainsay him."

She nodded. "Kit has a rifle, and we have Da's fowling piece. Bram, if you find a firelock for you and me, we'll all be armed."

Rankin shook his head. "You talk about a firelock, young miss, but what do you know about shooting?"

"I'll teach her," Hawkwood said.

Emma touched his forearm and smiled.

But damn if Rankin wasn't right. They were a thin reed to resist the Turnbulls, should they decide they were worth their time. "They aren't going to want an open war. All we have to do is show them we're serious and they'll move along. That's the way of hectors the world over."

Rankin pursed his lips. "You're all pudding-headed cullies. The Turnbulls can't let this pass. If people ain't scared of them, then they can't murder and steal. This silliness will probably get us all killed." He poured neat rum into his tankard and took a deep draught. "But damned if I'll run out on the only family I have." After another drink, he laughed. "I have to say, young Kit. I've never seen Ned in such dire straits. Old Man Turnbull about died when you were bearing down on that one-eyed varmint's arm. Hell, I was plumb sure you'd killed the other one."

"We shall persevere," Hawkwood said. "We'll be vigilant, and if they deign to bother us, we will show them off."

He just hoped to God they knew what they were doing. Because Rankin was probably right.

* * * * *

"THAT'S IT." HAWKWOOD WATCHED EMMA as she sighted his long rifle at a chunk of firewood about thirty yards away. "Hold it tight to your shoulder. Don't grip the forestock so hard." Her body pressed against him, and he reached his arms around her, perhaps more snugly than pedagogy required, steadying her hands. The faint scent of lavender on her skin made his heart race. *My God. I am moon-eyed over this girl. How did this come to pass?*

He tried to clear his mind. "Relax. You're squeezing the life out of it. Do you have the sights lined up?"

She nodded; her forehead creased with concentration.

"Take a deep breath. Now let it out. Come on, all the way out. Now take another one. Let half of it out. Swallow. Pull the set trigger. There, hear it click? Now just touch the forward trigger."

The hammer dropped, followed by a thunderclap and the rifle belching a cloud of gray-white smoke. The piece of firewood flipped into the air and skittered across the ground.

"Nicely done. That was an excellent shot."

She preened and blushed with his praise.

He looked into her eyes. "Keep in mind that shooting a piece of wood is a lot different from shooting a man. If it comes to it, do you think you can do that?"

She shrugged. "I've slaughtered hogs. I didn't have anything against the hogs. If one of those buggers,"–she spat– "crosses my path, he's a dead man."

He shook his head, grinning. "I do believe you're serious. Now load it and let's see you do it again."

* * * * *

WELL, HERE GOES, HAWKWOOD THOUGHT as he stood naked in the kitchen. From one of his leather trunks he removed the hunting shirt and leggings Emma had made for him before his surveying trip. He'd never tried them on. While he couldn't wear them everywhere, he could certainly wear them about a bit. Emma had taken the time to make the shirt, so the least he could do was be appreciative. Besides, his clothes had taken a beating since he arrived, and it would be damned near impossible to replace them in Virginia, no matter which side of the mountains he was on.

He donned the breechclout, shrugged the hunting shirt over his head, and secured the wool leggings with black silk garter ribbands. Last, he tied on the moccasins, marveling at the intricate designs wrought with dyed porcupine quills.

Not bad at all. With the waistband tied, the triple cape created the illusion of very broad shoulders and a wasp waist. Ironic, since the work and activity of the farm had cut any spare flesh from his frame while creating shoulders and arms more suited to a hod carrier than a courtier. Not that it mattered. His life was much more like that of a hod carrier than a courtier. The clothes were comfortable—well, once you got used to your arse hanging out in the breeze.

He walked out onto the porch where Emma, Hugh, and Rankin sat enjoying the coolness of the late afternoon thunderstorm that had driven them in from the fields. Sitting down beside her on the long puncheon bench, he stretched out his legs. "Nice rain, isn't it?"

Emma looked at him, and her eyes widened. She squealed in delight, then took his hands and stood, dragging him to his feet. "Why, Kit Hawkwood, you are one gorgeous man!"

Hugh and Rankin turned at the commotion. Rankin guffawed. "Kit, *mo buachaill,* you look like a fair timberbeast in them togs. Miss Emma, that is the finest hunting shirt in the Valley. Once the other men see that shirt, they'll all want to marry you."

Her cheeks reddened.

"And once them Irish morts get a gander of this"—Hawkwood flipped the hem of the hunting shirt, exposing his bare thighs above the leggings—"you'll have to use that long rifle to fight them off."

"Don't you worry about them other girls, Mr. Rankin." Emma gave Hawkwood a hug and a peck on the cheek that left him flushed. "I can take care of that problem."

Hugh hooted in laughter. "She's training Kit to steer clear of them wenches or she'll use the long rifle on him. That makes for a lot less work."

* * * * *

"What do you think is going to come of this, Bram?" Hawkwood asked. He was stripped to the waist as, together with Hugh, he muscled a stripped locust pole into a vertical position in a three-foot hole. As they held the pole erect, Rankin tamped stone and dirt around the post.

"I think that unless we get a couple more men on the place, you're going to work us all to death."

"You know what I mean. The Turnbulls."

"I don't know. Maybe nothing, maybe a lot. You can't predict what a passel of rogues like the Turnbulls will do. The only fly in the ointment, boy, is you dressing Ned and knocking Robbie Turnbull's cock in the dirt. Ned ain't likely to forget that. The question is, does he do something about it up front or does he skulk you like the scrub that he is." Rankin stood and dropped his earth tamper. "You boys can let go now."

They stood away from the post, admiring their work. Rankin reached into the pocket on the belly of his smock and drew out a fibrous mahogany-colored twist of chewing tobacco and a clasp knife. He cut a section from the twist, stuffed it into his left cheek, and began to work it.

Hawkwood placed his hands on his hips. "Cut me a piece of that,

Bram. I want to give it a try."

* * * * *

"STOP GAWPING AT ME!" EMMA SAID. "I'm not a raree-show."

Hawkwood and Hugh already sat astride their horses, with Hawkwood holding the reins of her horse, when she emerged from the house.

She had gone riding with him regularly since he had arrived in the Valley, and though she had previously been an infrequent rider, he'd found she had the instincts of a natural horsewoman. Her loose, confident riding style melded her and the animal into one creature, something some men spent years, even decades, trying to achieve. And she rode undeterred by the fact that the Pettigrew household did not possess a side saddle. She straddled the horse like a man, hiking her shift up about her waist, and modesty be damned.

Today was different though. She wore a hunting shirt like the one she'd made for Hawkwood, and her scarlet leggings were gartered with blue ribband. Her hair hung in a loose waist-length plait that fell from beneath a wide-brimmed brown felt hat. When she swung her right leg over the horse's back, Hawkwood was treated to a fleeting but prodigal view of long, finely shaped legs and a scarlet breechclout.

He handed her the reins and was rewarded with a wink as she saw his eyes wander down to where her leg was exposed between the hem of her hunting shirt the top of her leggings. Hugh looked on at the flirtation, all too damned amused by it.

They rode west toward the end of the Pettigrew property, all armed. Hawkwood rode with his long rifle balanced on his saddle's pommel and his infantry hanger strapped across his back. Hugh carried his father's fowling piece, and Emma sported a short, lightweight *fusil de chasse* that Rankin had procured by unexplained means.

"There! There it is!" Hugh nudged his horse into a trot and guided them into a hollow that sheltered a wide stream. "Da said we could build a dam here." With his finger, he traced a line across a point where the stream channeled through a cut scoured into solid granite. "The millpond would back up there." He pointed. "And we could build the millrace along that bank and put the sawmill right there near that boulder. The water comes from a spring about a half furlong from here. It never runs dry. Da said it could run a saw and turn a grindstone."

Hawkwood smiled at Hugh's enthusiasm. "We'd need to cut a road in here—"

"We can get some men to help on that," Emma said. "Once harvest is in, they'll work for grub and whiskey."

Hawkwood pulled his chin. "Yes. We can get a road in here and corduroy it, so the wagons don't get bogged down. I'd need to get a license from the county court, but that shouldn't be a problem."

"Welbourne could be a problem," she said.

Both Hawkwood and Hugh looked at her with some surprise.

"What? Surprised the girl has an idea?" When they stayed silent, she continued. "Anyway, Da said Welbourne has been talking about building a mill for some time. The county court won't license two mills this close together."

Hawkwood considered that. "Well then, I'll just have to get our license first. I think Billy Preston will help me out."

"One other thing," Hugh said. "We have to keep this to ourselves. Mr. Rankin is like family, but when he gets to drinking with that bunch at McDowell's place, he talks too much."

As they turned to ride out, Hawkwood kneed his horse, making it sidle into Emma's. He leaned on the cantle of her saddle with one hand, put the other hand on the nape of her neck, and pulled her lips to his.

She wrapped one arm around his neck and returned the kiss, then righted herself and tugged her broad-brimmed hat low on her brow. "Well, damme, Kit Hawkwood. I thought I was going to have to wait forever." She kicked her horse into a trot and rode after Hugh.

He watched for a moment. Her back was as erect and her shoulders as square as any dragoon's, and the long coppery plait and her adorable little arse bounced in time with the horse's stride. He might be calf-brained with lust, but he did believe he was in love with her. Digging his heels into his mount, he rode after her.

Just over the first hill from the stream, a dark plume of smoke spiraled into the afternoon sky. The easy ride transformed into a furious gallop for home. When they crested the hill that overlooked the farm, they could see the source. One of the outbuildings, a corn crib, was ablaze.

Chapter Twenty-Two

RANKIN STOOD BY WITH A SHOVEL, watching. There was nothing anyone could do beyond keeping the fire from spreading to the field and from there to other buildings. "Somebody set it on fire. I was over in the wood lot when I saw the smoke. There are hoof marks all around here. They came in and rode out the same way." He pointed to the southwest.

"Turnbulls?" Hawkwood asked.

"I suspect so."

Hawkwood spat. He'd hoped this conflict with the Turnbulls would not escalate into some sort of Scots border feud of tit-for-tat reprisals. Now, however, the only solution seemed to be to hit them back hard enough to make them chary about hitting the Pettigrew farm again.

"Hugh. You come with me. Emma, it might be best if you and Bram moved in with Sam Farris until we come back."

Emma opened her mouth, but Hawkwood held up his hand, silencing her before she could utter a sound. "Please, Emma. I know you can ride and shoot, but Hugh and I can't do what we may need to do if we're worried about your safety."

Tears filled her eyes, but her lips drew into a taut line. "We'll be at Sam's. We'll see you when you get back."

Once they were out of earshot, Hugh spoke. "I take it we ain't going to talk to them?"

"This turning-the-other-cheek shite is really overrated. Twice now Ned has tried to maim me. Your sister has twice been abused by them. Now they've burned our property. Eye for an eye is the rule."

Hugh nodded. "Woe for woe and blow for blow."

Two hours southwest, they cut across a track that showed frequent use by men and horses. They turned and followed the spoor. Hawkwood's heart pounded like a kettle drum, and, had he allowed it, his breath would have come in short wheezes.

What was he going to do when he found them? He couldn't very well just kill them. Skulking about and setting their houses alight was what a low-bred hedge bird would do, but he should do the right thing—go to Colonel Patton and tell him what happened and let the law prevail.

Hawkwood sniffed the air and caught the scents wood smoke, animal dung, and an overused jakes. He motioned for Hugh to stop. They dismounted, picketed their horses in a small copse, and set out through the chest-high grass.

The sun hung low in the sky when they arrived at a vantage point where they could view the Turnbull settlement. Hawkwood damned himself in silence because the sun's glare was directly in their eyes. They counted eight cabins, most of them hovels, really. The best one—he assumed it was Hairless Wat's—was a double-pen construction connected by a dogtrot, with no windows and two low doors. Two were three-sided lean-tos built similar to the McDowell's shebeen. Chickens scratched about, hogs rooted where they pleased, and a few head of cattle roamed free along with a dozen hobbled horses.

"What do we do?" Hugh whispered as he ducked below the bearded tops of the grass.

"I don't see anything worth burning." He stared through shaded eyes.

"Fuck it. Burn their houses."

"What if we kill someone? Then we'll be murderers."

Hugh gave him an incredulous stare. "You're shitting me. We've come here to hit them for burning our corn crib. If we kill one or two, there are that many less to deal with later. Who are these blackguards going to make complaint to? The law? If you're shy about hitting them, then let's be gone before we're found."

Hawkwood sighed. So what did they do then? The thought of hitting back was delicious. But the risks were great. What if they were caught in the act? They'd start a blood feud for certain. And what if the Turnbulls retaliated? There had to be a way to resolve this conflict and find a way of living together. "I'm going to go down there and talk to them. They can't want this tit-for-tat skirmishing any more than we do."

"What? That is bug-eating, bedlamite crazy. They'll gut you. How are you going to explain showing up at dusk on foot? They'll know what you were planning. Fuck it. I'm leaving. Are you coming with me, or are you going to kill yourself?"

They returned to their horses in silence, checking over their shoulders every few steps to see if they'd been discovered.

As they mounted, Hugh grabbed Hawkwood's sleeve. "Today this is just between you and me."

"What do you mean?"

"I mean my sister deserves a man who can care for her. That means someone who won't let her be abused and disrespected. That means someone who causes rogues and blackguards to walk small around him. Are you that man, Hawkwood? Because if you aren't, you'd best stay the hell away from Emma."

Not another word passed between them about the aborted raid on the Turnbulls. They retrieved Emma and Rankin from their temporary haven, giving the story that the Turnbulls were alert and anticipating retribution so they'd decided to take the better part of valor and slip away. Hawkwood thought he detected Farris giving him a cutty-eyed stare, but it could have been his own nagging guilty conscience.

The first night back at the Pettigrew farm, everyone stayed awake, taking turns manning a sentry post they established in the barn rafters. But all was quiet. The storm, it seemed, had passed. Or as Rankin said, "Maybe we're waiting for the other shoe to drop, and we're fighting with a one-legged man."

* * * * *

"KIT." EMMA CAME INTO THE KITCHEN with two brimming wooden milk pails dangling from a shoulder yoke. "It might not mean nothing, but I thought I saw smoke back to the west."

He took the milk pails from her, sat one of them on the floor, and poured the other into the butter churn. "Want to go have a look?" he asked Hugh.

Hugh shook his head. "Naw. Me and Mr. Rankin need to get started roofing that stable. With just the two of us, we'll need the rest of the week. Then there's that corn crib." He glared at Hawkwood. "You go ahead."

"I'll go with you. It sounds like more fun than churning butter. You saddle the horses and let me get my timberbeast togs on." Emma laughed and all but skipped from the kitchen.

Hawkwood eyed Hugh. "What's the matter with you? I'm not

accustomed to being gainsaid in such a manner."

Hugh stood and rolled his shoulders. "Kit, you ain't my da. My da would never have run from a fight."

"Fuck you, Hugh. And fuck your carping—"

Hugh took a swing at him, a wide and sweeping haymaker that aimed for Hawkwood's jaw. He blocked it just in time, but the sledgehammer impact to his arm drove him back a step. He counterpunched. Once. Twice. His blows landed square on Hugh's brow. Hugh roared and closed in to grapple with him.

They collided, each with a death grip on the other, and spun about in the smallish kitchen. Hawkwood lost balance when one foot landed in a milk pail. Hugh tried to throw him, but Hawkwood was stronger. He recovered his balance and swung Hugh to one side, slamming him against the trestle table and upending it.

The door from the dogtrot slammed open and Emma appeared. "Stop it! Stop it, the both of you! Leave you alone for five minutes, and I come back to find you fighting like heathens. Clean this mess up! Now!"

Hugh released his grip on Hawkwood's shirt, looked at Emma, and laughed. "I swear, sis, you sound just like Mam."

Her expression didn't soften. "What was going on here?"

Hugh gave a grin and wink. "We had a disagreement. We're fine now."

She gave Hawkwood a waspish look, and he nodded in agreement. "Fine. I'll saddle the horses while you clean this up."

Once she had left, Hugh offered his hand. Hawkwood took it without hesitation.

"Sorry about the punch. That was wrong of me. Maybe you were right the other night. Maybe we would have ended up dead. But we're coming to nut-cutting time where we either have to settle them or have to run. What are you going to do? You can't blow hot and cold. You take that ride with Emma. Think about her and what she'd think of you if she'd been there instead of me."

＊ ＊ ＊ ＊ ＊

HAWKWOOD HAD LEARNED HIS LESSON from approaching the Turnbulls' at sunset. This time he guided Emma in a wide clockwise loop to the north that allowed them to investigate the suspicious area with the rising sun at their backs. They soon spotted the stray plume of smoke.

"Make sure you're primed," he said. "Stay about ten yards off to my flank and behind me."

She nodded, lifted the frizzen, blew the priming powder out, and recharged from an old tin powder flask.

They dropped down a draw and entered a broad, shallow gulch that enclosed a deep and narrow runnel. Crouched low on their horses' necks and in single file, they worked their way toward the source of the smoke. At a sharp turn in the gully, Hawkwood saw the man. He was crouched on a flat granite crag overhanging an ankle-deep pool, and as they drew closer, it became clear that he was shaving. Hawkwood motioned for Emma to stop. A quick survey of the situation revealed he was alone.

"Good morning, sir," Hawkwood called.

The man started to his feet.

"What's your business here?"

"Name's Tom Shafto. Me, the wife, and our bairns are heading for Carolina."

Shafto? "I know you. I was there the day your cabin up on the New River was pulled down. What are you doing here? The Seneca Trail to Carolina is miles to the west. And you're heading in the wrong direction."

"Well, we wanted to rest for a spell. My Patsy is feeling poorly."

Hawkwood stared at Shafto. The man was thoroughly beaten down and Hawkwood was inclined to believe he was telling the truth.

"Where's your camp, Mr. Shafto?" Emma asked.

Shafto's mouth gaped.

She grinned. "You aren't mistaken. I'm a girl."

He pointed, and she goaded her horse up the wall of the gully and disappeared toward the smoke.

Hawkwood eyed him. "You must know you can't just stop here and set up camp. This is my land. I can't have you squatting."

Shafto's shoulders drooped. "We've been run out of so many places. All me and Patsy want is a piece of land where we can raise our bairns and be left in peace."

As they talked, several hounds bayed in the distance. Hawkwood recalled the rangy curs—ones that resembled Shafto in their dishevelment and expectation of a quick kick from strangers—lurking about the Shafto cabin. It turned out that Shafto and his wife had both come to Virginia as indentured servants. They'd married or taken up together, Hawkwood was unable to get a straight answer. He was also left with the suspicion that they were both runaway servants in the bargain. It seemed like the man was filled with good intentions but simply couldn't get the necessary traction to change his luck.

Emma trotted into view and guided her mount down into the draw with supreme confidence. Leaning close to Hawkwood, she whispered, "His wife's got a fever. She'll live but she needs rest. They've got four wee'uns that haven't been cared for. Of course,"—she nodded in the direction of Shafto— "he's a tousie one himself."

Hawkwood glanced at him. "What do you suggest?"

"Our Lord told us, 'Verily I say unto you, inasmuch as ye have done it unto one of the least of these my brethren, ye have done it unto me.' We need another man on the place. I could use another woman. There's plenty of work for the wee'uns to do too. Why don't we take them on as tenants? It would be the Christian thing to do, and they could be a godsend."

He considered that. "I don't know, Emma. He's looks like a scrub."

"He may be, Kit, but sometimes looks can deceive. If we let them stay and it don't work out, then they can go, and our conscience be clear."

He turned to Shafto. "I'll make you bargain, Mr. Shafto. You can build a cabin near my house. We'll see that you have enough to eat. If you like it, in a year or so we'll see about getting you your own land. In return, I expect you and yours to work, to work hard, and work hertsome." *My God.* When did he start talking like these Cohees? "If you can't do that, then you stay put until your wife can travel and then you have to be on your way. What say you?"

Shafto walked to Hawkwood, spat in his palm, and extended his hand. "I'm your man, sir."

Though disgusted, he had seen backcountry men do this before to seal a deal. He spat in his hand without hesitation, and they shook on it.

They straggled back to the farm together. Shafto led Hawkwood's horse with Patsy and two children on it. Emma rode with one child in front of her, while the oldest boy walked beside Hawkwood. The family's worldly goods comprised only a dangerously pitted cast iron skillet, a small stewpot, two blankets, and a small bag with Patsy's sewing and knitting needles. And three brindle hounds of uncertain pedigree.

As they approached, Hugh dropped the maul he was using to drive trunnels securing the rafter plate of the stable to a supporting post. Rankin, who was shaping a trunnel with a drawknife, looked up. They both ambled over to examine the newcomers.

Hawkwood smiled at Rankin and jerked his thumb toward Shafto. "You said you needed another man, so I brought you one." He tousled the Shafto boy's hair. "And I brought you a waterboy too."

* * * * *

THEY SAT, SHOULDER TIGHT TO SHOULDER, on the grassy bank above a limestone spring that fed one of the many streams that watered their meadow. Hawkwood took a single pebble from the cluster he'd gathered into one palm and idly lobbed it into the knee-deep pool formed by the spring. "That was brilliant, having Tom Shafto as a tenant. From what I see, he's a diligent worker and he understands farming."

He tossed another pebble, and the ripples cut across those still running out from the first impact. Then he bit his lower lip, tossed the handful of pebbles into the pond creating an arcing splash, and turned to Emma. "This is difficult for me to say, so hear me out, yeah? If we were in England or Ireland, most likely we would have never met. But we have, and I give thanks to the Almighty for our meeting. Were your father alive, I would ask him if I could call upon you with a view to asking for your hand."

She started to speak, but he motioned for her to be silent.

"Please, hear me out. I know I have no money and my prospects today are not what they were even a month ago. And I don't want to take unfair advantage of my legal duty as your guardian. But Emma Pettigrew,"—he clambered onto one knee and took her hands in his—"I would like to call upon you, and if you find my suit pleasing, I would be honored if you would be my wife."

Her eyes sparkled as she laughed. "Kit Hawkwood, the moment I laid eyes on you, I thought you were the grandest man I'd ever seen. I don't care"—she giggled and mimicked his Devon accent— "about your money or your prospects or your taking advantage of your position. I think you are good man, and you could be a bold man if you'd allow yourself. I have no doubt you will be a good husband to me and a good father to our children."

She placed both hands on the back of his neck, pulled his lips to hers, and kissed him hard. He dropped one hand to her hip, returned her kiss, and then probed her lips, ever so gently, with the tip of his tongue. She hesitated and tentatively parted her lips. Their teeth clacked together, and they laughed together, then started anew.

She met his tongue with hers, moaning low from the back of her throat. He fumbled, only for an instant, with her bodice laces as he pushed her back onto the sun-warmed turf. One hand found the hem of her shift, ran up her thigh carrying the shift with it, and caressed a firm, rounded buttock. His other hand grazed her belly and cupped a pert, smallish breast that felt soft and firm in his work-hardened palm. Nudging her thighs apart with his knee, he rasped for breath as blood pounded in his temples. For a second, he was amazed that his response to her was the same as his reaction in a fight—right down to the fear. He rolled over onto her and freed his painful cockstand from his breechclout.

But she wasn't some Irish trollop. She was a beautiful, trusting lass who was in love with him. This wasn't how their first time together should be—him into her mutton like some goose girl he'd tossed in the grass.

He toyed with her erect nipple, and she gasped and squirmed against him, hooking one ankle behind his knee and pulling his erection hard against her. He could feel her wet, wiry thatch grinding against his thigh in time to some unheard rhythm. He kissed down her neck, across the top of her breast, and licked at her nipple. He was intoxicated by her musk and enthralled by her slim, eager body, and tingled with desire and the prospect of possessing her.

Women were like luck. They offered themselves to you but once. If you didn't seize it when it was offered, you never get a second chance. He grasped a buttock and pulled her hard against his thigh. She gasped and arched her back. But on the other hand, if she was the lass he thought she was ...

He stopped and rolled onto his back, pulling her head to rest on his chest. "Sweetling, we need to stop before you find yourself ankled." He caught a glimpse of a rose-petal-red nipple and stroked it with his palm.

She sighed and snuggled close to his chest. After taking his right hand in hers, she pulled it to her lips and kissed his fingers. Her eyes seemed to pierce his soul. "So, why are you stopping? Aren't you're wondering if you'll ever get a second chance? That maybe I'll change my mind?"

"No! Of course not. I wouldn't think that." The bloody deuce! Did the mort read his mind? Maybe there was something to this second-sight nonsense.

She laughed. "You're an awful liar. You'd be a damned fool to not wonder. But you'd have been a bigger damned fool to take me." She leaned on an elbow and looked into his eyes. "Fair warning, even if you are my man, Kit Hawkwood, there's no winning with me." She laughed again and stood, taking him by the hands and pulling him to his feet. The lingering kiss she placed on his lips set his head to buzzing afresh and left him with another painful erection. "But because you didn't treat me like some doxy you'd diddle and toss off, I'll give you my prophecy."

She shucked her unlaced bodice and grass-stained shift and stood stark naked in the afternoon sun. She wasn't beautiful in the apple-dumpling, batter-pudding style fashionable in London salons and great houses in Tuckahoe Virginia. She was too tall, her face and arms were tanned, and her muscles rippled under a taut skin that didn't carry an ounce of spare flesh. The sunlight glinted copper-gold from her hair, glowed on her milk-white skin, and accentuated all the curves and contours of her body.

Smallpox had left a pebbling of light scars across her forehead and down her ribs, though it was washed out by the sun's glare. She had that fierce, imperfect, and untamable beauty that Hawkwood had come to appreciate about the Valley.

Emma spun in a slow circle with arms outstretched, face to the sky and her hair cascading over her shoulders and back. "All this will be yours."

He was breathless. Speechless. Incapable of thought.

She took a step and leapt feet first into the pool. "Don't just stand there." Standing knee deep in lucent water with her hands on her hips, she smiled up at him. "Let me see what I've bargained for."

Chapter Twenty-Three

HAWKWOOD AND EMMA RETURNED to the house, scandalously bedraggled and glowing with excitement, and announced their betrothal. Hugh whooped and pounded Hawkwood on the back at the news, and Rankin produced a cobalt-glazed stoneware jug of good Jamaica rum to celebrate. Patsy Shafto pressed her children into service to make a wildflower crown for Emma.

By a mechanism that Hawkwood didn't understand, for he would have sworn no one left the farm, the word spread. Over the next week, the Pettigrew farm hosted a steady stream of visitors who wanted to wish the newly engaged couple well and sniff about for a juicy nugget of gossip or a hint of scandal.

Emma showed a side of herself that Hawkwood had never witnessed. She was a gracious hostess, receiving guests with dignity and hospitality. A few of the visitors were rejected suitors—some philosophical about their loss and some who, Hawkwood could tell, would try to tar them with malicious gossip.

Others came to examine the living arrangements. Questions abounded. Was it possible that a pulchrie and high-spirited lass like that Emma Pettigrew wouldn't be sharing a bed with her handsome Tuckahoe? They were all but living together, since Hawkwood occupied the settle bed in the kitchen. Was she ankled, and did she have a jack-in-the-box? Bets were placed on Emma having a child very soon.

Hawkwood smirked at the thought. This wasn't their fault. They hadn't been scandalous, and, truth be told, it wasn't that easy to be scandalous among so many Irish. Talk all they would, in a few months she'd be in his bed.

"Then you'll want a wedding around Martinmas?" the ever-unctuous Reverend Huntsman asked.

The relationship between him and Hawkwood had been at arm's length ever since Hawkwood had stopped his business when he'd sought to use his religious duties as a means to woo Emma after the death of her family. Even though Huntsman carried significant influence as a Presbyterian minister in a heavily Presbyterian community, Hawkwood was a Church of England man and not impressed with Dissenter clergymen.

Even so, ever since that first encounter with Huntsman, he had held his piece with what he thought to be Huntsman's arrogance and pretentions, for the sake of Emma, who was a staunch Presbyterian.

Hawkwood and Emma exchanged longing gazes, and Huntsman averted his eyes. "Probably a little later than Martinmas," Hawkwood said. "We'll wait for the harvest to be gathered in so our neighbors can attend and share our joy."

"A proper wedding feast, hey?"

"We shall do as best as we can." He hesitated and considered his next move. He'd cast his lot with these people and could scarce afford to have the most influential aligned against him. He extended his hand to Huntsman. "Sir, I must beg your pardon for the manner in which I ill-used you on our first meeting. It was ungentlemanly and I'm truly sorry."

"Of course, sir." Huntsman shook his head, but his eyes showed he was fearful he was being made the butt of a joke.

"I know you Presbyterians don't go for glebes, but a man should have a place to call home. There's a piece of land I should like to donate for a meeting house. There's a fine spring on the parcel you can use for baptisms. If you find it acceptable, it's yours."

"Thankee, sir! That is most generous of you." His eyes flicked left and right as if searching for hidden informants, then he said in a low voice, "I must say, sir, that I've been in the Upper Valley for four years. The only man of the cloth the whole time. And not one of these people has offered me much more than a place to lay my head and a begrudging and niggardly meal. Thank you, sir. You are a true gentleman."

Hawkwood caught a glimpse of Emma as he spoke. She near glowed with pleasure to see him making amends with Huntsman. He felt like a scoundrel, what with Emma giving him that adoring look when he was just securing his flank. But he hadn't set out to deceive her and he wasn't. He needed to make things right with Huntsman.

When Clendenin arrived, Hawkwood had one arm about

Huntsman's shoulders as he laughed at a shared joke while Emma held onto the other. Clendenin slid from his horse, dropped the reins, took three long steps, and clasped Hawkwood in a bear hug. "Just came by to congratulate the bridegroom-to-be." He laughed and stepped back. "I would say I came to congratulate the better man, but there ain't no such son of a bitch." He winked at Huntsman. "Sorry about the language, Parson."

Clendenin made his best imitation of a courtly leg to Emma, hat held out away from his body. "Ah, fair Emma, you have broken my heart. I have longed for you for these past years."

She blushed and giggled. "Get on with you, Jemmy, you rogue. You'd have me like one of your Indian women, digging in the garden, half naked, and dropping a bairn once a year."

"But Emma, it would be an adventure. Not like this." He waved a hand to encompass the house and surrounding farm. "There's naught here but dirt to scratch in. That might be fine for this scrub you've decided to wed"—he gave Hawkwood a familiar hug about the shoulders— "but it doesn't mean *you* can't go a-roving with sweet Jemmy."

Hawkwood and Emma laughed. Huntsman seemed nonplussed at the exchange but, as everyone else was amused, he laughed nervously.

"What caused this to happen, Boo? One day you had no interest and the next you're all set to marry. Were you afraid one more visit from me might see Miss Emma succumb to my charms?"

Hawkwood thought he saw a glance exchanged between Emma and Clendenin. Emma flushed crimson. Then in his mind's eye, he saw Emma walking, prancing even, alongside Jemmy when he came to call. He remembered the toss of the head and the flick of the skirts as she looked him square in the eyes.

Wait. Would they? No. Of course not. They wouldn't. Would they?

Chapter Twenty-Four

HAWKWOOD AWOKE VERY EARLY. The air was hot and stale behind the shuttered windows, and contrary to his nature he found himself anxious to roll out of bed and be on his way.

The dormant embers in the fireplace provided only a faint light in the kitchen. He shucked his dank nightshirt and donned his hunting shirt over a breechclout. He added a possibles bag, a shot pouch slung over his right shoulder, and a powder flask over his left, then made a brief stop at the trestle table. A chunk from the wheel of heat-softened cheese, two johnnie cakes from the stack on the wooden trencher, and a few slices of dry smoked ham would chase his hunger away.

Outside, the air was already heavy with humidity and honeysuckle, and far too warm for real comfort. The goat-cropped grass underfoot was dry, promising an evening thunderstorm. He reached into his possibles bag and pulled out a leather pouch packed with bear grease, which he applied liberally to his face and ears. The rancid grease protected the skin from exposure to sun and cold, and during the summer, it repelled—or at least momentarily discouraged—gnats, flies, and mosquitoes.

He found Tom Shafto waiting in the barn, half asleep, with one horse saddled for him and another with an empty pack saddle.

"I'll be back in the morning, Tom. At the latest. Clendenin avers there are deer on the Upper James, and I hope he's right. Keep an eye out for trouble. I don't think the Turnbulls will be back, but you can't be too careful. Jemmy will be hanging about. If you see anything that makes you uneasy, give him a call."

"Sure thing, Mr. Hawkwood. Good hunting. Even if you don't get anything, it's good to be shed of the farm for a bit."

"Yea, verily, as the reverend would say. I need to clear my head."

He stopped after a couple of hours for a brief rest, enjoying a late breakfast while sitting atop a huge flatiron of a rock jutting out over a broad stream that fed into the James River some miles away. It flowed sleepily, the glassy surface broken now and again by large catfish inexplicably launching themselves toward the heavens and then smacking loudly as they reentered the water.

The sun rising over the Blue Ridge brought with it an eagle cutting lazy spirals in the robin's-egg blue sky. Hawkwood watched as the raptor folded its wings and plummeted. At the last moment, the eagle arrested its momentum in a flurry of wings, like oars backwatering a boat, came to a near hover and then skimmed low across the stream, its talons mere molecules above the water. Then softly, almost near supernatural, the eagle pressed its talons beneath the surface, leaving only the slightest perceptible wake. This was immediately followed by a powerful beat of wings, and the eagle forced its way skyward with a catfish as long as itself struggling in its grasp. He licked the last traces of the fried cornmeal from his fingers, mounted his horse, and continued his journey.

As the sun rose and with it the temperature, the bear grease on his face ran in viscous rivulets down his chest and barely deterred the halo of gnats and horse flies from feeding on him. His shirt was soaked with sweat and welded to his body. The air, liquid and sullen, fairly crackled with static electricity. There was going to be a hell of a storm this evening.

As though reading his thoughts, a rain crow cooed. He contemplated terminating his hunting trip, but the day away from work and the welcome solitude of hunting were too much to sacrifice.

Shortly after noon, he found a well-traveled game trail wending uphill from the river. The splayed hoof marks in the mud of the riverbank marked where several deer had come to drink. Well, damme. Jemmy had been right. He dismounted and picketed his mount and packhorse in the shade of a stand of sugar maples.

After kneeling to examine the prints, he determined the tracks were some hours old. Then he checked the wind direction. A light breeze came out of the northwest, carrying his scent away from this side of the river. He raised the frizzen to inspect the primer in the flash pan, and, satisfied that it would fire, slipped through the tall grass of the river bottom and began a gradual ascent toward a grove of young chestnuts.

The game trail ran through thickets of shoulder-high pokeweed festooned with purple berries and the tangles of greenbrier. Then it opened into a meadow of wild grasses, stinging nettles, and beggar's lice. He started when a covey of bobwhites thundered into the air scant yards in front of him. By the time he reached the tree line, his exposed skin had been scratched and stung and his leggings were plastered with the sticky beggar's lice seeds.

Hawkwood took a short rest for lunch. This, he reflected, was what man was meant to do—roam the primeval forest without care. No morning parades, no debts to be paid, no worries, no field to plow, no rails to split, and no cares. He fished into his possibles bag and found a strip of smoked ham and a liquefying chunk of cheese, then leaned against a tree, keeping it between himself and the clearing, and ate.

A hint of movement above the level of the grass across the meadow caught his eye.

A large buck cautiously exited the woods on the far side of the meadow. The buck froze and pivoted his head slowly, left to right and then back again, as if sensing something amiss. A light wind had picked up and was intermittently gusting from the buck toward Hawkwood, depriving the buck of his most effective early warning—the scent of man. The animal stood for a few minutes, and only when he minced forward did Hawkwood again move.

Crouching low behind a chestnut tree about six inches in diameter, Hawkwood raised his rifle in slow motion. The buck stopped and looked directly at him. Hawkwood hid his face behind the tree and willed the buck to look away. For an infinite minute, the white-tail stared at Hawkwood, until finally, seeing or hearing nothing untoward, the deer continued to walk into the glade. He stopped to nibble at the tops of the grass.

Hawkwood exhaled, steadied his gun, and took aim at a spot just above the base of the buck's throat. Ever so slowly, he squeezed the trigger. The hammer dropped and flashed the powder in the pan, and the rifle coughed and recoiled heavily into his shoulder. The buck started but not quickly enough. His front legs spraddled, and knees buckled, sending him head first to the loam. A cloud of sulfurous gray-white smoke wafted downwind, engulfing Hawkwood.

Evening now near by the time he'd dressed the deer and prepared to move back to where he'd left his horses. A pewter thunderhead piled up ominously above the pale violet of the mountains far to the west, bringing a premature dusk. Clouds roiled and lightning snapped between them and the mountain peaks. A scan of the sky told him he would have to bear the brunt of the storm before returning to the horses.

He used flint and steel from his tinderbox to start a small fire, and once it was blazing, he sharpened a stick, sliced thin strips from the buck's liver, and squatted as he broiled them over the flames.

What his old messmates would think if they could see him now? Here he was in the middle of the wilderness, naked for all intents and purposes. Up to his elbows in blood and entrails. Engaged to a wild Irish girl who could kill and scalp a person before cooking dinner. And he couldn't have been happier.

As he consumed his third slice of liver, he heard movement in the forest some distance to his right. He gulped down the strip and turned in the direction of the noise. The noise sounded again, this time some distance behind him, and he face it. If only he'd taken the time to reload the rifle.

A bear ambled onto the game trail about twenty-five yards away. Hawkwood guessed it was five feet long and weighed twenty stone. This was going to be really close. Could he reload before it attacked? And if he did, could he drop it? Fighting seemed sheer folly but the bear did not act as though it was amenable to letting Hawkwood walk away.

The bear raised onto its hind legs like an old man rising from his chair, its front paws folded primly in front. For a moment its nostrils pulsed furiously, seeking to identify the interloper, then it dropped back to all fours.

Hawkwood squatted and slowly picked up his rifle with one hand, using the other to pull a ball from his shot pouch and lift his powder flask. The bear returned his stare and emitted a growling moan that had a strangely human tenor to it. Rocking from left to right, the animal shook its head, stared at him again, and began clattering his teeth. It raked at the loam, scattering sticks and gobbets of matted leaves.

Not good. The bear was going to charge. Hawkwood dropped the ball into the muzzle without using a patch. Accuracy was less important than time in his current situation. He struck the butt of the rifle on the earth to seat the ball and then filled the priming pan. All the while he kept his eyes fixed on the malevolent porcine eyes of the bear.

He raised the rifle to his shoulder in a slow, steady movement, cocking it at the same time. As he did, the bear charged. The animal moved remarkably fast, much faster than one would have thought possible for a beast so lacking in grace. Hawkwood had only a fraction of a second to point the barrel at the bear's center of mass and fire. The powder flashed, and the gun recoiled into the pocket of his shoulder. Not certain he had killed the animal, he dropped the rifle and made a diving jump to the right, using the cover of the lingering gun smoke to evade the charge. He hit the ground and rolled, then glimpsed the bear somersault through the pall of gun smoke as he sprang to his feet, hunting knife drawn.

The bear finished its roll a scant two yards away. As it struggled to its feet, Hawkwood could tell his shot had struck the animal solidly in the left shoulder. The wound wasn't immediately fatal, but it had shattered the shoulder joint. As the bear tried to rise, its left leg collapsed, and it hit the ground hard on its wounded side, roaring in rage. Hawkwood went into a fighting crouch and retreated. The broken leg at least gave him a chance. Still, his pulse pounded in his temples and his breath came in ragged gasps.

As Hawkwood pondered his next move, the bear stood up on its hind legs, becoming about a half foot taller than him. Its head swiveled, the tiny pig eyes locked on him, and the animal took two steps and was on him.

The bear's plate-sized paw hissed through the air and struck him square on the side of his head. The world vanished in a blazing flash of white light, and he staggered away with long running steps to keep his balance. To go down would be to die. Amazingly, the blow was painless. His vision returned, and he spat a wad of blood and saliva. In the same blow, the bear had clawed his head behind his ear and cut a slash across his cheekbone.

"Can't wait for him or I'm done," he said through clenched teeth. The sound of his own voice, a wheezing pant, didn't provide the hope or encouragement he'd anticipated. "One more shot like that and I'm a goner. Only one thing to do." He gripped the handle of his hunting knife and charged. "Arrrrrgh!"

After three running steps, he hurtled into the beast. The bear seemed to be falling, but it took several hasty steps backward and regained its balance. Hawkwood drove the top of his head underneath the bear's jaw, butting it so hard that the bear's teeth clack together.

He burrowed his face deep into the rank fur near the bear's throat and locked his teeth onto a mouthful of skin and fur. At the same time, he thrust his left arm high under the bear's good foreleg, grabbing a handful of the bear's scalp from the rear and holding it in a death grip. Just as Hawkwood hit the bear, the bear roared and wrapped its good foreleg around Hawkwood, clawing at his back and blasting pain through his body.

Setting his teeth deep into the bear's hide, he powered his hunting knife forward. His arm jolted as the blade struck a rib. The animal hesitated, and Hawkwood had visions of the blade snapping. Then there was the sweet lack of resistance as seven inches of good Sheffield steel set in a cocobolo handle deflected downward and slid through the bear's diaphragm. He wrenched the blade sideways to do more damage, then pulled it free. And he stabbed again.

Thunder cracked, the air smoked with ozone, and the sun vanished, sinking the forest into darkness. The first sparrow-egg-sized drops of the long-anticipated thunderstorm slapped him.

The bear continued to rake Hawkwood's upper back with metronomic regularity, all the while thrashing its head to free it from his grip. Hawkwood's right arm worked like a piston on one of Mr. Newcomen's steam engines, stabbing the bear in the chest and guts. He could feel the warm wetness of blood saturating the thick, musky fur despite the driving rain. This same blood in unison with the torrential rain made the checkered handle of his knife slippery.

The bear had to be mortally wounded, but that offered cold comfort. Hawkwood's own back was as much a bloody ruin as that of any survivor of a flogging, so much so that it no longer bothered to register pain. If he slipped or lost his grip on the bear, he would be dead in a trice.

The rain lashed over them. Their feet churned the forest floor to muck, making their footing unsure and weakening Hawkwood's grip on the bear's scalp. Hawkwood dug his shoulder into the bear's chest, planted his feet, and heaved. The movement created a brief opening for Hawkwood to attack the bear's upper chest rather than continuing to ravage its lower ribs.

He again drove the knife into the bear's left side, midway between its lower ribs and ruined shoulder, trying to strike closer to its heart. His blade struck a rib directly and stuck fast in the bone, and he lost his grip on the handle. His hand slid down the blade, cutting his fingers nearly to the bone. He groaned as pain from an unexpected location hit his nervous system, and his teeth slipped from their grip on the bear's neck. The bear violently snapped its muzzle left and right.

Before Hawkwood could regain his grip on the knife and wrench it free, he lost his grip on the bear's scalp. Instantly a jagged vise clamped onto his left trapezius muscle. The bear's huge lower canine teeth slid in below his collarbone, and the beast set its teeth and applied more pressure. In his detached consciousness, Hawkwood heard himself howl as his collarbone cracked. The bear's upper canines plowed two bloody furrows in his back and scored channels in his shoulder blade.

Again, he bellowed in pain. The bear shook him, setting its teeth deeper, and then almost casually flicked its head and tossed him a couple of yards. He hit the ground flat of his back, and his breath whooshed from his lungs. The animal emitted another moaning roar and clacked its teeth. Even in the rain and growing darkness, Hawkwood saw the pencil-thick stream of bright red blood draining from the corner of the bear's mouth. He had a chance, if only he could stay alive.

He tried to rise to his feet but discovered his left arm couldn't bear weight. In desperation he used his heels and right elbow to scrabble backward, trying to gain distance. The bear stood its ground and didn't follow. Hawkwood rolled over and pushed himself to his feet, then weaved and staggered, trying to establish his footing in the sheeting rain. Finally, a tree steadied him.

Panting like a blown racehorse, he stopped to take inventory. Pain flashed from so many wounds that Hawkwood couldn't tell where he was seriously injured. As he explored with his right hand, he returned the bear's stare. There were gouges on the left side of his head behind the ear, as well as a slash on his cheek from the initial cuff. His left ear had been torn nearly in half. His collarbone was broken and his chest punctured and torn by the bear's teeth.

He could breathe with ease, though it came in raspy sobs, so his lungs weren't punctured, and his ribs weren't broken. Moving his left arm required great effort and pain, and even then, he had little range. He didn't bother trying to check his back, instead trying to push the thought of what it must look like—probably a field of harrowed flesh and exposed ribs—from his mind. Though his fingers pulsed blood from the knife slash, he could still flex them.

Fuck, he had to get out of here. He backed away, and the bear, standing stooped and drooling blood, watched as Hawkwood turned to run. Wait. Did he want to be Kit Hawkwood, the man who fought and killed a bear? Or should he be Kit Hawkwood, the man who got his arse kicked by a bear? These Cohees respected courage.

He eyed the bear grimly. It was a dead 'un, but if he left, the animal would go off into the brush to die and no one will find it. And he'd have these fucking scars and the sniggers behind his back for the rest of my life. But this was madness. He should be in Bedlam, eating bugs and being poked with sticks, for even thinking this. He needed to run for his life.

"No choice." The calmness of his voice surprised him. He couldn't leave until it was dead. He had to toe the line and get this over with.

He drew his tomahawk from the right side of his belt and used his left hand to force his right hand to close tightly around the haft since his fingers were stiff. Then he stalked the bear in small steps, trying to judge its reaction. The animal gave another of its moans and clacked its teeth but didn't move.

"Had enough, have we?" Hawkwood said. "There's a good fellow. Just stand still for a moment and let me split your fucking skull."

The bear took a quick step forward, and in a replay of the initial seconds of the encounter its paw rocketed forward. This time there was no slap. The paw closed on the nape of Hawkwood's neck and pulled him into a tight embrace. Hawkwood smelled the hot, foul exhalation of breath as the jaws dropped over his head. He screamed, hacked at the bear's side with the tomahawk, and twisted violently counterclockwise while pushing off with a knee braced against the bear's abdomen.

As he staggered free, he heard a ripping and popping noise from deep within his skull.

He was blind.

Chapter Twenty-Five

A HHH, FUCK! FUCK!" HAWKWOOD screamed as he staggered away. Dropping the tomahawk, he raised his right hand to his face. His mouth filled with bile as he felt mangled flesh where his eyes should have been. What the fuck was this? It couldn't be his face. His hand reached a few inches farther back on his head, and he felt bare bone. "By God, he's scalped me."

He found the edge of his ruined scalp at the bridge of his nose, slid his fingers underneath, squished it back into place, and wiped the blood from his eyes with his forearm. His vision returned, albeit through a thick haze. The bear continued to stand its ground, clacking its teeth and emitting its peculiar moan. Needing to clear his eyes, he took a chance and stared straight at the heavens, letting the rain sluice the blood from his eyes.

He hocked a wad of blood and saliva mixed with bile, then spat. "Fuck it all. Let's get this done."

Hawkwood picked up his tomahawk and gripped it at the end of the haft. He wished it had a wrist strap, not trusting his wounded hand to keep a tight grip, but he didn't. Placing his right foot pointed at the bear and the left foot perpendicular to the right, he extended his right arm and flexed it, holding the tomahawk perpendicular to the ground. Blood coursed down his face from his torn scalp, and he canted his head from side to side, trying to find a position where the blood would not run into his eyes.

He advanced a step and wondered what his old fencing master would think of a pupil facing a bear while armed with a tomahawk. The bear continued its gimlet-eyed stare over an open mouth drooling blood.

He feinted an attack, and the bear swatted at him. Another feint and another swat. Hawkwood carefully judged his distance. Ten feet? Twelve? He flexed his legs and hips. No damage. He should be able to cover that distance with a ballestra, but he had to kill the animal. He might not make it through another grapple.

Squatting a bit, Hawkwood concentrated past the throbbing pain and took a deep breath. At least it was easier to lunge since he was near naked. He wiped his forearm across his face to clear the blood and flexed the muscles in his right shoulder and arm. Another deep breath. Ah, fuck. He needed to get stuck into it.

With a scream, he bounded forward in a short hop and transitioned to a long lunge. The bear hesitated at the scream, then recovered quickly. It moved a step toward Hawkwood and reached for him with its paw. As Hawkwood extended into the lunge, he brought his forearm down and flicked his wrist. The tomahawk accelerated downward and struck the bear squarely in the center of the head, just above the line of the eyes.

Its Sheffield steel buried up to its full depth, but the bear's foreleg and paw struck Hawkwood solidly on his immobilized left arm. He bawled in pain as it raked its claws over his exposed ribs. Then the bear's legs went slack and the animal collapsed on Hawkwood, threatening to pin him to the ground. With his last reservoirs of strength, he rolled the animal to the left as it was falling and then collapsed to his knees beside the dead bear.

"There! Now you Cohee bastards tell me a story to top this one!" he shouted into the roaring storm.

* * * * *

THE SUN HUNG HIGH IN THE SKY AS Hawkwood stretched out in a stream, letting the cold water cleanse his wounds and loosen the thick crust of dried blood on his back. His horses were picketed no more than fifty yards away, but he couldn't bear the thought of walking—or more likely, crawling—to them, much less suffering the long ride home. For the moment, the pain was mere background noise that his mind had learned to cope with, although any movement brought dormant nerves back to consciousness and howling pain.

He heard the clopping of hooves and the murmur of voices and croaked out a call for help that set his cracked ribs dancing with rage.

"God Almighty, boy." A stooped middle-aged man slid from his saddle and splashed into the water. Hawkwood might have recognized him from the shooting match. "What happened to you?"

"Bear, I think," he grunted through clenched teeth. "Though it could have been Hairless Wat's woman."

The man and his companions, an adolescent boy and a burly man with a riot of red hair pulled into a ragged queue, guffawed. "Say, you're the Tuckahoe fella what lives at the Pettigrew place, ain't you? Here, let me get a look at you." His fingers gently probed the curve of Hawkwood's jaw, his ruined ear, and his lacerated scalp.

Hawkwood gritted his teeth and froze his facial features, determined to show no pain. He'd never hurt so bad in his life. But he'd killed a bear with a knife and tomahawk, and he'd be damned if he let anyone see him take notice of the wounds.

"Take my hand, boy." He looked at the big man. "Adam, get your hands under his shoulders. We're going to lift you out of this water, get you on your horse. Dan, you ride and find Granny Nixon. If anybody can fix this mess, she can."

Hawkwood tried to point. "I have a deer and my bear up that trace. We need to get them."

"Look at yourself, son. You're plumb torn up. We need to get you cared for."

He wasn't going anywhere without his bear. "The quicker you field dress that bear and get them loaded up, the quicker we can be gone. I killed that fucker fair and square. I'm not leaving without its carcass."

* * * * *

JUST AS THE BETROTHAL DREW VISITORS to Pettigrew place, so, too, did Hawkwood's convalescence. He found himself to be a veritable circus attraction. A three-headed goat wouldn't have drawn more interest. The old witch woman, Granny Nixon, took up residence nearly as soon as he was brought home. She brewed herbal concoctions that became a poultice she applied to his wounds each day, and it speeded the healing at a remarkable rate.

The attention and his improving health inspired him to tell and retell the story, embellishing and exaggerating in best Cohee style, leaving his audience alternating between rapt attention and doubled with laughter. The visitors marveled at the tight row of catgut suture where Granny Nixon had stitched his scalp back in place. *Good as new*, she had assured him. *Once the hair grows back out, no one will ever know ye were scalped.*

He left them agog when he insisted Emma lift the lint bandage protecting the hacked and mangled flesh on his back that was going to leave a tightly woven warp and woof of livid keloids that would be with him for life. His right hand was bandaged, so he shook with his left, even though that arm was tightly bound to his torso to allow his broken collarbone to heal.

Everyone brought food. The women helped Emma and Patsy Shafto with the day-to-day chores, and the men pitched in to help on the farm, giving Rankin the chance to do what he did best—sit in the shade, play his flageolet, and nip at his jug. All of this gave Maggie McDowell the chance to spend time with Hugh under the guise of helping Emma.

Hawkwood's wounds healed clean. The bear's pelt graced the parlor floor, and its claws were strung on a rawhide thong and hung around Hawkwood's neck. Both the buck and the bear were in brine-barrels in the smokehouse.

The only part of Granny Nixon's physic that didn't prove efficacious was her repair of his ear. When the bear had raked his head in the opening moments of their struggle, its claws tore the top third of his ear, leaving it attached by only a filament of cartilage. She'd stitched it into place, covered it with a poultice, and bandaged it tight to his head, but it didn't work.

When Emma removed the bandage to change the pomace of boiled leaves and bear grease, she found the ear was discolored. She sniffed and detected the faint odor of bad meat. "It ain't taking," she whispered. "It'll have to come off."

"Are you sure? Can't it be saved?" Tears welled in his eyes at the thought of having a cropped ear and what that meant in society.

She looked into his eyes. "Why, Kit. You come back home mauled half to death and you don't make a sound. Now you're getting teary-eyed on me?"

"You don't understand. These scars, and these on my face." He gestured weakly with his bandaged hand. "These are fighting scars. And this"—he waved his hand over his ruined ear— "means whenever I leave the Valley, people will think I'm a felon. That I've had my ear nailed to a pillory."

"Let them think what they will." She kissed him on the temple and pulled his bandaged head to her bosom. "The people that matter will know how you lost that ear. And you can always wear your hair loose."

"The people that matter?" He pushed back from her embrace and arched his eyebrow.

"The people that matter," she said. "Those people will know how this ear came to be. The rest can go straight to hell if they think less of you for it. Now are you ready? You faced a bear. I'm sure you can face my scissors."

Chapter Twenty-Six

HAWKWOOD STOOD ON THE PORCH, slowly windmilling his left arm. His collar bone had healed straight and true, and moving his arm no longer caused pain. The bandages were off his hand, and all the stitches had been drawn. One or two more days and he'd be ready to get back to work. Without Shafto on the farm, he knew Hugh would never have been able to keep up with what needed to be done with the buildings, crops, and livestock.

"Yo, Kit!" Hugh called. "Trouble!" He pointed across the meadow.

Hawkwood could see three horsemen approaching. Even at two furlongs, he could identify the ungainly, stiff-legged riders who flopped uncomfortably in their saddles as Hairless Wat Turnbull and his boys Ned and Tim.

Emma rushed out of the house at Hugh's yell, and her face blanched at the sight of the riders.

"Load all the firelocks. Prop them against the wall inside the door," Hawkwood told him, keeping his gaze fixed on the coming riders. "I don't want to threaten them, but I'm not going to be cowed by them either. Emma, would you mind going inside and helping Hugh?"

The three men reined in their mounts a scant few feet from the porch.

Hawkwood placed his fists on his hips. "What's your business here?"

"You're not going to invite us to alight and tie up?" Wat asked.

The eyes of Ned and Tim flicked about, likely taking account of who else might be nearby.

"I think not, Mr. Turnbull. It would be best if you stated your business and were on your way."

"Our business—or rather my boy Ned's business—is with Miss Emma. She's sweet on him, you know, and it hurt him mightily to hear that she'd agreed to marry a cock-robin such as you when a real man was in need of a wife."

Hawkwood raged inside, but he held his anger in check and gave Turnbull a disarming smile. Sod this blackguard and his gits, he'd cast his lot with these people and was betrothed to Emma. If he let this pass, he'd lose everyone. He'd be a laughingstock, and Emma would be shamed, assuming she would still want him. They would never be more evenly matched with the Turnbulls. They might as well settle this business now as later.

He kept his voice flat and even. "Seems to me, Wat, that Emma has already picked a real man. As I recall it, the last time I met Ned, I laced his jacket good." He paused and let the taunt hang in the air. "That was after I knocked Tim's cock in the dirt. What does she need with a fat, one-eyed ruffian like your boy?"

Wat smirked at him and shot tobacco juice. "My other boys had a taste of her. It's only fair that Ned gets the same seeing how he's their big brother."

Hawkwood's stewed. What the hell did he mean by that?

Tom Shafto came from around the house and approached the Turnbulls on their blindside, carrying the maul he'd been using to drive trunnels.

"Wat," Hawkwood said, deliberately omitting the honorific, "you've said your piece. Now I want you off my land."

"And if I say we're not leaving until Miss Emma—"

The door to the house slammed open, and Emma emerged with her *fusil* pointed squarely at Wat Turnbull. She was followed by Hugh with his fowling piece and Hawkwood's rifle. "Damn you to hell, Wat Turnbull!" she hissed. "And damn your one-eyed git and that"—she nodded in the direction of Tim— "bug-eating bedlamite. You come here to my house! To tell my man that I'd have anything to do with that …" She stopped midsentence and searched for words, her mouth working like a landed fish's. "That hog-grubbing slubber-degullion." She gave a menacing jab toward Ned with the gun barrel. "Now my man is a gentleman and asked you to leave polite. But I'm the daughter of Bart Pettigrew, and by God I'll salt your arse if you don't move."

Hugh stepped forward and slipped Hawkwood his long rifle.

Turnbull turned in the saddle to speak to Ned and, for the first time, became aware that Shafto stood only a few yards from them. He blinked and flexed his jaw as he evaluated the situation. "You win this one, Hawkwood. I'll give you that much. But this ain't over. Not by a long shot."

Minutes later, when Emma and Hawkwood were alone in the house, she collapsed in tears. He held her as she clung to him and heaved great racking sobs. "This won't end until they're dead or we're dead, Kit. They'll never leave us be."

She was right. It might just come to that. But the concern foremost in his mind was not red-handed war with the Turnbulls, but rather what Wat meant about his sons having a taste of Emma.

* * * * *

"GET ON WITH IT, YE HEN-HEAD," Robbie Turnbull grunted.

Willie scowled. "Do I have to?"

Robbie gave him a punch to the short ribs. "Go ahead, pick it up." He looked at the ever-befuddled Tim. "And you, keep the beast steady."

Tim patted the stolid Conestoga gelding on the side of the neck while Willie picked up the corn knife. He stood behind and to one side of the animal, crouched, and raised a trembling arm.

"Do it, damn your eyes," Robbie ordered.

Willie slashed with the knife, and the blade hit the horse's leg just above the point of the hock, severing the tendons and biting into the bone. The horse whinnied and toppled onto one side.

Willie dropped the knife. "This is a damned shame, Robbie. That's a beautiful animal."

Robbie waved him off. "Stop your whining. Let's get out of here."

"Wait," Tim said. "Shouldn't we kill it? I mean, we can't just leave it like this."

"You idiot, they ain't going to be scared if they find their horse dead. They will be when they find it hocked."

* * * * *

EMMA OPENED THE DOOR AT THE FIRST KNOCK. "Come in, Mr. Shafto. What brings you up here?"

Now six weeks past his mauling by the bear, Hawkwood sat in the kitchen, passing the time with Sam Farris. Though his wounds were healed, his endurance was lacking, and a small amount of work quickly sapped his energy. Shafto's visit piqued his interest though. The man rarely visited the house.

Emma led him into the kitchen. "Kit, Mr. Shafto is here to see you."

Shafto clutched his shabby felt hat over his chest. "Sorry to bother you, sir, but it's our plow horse. Somebody hocked the poor beast. I put him down. I can take you to see him if you're of a mind."

Hawkwood cursed under his breath. The horse played a critical part on their farm. The bay Conestoga pulled sledges and carts and the plow and harrow. While they had three other horses that could do some of the work, for the truly heavy lifting of hauling a wagon and pulling stumps or a sledge loaded with field stones, there was no substitute for that docile, hardworking beast. And he had no doubt who had mutilated their horse. "Damned Turnbulls."

"Aye, there's only one set of rogues in the country that'd do something as dirty as hocking a horse," Farris said. "This ain't going to get better."

Rankin came into the kitchen from the dog trot. "We'll have to get another before harvest comes in. We might be able to borrow one, but this mess with the Turnbulls could make it hard. Nobody's going to want their horse to end up hocked or get involved in the feud between you and them."

"Between us and them, Mr. Rankin." Emma said. "It is between this household and them. You need to decide if you can live with that."

Rankin looked at her hard, then lowered his eyes. "Right, Miss Emma. I didn't mean nothing by it. I'm with you."

"Where's the best place to get another?" Hawkwood asked. "Frederick Town or up in the Watauga Country?"

"Better price in the Watauga," Shafto said.

Rankin nodded in agreement.

"Of course, the horses are probably stolen from Pennsylvania." Shafto worked the brim of his hat. "Those boys steal them, drive them south, hold them for a year, and then sell them back to the Dutchers."

Hawkwood nodded. "Next week I should be able to make the trip. Bram, ask your friends at the shebeen for a recommendation for who to talk to and who to avoid."

Hugh came into the room. "Wait. I can go. I'm nearly eighteen."

"Hugh, please," Emma said. "Don't." Alarm showed in her eyes as she covered her mouth.

Hawkwood looked from her to him. "You can't go alone, Hugh. Can you get someone to go with you? Now mind you, I want to talk to the person. And it can't be Maggie McDowell."

Everyone laughed.

Emma hurried toward where Hawkwood sat. "But Hugh is too young, and the trip is too dangerous—"

"He's not your little brother anymore, he's a grown man." Hawkwood placed his hand on her arm. "We'll make sure he's traveling with someone reliable. He'll be safe as houses."

Farris snorted. "Hell, I'll go with the boy. I'm tired out hanging around here and listening to Kit tell his bear-fight story over and over. Hugh, what do you say we leave day after tomorrow? It'll be a week down and a week back. I'll have Mary stay here, just in case the Turnbulls act up again. And I'll get the chance to spend some of Kit's money."

* * * * *

HAWKWOOD HAD FINALLY STARTED TO feel strong again. His collarbone had set straight and healed solid, and no lasting damage had been done to the fingers by the knife blade. He'd returned to his daily regimen of pressing field stones to build strength, and, after his encounter with the Turnbulls near Woods Gap, he'd started running and swore he would be the fastest runner in the Valley.

"Time to call it a day, eh, Tom?" he said and dropped a flat fieldstone into place, capping the dry stacked stone wall he and Shafto were building.

They walked side by side to the water trough near the barn. Hawkwood shucked his sweat-soaked shirt and doused his head and torso in lukewarm water, then stretched his arm downward, flexed his triceps, and watched approvingly as it rippled beneath the drumhead-tight, tan skin. At the top of his shoulder he could see the stiff, pale pink lines of scar tissue that he knew covered his back like a cape.

"Tomorrow we need to finish thatching the corncrib and then we'll split more rails. Another two, three days and we'll be ready to start on the new fence line."

"Right. See you at cockcrow."

Hawkwood turned but stopped. A rider approached from south across the meadow. He pointed. "Who's that?"

Shafto sized him up. "There's just one man. He can't be up to mischief by himself and in broad daylight."

They waited as the rider approached. When he was a furlong or so away, Hawkwood could see two men riding the horse. He started walking toward the rider, and within a few steps, he recognized the rider as Maggie McDowell's father. "By God, that's Sam riding behind him!" He sprinted toward the rider.

Chapter Twenty-Seven

HAWKWOOD, McDOWELL, AND SHAFTO carried Farris into the house. Emma came in from the kitchen garden as they laid him on the bearskin on the parlor floor. His face was battered, his nose obviously broken, and eyes blackened and swollen shut. Blood had congealed about his mouth.

She took one look at him and brought her hands to her mouth. "God in heaven. Where is Hugh?"

Hawkwood used his hunting knife to slice away Farris's shirt. "Tom, you run and get Mistress Farris. Tell her Sam is here and he's hurt."

"Where is Hugh?" Emma asked again, her voice rising an octave. "Safe as houses, you said. Damn you!" She slapped Hawkwood across the face. "Damn you and damn him! Here, I've got him. I've tended enough beaten men to know what to do. You go find Hugh!"

* * * * *

"I THINK WE'VE LOOKED ALL WE CAN," McDowell said as he tossed the last of the breakfast tea on the campfire.

Hawkwood nodded in glum agreement. He and McDowell had scoured the area where Farris had been found for any trace of Hugh. Now, after three days, they had to call it quits.

"Good luck when you get home. That sister of his is a hellcat when you get her stirred up. But I guess you know that."

"She has every right to be. She didn't want him to go, but me and Sam insisted that nothing could go wrong. I don't know how I'm going to face her empty handed. Hell, if we'd found him dead, that would be one thing, but not finding him? She's just not going to understand."

They split up, both men heading home. Hawkwood wasn't sure of what awaited him, but it surely wasn't going to be hugs and kisses. Halfway home, he took a chance and turned his horse toward the Turnbull settlement.

At midmorning, he came within view of the settlement. It was situated, as were most Irish farms, in a small bowl-shaped hollow near a spring. The fields, unlike those on the Pettigrew farm, had not been cleared or plowed. Corn, beans, and squash grew in an untidy riot around and between tall dead-stand trees and alongside deadfall.

He swallowed hard, checked the priming in his rifle, and reached over his shoulder to finger the hilt of his hanger slung across his back. He knew one of those sons of bitches killed Hugh but needed to be certain before accusing them. It was probably just going to be him, Rankin, and Tom Shafto. Maybe Farris if he wasn't hurt too bad. And he couldn't count on Shafto or Rankin. Hell, he wasn't sure he could count on himself. Right now, he didn't trust his arse with a fart.

He clopped down the trail leading to the group of cabins. About fifty yards from the nearest one, he stopped. "Halloo! The house!" he called through cupped hands.

A pack of ragged curs began barking and howling at the invader.

The door to a dilapidated double-pen cabin creaked opened, and Ned Turnbull—bandy-legged, one-eyed, and malevolent—stepped out. "Well, well. If it ain't the bear killer himself. And now he's all decked out like he was a timberbeast instead of a Tuckahoe squireen. I thought you'd be laid up swiving that little girl of yours. She is a sweet piece, or so I'm told."

Hawkwood's temper rose. "Weren't you ever taught to speak of women with respect?"

Wat Turnbull came out of the largest cabin wearing a nightshirt and nothing else. The sun glowed on the weathered, yellowed ivory of his bare skull. Others assembled next to him. Hawkwood knew dimwitted Tim, vicious Robbie, and timorous Willie, then there were some he knew by sight but not by name. Behind them clustered their slovenly women and dirty, unkempt urchins.

"Hold your tongue, Ned," Turnbull said. "Come on in, Hawkwood. Tie up and 'light. You've nothing to fear from us."

"No disrespect, Mr. Turnbull, but I'll just stay where I am. Your boys seem to have developed a fondness for knocking me about."

The Turnbulls laughed at his jest.

If they were laughing, they weren't shooting or trying to gouge his top lights out. "I'm looking for Hugh Pettigrew. He and Sam Farris were waylaid on the road to Carolina. I was wondering if you might have heard about it."

"I ain't seen him." Turnbull looked at his men. "Any of you seen the Pettigrew boy?"

A shaking of heads followed as they moved closer to Hawkwood.

"How long's he been gone?" Turnbull came forward one small step at a time.

"Five days. I've been looking for him for three of those."

Robbie laughed. "He been gone five days, he's either dead or he's with that McDowell piece."

Hawkwood glared at him. "I've already knocked your cock in the dirt once over your nasty mouth and brutish ways. If you think I won't come down and slap your jaws again, you're mistaken."

Robbie flushed and made a motion to charge him. Hawkwood raised his long rifle, and the click of the hammer cocking rang like thunder, stopping Robbie in his tracks.

"No need for the firelock, Hawkwood," Turnbull said. "I gave you my word you were safe here. But now you've got what you're looking for, and you'd best be on your way."

He lowered his rifle and dropped the hammer to half-cock. "Perhaps. Sam Farris is still alive, and I expect him to be conscious by the time I get home."

Slack-jawed Tim spoke. "I heard, mind you, that the Pettigrew whelp is dead. Heard a man say that he bawled like a calf when he got a knife stuck in his puddings. Then they dropped him in a stream and—"

"Shut your gob, you lobcock." Robbie glowered at him.

Hawkwood felt as though he'd been punched in the guts. He was being taunted, but something about the challenge had a ring of truth. "What man was this, Tim? And who are *they*?"

Tim waved his hands. "Stranger." He glanced at Robbie from the corner of his eye. "Never seen him before. One of the timberbeast coves what were at the shooting match. Maybe. Coulda been them."

"Well, where were you when he told you this?"

"Boy, we've been more than fair with you," Turnbull said. "Now it would be best if you moved on."

Hawkwood pursed his lips. "This matter isn't settled, sir. Not by a damned sight. I might overlook my corncrib being burned and my horse being hocked, but I'll not overlook Hugh's murder. Mark my words, Wat, if one of your boys killed Hugh, I'll burn your whole goddam place to the ground."

Turnbull leered at him. "You're talking big for just the one of you. Now run along, boy. Go back and play with that girl of yours while you still can."

* * * * *

HAWKWOOD PACED THE POLISHED WOOD FLOOR of Welbourne's parlor like a sentry at guard mount. With every step he took, every second he waited, his anger simmered and perked. This visit to Welbourne inflamed the wound of Hugh's disappearance. Emma, a true child of the Valley Irish, had demanded blood for blood. Hawkwood had no objection to retribution, but the thought of igniting a war outside the law left him cold. As a result, a rift had developed between him and Emma, putting her credibility as a soothsayer into jeopardy.

Welbourne entered his parlor and rested his eyes on Hawkwood. The temerity of that boy, showing up at Chestnut Grove and demanding—not asking but demanding—an interview. He'd kept him waiting long enough to show him who was the supplicant, so he supposed it was time to see what this was all about.

"Mr. Welbourne." Hawkwood extended his hand. "It's so generous of you to receive me at no notice."

Welbourne kept his hands clasped behind his back. "I'm a busy man, sir. Please reveal what made your imposition necessary." He reveled when Hawkwood flushed. *How does it feel, my little boss cock? To have to take an insult and do nothing about it? Is it as much fun now as when you were flirting with my wife in front of everyone?*

"Hugh Pettigrew, sir. He's missing. There is reason to presume he's dead and that the perpetrators are some of the Turnbull clan. That lackwit, Tim Turnbull, as much as admitted that he'd killed Hugh. Sir, I'd like for you to issue a writ of *capias*."

Welbourne's mind worked. The last thing he or the company needed was an Irish blood feud involving men valuable to their enterprise. "I can issue all the writs in the world, young man, but no constable will carry a writ against the Turnbulls. He'd be lucky to escape with his skin."

"Then issue me the writ, sir. I will raise a *posse comitatus* and take them."

Welbourne shook his head, amazed. Hawkwood really didn't understand that he wasn't in England. "First, sir, you have no evidence against these men—"

"Bloody hell. They're boasting—"

"Quiet, sir!" he shouted. "Dammit all. You have no evidence that your ward hasn't simply decamped to greener pastures. Second, you have a personal animus toward these men and reason to seek their ruin." Hawkwood opened his mouth to speak, but Welbourne waved him to silence. "Let me finish. You are the one who came to me for favor. Third—and this, young sir, is the most important—if I issue you the warrant, there is no guarantee you can raise a *posse comitatus*. These Irish don't answer the call of the law, they answer the call of one of their leaders. One of their chieftains, if you will. I doubt a Tuckahoe is going to fare well trying to raise the Valley against some of their own."

"Let me try, sir!"

"What is it, Hawkwood? Has that Irish mort put you up to this? Is she leading you about by the sugar stick?" Welbourne laughed as Hawkwood's mouth dropped open. "Really, sir, you are most transparent. And were it only your name at stake, I would give you your writ and be damned. But it is my honor that will be blemished if I issue a writ and no one responds."

He paused to enjoy Hawkwood's humiliation and consider his next move. "Look here, Hawkwood. Despite our differences, I have to own that you're a brave and resourceful young man. A man who would bring credit to His Majesty's arms." Welbourne watched his face for any change of expression. "To advance your military career, and to see you out of Virginia because the partnership would rather you didn't crack a whip on how the company functions, we are prepared to make good your trimming at the hands of"—he hesitated, his brow furrowed—"at the hands of our friend Richard. Your passage home shall be on a ship chartered by the company, *gratis*, if you will. If you agree to leave the colony, we will even purchase your patent on the New River on favorable terms. If you take your fair lady with you, we will purchase her farm too. If she decides to stay, I'll arrange for another guardian."

Hawkwood took a step forward, his eyes icy cold and his teeth bared.

Welbourne skipped backward and held up his hands to ward off an attack.

"You think you can buy me off?" he shouted. "They killed a boy and they terrorize the country, and you won't lift a finger to stop them!"

One of the slaves peeked into the parlor, eyes bugged, and Welbourne gave him a look that pleaded for him to go find reinforcements. "Sir, I am trying to be fair to you. The Turnbulls, scum though they are, are useful tools. No one benefits from you starting some Irish blood feud with them. I'm giving you what you came to Virginia for. Think about it once the anger has passed. If you decline and decide to pursue this foolishness, don't blame me when you find the *posse comitatus* called out on you. Good day."

Welbourne wheeled and walked away as an overseer and three slaves appeared at the parlor door. He dismissed them with a wave of his hand.

Just outside the parlor, Sarah waited. "That went well," she said, her eyes laughing.

"He'll see the wisdom of the offer. His Irish trull will as well."

"You sell the lad short. He has a way of rising to the challenge."

He stared at her. "My God, Sarah. Don't tell me you are smitten by the boy."

She cocked her head and pressed her finger to her lips. "My only concern, dear Ran, is for us. We cannot be seen to lose. If you were not going to help him, then at least you should have shown him kindness and understanding. Now you've struck at his pride, and we don't know where that will lead."

* * * * *

HAWKWOOD AND EMMA SAT ON OPPOSITE ENDS of the puncheon bench on the porch, watching the squall line approach from the southwest. The deluge hit the house, and torrents cascaded off the shingle roof, splashed onto the packed, swept earth around the porch, puddled up, and then flowed out through eroded runlets that sought the low ground.

"I shall make an appeal to Colonel Patton. He is a just man," Hawkwood said, more to break the silence than anything else. His throat constricted, and his head and heart ached with the grief of his love dying before his eyes and being powerless to change the course of events. *We're just like the rain, drifting off into nothing, and there isn't any way of stopping it any more than I can stop the rain.*

Emma stopped cutting yellow squash into thick slices and dropping them into a rush basket on her lap. "Pah! The colonel is no different from Welbourne. He'll make you feel like he's on your side, but when push comes to shove, he's going to back the moneyed interests. He's one of them."

"Welbourne made me another proposition. He offered to make good all my losses and give me free passage to England. It would be nigh on eight hundred pounds. He offered to buy your farm too. We could leave and go back to England. Emma, my love for you hasn't changed. I wish nothing more than to be your husband. But if you no longer desire that, then you'd have money for a dowry that would attract a good husband."

She flinched, then she slid across the bench, placed a hand by his leg, and leaned in with her face scant inches from his. "Did I hear you right, sir? Did I hear you propose that we take Welbourne's blood money and run? Did he say, 'All these things will I give thee, if thou wilt fall down and worship me' while he was at it?"

"Really, Emma, it's not actually blood—"

"My brother is lying dead out there." She jabbed a finger toward the south. "He's not even been brought home to be buried with Mam and Da." Her face flushed with anger. "His fucking killers are right across that hill." She gave another jab of a finger. "And you, Kit, the man I've invited to my bed, are talking to me about selling out and fleeing to England and marrying me off to someone else."

Hawkwood edged away from her. At the moment he would have willingly faced another bear.

"Please, that isn't fair. I was telling you what Welbourne proposed, telling you your options, if you will. I don't want to see you wed anyone but me. But Welbourne is right. Even if he gives me the writ, who will rally to me?"

"The man who went blow for blow with One-Eyed Ned and killed a bear with a knife should be able to convince one or two men to ride with him to avenge a beautiful boy who was foully murdered. How about Maggie's da? You think he won't ride against Hugh's killer? If you had but a touch of faith in yourself, there'd be little you couldn't do."

She shook her head. "You hold my people in contempt and think I'm different from them. Kit, though I love you dearly, it breaks my heart that you feel so. I'm not different." She rested a hand on her bosom. "I'm Patsy Shafto. I'm Mary Farris. God help me, I'm whatever wench Hairless Wat has in his bed. I'm never going to be an English lady or a Church of Ireland woman. And I'd go to hell before I'd run and be shamed in front of my people."

"But, Emma, we must use the law. Eye for an eye isn't right—"

The knife flashed in her hand, and the tip hit Hawkwood's breeches at the knee. As neatly as she'd skin a squirrel, she laid them open to his hip. He yipped and pushed back against the cabin wall.

"You value the wrong things, Kit," she said. "You wouldn't wear the shirt I'd made you till you were damned near naked. Now you like it right well, eh? You couldn't go to see Welbourne dressed like a backcountryman, you had to go looking like a Tuckahoe. Did you think he'd listen to you if you were like him and not like my people? You think people don't notice that you think you're better than they are? That you think that even if they ain't bog-trotting Taigs, they ain't quite as good as an Englishman? They've offered you their friendship, and how have you met those offers?"

When the knife was safely away from him, he stood and looked at the ruins of his last set of breeches. "Damn it all! What would you have me do? Go outside the law and just kill them like dogs? Did you think that if the Turnbulls are as valuable to Patton as everyone seems to think … that if I do carry fire and sword to them—and if I prevail—that I might end up on a gallows in Williamsburg?" He dropped back onto the bench, exhausted by fighting with her. Exhausted by worrying about the Turnbulls. Exhausted by trying to save a love that she no longer seemed to care about.

Her shoulders heaved as she cried silently. He reached out to comfort her, but she pushed his hand away. Her touch was calm, gentle, and final.

"Ah, Kit. I loved you so." She stood, dried her eyes on her sleeve, stooped, and kissed him on the mouth. "I think you should call on Welbourne and see to your money." Then she walked into the house.

The rain paused as suddenly as it had started, and the last drips fell from the roof. Hawkwood thought he caught a glimpse of the sun breaking through in the western sky.

Chapter Twenty-Eight

A CAROLINA TRADER BROUGHT HUGH'S BODY HOME. The man had been bound from the Cherokee lands in the Carolina mountains to Frederick Town with a dozen packhorses loaded with deer hides. One of his drovers, sent to fetch water from Bearwallow Creek, had seen vultures circling and found Hugh's swollen, blackened body on a mud flat.

The cause of death was obvious to the coroner's jury, empaneled by Welbourne. Hugh had a broad knife wound just below his navel and had likely lived a day or two before passing. No doubt he had died hard.

He was buried next to his father on the Pettigrew farmstead in a coffin Tom Shafto built from hand-hewn planks taken from the barn. His shroud was the patchwork quilt his mother had made for his bed.

The day was hot as a blacksmith's forge and the air as dead as Hugh when Reverend Huntsman preached a funeral sermon based on Romans 12:19: "Avenge not yourselves, but rather give place unto wrath: for it is written, vengeance is mine; I will repay, saith the Lord." The mourners listened respectfully and agreed Huntsman had done himself proud.

For the sake of appearances, Emma held Hawkwood's arm. People murmured that they were a fine-looking couple, with her in her best dress and him wearing his hunting shirt and leggings. But the touch of her hand on his arm was polite, distant, and detached, almost as though she were not really there.

McDowell approached Hawkwood after he loaded his inconsolable daughter—carrying not only her grief but also a child—into their farm cart for the journey home. "Sorry about your loss. Hugh was a good'un and would have grew into a bold man. What the reverend said is right, son, but sometimes God don't smite as fast and as wide as He needs to. That's where a man has to take up the slack."

Without waiting for a response from Hawkwood, he touched his hat brim and walked away.

* * * * *

"THIS IS WHERE HE DIED," JEMMY CLENDENIN SAID, kneeling on one knee and pointing at a place on the forest floor where something had clawed through the leaves and loam and into the earth itself. "When the rain hit, this draw filled up and took him down there to the stream."

Hawkwood removed his broad-brimmed hat, the one with Emma's handmade black cockade, and held it over his breast as he knelt beside Clendenin.

Ah, Hugh. You were such a good lad—hardworking, lively, and quick-witted. I would have been so happy to claim you as my brother-in-law. I'll do as best as I can by Maggie because I know you loved her the way I love your sister. But I don't know what that will be, so if you can hear me and have a mind, I could use your help.

His eyes teared up and he blinked them rapidly. *Tell me how to fix this shitten mess I've made, because I've killed you by my actions as surely as if my hand held the knife. And I'm sorry for that, Hugh, and I will carry that debt with me forever. I wish it were me and not you in the ground, because then you and Emma would be safe and my troubles and the troubles I've caused would be at an end.*

Not wanting Clendenin to see his emotion, he rose and walked back to his horse.

"The Turnbulls did this, you know," Clendenin said. "They're talking big about it. They were never renowned for being scholars, that lot." He laughed a short, bitter laugh. "What're you going to do about them?"

Hawkwood cut a chunk of tobacco from the twist he carried in his possibles bag and stuffed it into his cheek. "Don't know. Don't even know that it matters what I do, because Hugh is still dead."

"Can't worry about the dead, Boo. 'Let the dead bury their dead.' Ain't that what your Good Book says? You got to worry about the living. That's a fine little girl you have there. It's got to be hard on her, losing her brother. You need to think about her. I can see she's blaming you for him being on the road. Hell, if she was to blame anybody, it should be Farris, right? I mean, he's alive and the boy is dead."

Hawkwood faced him. "What's your game, Jemmy? I see you with Welbourne. I see you with Patton. What do you care what I do?"

Clendenin grinned and shrugged. "My game is me, Boo. A man like me is always needed but not always wanted. You ain't like me. I'm always going to be that Irish trash what was raised by the Indians. Nobody in their right mind is going to send me back to Williamsburg or let me talk to the Virginia Council. But you? Shite, boy, you're Tuckahoe. You got a chance to be one of the big men in the Valley. You could be a Welbourne or a Lewis or even a Patton. So, I need to see if caring about you is worth it to me."

"And is it, Jemmy? Am I worth caring about?"

"Don't take this personal, Kit, 'cause I like you and you're a man I'd trust to cover my back in a fight, but I don't know. That's pretty much going to be up to you."

* * * * *

HAWKWOOD AND CLENDENIN PARTED COMPANY near the shebeen. Hawkwood had the need for neither drink nor companionship, and Rankin would be there with his cronies. The man was firmly in Emma's camp in spirit, though Hawkwood had doubt that he would actually saddle up and ride against the Turnbulls.

Maggie's father would be there too and maybe Maggie herself, and he couldn't bear the thought of seeing either of them. Dusk neared, and at a different time he would have headed home. Now he wasn't sure he had one.

Emma had changed as soon as Hugh disappeared. At first, she sulked out of sight, and when she did appear, she gave Hawkwood scant notice. He had hoped, after the kiss she'd given him on the porch, that a reconciliation was possible, but now it appeared that she was killing with cold premeditation whatever feelings she still had for him. The times they'd spent walking arm in arm and snuggling and the bouts of kissing and caressing that left them both winded seemed gone forever.

Then he came in from work in the fields and found that his belongings had been removed to the barn. He began taking meals with the Shaftos, and since that day he'd only had fleeting glimpses of Emma and nary a word had passed between them.

Unsure what else to do, he set out for Sam Farris's. He considered the man to be a friend and a mentor, and if anyone could help him through this, it would be Farris. Darkness soon fell, and he spent the night on a packed dirt floor in a none-too-clean cabin that was the abode of a young man and woman newly arrived in the Valley. Like sweet Jenny Crosslin, both were branded with a "T" on the brawn of their thumb.

Thieves, transported for life, and, more likely than not, indentured servants absconded from their masters. They might find that they'd made a damned bad bargain by running.

The next day, as Hawkwood neared the hollow that held the Farris farmstead, he could smell smoke. Not the faint trace of hearth smoke, but the stronger odor of a large fire. He checked the wind direction, and at the discovery that it was blowing from the Farris place, he kicked his horse into a gallop and primed his rifle while crouched above the saddle. He thundered down the narrow, rutted road to find their farmhouse completely ablaze. Some distance from the house, leaning against the large crimson wheels of a Conestoga wagon, were Sam and Mary Farris. They waved as he sawed his horse's reins to stop a few yards from them.

He dismounted. "Sam! What happened?"

"Nothing, Kit. We're just burning the house down."

"Why would you do that?"

"I told you before, my brother asked me to join him gunsmithing for some Pennsylvania traders. With Hugh getting killed and all, I decided that the time might be right to move. We're burning the house to collect the nails and hinges. I have to round up livestock and say a few goodbyes, then we'll be on the road in a week to ten days."

Hawkwood felt as though the breath had been knocked from him. He regarded Farris as one of the two men he could call true friends. He felt anger rising but fought it down.

"But we're friends, Sam. Why didn't you tell me? "

"I know, and I feel bad about it. But it's hard showing my face around here. Lots of folks blame me for Hugh getting killed. I know your girl does. What are you going to do?"

Hawkwood exhaled. "I don't know. I asked Welbourne for help, but he might as well have laughed in my face. I'm afraid I've lost Emma in the bargain."

"Oh, Kit." Mary touched his forearm. "You mustn't let that happen."

"Not my choice, Mary. She blames me for Hugh. Truth be told, I think she's accepted that Hugh wanted to make the trip. She just thinks I should have been with him."

"Then why?" she asked.

"Because Emma wants their hides tanned and nailed to the barn door," Sam said.

He nodded. "Yes, and—"

"Boy, there ain't no law here but you." Farris stabbed Hawkwood in the chest with a beefy forefinger. "If you don't get justice for Hugh, then there'll be none. Just keep in mind, there's no guarantee that if you try to get justice, you're going to end up anyplace but beside him."

Hawkwood nodded. He didn't want another fight over this subject. "You're right. I can see that."

But he'd go to Patton. Patton had helped him in that fight with Ned, so he had shown him some favor. These damned people were one step removed from painting themselves with woad and baying at the moon with their pride and blood feuds. He'd get justice for Hugh, and he'd get it the correct way, not *lex talionis*. He'd have them carted off to Williamsburg in chains, and he'd be there when they danced the gallows hornpipe.

Hawkwood turned to leave, then faced them again. "Sam, can I have a private word?"

Farris looked at Mary, and she stepped out of earshot.

"What happened, Sam?" he asked. "What really happened on the trail?"

Farris scowled. "I already told you and Emma. Me and Hugh were set upon by men and beaten. I don't remember anything else before waking up here."

And Hawkwood hadn't believed him then either. "You're a terrible liar, Sam. And that's to your credit. I'm guessing that lackwit Tim Turnbull was one of the men. But he's not smart enough to plan it, and he's certainly not big enough to beat either you or Hugh. Now that Robbie, he's a right turk, ain't he? He could do this. He could find a crew of bully bucks anywhere to help, because I don't think Wat knew about this, not that it matters."

Hawkwood crossed his arms. "As much as I dislike him, I don't think Ned was there either, because he wouldn't have used a knife on Hugh. He would have saved Hugh for Emma's sake. What I don't understand, Sam, is why you're alive. I mean, they killed Hugh, but the man most likely to hunt them down was you and you're here."

Farris sagged. "Robbie was the leader. Like you say, he had a half dozen hackums. They came into our camp just after dark and had us triced up before we knew what had happened. I think they just wanted to rough us up a bit, you know, take our gear and horses and scare us." He swallowed. "But Hugh was having none of it. I tried to calm him down, but then he put Robbie on his arse and Tim slipped a knife into him. Then they beat me till I was near dead. I think they were afraid two murders would be something even Welbourne couldn't overlook."

Farris sighed and stretched out his arms. "Maybe they figured I'd be ashamed and wouldn't tell. I don't know why I'm alive, Kit. All I know is that I'm glad that I am. I told you before, better a live dog than a dead lion."

Finally, the truth—and it was pretty much what Hawkwood had expected. "I understand. There was nothing you could have done. I just wish you'd have said earlier what happened."

He shrugged. "What difference would it make? Hugh would still be dead. You might be dead too, if that hellcat of yours knew for sure who did it. Hell, she'd saddle up and go after them herself. I don't know what you're going to do, but you have to decide if that girl is worth getting killed over." Farris shook his head. "And I can't give you no advice there."

* * * * *

"WHY ARE YOU HERE, KIT?" EMMA DEMANDED as she stood just off the porch, feet braced and hands on hips. "I'd thought we were shot of each other."

He slid from his horse, dropped the reins, and approached her. "Aye, you've made it clear that you're rid of me, but I'll never be rid of you."

"Shut up!" She pursed her lips as tears filled her eyes. "Don't come here trying to sweet talk your way back in. It won't work." She turned her back to him.

He put his hand on her shoulder, but she shrugged it off. He did it again, and this time her shoulder tensed but she made no move to resist his touch.

"I know who killed Hugh. I'm going to see justice done either my way or yours. I don't think your way is right or proper, but if the law won't act, then men must. I see that. I'm sorry I failed you. I'll not come here again, love. I just wanted to see you one last time to tell you I love you and that on my deathbed I'll regret losing you."

After turning away from her, he mounted his horse and urged it into a canter. It took all his willpower to keep from looking back—and to keep from crying.

Chapter Twenty-Nine

W HAT DO YOU THINK?" PATTON ASKED as he eyed
Welbourne and Preston from behind his desk in his office.
"Send him on his way, Colonel," Welbourne said.
"It's a shame that the Pettigrew boy was killed, but Hawkwood has rowed
with the Turnbulls ever since he arrived. The Turnbulls are blackguards,
for certain, but they are our blackguards. Without them, squatters would
be on our patents like a plague of locusts. My partners have subscribed
funds to make Hawkwood whole. He'll pack up and leave if you turn him
away."

Preston leaned his elbow on the sill of the open window and gazed
at Hawkwood, who paced the street in front of the county courthouse in
the gathering night, his long rifle cradled in the crook of his arm and his
hanger strapped across his back.

Hawkwood had arrived late in the afternoon, his horse lathered and
blown, and demanded an immediate audience with Patton. Patton had
just sat down to a perfectly good dinner with an attractive widow and had
already had an annoying day and did not want further annoyance. Though
he told Preston to have Hawkwood come back in the morning, the man
was having none of it.

Preston laughed.

"What's so funny, Billy?"

"Our man Kit certainly has your measure, Uncle. He quoted Luke
18: 'Though I fear not God, nor regard man; yet because this widow
troubleth me, I will avenge her, lest by her continual coming she weary
me.'"

Patton hesitated for a moment, then broke into loud laughter.

218

"Our problem, Uncle, is how do we win? Kit has a good case. There's no doubt that one or more of the Turnbull clan killed Hugh. We can't let that pass. But if we give him a writ, he's going to get killed and we'll look like fools. If we don't, everybody will say the Turnbulls are our creatures and they, acting on that perception, will simply engage in worse behavior." Preston shook his head. "Too bad. I liked Kit and had hopes that he and that Pettigrew girl would get married and improve the quality of the Valley."

"I must disagree, Mr. Preston," Welbourne said from his chair. "Hawkwood is hardly a man that will make the Valley a better place."

He grinned at him. "Why do you say that, Ran? Did you catch that little batter pudding of yours making calf eyes at him again?"

Welbourne flinched at the words.

Patton scratched his chin. "He was a lobster, right? An officer."

"Yes, he says he sold out because of personal difficulties, but I have it on good authority that he killed a man in a street brawl," Preston said. "That he's on the run makes him no different from most of the men in the county. In fact, Uncle, his story is remarkably like your Uncle John's."

Patton shrugged. "Most men out here are running from something. We'll not molest men who are leading inoffensive lives. Should we start doing that, we may all end up in chains in Williamsburg." He paused for a few moments, then nodded. "I think I know how for us to have our cake and eat it too. Get him in here."

Preston had finally summoned Hawkwood into Patton's office. Entering, he found Patton behind his desk, Welbourne in a chair, and Preston standing.

"Mr. Hawkwood, every time you show up in my town, you're in trouble and in need of something." Patton extended his hand in greeting. "I understand you wish to accuse one or more of the Turnbulls of the murder of your ward, Hugh Pettigrew—"

"Aye, sir. As Mr. Welbourne is here, I'm sure you're well aware of the situation." Hawkwood gave Welbourne the same icy stare he would give a miscreant redcoat before sending him to the halberds for a flogging. "As told him, Tim Turnbull did the killing, but Robbie set the scheme into motion. They robbed Hugh and my friend Sam Farris of their horses and belongings, including a quantity of coin I had entrusted to them, then they killed Hugh and left Sam for dead. They've bragged to half the county about their crime."

Patton nodded. "I know Sam Farris. Good man, he is."

"Sam will be a witness to that." He glanced at Welbourne to see if he knew that Farris was probably on the road to Pennsylvania by now. There was no change in his Welbourne's expression. "He'll post bond as a witness if need be."

"And you wish for me to issue you a writ of *capias* to allow you to apprehend Tim and Robbie Turnbull," Patton said.

"Yes, sir."

"What guarantee do I have that you can enforce the writ? I can't be issuing writs, will-ye-nill-ye, and not having them enforced."

Hawkwood considered that. "Sir, I don't know that I can execute the writ, but I'd like the chance to try for the sake of the law. Right now, the law is held in disrepute. No one respects it. If I raise friends and neighbors and settle these blackguards without your warrant, then I've done as much violence to the law as they have, and the authority of the Crown is further eroded." He swallowed, thinking of Emma. "I come here at great cost to myself, sir. The woman I had hoped to be my wife has rejected me because I didn't strike directly at that den of thieves and murderers. If you decline my request, sir, I will have no choice but to do it the way the Irish do. Eye for an eye. *Lex talionis*."

"That isn't necessary," Welbourne said. The flickering light of tallow candles made the splotches on his anger-mottled face stand out. "If the girl has jilted you, then leave the Valley. Take the money. Buy another commission. That is what you said you came here to do. That door is open to you."

"No, sir," Hawkwood insisted, his words flat and cold. "Your mistake was thinking I could be bought. And my mistake was thinking as much myself."

Patton waved his hand. "Enough of this bickering. This is my offer to you, Mr. Hawkwood. I'll give you your writ of *capias*."

Hawkwood couldn't suppress a grin.

"Now damme, young sir. Don't stand there looking like the cat that swallowed the canary. There's more. I want you as my constable in the Upper Valley. If you survive this adventure, then I'll expect you to serve in that capacity until I'm tired of you limping in here in need of something."

Hawkwood cradled his tricorne with his left arm and snapped to attention as if he were on parade. "Thank you, sir."

"Keep your thanks. You'll damn me to hell before this is over. Return in the morning and I'll have your writ. Then, sir, the hard part will start." He looked at Preston. "Billy, can you get Constable Hawkwood into suitable quarters for the night?"

* * * * *

PATTON WATCHED AS PRESTON AND HAWKWOOD left the room, then exhaled a heavy sigh and massaged his knees. "Well, that is done. Damme, Ran, changes in the weather cause me all manner of pains these days."

"Colonel … James," Welbourne said, "we've worked together, as friends and rivals, for nigh on ten years. I've never had cause to doubt you. Until tonight. What in the name of the Risen Christ do you think you're doing? By God, James, you're going to get him killed, and you're going to set the Turnbulls loose on us in the bargain."

"Now, Ran." Patton poured two fingers of dark Jamaica rum into a good crystal goblet. He swirled it and watched the light play on the rich amber of the liquid. "You have to admit the lad is resourceful. I mean, he'd scarcely been with your surveyors a week when he discovered your long chains. And he's a bold'un. You were there when he tangled with Ned Turnbull. Our man Clendenin tells me he learns fast and is a fair scout. He's going after Wat's clan no matter what I do. So, as he so eloquently put it, for the sake of the law, it is better that he does it with a writ than as a feud. What happens then?"

Welbourne rubbed his hand over his face. "I suppose he gets killed."

"Maybe. Or maybe he settles the Turnbull problem for us. But now he's my constable. If he gets killed, I will declare the Turnbulls rebels for killing an officer of the county court and I'll call out the militia. So, the law is upheld, and we are rid of the Turnbulls. If he lives through it, I have a man who can impose order on the Upper Valley and, if need be, raise men to fight the French and their Indians when that day comes. I like young Hawkwood and wish him well, but now he's on his own."

"You think he'll stay now that the Pettigrew girl has cut him loose?"

"He'll stay. He's smitten with the mort,"—he laughed— "and your Sarah might need some amusement on occasion, eh?"

Welbourne flushed and his lips narrowed to a livid, knife-thin line.

* * * * *

THE DAY WAS AS HOT AS THE HINGES of hell. Not the hint of a breeze stirred the syrupy air, and even the gnats had decided it was too hot to venture out into the merciless sun.

Hawkwood sat near his hobbled horse in the shade of an ancient chestnut, morose and dejected. Patton's warning was prophetic. For two days he'd haunted the dry goods stores, trading company warehouses, legal ordinaries, and illegal shebeens, trying to find hard, bold, and reckless men who would join him. He called on farmsteads too. All expressed sympathy, and some evinced interest, but in the end, none answered his call.

As he sat there, he did something he hadn't done since he'd put on long pants. He covered his face with his hands and he cried. Not the moist eyes that resulted when a favorite horse or hound had to be put down. And not the manly tears that fell when a friend or wife passed. He sobbed like a terrified child.

He cried for the man he'd killed in Ireland and for his own lost life in England. For the blind trust he'd placed in Crosslin. For Emma. For his failure to protect her. For his inability to raise men. For the utter unfairness that had driven him from a profession he loved to the wilderness west of the Blue Ridge and the heathen Irish who lived there.

Then he stopped.

"I asked for this. Now I have it. Sitting here mewling like a little girl isn't going to do anything." He stood and paced beneath the tree. "Looks like everyone was right. All I can rely on is my own strong right hand. I have my writ, so I'm acting within the law. I have a damned nice rifle. There ain't so many of them that I can't kill half of them and run the other half off. If I can't raise men, then I just won't take them head on. I clip them one at a time and put the fear of God into them."

With newfound though brittle resolve, Hawkwood led his horse from the shade of the tree and though the sweltering heat to an icy spring surrounded by a marsh of cat tails in a stand of river birch. He knelt by the pool, scooped water with cupped hands, and drank.

Suddenly, he recalled Reverend Huntsman's nasal Ulster whine, *"And the Lord said unto Gideon, by the three hundred men that lapped will I save you."* He couldn't remember the sermon, but the words made him laugh. "Well, damme, if that isn't something. I don't know if this is a sign or I'm just mad as a bloody hatter."

He washed his face, sluiced water over his head and neck, and led his horse across the field to town. While mired in self-pity, he had not noticed the bank of charcoal clouds pile up and lightning crackle over the Appalachians. Another tumultuous night awaited.

Tomorrow he would hit the trail early and head home, stopping at McDowell's place to see if he could raise a few men there. McDowell might come since Maggie was carrying Hugh's child. He wouldn't ask Rankin. The man would go, but his heart wouldn't be in it. Tom Shafto would get himself killed. But there might be a brace of timberbeasts who were spoiling for a fight. Then he'd start dropping the Turnbulls one by one until they'd had enough.

A raindrop hit the edge of his hat and shattered into spray. Another exploded against his hunting shirt. Across the meadow to the west, he could see the squall line, a shimmering indigo curtain that obscured the mountains beyond, flowing toward him. He swung into the saddle and raced the storm to safety, finding a stable moments before the storm overtook him.

Two older men sheltered inside, both wearing the loose smocks, nankeen trousers, and clogs of itinerant farm laborers. They were probably forty but could pass for half again that age. Both nodded in greeting, and the one who was sipping from a stoneware demijohn passed it to Hawkwood.

He took a slug. His eyes watered as the corn whiskey burned, but he choked it down without expression, then he reached into his possibles bag and pulled out his twist of chewing tobacco. "Chaw?" He flipped it to the man who had given him the whiskey.

The man cut a generous plug, then cut another one, a bit smaller, that he stuffed into his smock. He passed the twist to his companion, who took the rest.

"What's troubling you, *mo buachaill?*" the one with the demijohn asked. "You look like the weight of the world is on your shoulders. Nothing can be that bad."

"Nothing much." Annoyed at the intrusion into his solitude, he unbuckled the girth strap on his saddle, pulled the saddle and pad free, and looked around for a curry comb. "The woman I was to wed has jilted me. I've lost all my money. I have to revenge the death of a friend that will inevitably result in my death." He pulled the comb down his mount's withers and shoulder.

The men hooted. "That's a good one, lad. Things have got to start looking up for you."

"I need men. Hard men to help me bring some brigands to justice. Where do I find them?"

The one with the whiskey jug laughed. "All the hard men in this county are brigands. The rest of us are farmers."

Hawkwood tossed his tricorne near his saddle, untied his sweaty and untidy queue, and Welsh-combed his shoulder-length hair until it hung straight and untangled.

The two men exchanged a knowing glance. "Looks like we have

more in common than I thought, lad." The man moved his hair to reveal an ear that drooped over a rough tear.

"I don't think so." Hawkwood dropped onto the hay and rested his head on his saddle. "A bear ate mine."

Chapter Thirty

AS HAWKWOOD WATCHED, EMMA TWIRLED in the grass meadow near a spring. She smiled that wanton yet innocent smile that he'd seen on no other woman, and the sun glowed on her flawless skin as she sang *"A Blacksmith Courted Me."* Then she called his name and beckoned him—and he started awake.

Though unable to go back to sleep, he waited until an hour after dawn before heading out. He had hoped the rain would stop with the coming of day, but it continued, unrelenting. The woman who brought breakfast to the stable was surprised to find another border plus a horse there but took it in stride. The parched corn boiled in milk was bland and the appearance unappetizing, but it would stay with him for hours. He left his hostess a shilling, one of his decreasing supply, for the grain and hay his horse had consumed.

Once he'd saddled his horse, he loaded his rifle, carefully plugging the muzzle with a pine stopper and, after he had ensured the pan was empty and dry, covered the lock with an oiled leather boot. Only then did he slip on his oilskin cloak, mount, and ride out into the lukewarm deluge.

He found himself calm. *Iacta alea est*, his Latin master would have said: The die is cast. The Rubicon is crossed. Of course, his Latin master would have run outside screaming at the thought of what Hawkwood was about to undertake.

He would pay a quick visit to the place he still thought of as home to check with Shafto and Rankin to see if either knew of likely men he could enlist—and to make sure Emma was faring well. To be honest, he really wanted to see her again. Then he would skulk near the Turnbull

settlement and start potting them one by one. Ideally, he would bring
Robbie to Williamsburg and see him hanged, but he wasn't going to take
chances to achieve that desire. Robbie shot dead by the roadside was just
as satisfactory as the jinglebrains dangling from a gallows.

After about two hours riding in the downpour, the monotonous
tableau of farms, fields, and pastures gave way to forest. What a welcome
change to be riding in the shelter provided by the limbs of centuries-old
massive trees. The trail climbed very gradually, and he came upon a
Conestoga wagon occupied by a large family of Palatine Germans. The
rain had turned the road to a morass, and the wagon couldn't negotiate
the climb, so they had unharnessed the horses and taken shelter in the
wagon until the rain stopped and the trail dried.

Hawkwood dismounted.

"Terrible day to be traveling." The head of the household spoke in
accented English. He was a bulky, hard-looking man in his thirties with a
battered felt hat and unkempt chinstrap beard.

"Indeed," Hawkwood said, clearly surprising the man when he
answered in Hanoverian-accented German. He was then invited up into
the crowded wagon.

As best he could tell, it held the man and his wife, an older couple he
believed to be the wife's parents, and five children. The oldest was a girl
barely into her adolescent years, and the wife was heavily pregnant. They
had a small fire blazing under a canvas hood attached to one of the large
rear wheels, and soon he was sipping a cobalt-glazed mug of hot tea.

"We're bound for the Carolinas," the man said. "Too many of these
damned Irish moving into the Lower Valley. I only hope we make it
through the next week without being killed by the lawless dogs."

"They aren't that bad." Damme, was he defending them? What the
hell had happened to him? "They can be quite kind to a stranger in need."

The man barked a laugh. "Yes, if they don't cut your throat first."

"There are brigands on the road. Are you armed?"

He shook his head. "There is little game in the Valley and no
Indians. We had no need of a firelock. Until the Irish moved in."

When the rain eventually slackened, Hawkwood said goodbye,
climbed down from the wagon, slid on his oilskin, and untied his horse.

"Are you sure you can't travel with us?" the man asked. "We could
feed you."

Hawkwood smiled, shook his head, and nudged his horse back onto
the trail.

Within a half hour the forest ended, far too quick for Hawkwood's taste, and the road headed downhill across a river that was barely hock deep at the wagon ford. In a day or so, when the runoff from the mountains hit the river, it would be hazardous to cross, but for the time the ford was shallow and the current slow. Across the river, the road started uphill into another expanse of forest.

He was nearly to the edge of its nominal shelter from the rain when he saw the two men, backs turned to the ford, in the shelter of a spreading oak. One man, hunched over a horse's hoof he was examining, was an axe handle wide across the shoulders. His partner was lanky and wearing excellent top boots and a very nice waistcoat.

"Son of a bitch," Hawkwood muttered. "He's not going to rob me again." The lock of his rifle was dry, sheltered under both the leather boot and his oilskin. He opened his powder flask under the oilskin and primed the pan by feel, then jammed his hat down low over his eyes and continued up the road as if oblivious to the men.

The big man stood and turned. Ute Perkins, who obviously didn't recognize Hawkwood under the low-pulled hat and oilskin, smiled. "Good day, sir. Where are you bound?"

Hawkwood pulled his hat brim up. "Ute, you have to start using a different line." Movement in woods to his left caught his eye. "Tell your boys to stand down or I swear I'll kill you where you stand."

Perkins laughed. "In this rain? How are you going to do that?"

"With this perfectly dry rifle." He shifted his horse a little so Perkins could see the rifle barrel pointed at his gut, then cocked the hammer. "We've danced this dance for the last time, Ute. The colonel has made me a constable for the Upper Valley. I want you to ply your trade out of my territory."

Perkins placed his hands on his hips, threw his head back, and roared. "Well, stap me, Hoss. He made a good choice. When I saw you fight One-Eyed Ned, I said to myself that you were a bold'un, a regular Captain Hackum. How's that pretty lass doing? I heard you two were going to jump the broom. Can I dance at your wedding?"

Hawkwood gave a rueful laugh. "Her brother was murdered by the Turnbull clan, so she's not in the marrying mood right now. I'm going to try to raise a *posse comitatus*. If I can't—and I don't know that I can, truth be told—then I'm going after them myself."

Perkins whistled and shook his head. "That's a hard row to hoe, Hoss. The Turnbulls are a tough bunch."

Hawkwood shrugged. "Maybe. Maybe they're tough because no one's ever tried them. One way or another, I'm going to find out. Either you're going to see a brace of them dangling from a gallows tree or you're going to see me stretched out, toes up."

Perkins turned to his companion. "See, ye doubted me when I told you he was a right gamecock." Then he jutted his chin at Hawkwood. "Can you point that rifle somewhere else, Hoss? I don't want your horse to start and for Ute Perkins to meet an untimely end."

Hawkwood nodded and dropped the hammer to half-cock. The old laborer's observation that all the hard men in the county were brigands came to mind. What did he have to lose by asking? "If you and your lads are inclined to ride with me, I wouldn't turn you down. Not for me, mind you, and God knows not for the law, but for sake of the Pettigrew boy. I'll use whatever little influence I have with the colonel to get your slate wiped clean."

Perkins scratched his beard. "Ute Perkins on the side of the law. I could dine out on that story for the rest of my days. It'll take me some time to round up my men. Where will you be?"

"Inquire at McDowell's shebeen. Someone there'll know. They'll also know if I'm already dead, and that'll save you some trouble. By the by, Ute, there's a wagon full of Dutchers back across the river. Could you get one of your men to see them as far as the Watauga Country? Seems that they're a bit afraid of the Irish. I tried to calm them down, but they were having none of it."

Perkins and his companion laughed. "Sure thing, Hawkwood ... I mean Constable."

Hawkwood found shelter for the night at an ordinary that was shabby even by Valley Irish standards. Rather than hazard the squadrons of black cavalry—the plague of fleas, lice, and bedbugs he feared he'd find in the bedding—he spent the night in the stable with the oilskin draped over his head to ward off the rain cascading through the crude shingle roof. The rain abated in the wee hours of the morning, and he left early without waiting to eat. Surely the Turnbulls were less deadly than the ordinary's food.

As he approached the Pettigrew farm, the heavy sour smell of smoldering wood wafted on the thick, moist air. He galloped up to the wreckage, jumped from the saddle, and waded into the smoking timbers. Dread rose in his throat as he kicked at every lump of ash.

The house was half-burned, having been set afire from the inside to foil the rain beating down outside. The fire had started in the dogtrot between the boxes but had burned out before reaching the kitchen area. The cabin box that was the parlor and bedchambers had collapsed and was still smoking.

"Don't fret, Mr. Hawkwood," Shafto said from behind him. "She ain't in there. They took her."

"Who took her? The Turnbulls?"

"Some bully bucks they hired. I counted four of them. They burned the place yesterday afternoon. Told me and Patsy to mind our own business. Robbie led the pack, but none of them were his folks. It looked like Robbie gave her to them. You know, like she was a present or something."

"Where'd they go?"

"South, toward Watauga, I imagine. That's where you'd hire men like that. What're you going to do?"

"Being the damned fool that I am, Tom, I'm going to bring her back. In two days' time, check for me at McDowell's shebeen. Some hard men from up the Valley should show up around then to help me out. They're led by a man named Ute Perkins. Heard of him?"

Shafto nodded, his mouth agape.

"Tell Ute that if I'm not back in three days, I'm not coming back. Tell him what you know and that I'd be forever grateful if he took revenge on my behalf. Not for me. For Hugh and Emma. Understand?"

Hawkwood, trailed by Shafto, went into the unburned half of the house, which still reeked of wet smoke and ashes. "Did they take my baggage?"

"No, sir," Shafto said. "It's still in the barn where you … you know… when Miss Emma … ah…"

"You can say it, Tom. When she threw me out."

He looked around the place with Shafto in tow. Though the one half of the house had been heavily damaged, the kitchen was largely untouched. Some of the food had been taken, but otherwise it had been neither damaged nor plundered. "Tom, could I trouble you to move everything you can down to your place?" he asked. "I don't want scavengers coming in here. Help yourself to the food but keep the rest secure for Miss Emma. She'll be needing it. I'd be grateful if you stuck around to help her rebuild. Can you do that?"

Shafto nodded. "Aye, sir, I will. You can count on me."

In the barn were his bags from his first trip to the Valley, what seemed like years ago. He opened an oxhide valise onto the straw-strewn floor and unbuckled the straps. Inside were his regimentals. He pulled out his crimson silk officer's sash, unfolded it, and combed the tassels with his fingers, then slid it over his right shoulder so the knot rested on his left hip. Next, he fastened his silver gorget about his neck and finally slung his hanger over his back, so the hilt poked above his left shoulder.

He waved goodbye to Shafto, mounted his horse, and picked up the trail the raiders had left with ease. In the rain they'd carved a muddy gash across the wheat field, heading south and west, striking for the Seneca Trail. The tracks indicated they weren't in any great hurry. He was outnumbered four to one, but they weren't moving fast or expecting pursuit. He should be able to take them if he played it smart.

Hawkwood used every trick Clendenin had mentioned in their campfire conversations to close the distance without being seen. He galloped up hills, stopped just short of the crest, and crept forward, standing in his stirrups, until he could see the downslope and the next rise. Where his quarry had meandered around high ground, he found several opportunities to anticipate their path, cut cross country, and lop off distance. The first night he pressed on until darkness obscured the spoor.

He sat awake most of the night and gave a silent prayer of thanksgiving when the rain ceased in the early hours of the new day. Breakfast was a palmful of parched corn washed down with water, and before dawn he was moving again, trotting at a pace that conserved his strength but chewed up the distance while he led his horse. At the twilight of false dawn, he swung into the saddle and settled in for another day in pursuit—a day that should bring the matter to a close. He'd gained on his prey, and as long as they didn't know he was behind them, he should run onto them around noon.

He'd been in the saddle scarcely an hour when he came across the remnants of their camp. Trampled grass where horses had grazed—they'd hobbled the horses rather than picketing them or tying them, further evidence that they thought they were safe. Embers still glowed in the campfire, and grass was flattened where they had slept. Hawkwood counted five spots, and one of them, he assumed Emma's, was near a small tree where the bark had been chaffed by a rope.

He knelt and placed his hand on her sleeping place. "Hold on, sweetling. Just a few more hours."

Hawkwood could see where they were going to cut the Seneca Trail in less than a mile and made the decision to try to get in front of them rather than take them from behind. He raked the horse with his heels and cantered due south. After about three miles, he climbed a gentle ridge and reined his horse to a stop.

"My God. I've never seen the like of that."

Off to his left, soaring above a thickly wooded river bottom, was a majestic natural stone arch. It soared, easily two hundred feet in the air, above the smallish river that had scored the tunnel through it and was at least a hundred feet long and just as wide. The dark line of the Seneca Trail wound from the north, crossing the tawny striated stone face of the arch.

He sheltered his eyes from the sun peeking over the Blue Ridge and scanned the trail back to the north. All the while, he damned the Tuckahoe constable who had taken his spyglass along with his coat.

There. In the faint mist of a saddle between two hillocks was a tight knot of riders.

Chapter Thirty-One

H AWKWOOD SQUINTED AND WILLED the image closer. Two of the riders merged into one figure. He guessed them to be Emma and the man managing her horse. The other three didn't seem to be in any identifiable formation.

"I can hit them right here," he muttered. "They might turn back north, but if I were a Carolina brigand, I'd spur my horse and head across that arch." That settled it. If they got past him, it would be a long chase against men who were on guard. And if he pressed them too hard, they might kill Emma.

He slid beneath the skyline and sprinted back to his horse, then mounted and drove the mare down toward the riverbed. They dodged and jumped their way through a boulder field, sparks flying as her iron shoes struck thin-sodded slabs of stone. About fifty yards from the river, the open meadow gave way to dense undergrowth. Hawkwood dismounted and kicked and pushed his way through.

Greenbriers clawed at his bare thighs, tore at his hunting shirt, and ripped his hat away. At one point he was caught by his hair, but he freed himself by grabbing his hair close to the scalp and jerking his head to one side. He buried his eyes in the crook of his arm to protect them from the thorns, lowered his head, and churned his legs. His weight, strength, and determination overcame the briers, and he broke through that barrier into the dense forest.

Hauling his horse behind him by the reins, he plunged downhill. The hillside was steep and his mount tried to balk, but momentum carried them both forward, the horse with rigid front legs and sliding on its haunches. Their slide ended above a low cliff that overhung the river. He did a quick visual check of the extent of the cliff, spotted a shallow reentrant intersecting the river, and led the horse in that direction. They splashed through the hip-deep water, clambered up the far bank, and fought their way through brush and brambles climbing out of the riverbed.

As soon as he was in the open field above the river, he vaulted into the saddle, breathing heavily, and forced his tired mount into a gallop.

The Seneca Trail paralleled the riverbed for a distance on the north side, hooked sharply south, disappeared into the forest that grew atop the limestone bridge, and reappeared on the south side of the arch. Hawkwood picked his ground in a wooded copse about a hundred yards from where the trail emerged from the forest growing on the arch. On either side was the steep and fatal drop to the river below. He could stop them here, or, if things went bad, force them to flee back north. After tying his horse in the forest, he loaded his rifle and crawled until he reached a firing position.

The group was now only a furlong off, ambling down the trail headed for the limestone causeway. His heart thudded, driving his blood to kettledrum intensity in his ears. His mouth was parched. Into his cheek he stuffed three musket balls for rapid reload and sucked on them until he could spit. Focusing on picking briars from his hands and legs helped calm him.

The first man came into view, small and looking as though he'd been cobbled together from stray bits of rawhide rope. A larger man with white-blond hair falling loose about his shoulders trailed him by a few feet. Behind him was a middling man, wearing a cast-off red coat with blue facings, who held the reins of Emma's horse. The last man wore a butternut hunting shirt and leggings that marked him as a true backcountryman.

The sight of Emma thrilled Hawkwood. She may have been captive, but she was unconquered. When the two of them had rode together on the farm, she hiked her skirt and shift up to her hips. Now she had her skirts tucked tightly about her legs, covering herself from just below her knees. She was angry, and her mouth moved in staccato bursts.

"Giving them hell, are we?" he muttered. "I've been on the receiving end of that volley fire before. I may be doing this bunch a favor by killing them." By her mannerisms, she was alert, tense, and looking for the chance to escape.

Hawkwood sighted on the lead man. He supposed he should call on them to surrender, but the hell with that. If they couldn't take a joke, then they shouldn't have hired on with the Turnbulls. He cocked the hammer, pulled the set trigger, placed the sight on the bridge of the first man's nose, and touched the firing trigger. The ball blew through his face, exploding from the back of his head in an eruption of pinkish froth.

Hawkwood jumped to his feet and rushed into the clearing. "Emma!" he bellowed. "To me!"

She grasped her horse's mane and dug in her heels. The horse bolted forward, dragging the reins from the grip of the man leading it, then thundered past the corpse of the leading man and raced toward Hawkwood.

Hawkwood poured powder down the barrel, spat in an unpatched ball, slapped the butt on the ground to seat the ball, primed the pan, and took aim at the men behind Emma. "Hold you, men!" he yelled. "In the name of the king, drop your firelocks and climb down off your horses! Don't try to run! My men are right behind you!"

Emma pulled up beside him in a shower of mud divots, jumped from the saddle, and ran to him. "Kit! How—"

"Never mind. Just take my knife and free yourself." He looked at her, daring to take his eyes off the men for a moment, and gave her a smile and a wink. "My horse is tied on the far side of this wood. Go there. We may have to run for it."

She pulled the knife from his belt and ran away behind him, leading her horse.

"Eh, fuck off, you!" came the reply. One of them fired at him, but the ball, aimed from the back of an unsteady horse, didn't come near.

"Is that your answer?" Hawkwood shouted back and sighted on the big blond-haired man. The ball wasn't patched and the sights wouldn't be accurate, so he aimed at center of his chest and pulled the trigger. The man howled in pain as the ball struck his inner thigh, a scant couple of inches from his nutmegs. The ball passed through his leg and into his horse, which took two steps sideways and collapsed.

Hawkwood reloaded the rifle, this time using the ramrod on a patched ball. "Last chance, boys! I'll kill every goddam one of you if you don't do as I say."

They hesitated, then the man who had been leading Emma's horse slid from his saddle and laid his musket on the ground.

"Emma! I need your help!"

Hawkwood ordered the men to lay face down on the road and approached them with rifle at the ready. Emma ran in and took their muskets. He glared at all of them. "Men. You burned my house. You took my woman. I never did you a wrong. In fact, I don't know you from Adam. But I am an Augusta County constable. Yeah?" He gestured at a massive maple with a thick, low-slung limb. "And I am inclined to hang the three of you from yon tree."

They all babbled apologies and excuses. Need of money. Wife and babes at home. Drink and bad company.

"Shut up," he growled. "The lot of you just shut your gobs. As a one-time favor, because you didn't harm this lass, I'm letting you men go home. Yeah? Go home and tell your friends and neighbors that if they want to ply their hedge-bird ways in my county, if they want to play moss-trooper around my people, I swear by the Great Jehovah that I will hunt them down and burn their houses about their ears. Yeah? Understand?"

The all nodded their silent assent.

"You can go. Take that mewling bully-huff"—he jabbed his rifle at the wounded man— "with you."

The man in the red coat reached for the reins of his horse.

Hawkwood held up his hand. "You can go. Your horses and firelocks stay with me." When the man started to protest, Hawkwood cut him off. "You're alive. If I take you to Williamsburg, you'll hang. Hell, my people may hang you before you get to Williamsburg."

"Just a second, Kit," Emma said. "I have need of something." She pointed a musket at the man in hunting shirt. "You, doff your clothes."

He hesitated.

"Now!"

When he was stark naked, standing in the road with his hands covering his privates, Emma took his clothes. Then the two able men, one of them without a stitch of clothing, supported their compatriot as they started down the long road toward the Carolinas.

She grabbed his arm with both of hers and nestled her head against the point of his shoulder. "You were a grand sight, Kit. Maybe not as grand as the first time I laid eyes on you, but grand nonetheless."

* * * * *

HAWKWOOD AND EMMA RODE HARD, heading home. Hardly a word passed between them. When they camped for the evening, she changed from her skirts into the clothes she'd taken from one of her captors.

"What's this about being a constable?" she asked as she sat close by him at the fire.

She listened as he filled her in on the happenings, then grinned. "I'm proud of you. And I'm not letting you out of my sight ever again." After wrapping her arms around his neck, she pulled his face down to hers for a deep, languorous kiss.

He drew back. "Wait. Wait. Last we saw one another; you didn't want to see me again and you blamed me for Hugh."

She kept her arms about his neck and pressed her head against his chest. "Aye. But I see now that he was a man and had the right to make a man's choice. Hugh died as a bold man should—on his feet and facing his enemies. I had no right to blame you for his death." She moved her head so she could look at him. "I've had time to think since you've been gone. You infuriate me, Kit Hawkwood. You are stubborn and unreasonable. You make me fit to chew nails. And you say the wrong thing at the worst time. But you are so kind and gentle, and you show up to rescue me when you had no reason."

He kissed her on the forehead. "You know you promised to marry me, and I intend to hold you to that."

She pulled away. "After all that has happened, I doubt that you will want me for your wife."

He closed his eyes and stroked her hair. "That's silliness talking. Why would I ever not want you to be my wife? The fight we had is behind us."

Her lower lip trembled, and tears welled in her eyes, then she turned away from him. "Ah, Kit, I should have told you long ago. That day the Turnbulls came calling, the day you had your first fight with Ned ... well, they raped me. Tim, and Robbie, and God knows who else. They took me in my bed. They spread my legs, and they rooted around inside me. I stopped any git they may have sired on me, and I swore to go on with my life and forget and not live in fear."

Tears streamed down her cheeks when she faced him. "Do you know that I've slept every night since then on the floor of my bedchamber? That I can't touch the bed without seeing one or the other of them grunting and snorting like hogs. Now they've killed Hugh and they're still walking about without a care in the world."

"Oh, my God," he whispered, holding his face in both hands. Images flashed of Emma naked under a blanket on the porch, Granny Nixon's unexplained visit, and the snide remarks by Wat and the others. "I was so fucking blind."

"I'm sure they've told half the county by now. I understand if you no longer want me."

He wrapped her in his arms, burying his face in her hair so she wouldn't see his tears. "I thought my heart would break when you sent me away."

"Aye. Mine as well." Her nails played over the ridges of scars on his back.

"Tomorrow we'll be home. The Shaftos are still at the farm. You can stay with them until this is finished. Never fear about vengeance for Hugh. I have men meeting me at the shebeen, and we're going for the murdering blackguards who killed Hugh and hurt you."

Emma shook her head. "No. They've taken a lot from me. They took my maidenhead. They killed my brother. They burned my home. This is my fight as much as yours. I can ride and I can shoot. You'll need every man or woman who can do that. We're a threefold cord—you and me and our love. The Bible tells us 'a threefold cord is not quickly broken.'"

Hawkwood broke off a stalk of grass, twisted it into a ring-sized loop, and took her hand. "I, Christopher, take thee Emma to my wedded wife, to have and to hold from this day forward ..."

She placed her hand on his cheek. "For better for worse, for richer for poorer, in sickness and in health, to love and to cherish, till death us do part."

He slid the grass loop over her ring finger. "With this ring I thee wed, with my body I thee worship, and with all my worldly goods I thee endow." He kissed her.

She responded in kind, placed her hands on his shoulders, and pushed him to the ground. After throwing one long leg over his hips, she sat astride him looking down. "You'll recall," she said, doffing her shirt, "that I did prophesy that this would be yours."

Chapter Thirty-Two

HAWKWOOD AND EMMA DISMOUNTED JUST outside McDowell's shebeen. A dozen or more men were gathered about the fire in the early evening gloom. He recognized Rankin, who avoided his gaze, and a couple of Rankin's cronies. Also, there were some backcountrymen and a couple of Scots who ran pack horse trains carrying deer pelts one way and trade goods the other into Cherokee country.

While Hawkwood's sash and gorget caused some comment, Emma's clothing created a stir. Though dressed in a hunting shirt, leggings, and a kerchief like he was, no one mistook her for anything but a woman. She'd made a broad sash belt from a length of blue checkered cloth and tied it tight about her waist, accentuating the curve of her hips and the fullness of her breasts.

McDowell emerged from the gloom of the shebeen, wiping his hands on a soiled towel. "Hello, Hawkwood. Glad to see the lass is safe, but you can't bring her in here."

Hawkwood ignored him. "I'm here for men. I'm a constable for Augusta County, and I bear a writ from the county court to bring Robbie and Tim Turnbull to account for the murder of Hugh Pettigrew. Who'll ride with me?"

All conversation ceased.

"Come on, Hawkwood," McDowell said in a low voice. "Emma shouldn't be here."

"Your daughter is carrying Hugh's bairn. You should be thinking about saddling up and killing the sons of bitches who murdered your grandchild's father."

The men about the fire stirred sheepishly.

Hawkwood looked around at all of them. "So, the only man who'll ride with me is the girl?"

"Bugger off, Hawkwood," a rough voice said. "Take your jade with you."

He turned to face Tim Turnbull, accompanied by three strangers, and smiled. "Just the man I was looking for."

"What are you grinning about? You're done in this Valley. If you're lucky, you won't end up with a knife in your guts too."

"I'm grinning because I have you, Tim."

"Do you now?" He turned to the men at the fire. "I can recommend the mort. She's not much to look at, but once you're in her mutton, she's a damned fine romp."

No one in the shebeen made a move or a sound.

Hawkwood took a step and backhanded Tim across the mouth. One of his men moved to his assistance, and a flash split the dusk gloom with a booming report. The twilight air filled with gray smoke and the smell of sulphur, and the crowd that had gathered to watch the imminent fight scattered like a covey of quail. Emma's shot, a ball topped with three buckshot, had furrowed the ground at the man's feet. After dropping her musket, she grabbed Hawkwood's rifle from his horse and cocked it.

"I'll kill the next man that moves." She said, "In case you don't know, my man killed a bear with his hands. He fought One-Eyed Ned to a standstill and still has both his toplights. If you take another step, them what I don't kill, he will do for."

They made no motion to move, and the men who'd scattered from the fire gathered and conversation hummed.

"Why'd you kill the boy, Tim?" Hawkwood asked.

Tim spat a gob of blood and saliva and lunged at Hawkwood. Hawkwood stepped inside the roundhouse punch, grabbed his shirt with both hands, and gave him a ferocious head butt in the nose. The sound of the bone breaking and cartilage tearing seemed as loud as the gunshot. Hawkwood tossed him to the ground like a sack of meal and stepped on his throat, then reached over his left shoulder and grasped the hilt of his hanger. It sighed as it was drawn from its scabbard and then flickered in the twilight. The blade stopped with the point on Tim's abdomen, just below the navel.

"You know that Hugh probably lived a day or more after you stuck him? A fine lad." He looked around at the men. "The father of Maggie McDowell's bairn." Then he faced Tim, who seemed to only barely comprehend what had happened to him. "Lying in the wastelands, alone, the pain eating at him. There was no call for that, Tim. You had no quarrel with him. You had no quarrel with Sam Farris when you and your boys beat him nearly to death. You're going to hell, but you're going to get a taste of it before you leave this world."

Tim howled and squirmed as Hawkwood's foot pressed down hard on his neck. He grabbed his leg with both hands and fought to remove the weight from his throat, but Hawkwood didn't relent.

Emma grabbed Tim's ankles and pinned them down with her knees. "Hey, Tim. How does it feel to have someone spread your legs?"

Hawkwood lifted the hanger and pointed it at the men Tim had brought with him. "Don't you boys move! Don't even breathe. This is between me and Tim. You can stay and watch, or you can mount up and clear out. But if you try to interfere, you're dead men." He glanced at Emma. "Can you do this?"

She swallowed hard and nodded.

He placed the point back on Tim's belly and leaned his weight on it. The steel hesitated for a moment, then slid without resistance through Tim's guts and out his back. For a second or two, Tim let out an animal-like screeching keen. Emma released his ankles as Hawkwood pulled the hanger free and stepped back. Tim coiled and writhed like a worm on a hot griddle.

Hawkwood pointed the bloody hanger at Tim's men. "You go tell Wat and Ned and the rest of that bunch that I'm coming after them with a writ and I'm bringing fire and sword. Tell them Tim died like a dog and I expect they'll do the same. I have no quarrel with you men. But if you're with Wat when I get there, I'll kill you without mercy. Now go."

Tim howled, tried to stand, and fell at the edge of the fire. His shirt flamed up, and he bawled again as he rolled away from the fire.

The men in the crowd glanced at each other, unsettled. They probably wouldn't take too much more of this. There was a fine line between being hard and being cruel. Hawkwood didn't want to overstep that line and lose their respect.

He stepped on Tim's ear to pin his head to the ground and drove the sword through the screaming, thrashing man's throat. Blood jetted onto the dirt, and Tim shook and fell silent. Emma pressed his rifle into his hands.

Hawkwood turned to McDowell. "Can the lass stay now?"

McDowell nodded. "Aye, she can. Let me go get my firelock and possibles bag and tell Maggie what I'm up to."

The men moved into the firelight, some to look at Tim's bloodless corpse and others to congratulate Hawkwood.

"Men, I'm calling on you one last time to ride with me to rid the country of the Turnbulls and to avenge the murder of one of our own. My woman and I will ride alone if need be. If you're inclined to ride, we rondy at the Pettigrew place tomorrow no later than midday."

When he turned from the crowd, he was face-to-face with Ute Perkins and eight men.

"That was quite a show, Hoss," Perkins said. "You are indeed a man of many parts."

* * * * *

WHEN HAWKWOOD CHECKED THE SUN, it hung directly overhead.

"I guess we're all there is," Ute said, leaning on forearms crossed on his pommel.

"I suppose so." Hawkwood sized up the small group mustered at the Pettigrew farm. He and Emma. Ute and his men. And McDowell. Shafto had wanted to ride, using one of the horses and muskets Hawkwood had taken when rescuing Emma, but Hawkwood told him no. Someone had to stay at the farm, and Shafto's inexperience with firearms made him of little use and put him as risk. Rankin wasn't anywhere to be seen, not surprising since he wasn't a fighter. "Last night I thought I had every man-jack of them. I would have sworn they would all ride with me."

"Last night you did. Dawn is always different," said Ute. "Are we still going? We should be even-matched. But if those Carolina boys didn't scare off, they'll sure outnumber us."

Hawkwood squirted a stream of tobacco juice from the corner of his mouth and wiped his lips with a drag of his shirt sleeve. "We're in it. Yeah? Men, we don't have as many as I'd hoped, so if any of you want to leave, there's no hard feelings."

No one moved.

He swung into the saddle. "Let's go and get this done then."

A hundred yards from the house, a gunshot came from behind them. Hawkwood wheeled his horse about to face the threat, but it was Clendenin, his horse nearly blown and foaming with sweat.

He thundered to a halt at Hawkwood's side. "They say you're going to do for the Turnbulls. Is that right?"

"Sure is."

He nodded. "Well, Boo, I guess you need all the help you can get."

As they plodded to the south and the Turnbull settlement, they met more men. The Scots traders and their drovers were waiting on the road and fell in without saying a word. Every few minutes, a new man would either ride up hard on the rear of the group or be found sitting astride his horse at trail side, waiting for them to pass.

"You see, Hoss," Perkins said. "You need to believe before you can make it happen. Just like Peter walking on the stormy seas."

Hawkwood glanced at him. "Only problem with that … is when you look down and realize you're trying to walk on water."

The last man to join them was Sam Farris. He caught up from the rear, riding an exhausted horse.

Hawkwood could hardly believe it. "Sam. Why are you here? I thought you were on the road to Pennsylvania."

"Mary's on the road to Pennsylvania," he said, leading his horse by the halter. "I'll catch up with her when this is finished. I owe it to Hugh. And I owe it to you, and to myself, to see this through."

"I thought it was better to be a live dog than a dead lion."

Farris shrugged. "True that. But nothing wrong with being a live lion, is there?"

As they rode, Clendenin ranged ahead scouting. In late afternoon, the group found him holding his horse and standing in the middle of the trail.

"Man up ahead, coming this way," he said. "He ain't paying much attention."

Hawkwood's men sought concealment in the brush on both sides of the trail. A young man, barely out of his adolescent years and dressed in nankeen trousers over Hessian boots and dirty linen smock, rode into view.

Emma gasped. "He's one of them." She flushed and cocked her musket.

At the click of the hammer, the man hesitated, then his eyes widened. Panicked, he sawed at the reins to turn his horse about. One of Perkins's men was on him in a flash, grabbing the reins with one hand and hauling him from the saddle with the other. Perkins pulled him to his feet as Emma rushed from cover with her musket pointed at him.

Clendenin caught up with her, pushed her musket barrel toward the ground, and looked the man square in the eye. "Well, little Willie Turnbull. What brings you out this way?"

The color drained from his face as his Adam's apple pulsed spasmodically.

Hawkwood pulled Emma to one side. "Was he one of the ones who

…" He couldn't finish.

She nodded. "He was one of them."

Hawkwood was very conscious that all eyes were on him. He knew they would be judging his next actions. He was at a crossroads. He could enforce the law and sent the Turnbull boy to Williamsburg for trial. Or he could be the law and finish the matter himself. Much to his surprise the decision was very easy.

"Ute. Get one of your men to throw a halter over yon limb."

"Aye." Perkins pointed to one of his men.

Hawkwood turned to the rest of the men. "If anyone has an objection, you're welcome to leave now. I'll not make any man have a part in this against his will." He surveyed their faces—lips tight and jaws set, with unswerving and relentless justice in their gaze. "Yeah? Then get him up."

The Turnbull boy was forced onto his horse, the noose was slipped over his head and tightened, and then the horse whipped out from under him. Whether stubborn to the end or struck dumb with terror, Willie Turnbull died without speaking a word.

It was nearly dusk when they reached the Turnbull compound. Hawkwood's throat tightened as he recognized the area where he and Hugh had bickered over their abortive raid. Horses were tied in a stand of trees, and one of Perkins's men, an older man with one dead eye, was left in charge of them. He claimed he was better with horses than with a musket and tried, only half in jest, to cajole Emma into staying with him.

When everyone was in position, Hawkwood mounted and rode down to the settlement.

"Wat! Ned! Robbie! I've come for you. Either come out or send your women and children out."

Chapter Thirty-Three

WAT TURNBULL, WEARING THE ONLY SET of clothes Hawkwood had ever seen him wear, walked out of his cabin. He approached with the confidence of a man who had faced down many problems in his life and who knew this one would be no exception. Hawkwood dismounted to talk to him.

"Constable Hawkwood," Turnbull said. "I do have that right, don't I? And that is a bonny sash you're wearing. I heard tell you was a lobster. What do you want with me and my sons? You've already killed one of them with no cause."

"Two, Wat. I've killed two. I hanged Willie not two miles down the road."

The old man's eyes bugged and his shoulders sagged.

"I'm here to take the three of you to Williamsburg, and I intend to see you hang. Or I can kill you here. I don't much care anymore."

"Thanks for the offer, Constable, but I'll take my chances here."

Hawkwood recognized that this was not the Wat Turnbull who had terrorized the Valley, he wasn't the same man who had led the attack on the Pettigrew farmstead. He was a beaten man, trying to play it game until the end. He was still dangerous, but he was scared and looking for a way out.

"It's your choice, Wat. Send your women and children out. No reason to get them hurt."

"I'll think about it."

Hawkwood posted a few men to prevent anyone from escaping from the settlement, and Perkins took on the task of rounding up the Turnbull horses. "The quicker we get stuck into this, the quicker we get it over with," he told them. "I know a lot of you have done a bit of fighting, but this is different from skirmishing. If we're careful about it, none of us need be hurt. We're going to take one cabin at a time. Jemmy, I want you to pick three or four marksmen who can keep the area between the cabins swept clean. We can't have them concentrating in the big cabin. Take my rifle. I'm not going to need it. I need a couple of men to clear the cabins with me. It'll be close work. If you can't use a blade, you don't want this."

"I'll go with you, Mr. Hawkwood," Shafto said.

Hawkwood turned. "Tom, what in the name of God are you doing here?"

"Trying to be a man for once in my life. I don't have a firelock, but I brought my mallet."

Two other men stepped forward, both backcountrymen with tomahawks and hunting knives.

"Sam, you control the shooting. Keep a steady fire going at them. Even if they aren't firing at you, keep shot going through the windows and doors." Hawkwood drew his hanger. "Emma, stay near Sam. Please. Shoot or reload for one of the men, but just don't follow me."

She nodded, but her eyes and the set of her mouth told him she was just avoiding an argument.

He pulled her close and kissed her. "Dammit, don't follow me."

When Farris fired the first shot, Hawkwood and his men sprinted to the nearest cabin at a blind corner. Like so much else about the Turnbull place, the arrangement of the cabins was a slapdash affair influenced by their own native slovenliness and the fact that they didn't have to worry that their settlement would be attacked. His chest was heaving when he threw himself against the wall. The door and single window opened facing another cabin. He heard digging, and a hole appeared in the clay chinking between two logs. Hawkwood braced himself and lunged, running his sword in through the hole. Screams filled the cabin as he withdrew the blood-wetted blade.

"Down through the roof!" he ordered.

One of the men boosted Shafto onto the low shingle roof. Shafto ripped away a yard-square opening and dropped into the cabin. The other three followed him up over the eave and inside. By the time Hawkwood got in the cabin, the fight was over. His thrust had wounded the only combatant in the house, and Shafto had finished him off with a quick stroke of the mallet.

As the men pushed aside the lower courses of shingles, opening the back roof and waving the marksmen forward, Hawkwood dealt with the stick-thin woman in a dirty shift who was crying over the body of the dead man. Four young children cowered in the corner. "Madam." He shook her by the shoulder. "Take your young'uns and leave. There'll be hot work here in a few minutes."

She looked at him with a bland, trusting expression, then enfolded her children in her arms and led them out of the cabin.

The bark of muskets sounded outside as Clendenin's men pinned people inside their cabins and the Turnbulls and their men returned fire. Hawkwood peeked around the door jamb and saw a steady trickle of women and children running from the cabins and toward the woods.

Hawkwood's men crouched behind the wall, and he pointed out their next objective—a lean-to with the open side facing them. He had one of Farris's men shoot through the deer pelt curtain to draw a reaction, then the four of them raced across the open space without even a single ball directed at them. Hawkwood pushed his way through the gap between a wall and the deerskins with his hanger at the ready.

A musket discharged.

The flash blinded him, and his ears thrummed, and a hot sulphurous blast passed him. He flung himself, hacking with his sword, in the direction of the shot. His blade hit the pine log wall and rebounded, so he punched using the handguard as brass knuckles. He connected with someone in the dark, and a woman shrieked. At that moment the skin curtain tore away, revealing only a dirty young woman and her baby in the lean-to. His stomach knotted and churned as the image of the Serb villages his Grenzers had rampaged through flashed before him. He'd nearly killed her.

"Get up! Grab your babe and get out! You men! Start knocking the chink from between those logs."

By dusk the outer cabins were secured. After Hawkwood had stormed two of them, the men in the outlying cabins retreated to Wat Turnbull's larger cabin, undeterred by the rifle fire directed at them, and sent their families fleeing to the woods. Leaving half a dozen men in place to guard against any attempt by the Turnbulls to break out, Hawkwood gathered his men at the lean-to. They built a bonfire of shingles near the open side and waited for dawn.

"Why don't we just burn them out?" Clendenin asked.

Hawkwood shook his head. "There are probably women and children in there. I don't want to be a party to that. They don't have water and but damned little food. They'll come out."

"Why're you squeamish about burning 'em? We hanged one of them boys on the way over here, and you gutted another one last evening."

"That's different. They were grown men. They had it coming."

"Nits make lice, Boo. You let them women and kids run away, those kids are going to grow up and come back looking for you."

"That's a chance we've got to take," Emma said. "We can't be killing folks that don't have any say in their predicament."

The men murmured their assent.

Clendenin shook his head. "Don't say I didn't warn you, Boo. Don't ever say I didn't warn you."

A horse approached, and Welbourne emerged from the darkness into the firelight. He alighted and looked around at them. "You boys need to go home. I can handle it from here on. There's no need for more bloodshed."

Hawkwood towered over the rotund little man, who untied the scarf that kept his hat and periwig secure on his head while on horseback. "We'll go home when we're done."

"You are done, Hawkwood." Welbourne flushed with anger. "You've done enough damage already. I know you're trying to impress your private mutton—"

"Would I be that private mutton, sir?" Emma asked.

He spun toward her. "My God, man. You have the girl out here too?"

Hawkwood grinned. "I've discovered that when she puts her mind to something, there is damn all you can do to change it. I'll make a bargain with you. None of my boys have been hurt yet, and I'd like to keep it that way. You tell them to send out Robbie, and if they do that, then Ned and Wat and the rest can go. Otherwise, we're just going to wait until they have to come out and shoot them down like dogs."

"Be reasonable, men. You know the Turnbulls, and I'll allow they can be a rough bunch, but if the French and their Indians come, you'll be glad they're here. And who else is going to keep squatters off the land?"

"French and Indians ain't here," McDowell growled. "Neither is the father of my grandchild."

"Only man that cares about squatters is the man who claims to own the land," Farris added, taking a nip from a whiskey jar and passing it to the man next to him. "You call them squatters. I call them neighbors. Hawkwood ain't the only man here with a reason. They beat me near to death and killed a good man."

Perkins stepped out of the shadows, and Welbourne's eyes widened.

"I think it would be best if you mounted up and went out the way you came in."

Welbourne faced Hawkwood. "Does the colonel know you have this rascal among your men?"

"I didn't ask him." Hawkwood shrugged. "And he didn't say anything about it. Take Mr. Perkins's advice. Head on back home and check on your wife. She may be lonely. Or not."

Welbourne huffed and mounted his horse. Rather than retying his scarf, he removed his hat and wig and tucked them under his arm. "You'll regret this. All of you will. But you, Hawkwood, you will regret this most of all."

"It's possible, I'll warrant," someone said from in the darkness." But it won't be a big regret."

Rankin. The old man approached Hawkwood like a cur expecting a kick. "I'm here. And I'm ready to help if you'll have me."

Emma threw her arms around him and snuggled her head into his chest. "Mr. Rankin, you are about all the family I have left. Of course, we'll have you."

* * * * *

DAWN BROKE, AND THE MEN who had been sleeping stirred and stretched. By habit, Emma had risen well before dawn, built the fire up, and boiled a kettle of parched corn into mush with spring water instead of milk. One of the Scots contributed enough tea leaves for everyone to have a small cupful.

"She's a keeper," Perkins murmured to Hawkwood.

Hawkwood stood and addressed the men. "The sooner we're started, the sooner we're done. Yeah?"

A low, rumbling chuckle ran through the group like a distant thunderhead.

He walked toward the main Turnbull house, hands over his head and holding a white kerchief on a stick. "Wat!" he shouted. "Come out. I want a parley."

The door opened, and Ned came out carrying a musket. "Come to surrender, did you?" He laughed.

"Where's the old man, Ned?"

"Gone. He put on a dress and ran away with the women yesterday."

He should've seen that coming. "I should've known Hairless Wat wasn't going to wait for the hammer to fall."

"The old man's a survivor. Someone's going to have to knock him in the head on Judgment Day. You know I didn't have nothing to do with what happened to Emma, don't you?"

"You could've stopped it, Ned, and you didn't."

"True that. A man lives long enough and he does things he regrets. I don't know that I could've stopped it, but I didn't try." He gave a wry laugh. "Shame is, I've been sweet on her since the first day I laid eyes on her. I know I didn't mean nothing to her, but I never wanted anything to happen to her. I'm not asking for quarter, you understand, just that, man to man, I want you to know I wouldn't do anything to hurt that girl."

"And Hugh?"

"I think you figured that out. Robbie made the plan, and Tim, being the cod's head he is … was … got out of control. They didn't intend to kill the boy. It just happened. I know that don't matter none, but it's a fact."

"You got women and children in there?" Hawkwood asked.

"Yep."

"I think there's been enough killing in the main. The only business I have is with Robbie and men who raped Emma. You give them to and you can take the other men, the women, and children and walk out of here. I'll let the boys who were there when Hugh was killed go too. Go to Carolina. Go to Pennsylvania. I don't care. Just get out of the Valley, and don't let any of your people come back. Can you do that?"

Hawkwood took a step closer. "This ain't you asking for quarter. This is me saying I don't have business with you. I don't hold these against you." He indicated the livid scars running from the corners of his eyes down alongside his nose. "And there's no reason for any more of these bairns to grow up without fathers than there already are. I'm looking for justice, Ned, not vengeance."

Ned shook his head. "I can't give them to you."

"You'll think of something. Because you know I'll kill everyone in that house to get them." He turned to walk back to his men, but then stopped and faced him. "Strange as this sounds, you taught me some lessons I won't forget. Whatever you decide, I owe you for them." He spat in his hand and held it out.

Ned spat in his and shook it.

And the wait began.

Finally, Farris checked the sun. "Nearly noon, Kit. We need to do something or we're going to start losing men. This ain't an army laying siege. These men have farms to tend to."

"They're coming out!" one of the men called.

They gathered and watched as two dozen men, women, and children left the house and moved in a loose gaggle toward Hawkwood's men.

Hawkwood, Clendenin, and Emma stood apart from the others as they examined each of the refugees, looking for men disguised as women and men whom Emma could recognize as being among those who had attacked her.

"Thought I'd lift your scalp for sure, Ned," Clendenin said. "Lucky it was Kit and not me chasing you."

Ned grinned. "If it was you, Jemmy, I never would have had to come out." He looked around the hollow as if committing it to memory. "I'm going to miss this place. Been here nigh on ten years. It's as much a home as I've ever had. I don't bear you men any ill will. You had a right to come for us, and you've done right by us. Robbie and the two men you want are in the house. They are armed. It's up to you to get them out."

* * * * *

"READY?" HAWKWOOD ASKED.

Shafto and three volunteers, a Scot and the two men who'd been with him the day before, nodded or grunted in assent.

"Let's be at it then." He peeked around the woodpile that sheltered them. "Go!"

Hawkwood and the other men raced across the seventy yards of open ground as the rest of the men pelted the Turnbull house with musket fire. Hawkwood's mouth was desert dry and blood hammered in his temples. A musket barrel poked out from between two logs. Time slowed and his legs felt as heavy as plowshares. The barrel foreshortened and fired in their general direction, but the shot didn't come close. Then they were there.

They fell against the wall of the Turnbull house and waited for their heaving chests to still. The plan was simple. Shafto would take the door down with his mallet, and then everyone would pile into the house. Once they were inside, the rest of the group would stop shooting and join them. It would be a short, desperate, and dirty fight with knife and tomahawk.

Across the field they had crossed, another figure leapt up and race toward them. Emma. He held his breath as she pelted toward them. While he and his group had had the advantage of surprise, the men in the house were watching when she began her run. Musket balls and buckshot whipped through the tall grass at her side. In a moment she was flopped on the ground beside them. He gave her an angry look and pointed at the ground, indicating for her to stay put.

She gave him a pout and shook her head like a stubborn child.

With another gesture, he indicated for her to stay beside the Scot who was to be the last man into the house.

Shafto leaned against the log wall, panting. Hawkwood pointed at the door and Shafto nodded. He took a deep breath and dealt the door's lower hinge a bone-jarring blow. Though the rough plank door was barred on the inside, the mallet drove the lower half of the door from its leather hinge. Shafto ducked back behind the door jamb and dodged a volley of musket fire from inside the house that blew large splinters from the door. The gunshots were still hanging in the air when Shafto sprang to his feet and gave the door a second mallet stroke that wrenched it free from the upper hinges. One of the backcountrymen grabbed the top of the door hauled it free of the jamb. Hawkwood dove under the bar into the parlor of the house. The air in the room was stiff with gun smoke. He perceived movement in the unlit gloom and smoke and struck at it with his sword. Someone screamed and cursed. His men pushed through the broken door behind him.

"Clear the dogtrot and hold up!" Hawkwood yelled. He didn't know the location of the men in the house and didn't want anyone rushing into the other half of the house and finding someone with a loaded musket on the far side. He also didn't want someone to surprise them by way of the dogtrot.

Emma appeared at his side.

"Dammit, don't you ever listen to me? I told you to stay back," he said.

"I'll be right behind you. My musket is loaded with buckshot. And if I waited on you to make up your mind, where would we be? Eh?"

The man Hawkwood had wounded was cornered and tomahawked by one of the men. The Scot's broadsword brought death to the other hiding in the upper sleeping chambers. Only Robbie remained.

"Robbie," he called down the dogtrot. "Come out. It's over. It's going to go hard on you if we have to come in and get you." From inside the other section of the cabin came a furious scrabbling sound, like a trapped animal trying to claw its way to freedom. "Hit the door, Tom."

The interior door wasn't barred and exploded inward under the impact of the mallet. Hawkwood was catapulted into the room by the rush of the men behind him.

"By God," the Scot said. "I believe he's flown. How'd he do that?"

Hawkwood couldn't believe it. "Turn the place upside down! I want him dead!"

Emma touched him on the shoulder, held her finger to her lips, and gestured at the hearth with her musket. The obvious dawned on him. Robbie had crawled up the chimney. The wattle-and-daub structure would be too narrow at the top to allow him to escape, but it could provide a hiding place until he had the chance to make a run for it.

She cocked her musket, walked over to the hearth, squatted, and inserted the muzzle up the chimney opening. "Robbie! Is that you?"

A strangled whimper came from inside the chimney. Shafto and the other men stopped searching the room and watched. .

She probed with the gun barrel. "Robbie, it is you? You aren't acting as bold as you were in my bedchamber. There you were quite a damme-boy. But as they say, if you'd fought like a man, you wouldn't be hanged like a dog."

Hawkwood struck the wall with the hilt of his sword. "Robbie, we know you're in there. Come out."

Scratching sounded as he tried to force his way higher up the chimney. One man laughed, then all of them were doubled over, laughing at Robbie caught in the chimney and with relief that the fighting was over and they were still alive.

The room filled with thunder, and flecks of daub flew from the wall. Emma had fired her musket straight up the chimney. She dropped it as if it were a snake, stood, and tears coursed down her cheeks, then she fell to her knees on the packed-clay floor. Clenching her fists, she hugged herself as she sobbed and her shoulders heaved.

Hawkwood moved to comfort her.

"No!" she shrieked. "All of you get the hell out! Leave me alone!"

As Hawkwood turned, Robbie's corpse, one leg nearly severed from the blast, slid down the chimney and came to rest on the cold ashes in the hearth.

* * * * *

"SEEMS LIKE A SHAME TO BURN IT," Farris said as flames licked out of the door of Turnbull's cabin and the bark of the untrimmed logs caught fire.

The men stood around a small mound of tools, firearms, and cooking utensils that had been deemed worth carting away, while the

Scots piled them into lots to be divvied up among the men. To their surprise, a clan that had lived on robbery and extortion left behind so little to show for its efforts.

Emma, composed but with her eyes still red from crying, sidled up to Hawkwood and gripped one bicep with both of her arms. "Evil lived here, Mr. Farris. If someone else wants to live here, let them build afresh."

"Kit." Clendenin nodded across the meadow. "Looks like Welbourne didn't like your answer. He's come back and brought help."

The portly figure of Welbourne cantered toward them with a dozen men in tow. As they drew closer, Hawkwood's stomach constricted. John Bull and Scarecrow were with him. They pulled to a halt only a few feet from Hawkwood and his men. Two were Welbourne's farmhands, but the rest he took to be companions of his pursuers.

"That's him, men." Welbourne pointed at Hawkwood. "You can take him."

"What's the problem, Mr. Welbourne?" Hawkwood asked.

"What damned impertinence!" John Bull said. "You, sir, are a murderer, and we are here to take you to face justice."

Emma's grip on his arm tightened.

Hawkwood perceived some shuffling of feet and shifting of weight among his men. He saw Perkins cock his musket and move off to one side of the group. Hawkwood knew all it took was a single word and everyone with Welbourne was dead. There was a certain attraction, he had to admit. He wasn't sure Burchill could ever be effectively deterred and he now knew the depths of Welbourne's animosity. He could settle it all now without objection. And the knowledge of what he could do acted as a restraint on him.

"Mr. Burchill. I warned you last time. If you want to fight, we can fight. One more corpse laying out here, more or less, makes no matter to me. The rest of you boys"—he jabbed the flat edge of his hand in their direction—"need to decide if I'm worth getting killed over just because Mr. Burchill wants to get paid when he gets back to Ireland."

One of the men riding with them hawked and spat. "I didn't sign on to get killed. I'm going home. Any of you boys going with me?"

One after another, they turned their horses and rode away.

"What's it going to be, boys?" Hawkwood asked John Bull and Scarecrow. "Are you going to leave me and mine in peace, or do we finish this right now?" He tucked the stock of his rifle under his arm and cocked the hammer.

"This ain't over, Hawkwood," John Bull said.

"You're wrong. It is over. It ends today. Whether you like it or not, justice has been served. You may think I've escaped. I haven't. Had the course of justice been permitted to run without a rich man trying to see me hanged out of spite if I were convicted, I would have been transported to Virginia for life. That's where I am. More than that will have to await God's judgment."

Hawkwood turned to his men. "Let's go, boys. We're done here. Me and my lass are off to find Reverend Huntsman, and I'll buy enough liquor to make you all blind-staggering drunk if you'll dance with my bride at our wedding." Then he faced John Bull and Scarecrow. "You're invited too. You've ridden long and hard, and I don't want you to leave with nothing."

As Welbourne and his party receded in the distance, Perkins sidled up to Hawkwood. "You handled this damned well, Constable. We didn't kill any more than we had to, and I suspect your problem with the thief-taker is at an end. Though your problems with Welbourne are just starting."

"What are you and your boys going to do?" Hawkwood asked. "I can't let you ply your trade in my territory."

"We'll probably move down Valley. There is better pickings there anyway. By the way,"—he handed Hawkwood the *doppelstutzen* that had been lifted from him near Staunton— "you can have this back. It ain't to my taste, and I couldn't even find a buyer for it." He winked at Hawkwood. "But don't get no ideas about getting anything else back. I'm a highwayman, and I have a reputation to worry about."

.

Chapter Thirty-Four

PATTON SIPPED FROM A tankard of grog as he sat behind his desk. "The Turnbulls are truly gone, eh? That gives Williamsburg one less reason to muck about in our affairs."

"Indeed, Uncle." Preston slouched a bit in his chair and stretched his long legs out, feet apart. "Our friend Kit is quite the local hero. He avenged his loss but had the good sense not to turn a victory into a slaughter. I must say, I was surprised that he let One-Eyed Ned go. I would have wagered a substantial sum that he would have had Ned dangling from the nearest tree."

"The boy is an English gentleman. Most every man in the Valley would have slain every last creature in the Turnbull settlement. He didn't because he believes in the law and in justice." He took another drink. "I would have thought these past months would have taught him that law and justice are only as powerful as his own hand. He may ape our dress and our manners, but he will ever be Tuckahoe and we Cohees."

"That may not be all bad. Men, even our backcountrymen and timberbeasts, follow a gentleman cheerly if he knows what he's about, where they would quarrel among themselves over precedence. Kit has proven himself, and he will be able to rally men to him if need be. As you say, he respects the law, and so long as you are the law, he will be your man."

Patton considered that. "You may be right, Billy. Or he may prove to be more trouble than he is worth."

* * * * *

"YOU CAN'T JUST RUN!" Welbourne's face turned a mottled purple with rage. He leapt from his chair and had to restrain himself from striking the bog-trotting thief-taker. "A hundred-pound reward plus the reward your employer is offering lies a-waiting. He and the rest of those Cohees are as drunk as lords after his wedding. I can raise some men. We can take him while he's asleep or abed with his wench."

The stout Cork thief-taker, Burchill, hooked his thumbs in his waistband and leaned toward him. "Money," he said, shaking his head, "is of no use to me if I am dead. He's had two chances to kill me. I daresay that making a third run at him could be fatal. You saw those men Hawkwood had about him. You can raise a handful of farmers, but his followers will kill without hesitation. And if I do snatch him from his bed, do you think I can get him across the mountains? No, sir. I'm afraid that my employer must content himself with Hawkwood's permanent exile. Or he can hire some bigger bird-wit than myself to try again." He jammed his hat onto his head. "Good day, sir."

Welbourne watched from the window as Burchill and the Essex County constable, Boulware, rode away. Damn them. Damn them to hell. It wasn't their failure to take Hawkwood that he minded as much as the humiliation of Hawkwood sending him away like he was his lackey. This was a long game. What was it the French said? *La vengeance est un plat qui se mange froid.* Revenge was a dish best served cold, and he would serve him up in due course.

"Dear Ran, are we still plotting the boy's demise?" Sarah said from beside him. She had entered the room so quietly that he hadn't realized it.

"He made a fool of me in front of the Cohees." Welbourne clenched his jaw. "If I let that pass, everything will slip from my grasp."

"The Turnbulls were expendable. Like so much bum fodder. You can buy them by the dozen in Carolina. Leave the boy be, Ran. He has his girl, and they'll soon have children. The only thing these Irish are industrious about is making babies."

Welbourne saw the wisdom in her advice but the thought of taking revenge on Hawkwood loomed large in his imagination. Right now, Hawkwood was untouchable but he'd shown himself to be reckless and impetuous. There was time enough to get his own back in the future and the best way of doing that was to let Hawkwood believe he was safe.

"I'll leave him alone for the time being. You're right, that mort will probably keep him sapped of ardor and ambition for anything other than rutting. But he can't be bought or intimidated, and that makes him damned inconvenient." He eyed her. "And you, my love, keep your eyes and hands off him."

* * * * *

WAT TURNBULL SQUATTED BY A SMALL FIRE in front of a lean-to. He had run hard for two days, killing one horse in the process, before coming to rest here in the mountains of the Watauga Country. His first thought had been to head to the Forks of the Ohio and trade with the Shawnee and Lenape again, but on further reflection he decided that the same Indians who had lifted his scalp might recall him. So he'd turned his horse south and run for Carolina. His plans at the moment were in flux.

He started as a horseman rode up in the dark and dismounted. Standing, he pulled a knife from his boot top.

"Hello, Pa," a familiar voice said. Moments later, Ned walked into the firelight.

Turnbull relaxed and sat down. "Tie up and 'light, boy. I'm surprised to see you. Hawkwood hated you worse than a week-old fish. I thought he would do for you for certain."

Ned shrugged. "He wanted Robbie and the boys that helped him rape Emma. He let the rest of us go."

"Robbie gave himself up so the rest of you could go free?" Turnbull guffawed. "Pardon me for saying so, but Robbie never cared about anyone but himself. Why did be become noble all of a sudden?"

"He didn't. He wasn't given a choice."

"I'm sure you did what you needed to do. Why'd you chase me down?"

Ned took a seat beside him. "A man has to go somewhere. What do we do now, Pa?"

"I don't know." He sighed. "But something will turn up. Something always does."

* * * * *

ON A HOT DAY AT THE END OF LATE INDIAN SUMMER, the tall clouds boiled up over the Blue Ridge, auguring an evening thunderstorm. Hawkwood and Shafto had been splitting rails since dawn. Rankin was supposed to be working with them, but he was lounging on a patch of grass under a large pin oak tree, nipping from his jug and playing the flageolet. The two oldest Shafto children held the wedges as Hawkwood and Shafto drove them into the logs.

Hawkwood's hair, tied back in a loose queue, had plastered to his head with sweat as he worked in breechclout and moccasins. He flexed his back, lifted the maul, and powered it in a blurred arc to slam into the wedge the oldest Shafto boy was holding. The boy winced at the impact but didn't flinch. Another rail done. Just a few thousand more and they'd be ready to start on the next fence.

He leaned on the handle of his maul and surveyed his work. His arms ached, his back was tired, and his hands were bruised and sore, but he was at peace with the world. Women's voices carried on the breeze, and he turned as Emma and Patsy Shafto joined them. Patsy carried their midday meal in buckets suspended from a shoulder yoke—milk still cold from the spring house, bread, and cheese.

Emma smiled as she neared him. "You look good enough to eat." She traced a fingernail over the muscles in his arm and then along the verge of the mass of scars atop his shoulder and down the center of his chest.

"Stop it, you two," Rankin said. "The boy's already near naked. Nothing good will come of provoking him."

"Pah, Bram Rankin!" She stuck her tongue out at him and stroked her belly, which was beginning to push hard against her shift, then laughed the throaty laugh that sent fire racing through Hawkwood's blood. "Damned little you know about what's good."

Hawkwood spat out his cud of tobacco, dipped a tin mug into the bucket of milk, and drank deep as Emma lowered herself to the ground by Rankin. Rankin started playing *"A Blacksmith Courted Me,"* and Emma closed her eyes, leaned her head back, and sang.

Hawkwood shook his head in wonder of it all. Who would have ever thought that he would come to be splitting rails, wearing little more than his birthday suit, in the Virginia backcountry? That he would fall in love with a wild Irish lass and become a father? His throat knotted as he looked at Emma, so beautiful and strong and confident, her belly swelling with their child-to-be.

Once his meal was finished, he took the twist of tobacco from his possibles bag, cut a piece, and started chewing. Who would have believed he'd come to like this vile stuff, too?

"Company a-coming, Mr. Hawkwood." Shafto pointed down the narrow track that ran some miles to join the Seneca Trail.

Two men in good clothes and riding fine horses approached. Kit gave them a wary glance and edged toward his rifle, which leaned against the oak.

The lead rider, a man of middling height who wore a stylish wig under an oversized beaver tricorne awash with plumes and gold lace, stopped and gave them a distasteful look. Hawkwood approached him.

"Good man," the rider said. "Where may I find your master?"

Hawkwood looked down, jetted a stream of tobacco juice on the road, wiped his mouth with a sweaty forearm, and then laughed. "Well, sir, I don't reckon that son of a bitch has been born."

Historical Note

The geography of the Shenandoah Valley created a social environment unlike any other found in the English colonies of North America.

The Blue Ridge Mountains only had a few passes south of the Manassas Gap. The most prominent were Jarman's Gap and Rockfish Gap. The primary line of drift into the Valley was from the port of Philadelphia to Carlisle and down the Cumberland Valley and into Virginia. To the north, the Lower Valley (so-called because the rivers in the Shenandoah ran down to the Potomac), was heavily German. The Upper Valley was mostly what we, today, call Scots Irish, though, at the time, they referred to themselves as just Irish. The two groups mingled only tentatively. Marriage records indicate that intermarriage between the Scots Irish and Germans was uncommon until after the Civil War

The Blue Ridge also cut off the Valley from Virginia's Tidewater and the mostly English population there. The Valley Irish, the Cohees (named as such by the English because of their fondness for using 'quoth he' in conversation which sounded like 'cohee'), mixed no more easily with English Tuckahoes than they did with Germans.

The Virginia frontier of the 1750s, like the frontier in North Carolina and Pennsylvania, tended to be a fairly lawless place. Some modern scholars have tried to paper over this fact by creating a, in my view, fanciful view of Valley Irish society. The fact remains that travelers' journals of the era express fear at having to pass through the "Irish Tracts."

What separated the Virginia frontier from its neighbors to the north and south was that Virginia's government created a ruling hierarchy that, at least superficially, tried to enforce some kind of order. This hierarchy were also men on the make who used their formal power to enrich themselves. James Patton, John Lewis, William Beverly, Benjamin Borden and other worthies might have been loyal subjects interested in expanding Britain's borders, but they were definitely in hot pursuit of personal wealth and influence. They weren't necessarily unscrupulous, though you could be forgiven for thinking them so, but they were not to be trusted in any dealing which could put them at a disadvantage. This homegrown oligarchy handed out land grants and offices in return for personal loyalty. Without that patronage, land ownership was impossible, and a substantial underclass was created that had no firm title to the land they settled.

Robbers and brigands were not uncommon in the backcountry. The highwayman, Ute Perkins, was real and the skimpy record he left behind comports with the life I've given him. Criminal enterprises, like the Turnbulls, that masqueraded as families were not unusual on the colonial frontier.

Kit Hawkwood, while a figment of my imagination, faced a dilemma that daunted many young men of modest means who wished a military career. The expenses of an officer exceeded what he was paid, indeed, in official parlance an officer was paid a stipend, not a salary. Unless a young officer had outside income, he was operating at a deficit. Though Kit doesn't realize it, he's dodged a bullet by being forced to flee Britain. Hawkwood's peregrination about Europe was not all that unusual and, as one of Sir Peter Halkett's officers at Prestonpans, he would have found a chilly reception for him outside his regiment because of Halkett's refusal to break his parole and return to field against the Scottish rebels in The 'Forty-Five. His background with the 44th Foot will play into what lies ahead for him. His pursuit by a hired "thief taker" is how the law was enforced in Britain under George II. The notion of a dedicated police force was something Britons were hostile to. To prosecute a crime, the victim had to arrest the malefactor and hire a prosecutor. It was Kit's bad luck to run afoul of a man of means.

Some of the incidents in this novel may be familiar as I have "borrowed" them and placed my characters in central roles. Travelers' journals of the time held views of the "wild Irish" that ranged from contempt to grave apprehension. As most of the Valley Irish left no written records behind, I've filled in the gaps using best guesses, imagination, and a modern analog. The attitudes and outlooks of many of the characters will not be a surprise to anyone who has spent any time around people from that reservoir of Scots Irish culture, the Appalachian foothills.

So now Kit is no longer a wanted man, he seems to be happily married and content with a baby on the way. Young men can be restless, young women fickle, and a baby and a farm can be a lot of hard work and there is a war on the horizon. We'll have to find out what happens together.

Personal Note to My Readers

I hope you've enjoyed participating in the lives of Kit and Emma as much as I have. If you have, I'd be grateful if you would take the time to post a review on Amazon.com.

Reviews are critical to the success of a book on any of the online platforms because reviews determine the level of attention the book gets from the publisher. It is really simple. Go to the review section of *A Threefold Cord* on Amazon and click the button that says, "Write a customer review." The review doesn't have to be long, just a few sentences that describe (hopefully) why you like the setting and characters and why someone else should buy it.

You can connect with on Facebook where I not only talk about Kit Hawkwood and company but chronicle real happenings on the Virginia and Pennsylvania frontiers on the eve of the American Revolution. Your comments and feedback are always welcome.

Made in the USA
Monee, IL
15 January 2021